OTHER WORKS IN PROGRESS BY AUTHOR

NOVELS
"Tunnel Vision"
"Aftermath"

SHORT STORIES
"With malice aforethought"
"This is another mess you've got me into"
"Absence makes the heart grow fonder"
"An away break"
"Point of view"
"We'll be asking questions later"
(Published by New Fiction)

Published in, 2013
Slightly revised from the original Kindle version, released in May 2013.
© Robert Boenke 10-05-2013 Registration No. 284669295

This book is a work of fiction. All the characters are entirely fictitious and is based on the possible use of Red Mercury and its theoretical potential.

It is a conspiracy theory.

ACKNOWLEDGEMENTS

Thanks to my wife Lin for her continued support throughout the birth of this novel. To Kathy Burman Editor and critic.
To Lindsey Robinson for his opinion. With special thanks to Paul Burr, Author, for his assistance in getting this novel online with Kindle and CreateSpace.

CHAPTER 1
Late October 1993

In the Surete Headquarters in Aix-en-Provence, Inspector Renard was completing a morning of departmental strength assessments with the Regional Staffing Officer. He sighed to himself as M'sieu Floccard closed his file, put it into his briefcase and stood to leave. There had been no rapport between the two men and throughout their discussions Floccard had made so many indications on how well equipped Renard's station was he felt that his request for a further two officers to strengthen the shift system was unlikely to be granted. Not that men were unavailable, it was all about budget expenditure, size of area, numbers of officers seemed to count rather than need based on caseload. His experience counted for nothing and that was what was frustrating the Inspector.

"Au revoir Inspector." Floccard held out his hand. Renard, who knew to expect a limp damp grasp, took the offering with some reluctance which he hoped did not show on his face.

"Au revoir M'sieu. When will I know whether my request is accepted or not?" he asked.

"We will not keep you waiting long" the thin balding figure of around forty five replied. The man wore a grey suit and brown shoes, a combination that Renard would have attributed more to a psychopath than a bureaucrat he thought to himself grinning inwardly. It was likely to be the only amusement he was likely to get at the other man's expense, he reminded himself, as he watched Floccard turn and leave his office.

"Leave the door open M'sieu" he called to the departing figure as he looked down at his desk and the files and forms littered across it. Not that a mess was anything other than normal for the Inspector's desk but he preferred it to be littered with the files of criminal investigations to that of admin and staff matters. He called through the open door to his secretary.

"Annie?"

"Inspector?"

"Could you do something with this lot while I'm at lunch."

"Oui." came the woman's voice from the outer office. He was pleased he was unable to catch her eye while making such an unpopular request. But that's how it goes he told himself as he came round the desk and took his coat from the old hat stand in the corner. The office had probably looked modern in the fifties, probably the last time it was decorated too, he thought.

"Is Lascaux in?" he called.

"Oui M'sieu, he is waiting in his office for your meeting to finish."

"Right."

Inspector Pierre Renard was a stocky man with the dark complexion and dark hair that told that his ancestors had crossed the Mediterranean at sometime in the past. He had brown eyes in a sharp featured face. His nose, normally described as aquiline, shadowed the moustache which he kept trimmed to perfection.

It was his only contribution to sartorial elegance. His clothes looked lived-in and this appearance belied his position, an effect, some believed, he cultivated on purpose. He stopped outside Lascaux's office, enclosed by a glass partitioned wall off a central corridor. This in turn led to the lift and staircase. His suite of offices was on the first floor of a cement rendered building that looked out onto the Rue Gaston de Saporta, close to the Musee du Vieil. Windows at the back of the building had a less pleasant aspect, but at least the offices were in the centre of town. There was a yard where police cars were corralled and on the far side were the kennels and pound. The cells were in the basement of the building. The ground floor was given over to reception, holding areas and communications.

Pierre Renard, who had been in charge of this station for the last eleven years, had decided it was time for lunch at the corner Tabac with his friend and colleague Maurice Lascaux.

As he passed Annie's desk he said "I'll be at the Tabac if anything desperate occurs."

"Such as?" said Annie wryly.

"Outbreak of World War 3 and nothing less" he replied, the depression of his earlier meeting already beginning to lift at the thought of lunch.

"Maurice" he called through the door to Lascaux's office.

"Coming Inspector" said Lascaux getting up from his desk where he'd been sitting with his coat on in anticipation of the invitation.

Pierre looked at him with amusement "I've kept you waiting?"

"Oh no, I was beginning to feel the chill" Maurice responded. "Come let's go. Bye Annie."

At the cafe they ordered their food and a bottle of red wine to go with it. They occupied their favourite table and like so many other colleagues talked shop while they lunched. They ordered coffee to finish but they were destined never to drink it.

Pierre who was facing the door saw his latest recruit arrive looking decidedly worried. He frowned and Maurice seeing something had attracted Pierre's attention, turned towards the door.

Paul Giscard, the youngest officer on the station, spotted them and rushed over.

Before he could begin explaining the problem Pierre raised a hand and said "Calm down and tell me what's up slowly and quietly." He emphasised this last remark by looking exaggeratedly around the cafe which had quietened, sensing a drama. "Here, sit down" he indicated a chair.

Paul sat down and leant across the table. "They've found a body Sir. Inside the mountain while they were potholing." He added.

"They?"

"Some potholers Sir, up around Les Girons."

"When?"

"We got a call ten minutes ago. The leader had a mobile phone and phoned us from the site."

"We have directions?"

"Yes Sir. It's not easy to get to. They took a four wheeler and then trekked to the site. The quickest way up is by helicopter."

Despite the seriousness of the situation Pierre could not resist a smile at the young officer's enthusiasm at the prospect of some action. "OK Paul I'll be back in a moment. Please find out where everybody is and who is available to drive up there. Oh and by the way get hold of Jean Girand, I want him as Scene of Crimes Officer. He's to drop whatever else he's doing, OK?"

The young constable rushed off as Pierre and Maurice settled their lunch bill, regretting their lack of a coffee. The patron gave a Gallic shrug, he'd heard enough of the conversation to begin a good piece of speculative gossip.

As they walked back he asked Maurice whether they should set up an incident room and get hold of a forensic specialist.

"Let's see what we find, although it may be a good idea to get someone along early. Even if it turns out to be an accident there will still have to be an autopsy to determine the cause of death. Someone who may have to do a little pot holing."

"He won't be the only one." Pierre added "he

may need experts to get the body out, assuming that's possible" he looked thoughtful. "I wonder how far in the body is, not that I'd have towed a body too far into a mountain."

"Nor I" replied Maurice" however we may never know how it got there, shall I call up the chopper?"

"Yes, I guess so, though I hate those things."

When Renard reached his office he told Annie to let his wife know that he didn't have any idea when he would get home that day but that he would ring her later.

Annie grimaced, she knew she would be quizzed and have to listen yet again to the complaints of a policeman's wife.

"And could you get me a mobile?"

"Sir."

Lascaux rushed in knocking on the door jamb as he did so. "We've located Girand, he'll be here in about ten minutes, he was out on a routine patrol and we picked him up on the car radio." He looked down at Pierre's shoes. "You'll need more than that. It can be quite treacherous underfoot up there."

"I know. I've got walking boots, socks and a parka in the boot of my car. In fact we'll use my car to get to the airport. Is the chopper ready or are they stripping it down again?" he asked sarcastically. They rarely had call for the police helicopter, but it seemed to Pierre on the occasions it was required it was either, being serviced, tested or repaired. In view of

In Pursuit of the Red Kite

the little use it got he had remarked exasperatedly, on more than one occasion that somebody must be hiring it out privately to supplement their income.

"No, it's on standby."

They had to drive five kilometres to the small private airfield outside Aix where they housed the machine.

"Arrange a back up team Maurice to drive there and include young Paul, it will do him good to get out and do something a little different. They'll need a 4x4." he paused "What about forensics?"

"She'll meet you at the airport."

"She? I thought the hospital forensic staff were both male."

"Apparently not Sir. She's new and she has had some experience in potholing as luck would have it." He smiled enjoying the expression on his chief's face at having to take a new unknown and, for him, untested scientist into the field.

"H'm" was all Pierre said. His phone rang.

"Reception Sir, Girand has arrived."

"Ask him to wait" he hung up. "Annie where's that mobile?"

"Coming Sir" Annie appeared in the doorway and handed him a compact black mobile.

"Batteries?"

"Just put new ones in Sir" said Annie smugly.

"Thanks. See you later then and don't forget

to ring my wife."

"Yes Sir. Good luck." Annie knew he hated the helicopter.

Downstairs Girand was waiting at the desk. They went through to the back of the office and out into the yard to collect Pierre's car. As they drove to the airfield Pierre was quiet and Girand, respecting his mood, did not indulge in small talk. With a clear flight they should be over the site in anything from fifteen to twenty minutes depending on wind direction and how easily they could locate the group of potholers.

They had several hours of daylight yet but Lascaux was going to telephone ahead and ask the potholers to light a bonfire as a signal to show the helicopter that they were in the right locality.

The potholers were professionals and seemed well organised. They had given good map and compass references and there was almost no need for

the bonfire but it would save Girand circling the area.

At the airfield Marie Lemerle the forensic pathologist was already waiting for them. She was kitted out for the ordeal ahead and she had a haversack with her containing her field kit.

Pierre thought she looked around thirty, maybe a little younger. She was a small framed woman with short blond hair. She was unremarkable in appearance except for the look of a deep intelligence behind her blue eyes.

In Pursuit of the Red Kite

There was no possibility of conversation on the trip above the noise of the helicopter and therefore no chance of him finding out more about her.

When they arrived they found the group had set the fire near a piece of fairly level ground in order to provide a good landing site.

Once they'd landed Pierre introduced himself to the leader of the potholing group who came from Avignon and explained that there would also be a 4x4 coming by road with more assistance. The leader, a young Frenchman named Leon De Clerk, looked shaken by his experience although it must have been over two hours since he had first discovered the body. He told Pierre how he had been leading the team of three others, two men and a girl, through a series of tunnels and caves which had been discovered by his club some years earlier but had not been visited in the last nine months by any of his colleagues.

Leon advised them that the body had been

found in a small cave not far into the system. It was located at the foot of an almost vertical shaft which suggested that the victim must have fallen from above. They would have to approach the shaft via a tunnel where it was necessary to crawl on all fours for much of its length. Ventilation was good throughout the system and the first indication of the presence of a body was when they became aware of the sweet smell of decomposition. It was the helmet lamp that had picked up the half decomposed head grinning at him that had caused the shock to the leader. A sight he stated that he would never forget.

"Have any of you touched anything?" was Pierre's first question.

The look on their faces was sufficient to confirm the negative they all voiced.

"Have you any idea how it might have got there?" he added.

"Well as I said the system is well ventilated by chimneys and fissures that must come from higher up the mountain, so he could have fallen from above. The only other way in is the way we entered" said Leon.

"You said him?" queried Pierre.

"I am reasonably sure it is a man."

"Did it look as though the body had been dragged in through a tunnel?"

"Almost impossible to tell. You must remember we were not expecting to find a body, so we may have obliterated any traces on the way in....I'm sorry" he added.

"Oh that's OK" said Pierre, "it must have been a terrible fright for all of you" he sympathised. "How long will it take to get to the spot?"

"About fifteen minutes" Leon said.

"I'm afraid I'm going to have to ask you or one of your team to lead us in."

"Yes I know, I'll do it" said Leon.

A good leader thought Pierre. He doesn't like it but he won't delegate. He looked at Jean and Marie who had been following the conversation without interruption.

"Are we ready? Is there anything you need from the helicopter?"

"At some time we'll need a body bag" said Marie.

"There will be one coming up in the car" replied Pierre.

"Anything else?"

"No" they both replied.

"OK, I'll phone headquarters with a brief report and then we'll go in. They can speak to the car and let them know what's happening."

He spoke to Lascaux who asked little and promised he would speak with the rest of the unit.

""Oh I have not spoken to the press yet, although I have had one or two calls. No doubt the cafe society has been talking."

"No, keep them out of it for the moment" Pierre agreed.

The mouth of the cave was some 300 metres away from the landing site up a gentle slope into a loose moraine at the base of an escarpment. High up Pierre could see a further level area and then set back behind this the mountains climbed into a broken sky. Thankfully it was not raining he thought to himself as they began the trek to the cave. The leader of the Avignon group walked ahead with Jean Girand and Marie accompanied him.

In Pursuit of the Red Kite

"Are you an expert potholer?" he asked her.

She grinned at him. "No, certainly not", then by way of explanation added "It's my boyfriend who is really keen and I guess I've become involved through him. We mainly do it in summer which is less hazardous. Less risk from underground streams and it's not so cold although the temperature variation inside the mountains remains fairly constant.

"You obviously don't suffer from claustrophobia" he smiled.

"No, and I hope you don't."

"Well I never have before but I've never done anything like this before."

The ground became rougher under their feet and they had to pay more attention to their progress. As they neared the base of the escarpment the face began to loom above them and they lost sight of the upper plateau. Some of the rocks were large and looked to have fallen relatively recently. Pierre looked up and shivered. He didn't fancy being hit by debris. He looked at the others, no one else seemed over concerned.

When they reached the cave mouth Pierre was surprised it had been discovered at all. It lay behind a large collection of boulders and could only be approached from one direction. The opening was big enough for them to walk into. Before entering Marie handed each of them a sterilised face mask and suggested they wear it at all times while they were inside the mountain just as a precaution. Each produced a torch and followed Leon as he entered the system along a tunnel that averaged about one and a half times the height of a man and was of similar width.

The walls were dry and the floor coated with dust through which pieces of smoothed rock protruded, eroded Pierre assumed by the action of water. The tunnel changed direction suddenly and narrowed as they began to climb. They could feel a draught of air on their faces. Leon, who was leading, slowed as they entered a small chamber with a high vaulted ceiling. He shone his torch around and indicated three separate exit tunnels all smaller than the one they had entered by. Pierre estimated they had come about eight hundred metres into the mountain.

Leon indicated the exit directly opposite. "Almost as soon as we enter we will have to get down and crawl on hands and knees" he said "and before we go any further I would like us to rope up."

They did as he suggested and he seemed to spend an unnecessarily long time testing the knots and everybody's kit. Pierre suspected that this was due to an increasing reluctance to meet up with the body again. At last Leon seemed satisfied and led them on the final section of the route. Having entered this new tunnel they soon began to smell putrefaction on the faint wind blowing through the system. It was not pleasant. Nor, Pierre thought was the sight of what remained of the body they discovered in the inner chamber. It lay on its side facing the entrance, the clothing torn in places. Pierre shone his flashlight all around the small space, there was nothing remarkable about it, there was a further exit but Leon said it was not the one they were to take. The breeze here seemed to be entering from above and by the light of his torch Pierre saw a jagged hole that disappeared upwards. More interestingly he noticed, was a rucksack hanging from an outcropping of rock around which a shoulder loop had got caught.

"I think that's how the body got here" he said aloud.

Marie knelt beside the body. Jean Girand stood back watching her as she gently investigated the clothing.

"I'm sure it's a man by the facial hair, the style of clothing and the size of the feet" she paused "before I start cutting away some of this cloth do you want to take some photographs?" she directed at Jean.

As if woken from a bad dream, he started "Oh, yes of course" then as professionalism resurfaced he added "Any obvious sign as to cause of death?"

"There are a number of contusions on the skull but I think from the amount of blood on the lower chest, I suspect he died from a knife wound. Of course it's possible he may have been shot, but I think that's unlikely. There is no apparent exit wound although that's not in itself conclusive."

She looked up at Pierre "I can only carry out a proper examination back at the morgue. I think it best if we wrap his hands to protect for fingerprints before we bag him. Then we get him out with as little damage as possible.

"Agreed" said Pierre. He looked at Leon who

was staying as far away from the body as possible. "I think you have done enough young man. We'll all go back outside, unless either of you has a burning desire to wait here until the body bag arrives?" He looked at Jean and Marie.

"No" Marie said "we'll come out too, that is, when Jean has taken all the photographs he wants."

"Leon I want you to clearly mark the right tunnels to get us back in but you don't have to go back in again." Pierre said. Leon looked extremely relieved.

"We will need to take preliminary statements from you now and would ask you to come down to the station, in the next few days to formalise them."

"That is no problem as we had planned to spend the next two days in the area. Are you from a local station?"

"No, Central Headquarters in Aix" Pierre informed him. He turned to Jean "We'll need a ladder in there to get the rucksack down." He looked at Jean with a wicked glint in his eye "Maybe you had better see if there is anything else up there."

Jean groaned to himself, he was no climber. But, he knew a man who was; maybe he would abseil down

"I'll come back tomorrow" he replied.

"OK, let's wait outside for the team."

They crawled back out of the chamber leaving the body in peace for the last time. Within the next couple of hours it would be manhandled down to the helicopter by the forensics team from the station. From there it would be airlifted to Aix and then driven to the mortuary for Marie to carry out an autopsy.

On Saturday morning Jean collected an extendable aluminium ladder although due to the limited access doubted it would be of any use together with ropes and climbing gear which he loaded onto the Range Rover. Then he called for his friend Roger Le Brun and they began the drive up to the tunnel. They would meet Leon at his overnight camp and go back to the caves to retrieve any other evidence that might give a clue as to what had happened.

Leon and his group would then follow Jean back to Aix to give their statements. The trip was uneventful and apart from retrieving the rucksack from its snag on the rock face and some small traces of what could have been dried blood there was nothing more to see.

Roger, having anticipated a morning's climbing having retrieved the rucksack, continued up the fissure until he came out into the back of the small cave.

He made his way back down to the lower plateau and told Jean he'd found the entry point almost directly above where they had just entered the tunnels. Jean radioed headquarters and told them that he had retrieved the rucksack. He had not attempted to find out its contents. The Scene of Crimes Officer knew the rules.

Pierre had left instructions that as soon as anything further was discovered he should be contacted at home and he would return to the office as

In Pursuit of the Red Kite

necessary. Once the investigation got under way he would have little time to call his own.

It was mid afternoon when Maurice telephoned. Pierre could tell from his tone that it was something serious.

"Inspector?"

"Yes Maurice. What's the trouble. What have you found?"

"I'm afraid it's a murder investigation we have here, the victim was stabbed."

Pierre drew breath for a moment "What else Maurice?"

"Very little Inspector. The rucksack contained what one might expect of a hiker. There was enough money for him to pay cash for most of his likely needs, but no credit cards or travel documents."

"So we have no idea whether he is French or a foreign hiker, if so how long he has been in France?"

"No. Oh, Inspector we found remnants of bread which looked home-made which had become hard and not decomposed. I suppose the absence of damp in the system saved it."

"Any weapons?"

"Yes, a Walther and a Glock and what's odd is they had both been damaged and made unusable."

"I wonder why?"

"Well maybe our killer has a social

conscience and made sure that if they were found they could not be used. Other than that nothing, although most hikers and campers I've ever met will have a decent knife with them."

"I suspect the killer took it with him ..... Have we heard anything from Marie yet on the body?"

"Yes. Her initial findings are that he was stabbed and probably died as a result. If not the injuries he sustained falling down the fissure would have finished him off. Oh, and the body's been there about a month she reckons."

"I see."

"She may be able to be more precise on that depending on what more she discovers."

"Maurice. You will have to tell her to hold everything and stow the body, I'm coming in. I need to notify the Deuxieme Bureau and let them know that we have a body of unknown nationality in the morgue." Pierre felt depressed, he could see the paper work and reports clogging his office for weeks to come and, as if that was not enough, his office would be taken over by the Bureau as they investigated what could now become an International incident unless they find further evidence proving the body to be a National, which now seemed unlikely.

CHAPTER 2

Late September 1993

Once again the call to prayer broke into his sleep. However as he awakened he reminded himself it was for the last time that his presence at Matins would be demanded.

A small window looked out across a paved area on to an old brick wall approximately two and a half metres high and on which ivy had made a permanent home. His only concession to comfort being a rush mat. But despite its age and basic construction the cell was dry.

Known only as Brother Alan to the Franciscans he threw back the coarse blankets and got up off the timber framed bed. As he stretched out he could almost bridge the width of the space.

From the pale light entering his cell through the window he could see sufficiently to light the candle on the washstand. He filled the chipped enamel bowl from the equally chipped enamel jug then he paused before washing, as, in the distance he heard a reminder of the call to morning prayers.

Alan had never been one to lie in bed in the mornings. He found that during the winter months, when the nights were so cold, it was almost preferable to be up and active rather than try and keep warm using the same amount of bedding the Friars seemed able to survive with. He'd never regarded himself as soft, but he knew he could not have faced a lifetime living this way within the narrow confines of the Friary and its walled gardens. His two year stay was more than enough. He assumed that it was not unlike being in an open prison without all the associated comforts. As he washed in the cold water, Alan reflected on the fact that his time there had not been entirely of his choosing. The operation he had been involved in had been successful and he had needed to go into deep cover or risk the very real prospect of capture with the high probability of a very painful and lingering death.

Buried deep in the French countryside both he and his employers felt sure he would be safe from reprisals, although there was no one who would give him any written guarantees. The Friary consisted of private and guest cells, a dining hall, a chapel, library and a vegetable garden. There was also a small dispensary that was the province of Brother Jean who was both doctor and nurse to the community. In all there were currently eighteen permanent brothers in residence. He had learned that originally there had been more than fifty Friars occupying the building.

The distant ringing of the bell reminded him that he was expected to attend the service. He quickly finished his wash, slipped the brown cassock over his head, put his feet into the rope soled sandals and, before leaving the cell, blew out the candle.

His cell led directly off the cloisters in the centre of which was a neatly laid out herb garden most of which was in dark shadow as the early morning light had not yet risen above the surrounding roofs.

As he emerged from the cloister and made his way through the dimly lit corridors he remembered how after the first week of arriving he could not believe that he had agreed to his two year incarceration. His stay with the Friars had in fact turned out to be more enjoyable than he had imagined. Perhaps 'enjoyable' was not the right word he corrected himself. Alan's passage along the corridors was accompanied by the leaping shadows created by the flickering candles on the walls. He was the last to arrive at the Chapel. Brother Dominic looked at him over the top of his half framed spectacles in silent remonstration before commencing the service. Alan quickly knelt at his pew.

Aged thirty one Alan was still a very fit man. His early career in the SAS had instilled in him a health and fitness regime that was now habitual and he had devised a routine suited to his restricted surroundings. He stood about five foot ten and was broadly built. His hair was almost black and his brown eyes and light brown skin tone were inherited from his father. His father, a Regular in the British Army and an Italian by birth, was originally from Naples, his mother was English and Alan had been born and brought up in England. His mother had died of cancer when he was nine years old.

Alan had been raised by his father who had died five years ago. There had been no siblings or distant relatives that he was aware of and he had not been able to settle to any long term partnerships. There had been one relationship, in his early twenties, that had progressed on to an engagement but as time passed his wife to be had realised that he was more firmly wedded to the service and had called it off rather than spend a life possibly largely on her own. Alan looked back on this at times and wondered if she had been right. Maybe one day someone might come along but under the present circumstances a partner could be in as much danger as himself and provide a lever with which to force him out of hiding. While living in the Friary, Alan had let his hair grow long and it now merged into his sideburns and beard. This was due as much to the impracticalities of shaving as it was for the need to help disguise his appearance.

Following Matins, the Brothers proceeded silently to the dining hall where breakfast would consist of home baked bread, goats milk and cheese. Breakfasts were usually silent affairs.

Alan had not been alone in the operation. He had had a Russian partner who had also elected to disappear from society and his whereabouts had been kept from Alan. He reasoned that if he was captured he would be unable to disclose the Russians hiding place under torture.

Each had decided where his refuge would be. It had been agreed that they should remain out of circulation for at least two years. Alan wondered if like himself the Russian was also about to re-emerge from hiding and what he would do in the future. Both knew that they could not go back to any earlier existence as that would be a certain route to disaster. A watch would indeed be kept for any contact between his old employers and himself. His enemy's arm was long.

This state of affairs had been appreciated by all parties and a handsome payment had been made to Alan in lieu of any further promise of employment. It was 'The Golden Handshake' so popular in business circles for departing executives who were no longer required by their employers.

Alan had acquired a bank account in Geneva into which a bonus payment was to be added after his two years in hiding. In a personal box in the vault of the same bank was a new set of identity documents.

He had left instructions with his solicitors that if he did not contact them within two years and two weeks of the date he had given them before going into hiding then they were to go to the press with a short report setting out details of the special operation that had led to his current circumstances. This was to provide him with, he hoped, some form of insurance for the future. He had also left with them his will giving access to his assets in the Swiss account. No beneficiary had been named and unless Alan survived to include one then any monies would be equally divided among a prepared list of charities. This too would be acted on after the same time frame. He would need to make contact with his solicitors as a first priority once he had left the Friary and before the following two weeks expired having firstly ensured that all was in order in Geneva.

Despite the fact that enforced confinement was for his own personal safety and for which, Alan constantly reminded himself, he was being handsomely reimbursed, there had been times when he found the situation difficult to come to terms with. In order to make the passage of time more endurable he had taken to learning more about gardening and had helped the Brothers with the growing of vegetables for their food. He had also, again with their help, learned how to sketch and although there was a limitation of subject matter, had become reasonably good at it, or that's what they kindly told him.

The Friary was located in the Montagne de Lure region of Southern France in the Bas Alpes. The nearest habitation was the village of Lardiers.

On leaving the Friary Alan had decided he would head south, bypassing Lardiers and following hiking tracks down towards Forcalquier.

He was brought back from his reverie by a cough and looked up to see Brother Ignatius, the Abbott, watching him.

Alan smiled. He had become friends with the Abbott who had first opened the stout wooden door to the Friary on his arrival. Brother Ignatius smiled back although there was a look of sadness on his face. He had welcomed the companionship of the last two years. It had been good to discuss the outside world with the Friar even though Alan's views on religion were at best a little vague and it had become a subject, not unlike politics, best avoided between them.

Brother Ignatius had never probed too deeply the reason behind him seeking sanctuary which Alan had appreciated.

Having finished breakfast Alan returned to his

cell for the last time where he removed the cassock and rope sandals and put on the clothes in which he had arrived two years earlier and which still fitted. At the cell door he turned and took one last look at his home for the past two years.

He collected the rucksack of his personal belongings from the Abbott's office and there was an awkward moment when Ignatius held out his hand and said,

"So the time has come my son. May God protect you, and spare a thought for us sometimes."

"I will" said Alan, a sudden lump in his throat and instead of taking the outstretched hand, he stepped forward and hugged Ignatius. Then he turned and left the office without looking back. Was the Abbott aware of the contents of the rucksack. It looked untouched. Inside, carefully wrapped inside his tent was his handgun, a Glock and his double bladed service dagger.

He made his way to the entrance of the Friary where the other brothers had congregated to wish him well on his journey .

At the wooden entrance doors stood Brother Claude with a small package which he handed to Alan.

"Food for two days" he said in explanation.

"Thanks" Alan smiled and after a moment's hesitation, walked out into the bright morning sunshine. The air was crystal clear and as he stood with his back to the collection of buildings and took in the spectacular view he heard the wooden door creak shut behind him. He knew without turning round that Brother Claude would be watching him through the postern window.

In front of him was the narrow track that would take him back down the mountain and back towards civilisation. The mountains, as the Brothers had referred to them, were more like low imitations of what Alan thought of as mountains. The area between the Friary and Aix-en-Provence, where Alan was headed, consisted of several ranges of these weathered and eroded limestone crags between which were the farmed and forested plains of the region.

Alan stood for some minutes just savouring the view before picking up the rucksack and beginning his journey back to what? A new life and no longer as Alan Spinetti, after his father, but Alan Marks, after his mother?

Once the impact of the scenery had diminished he began to consider how best to proceed. The Friary was situated in a region where serious hikers rather than family groups would be found. This meant that there were more likely to be people about during the week not just at weekends. Brother

Ignatius had told him, he recalled, that the region was also a destination for potholers. The chances therefore of leaving the area unnoticed were slim. While in the Friary he had made no plans other than heading for Switzerland and his deposit box where new identity awaited him. Would he now be safe or would he spend the rest of his life looking over his shoulder. His job training had created the habit of remaining aware of his immediate surroundings at all times so the answer to this question was obvious. Nevertheless he tried to push this thought from his mind as he headed down the loosely defined track. Despite having good walking boots, he knew he would have to take it easy for a while, as his feet had not been this restricted for the past two years. He didn't want blisters or to bruise his toes by taking the downhill track too fast. He concentrated on his footing as the ground over which he was headed was extremely rough in places.

From time to time he reminded himself he was in no hurry. As yet he had no real destination and he had plenty of time to come up with a plan for his future. He didn't know what, under his new identity, his old employers at "The Firm" might have in store for him. Would there now be a total separation from the service, which would be wise, or would they still try to retain him in some godforsaken outpost where they could keep a fatherly eye on him. That is, if in fact that was what he now wanted. Part of him wanted to get out and lead a more normal life; have a family before he got too old to enjoy it. At that thought he broke into a broad smile.

After about two hours walking the track broadened into a path. To the left it headed north and up into the mountains, to the right, down towards a range of hills which were fairly heavily forested as you went lower.

Alan planned to take a wide loop round any villages on the way. Despite his appearance as a hiker he did not want to be seen in the vicinity if possible and so far he had been lucky and not met a soul.

In Pursuit of the Red Kite

At a divide of the track he stopped and spent a few moments looking north. He turned and headed south, his destination Aix-en-Provence and from there by train to Switzerland. This was the most tricky part as he would have to travel on his old identity in order to cross borders. At some point on his walk that morning he had decided to leave France as quickly as possible.

The early morning promise of a fine day had been kept and as the day warmed, he decided he would break for an early lunch and eat some of the food provided by the Brothers. At this height the landscape was still rugged with rocky outcrops and cliff edges to some parts of the path. The grass was short and stunted and the occasional tree, beaten into shape by exposure, began to appear.

A short way ahead and off the track, was a large outcrop in the rock face with a small area of scree in front of it before reaching the edge of a cliff, the height of which he could not determine. He made for the outcrop; he would sit with his back to the rock and look out over the valley. As he got closer he saw that a path wound beyond the outcrop and seemed to head down into the valley he was making for. This would keep him off the main track. He would need to take care of his footing on the scree; he did not want to take the short cut to the valley floor.

He sat and took out the pack of food the Brothers had prepared, opened it up and selected some bread which they had thoughtfully sliced. From another wrapped pack he found some cheese and with his knife cut off a small portion. He would have to make it last. He had filled his water flask before

In Pursuit of the Red Kite

leaving the Friary and had drunk sparingly from it. He laid it on the rocks alongside the small patch of grass on which he sat. Apart from the sound of him chewing his food, the only other sounds came from the birds spiralling on the thermals calling to each other and that of the occasional cricket. He leant back into the rock face before closing his eyes. He was in no hurry and the midday warmth was too good to resist. It had taken him three days to get to the Friary on his way to his forced seclusion and unless he decided to pick up a lift, it would take him the same time to hike into Aix.

Despite being an army child the family had not had to move from their base camp like many army families to follow the needs or deployment of the Forces around the globe. This was due to his father having been wounded in action in Northern Ireland. His wounds were such that he could not return to active service so the army had found him a desk job in the Colchester Barracks. His father realised he had been luckier than some and made the best of it. It also meant that he would not need to provide a roof over the heads of his young family.

Alan had attended local schools and whereas he had been a reasonable student he was never going to be a genius. Where he managed to rise above his fellow students was in languages. He was bi-lingual due to his father insisting that he would learn to speak Italian as well as his native English. At school he did well in French and German and did not appear to have any problem going from one to the other halfway through a conversation.

He was a very physical child and would take

part at any school sport on offer. Also he would take any opportunity to get involved with the rookies on the camp until he was old enough to join the cadet force.

With his father's[2] encouragement he aimed to join the SAS and was finally accepted into this elite force. He regretted that his mother had not survived to see what he considered to be his success although she may not have approved of his career path.

While he was in training he did sometimes wonder if a forces career would be all he wanted from life. It was shortly after completion of his training and after returning from a disastrous operation in Iraq that he was called to the Captain's office and introduced to a man in a suit. Introduction was the wrong word as he never did get the man's name. The Captain had made a point of tidying up his papers and putting them in his desk drawer before getting up and leaving the room. The man in the suit walked round the desk and sat in the Captains' chair. He had waved Alan to take a seat in front of the desk.

"I expect you would like to know what this is all about?" he began

"Well yes I would" Alan had replied.

The Suit leaned back in his chair and took a minute before replying.

"I represent a Government department that is closely linked to the army and sometimes we approach certain individuals that we feel would be suited to our needs."

Alan remembered that at the time he had said

nothing. He had waited for the Suit to carry on.

Seeing there had been no response by way of a question the Suit went on to expand his approach. He looked directly at Alan and steepled his hands in front of himself before continuing.

"You have certain talents that we could use. You are in peak physical condition. You speak several languages without difficulty which means you can operate beyond our borders. I believe you are wondering where to go from here now that you have qualified in the SAS."

"What makes you assume that?" Alan had interrupted him.

"From reports received from your superior officers." he paused "you probably think that all that is assessed here is your suitability to fight. If so you would be extremely wrong."

Again Alan had not immediately responded so the Suit went on.

"We believe that you would fit in well with the service I represent."

"Which is?" Alan asked.

"At this point I will not go further." the Suit stood up. "More will be explained should you decide to move on from your current position and there will be no recrimination should you decide to stay where you are." He got up, did not offer his hand and left the office .The Captain who must have been waiting in the outer office, had returned to his seat and looked enquiringly at Alan.

Alan, not knowing what to say had simply shrugged. "What should I do Sir?" he'd asked.

"Sorry soldier this is your decision alone" the Captain had replied "but if you wish to speak to them let me know"

With that he had dismissed Alan who went away to ponder on the somewhat strange meeting. Much later he was to realise that by leaving him with unanswered questions he had been psychologically played by the man in the suit. Knowing the curiosity of youth was all it had taken to get him hooked.

CHAPTER 3

November 1993

Harry McReady looked down onto the lights slowly moving on the river. By turning his head he could see several of the illuminated bridges crossing the Thames. To his left was Vauxhall Bridge still wet from an earlier shower, the road surface picking up the reflections from the slow moving vehicles passing between the north and south sides of the Thames. An overcast sky had seemed to make evening arrive early. He looked down at his watch as he walked back to his desk. It was 6.30 pm, his day was not yet over. Reaching for the phone, more out of habit than concern, he rang his wife to tell her he would be late home again.

At MI6's headquarters Harry was the deputy to the current Director General, Sir Ian Rush. He and Sir Ian had spent all day attending emergency meetings and press conferences concerning the latest IRA bombing where their role was to support their political masters in dealing with the media.

He sat down and stared at the neatly arranged pile of folders Amanda had left on his desk, swore to himself and got up to make himself a cup of coffee remembering the Canary Wharf bombing on 16th November 1992. The IRA were now back in action on the mainland. Harry shared the cynical view of those who had believed that the cease fire had been for one purpose only, to re-arm, recruit and retrain its members and strengthen the brigade. The cynics had been proved correct. By manipulative campaigning the IRA leaders had been able to get many of their more hardened members out of jail during the stay of hostilities.

Following the latest bombing the media's opinion was that the IRA had become frustrated by lack of progress in the peace process and was now exerting more pressure on John Major's Tory Party to permit the IRA a political voice. Harry knew the reverse would happen. No government, Tory or Labour, could allow themselves to be pressurised in this way. The IRA would be back in business for the foreseeable future.

During the coming week Sinn Fein would issue a press release from the IRA stating that a new campaign was under way and that the path back to the peace process would be difficult if not impossible.

He got up and stood again at the window looking down on the river. To Harry this was the perk of the job. A room with a view though there was no sound to the picture. The window system was so designed as to prevent penetration by the most sophisticated of listening devices. He reminded himself that he could see out but not be seen. The layers of reflective glass and sound screening stopped sound emissions as well as visual intrusion. In his opinion this Government had no chance of success on what was called the "Irish Question" and he thought they were unlikely to get re-elected at the next election. John Major had Harry's sympathy. Harry

In Pursuit of the Red Kite

thought Major had tried hard for a lasting peace. His problem, according to Harry, was that Major had played using a straight bat, forgetting that the Irish did not play cricket.

Had Major adopted a more forceful or covert operation he would only have raised world and media opinion against himself and the party. This despite the fact that it was a commonly held belief that most men of influence in the IRA were known to the security forces and that a properly orchestrated strike could swiftly bring down the army with little or no danger to the general public.

John Major's critics remembered Thatcher's Falklands Campaign and her policy of 'no negotiation' and wondered why he did not follow suit and take a more positive attitude. They conveniently forgot that she too had not dealt with the problem of Ireland.

Harry straightened up, catching his reflection in the window. He smiled and said aloud "Now for any other business". He returned to his desk and put the remains of his coffee down.

With the end of the Cold War the British Government had felt that a large covert network within Russia and the Eastern Bloc countries was no longer required. It was not a view that Harry shared although publicly he had not voiced any opinion, a point which he felt had helped him retain his position when the service was reviewed and reorganised in line with the new spirit of Detente. Those that hired and fired had seen him as a man capable of dealing with politicians and diplomats without ruffling too many feathers. A man who could move with the times. A safe pair of hands.

Harry in his late forties enjoyed a stable marriage, or so he was informed by his wife. They had two sons both in their twenties and now living away from home. One with his girlfriend in Beckenham and the other travelling in Thailand, or so he believed. It was some months since they had heard from Tim, and Harry at times wondered whether he should be showing more paternal concern. When it had come to careers, both the boys had made it perfectly clear that they had no intention of following their father's lead by joining the diplomatic circus, as they had put it.

To those that did not know him he appeared to be carrying the worries of the world on his shoulders. The reality was quite different. He had a clear and incisive mind with a sardonic wit which had not made him as many friends among his colleagues as he might have wished.

He drained his coffee and pulled the pile of folders towards him to begin the rest of the day's work. He paused, an almost hunted look in his eye, as the task in front of him appeared to take on ever increasing proportions. He stood up clutching his cup "Coffee, that's what I need" he said aloud, further putting off the evil moment.

Fresh coffee made and back at his desk, he took his coat off and placed it on the back of his

In Pursuit of the Red Kite

chair, sat down, squared his shoulders determinedly and opened the top file.

It was a little later that he felt a presence and looked up with a start to see Amanda standing in the doorway.

"What are you still doing here?" he demanded, then smiled and added in a softer tone by way of apology "You made me jump."

"Sorry, didn't mean to wake you" Amanda smiled back, no offence taken.

She crossed over to his desk and added another thin folder to the pile in front of him. The file was headed simply "Red Kite."

"What's this?"

"One I forgot to leave earlier" she told him.

He remained looking quizzical so she took pity on him and added

"It's from the previous administration. It was automatically pulled after two years. Or that was the instruction. Probably some form of monitoring or review."

This was not new to Harry, the system contained many cases that were inactive for a period of time or simply required a regular overview.

"OK, I'll read it through and see what action we need to take if any." He looked down at the brown folder as Amanda watched him and read the simple white label saying "Red Kite". He looked up at her and asked. "Are you finished for the night?"

"Yes I'm just about on my way now" she replied.

Amanda was the mainstay of the office. That type which all organisations need. Virtually unflappable, intelligent and capable of lending a hand in an emergency to matters that were beyond her job description as personal assistant and secretary to Sir Ian Rush.

In her mid-forties, and still an attractive woman, Harry could remember earlier times in the last twenty years or so that he had known her, when his feelings towards her had been less than professional. But that was some time ago. Still, he thought to himself, she remains very desirable. She had never lost her figure and the friendly petite face in a dark brown bonnet of hair had aged her very little. She was always conservatively dressed and Harry was sure she was well aware of how she was viewed at the office. Like Harry, she had moved up through the ranks of the service, though not always directly with him.

In addition to all her other talents, Amanda had embraced computer technology and IT, both of which had enhanced her performance. Harry was fairly computer literate but not in the same league.

"Oh, while I remember" he said "I've a meeting at 10.00am with the Home Secretary and Sir."

Amanda waited for him to continue.

"I'll come into the office first and we'll go

In Pursuit of the Red Kite

together from here"

"By car?" she asked.

"Yes. Get Sir's chauffeur to stand by and tell him to allow at least twenty minutes for us to get there." He looked out of the window with the light reflecting off the Thames. Not far as the crow flies, but by road in the late rush hour either the Palace or Downing Street could take as long as half an hour to reach.

"OK. Goodnight" said Amanda, as Harry turned back in time to see her leave the room.

As he had done so often in the past Harry considered her retreating figure, the legs clad in black tights, he assumed, a fashion that did not date and one that most women knew to be universally acceptable and usually flattering. "Thank God for black tights" Harry said aloud to the empty room.

Amanda had a partner although no one had met him. It appeared they lived separately and he was apparently as devoted to his career as Amanda was to hers. Harry thought it was an odd basis for a relationship, but if it worked, good luck to them.

He found he was still holding the "Red Kite" file. Inside was a single sheet of paper which referred to a second file for DG's eyes only. As a cryptic reminder there was a single line of type which said:

"The Red Kite flies again in September 1993."

Harry snorted at the text. There were times, of increasing number lately, when he found this style of reference irritating and ridiculous. In the morning he would tell Sir Ian that he had a legacy from the past administration that needed some action. He could just imagine his chief's expression of mild irritation when he was faced with an issue he would have to deal with himself, one that couldn't be delegated to a lesser mortal.

He smiled to himself and wondered what the file referred to.

In reaching and maintaining his position at MI6, Harry had worked at his own philosophy on success which was not to be over ambitious. He had realised early in life that few wanted to be number two, it was seen as being un-ambitious, it was not a threat to those chasing the ultimate power position and was probably the most secure position in the firm. He also discovered that where internal politics were concerned he would share the concerns and ambitions of the upwardly mobile and would be a sounding board for the policy making decisions taken by the Director General.

He was the middle man trusted by both sides and he had little fear of anyone wishing to usurp him.

At 9.30 the following morning Sir Ian Rush looked into Harry's office "We'll be off in about ten minutes, is there anything I need to know?"

"Amazing," thought Harry, not for the first time. We spend all the previous day together and we'll probably spend all of today together and still he expects me to brief him on all departmental issues. From past experience he knew it was not a good idea to give the chief any indication that he was not on the ball. Such a lack of perfection would not be met with any sympathy.

Sir Ian was neither concerned that Harry had a home to go to nor that he needed any sleep. There was nothing of any major import to report and as his mental mutterings subsided he replied. "Not much, I'll bring you up to date as we drive." He paused and picked up the 'Red Kite' file. "There is this you need to look into. It's something from the previous administration."

Sir Ian looked at him questioningly, so he added

"I can tell you nothing about it except that the boss kept it close to her chest at all times."

Sir Ian took the file, flipped it open and read the single line of text before closing it and handing it back to Harry.

"Remind me when I get back tonight. I'll pull the file and see what it's all about." He looked down at his watch "We'd better go" and as he turned to leave added, more to himself than Harry "Another day at the asylum."

On his return to the office that evening Sir Ian's temper was decidedly frayed. He had spent a most frustrating day in meetings that seemed to be conducted at the outset by asking his opinion and be concluded only when his advice or opinion had been meticulously dismembered and then ignored.

He found himself longing for a return to the past where a politician's attitude had been, when confronted by an awkward situation to say "Deal with it, but keep me informed." Now they felt able to advise you on how to conduct your operations. He sighed, the only small comfort was that at these security "committee meetings" the other security forces attending fared no better.

Sir Ian Rush had earned his Knighthood from services to the State. He had served as UK Ambassador in many of the less likely outposts of Europe and spent some time in Moscow. He had a reputation for ruthlessness and did not suffer fools gladly. This reputation had often made him seem unapproachable especially by the more junior members of staff. His family home was in Surrey and it was there that he spent most of his weekends. The rest of the week was spent at the RAC Club in Pall Mall where he found the facilities on offer suited him better than some of the other clubs nearby. There was a gymnasium and pool which he used early in the morning before the working day began. Jogging was not his style, much to the relief of security who were always unhappy with any potential target causing them unnecessary work in providing protection.

He had been educated at a minor public school where he proved competent but not outstanding. His main love except for sport had been the Cadet Corps. From school he had gone into the army and taken an active interest in military history. He was an officer at twenty one and had then enlisted with the Para's 33rd Brigade and had seen action by secondment to NATO in Africa.

True to his promise Sir Ian had resolved to read the 'Red Kite' file that evening. The file was duly delivered in a sealed envelope by a man from

In Pursuit of the Red Kite

records accompanied by a frustrated looking Amanda. Frustrated because she was not allowed to handle the file herself or deliver it to her boss. After he had signed for it the man from records disappeared, Amanda remained however seeming to want to vent her exasperation, but when she found Sir Ian's unsmiling gaze on her she changed her mind, excused herself and left him alone with the document.

He took out the file marked "'Top Secret 'DG's eyes only." As he began to read Sir Ian's interest began to take hold. He vaguely remembered gossip of a joint operation between MI6 and the Russian KGB. The gossip had never been confirmed and like so many security issues other pressing matters had soon consigned it to no more than a dying rumour.

"So there had been a joint undercover operation between the powers", Sir Ian mused, "and now I'm in a position to know just what it was about."

The file set out to illustrate the concerns of the Western Powers at the end of the Gulf War and how they had tried to ensure that Saddam Hussein would be prevented creating a similar scenario in the future and to prevent Iraq from having a nuclear capability.

Much to the confusion of the man in the street Saddam had not been personally brought to task or removed from any position of power in the Middle East. To many the war had seemed to fizzle out like a damp squib once the Iraqis had been beaten in the dessert and driven back within their own borders. It seemed that the joint political and military view was that Saddam would always pose a threat, but that if it were contained, then on balance he would continue to hold together many of the minor ethnic groups within what was known as Iraq. Without him it was felt civil war would follow and the whole uneasy peace in the Middle East would be threatened. The plight of the Kurds within Iraq was to be forgotten for political expediency and for the sake of the bigger picture.

Notwithstanding Human Rights issues this philosophy was vindicated on the basis that soon after the break- up of Yugoslavia civil war erupted between Croats and Serbs and ethnic cleansing caused horror among the Western Alliances.

As the situation in the Balkans flared many remembered that this region had already caused one world war and NATO was mobilised to try to prevent a similar tragedy occurring.

The file told how it had been agreed between the Super Powers that Saddam would need to be kept impoverished and should not be allowed to build up a significant war chest from which he could purchase the necessary hardware to again pose a serious threat to the civilised world.

What was unclear from the file was who had come up with the particular operation that was to follow. It had been sanctioned at the highest level and involved MI6 and the KGB in Moscow.

It was a cleverly woven plot, it used the obvious and the credible to make it plausible. Knowing that Saddam would relentlessly try to rebuild his credibility in the Arab world and knowing of his wish to regain face at home, he would seek any

In Pursuit of the Red Kite

available method to take revenge on the West. The ruse was to offer him a new super-weapon that would put him one step ahead, but it had to be costly to drain his financial resources. It would need to be obtainable from a covert source friendly to Iraq and to have technical credibility.

It had been agreed that following the break-up of the old Soviet Union there was a plausible and friendly market place for weaponry. What was to prove more difficult was finding the super-weapon that would satisfy the Iraqi leader.

It may have been from the developing "Detente" between Britain and Russia that the rumoured development of a suitable product suggested itself. The material had a common working name among scientists and was known as 'Red Mercury'.

Ever since Red Mercury was rumoured to have been produced in 1965, there had been much learned scepticism throughout the world of chemical explosives as to its existence or potential capabilities. It is claimed the material was first produced in a nuclear research centre at Dubna, near Moscow, in a cyclotron.

Red Mercury, which according to some scientists is a myth, is reputedly a uniquely powerful chemical which could be used in fusion weapons as an explosive catalyst. The theory was that if it can be compressed to fuse with Tritium atoms then this would produce a thermonuclear explosion.

American nuclear physicists and a former director of the Stockholm Peace Research Institute have gone on record as to being worried that Red Mercury will make it much easier for non nuclear powers and even terrorist groups to construct small thermonuclear fusion devices. The claims surrounding this material report that a bomb the approximate size of a baseball would be capable of killing anyone within a 600 metre radius of the explosion. It could be delivered as a conventional warhead or as part of a portable terrorist arsenal capable of remote detonation.

It seemed that much of the work and expertise on the product and its potential emanates from the USA, South Africa, Russia, Germany and Austria, where investigation into its use for non-military purposes suggests that the amount of chemical energy produced for peaceful purposes could possibly revolutionise space travel as a new super fuel.

Red Mercury was given its name from the compound of mercury and mercury antimony oxide ($Hg_2\ Sb_2O_7$) which is described as 'Cherry Red' in colour and is semi-liquid or a gel.

Sir Ian found that he had been tensing himself as he read the file. He put it down, stretched and got up to make himself a coffee. Amanda would have made it for him had she been there. He had no choice but make it himself as he didn't want to break his concentration while the office was quiet. He strolled across to the window as the kettle boiled and stared down at a similar view to that which Harry had looked on the night before.

Seated again, he continued with the file which went on to describe how there seemed to be a clandestine interest in the material and its potential and how a sales director for an international chemical business involved in producing 'Red Mercury', had been mysteriously murdered in 1991. This incident had enhanced its reputation.

Sir Ian smiled to himself as he understood the psychology of the plot and how a credible hoax could be evolved. There was sufficient scientific awareness of the product and its supposed potential. A man like Saddam would also be aware of the efficiency of a terrorist campaign with such a small portable device. He could take the war to any nation.

It was natural selection that placed Russia as the vendor.

The black market trade in weapons from the Soviet Bloc was well known worldwide. A situation emphatically denied by the Russian Politicians thereby making the lie more believable.

It had been agreed that both Russia and Britain would field a 'Salesman' whose personal history had to show a disillusionment with their own country or be sufficiently corrupt to give a plausible cause for their actions. Sir Ian smiled to himself again as he imagined why there were two joint operatives. Despite 'detente' there still remained a healthy atmosphere of distrust between the respective governments. Sir Ian's amusement was interrupted by the phone. He picked up the receiver

"Yes?"

"DCI McCullock of the Yard, Sir" said Amanda.

She was still at her desk, she could have made the coffee, he thought. "Put it through to Harry."

"He has asked particularly for you, Sir."

"Damn", his concentration now broken Sir Ian said "put him through."

"McCullock here."

"Yes Inspector?" said Sir Ian allowing exasperation to show in his voice.

McCullock did not rise. He spent most of his life dealing with Prima Donnas, or so it seemed.

"We have received fairly reliable information on the IRA cell who hit Canary Wharf."

"Yes?"

"It was a three man team with no previous form on the mainland."

"Corroboration?"

"It seems to fit the signature on the bomb" replied McCullock.

"Who says?" Said Sir Ian somewhat rudely.

"The bomb squad have a lad who spent time in Belfast before the ceasefire. He is as convinced as can be from the traces found on the debris as to the type of bomb and how it was detonated." He paused, but Sir Ian decided to outwait him.

"He put a name forward. Sean McGuire. His was one of the names given us for the unit."

"And?"

"The unit is back in Ireland. They flew out by Ryan Air from Stansted the same evening."

"Jesus Christ man, what happened to Security and have you told Five" exploded Sir Ian.

"They seem to have travelled as separate families complete with children, false names and undoubtedly fake documents and yes I've told Five."

"Why weren't they stopped?" Sir Ian realised that the question was unanswerable.

"Firstly we did not have the information we now have, secondly we have no photograph of Sean McGuire and thirdly one of the team we now know to be a woman. We cannot arrest every person flying to Ireland and lastly we believe they were already in the air when the explosion went off," he fired back at Sir Ian. Then in a more resigned voice he added

"By the time the incident was confirmed and the alert went out they had landed and disappeared."

"You want Six to follow it up?"

Sir Ian could sense the reluctance of the request that was to follow. None of the services liked calling for support, each believing they were superior to the other.

"Yes, I guess so."

"OK. Harry will be your point of contact at Six. Any snippet of information must be passed on."

"No doubt you'll return the favour" said McCullock.

For the first time since the conversation had

started Sir Ian smiled

"Of course, dear boy!"

"Thanks", McCullock hung up and as if by magic Amanda knocked on his door.

"Come" ordered Sir Ian.

"I have had Lady Rush on the line Sir asking me to remind you of your dinner at the Grange this evening." Sir Ian looked at his watch, a lesser man

may have cursed.

"The car is outside, Sir."

"Most efficient, Amanda" Sir Ian acknowledged with just a hint of sarcasm. "Please put the file away for me."

"Am I allowed to" she realised that was a cheap shot but it nevertheless gave her some pleasure as Sir Ian looking exasperated asked her to recall security. He would have to wait now until they turned up.

"I'll have to finish it later and I suppose you're right it should be returned below stairs overnight."

Sir Ian's eyes did not follow Amanda's figure out of the room. Unlike Harry he had little interest in the fairer sex. His own marriage was one of convenience. It was power and money that drove Sir Ian. Money was not in short supply; he had fared well from the industry of earlier generations. Power was the motive for his existence.

Once they had left the suburbs behind and he had scanned the headlines from the Evening Standard he relaxed back into the rear of his car. Michael his chauffeur knew better than to try and engage his boss in trivial conversation.

As they turned off the A3 and headed for Dorking, Sir Ian thought again about the 'Red Kite' file and remembered the clean cut young face that had stared back at him from the photograph attached to it. There was a touch of the Mediterranean in the features he recalled, but the photograph gave no indication of the character of the individual named Alan Marks.

Sir Ian cynically wondered what he had done wrong that had qualified Alan for the attentions of MI6 and his selection as a suitably corrupted or disillusioned national. By tomorrow, given the opportunity, no doubt the file would reveal all. For now, he thought, looking out of the window, a nights' excitement at the Grange mixing with those his wife emphatically referred to as 'the right people' was something he could well do without.

In Pursuit of the Red Kite

CHAPTER 4

Late September 1993

Having eaten Alan decided to explore his surroundings before taking a nap.

He rounded the outcrop against which he had been sitting where he discovered a small cave eroded into its face. On investigation he found it was not very deep and daylight reached right into the back wall. At the rear he found a small hole in the floor, just large enough for him to fall through if not careful. He tossed a stone down and could hear it bouncing into the depths. As the sound diminished into silence, Alan realised that it was very deep.

He looked around and found some cigarette butts on the floor but little other sign that the cave was used by people or animals. Outside he opened his rucksack, took out the package, un-wrapped it and broke off a chunk of bread and some cheese.

He leant back and closed his eyes. He felt good as he again took in the twin pleasures of peace and freedom. He felt he had time to lie down and rest a little longer. He placed his arm across his eyes to cut out the glare from the sky which penetrated his closed lids.

He awoke with a start, what was it that had disturbed him? He didn't move, just listened. The birds and crickets continued as before. Gently he raised his arm a fraction so that his eyes could become accustomed to the brightness of the sky. When he opened them his vision was severely restricted. As he

In Pursuit of the Red Kite

was about to remove his arm, he heard a small sound. It was the scree warning him; nothing could cross it without making a noise. What sort of animal might it be he wondered. By way of an answer he heard something rushing towards him and a dark shape entered his thin line of vision.

Alan rolled sharply to his left while twisting the angle of his body. He lashed out with his feet at where he thought the shape would be as a body crashed onto the spot he had occupied only moments before. He continued to move away as he rolled into a crouch and then stood up. His assailant, whom he could now see was a man, lay where he had fallen, no doubt winded. Alan took no chances, he threw himself on top of the man and put him in a hammer lock. His natural instinct had been to kill, but now that he had the advantage he wanted to know why he was being attacked. With his free arm the figure signalled submission. Alan leant back and pulled the hood of the anorak the man was wearing, off his head, to reveal close cropped blonde hair and as he turned his head, the features of Nikolai Petrofkia.

Alan let go of the arm lock and kneeled back keeping his body weight on top of the Russian. It was then that he saw the blood pooling out from beneath Nikolai's body. He rolled him over to see a mass of blood soaking the clothing round a protruding handle of a knife that had entered the body in the upper middle torso. From the amount of blood there was almost certainly arterial damage. His one time friend and colleague had no chance of surviving the wound; it was only a matter of time. Nikolai's eyes were closed and his face was contorted with pain. Every

In Pursuit of the Red Kite

breath was difficult. Alan squatted down beside him.

"Why Nikolai?"

Nikolai's eyes opened and he tried to smile through the obvious pain. "One way or another SAS, you're a dead man."

Alan felt no anger and was surprised at his own detachment. He needed an explanation as to why his one-time colleague had tried to kill him and he was sure his future survival depended on what he could extract from the Russian. Time was short but he would try the soft approach first and if there was no co-operation he would, of necessity, resort to other tactics however unpleasant that might prove.

"Can I make you more comfortable?" he asked.

Nikolai went to laugh but only choked and spat blood. He lay back and wheezed. "You're too soft SAS".

Alan ignored the jibe and tried once more. "Would you like some water?"

"Water" grunted Nikolai

Alan crouched behind him, raised his head and put the water bottle to the Russians lips. Despite the man's condition, Alan kept a wary eye on the Russians hand in case he made a last desperate attempt to withdraw the knife and complete the job he had set out to do.

"Why Nikolai?" he repeated.

"Orders" Nikolai replied.

"From whom?"

Nikolai glared at him and then winced in agony. "Use your imagination SAS. Orders only come from one source" he closed his eyes.

Alan remembered the clinical expression he had seen in the Russians eyes on the last time they had met and before each went into hiding. Nikolai had been assessing what condition he was in physically. Alan contemplated the implications of the Russian's reply. His orders must have come directly from the KGB. Was it before they went into hiding? No, it couldn't have been – two years had passed. He looked over at Nikolai and wondered how much more he might learn before the man died. Was this part of an agreement between his own government and the Russians or was it just the Soviets cleaning up the operation regardless of liaison. He had not received similar orders to take out Nikolai and knew that if he had, he would have refused.

"I don't buy it Nikolai" said Alan more to himself than the dying man.

"Then you are a fool SAS man" said Nikolai opening his eyes and looking quizzically at Alan." "I know I am dying, so let me tell you what I was told."

He seemed to have decided to help and Alan was relieved; he had not fancied trying to extract information from a dying man. Nikolai gasped as another spasm hit him. Having decided he was going to talk the Russian was trying to hang on.

As he waited Alan was aware of the sun's burning rays. The sounds of nature were unabated, the drama being played out between the two men was of no significance to them.

"I was told" Nikolai began "the SAS no longer trust their own to keep silent on covert operations. If what you and I did ever became public knowledge, our nations would suffer at the hand of world opinion and both our masters would be sacrificed to satisfy in part, the outcry that would follow." He coughed and spat up more blood. As he looked at Alan his eyes took on a slightly frantic expression as if he may not finish what he had set out to say.

"Public opinion would be so focused on them that their enemies at home and abroad would have a field day. Of even more concern is the backlash of terrorism that would almost certainly follow from Iraq."

So he and probably Nikolai were to be sacrificed for expediency. So why did Nikolai seem to think that he would not suffer the same fate. Alan believed he understood the way political reasoning worked and just what might have caused such a course of action. It didn't help to understand. Sadly the politicians had a cause for concern. It had been given them by Sir Peter de la Billiere, who despite the SAS code had produced Gulf War memoirs which had in turn persuaded Andy McNab to write his first novel "Bravo Two Zero", an account of the incompetence of the Allied forces in providing back-up support to SAS field operations in the Gulf War.

No other serving officer in the SAS could now be relied on to maintain silence on company

In Pursuit of the Red Kite

actions and covert operations. He owed McNab! What Alan was unaware of was that the Service was trying to repair its damaged image. The public were made aware of it when the moralising media delighted in reporting that Sir Peter had not been invited to the services annual dinner.

Alan was brought back from his short reverie as Nikolai began to choke and clutch at his stomach. The spasms seemed to take forever as he was forced to watch his former partner die in agony. At last it was over and Alan leant over the now peaceful Nikolai and closed his eyes. "If they were after me they were after you too" he said to the corpse.

He realised that his plans to return to England and report to MI6 were no longer an option. He told himself that if he were to continue to survive it was imperative that British and Russian intelligence must not discover he had broken cover and there must be no trail to follow. First however he had an unpleasant task to perform. He would have to hide Nikolai's body. The Russian could not have picked a better location for the ambush. The hole at the rear of the small cave would be a perfect resting place. Alan only hoped it would be wide enough and that the body would not be stuck at the top of the shaft.

He dragged the body by the feet to the edge of the opening, eased the legs over the edge and with a lot of effort he lifted the torso below the arms and shuffled forward. The last manoeuvre was to make sure the arms were out straight above the head to reduce the risk of jamming on its way down. With a last shove of his foot Nikolai disappeared from sight, the sounds that followed caused him to wince and he had to remind himself the man was dead.

Alan left the cave perspiring from his efforts. He kicked the scree around to reduce the evidence, although some of the blood had already dried to a dull rusty colour and would soon be washed away into the rocks. Before he moved on he had to find Nikolai's rucksack and equipment which would follow him to the grave. He did not have too much trouble, there were not that many places to search. Alan found it behind a large boulder within 150 yards of the cave.

Now that it was over Alan wanted to put as much distance as he could between himself and the place where he may have died if it hadn't been for the fates deciding the Russian would fall on his own knife. That night he would head east and circle the village of Les Girons. He sighed, within hours of leaving the monastery he was again a fugitive. Alan sat inside the cave mouth out of sight from all directions. He would try and sleep again before recommencing the journey, the destination now clearly determined by events. Were MI6 party to Nikolai's actions or not. He would not take any chances in trying to find the answer to that question he told himself.

He was not naive. The fact that the Russians had so far failed in their attempt to kill him did not mean he was safe. If it had been felt sufficiently important that he should die then sooner or later someone else would be on his trail.

He hoped it would be no time soon as he needed to get away and establish his new identity before any trail became too easy to follow.

In Pursuit of the Red Kite

He went back to his camp site to remove any further trace of what had happened before a curious hiker came across the sight of too much blood just off the track. He packed his possessions into his rucksack and with a last look around took it to the cave.

He gathered up Nikolai's rucksack, carried it back to the cave where it followed the body's hiding place. Not however before Alan had searched its contents to see if there was anything that would be of use to him. He took the passport and the food and a more up to date map. Alan kept the knife which he had taken from Nikolai's body. He had cleaned it on the grass and now returned it to the sheath before putting it into his own rucksack. He resisted the Walther PPK two guns were one too many. The Glock would anyway only get him as far as any border crossing where it would have to be left behind.

Alan sat inside the cave mouth out of sight from all directions. He had to admit that he was a little shaken up by what had happened so soon after leaving his refuge. He would not now venture further in daylight and he would try to sleep before recommencing his journey.

That night he would head east and continue to circle any villages. He would stay well away from habitation.

It was only as he lay there trying to get off to sleep he worked out how easy it had been for his refuge to be traced. While he and Nikolai had been in Iraq they had both been kitted out by the Russians and Nikolai had told him that a tracking device had been built into their equipment in case a clandestine extraction had become necessary. 'What an idiot' he told himself. He had used the same rucksack when he had decided to hide out in the Friary. He would now have to abandon it as soon as he could get himself some new kit although it was extremely unlikely that any battery was still operating. In the meantime he knew he may well be tracked by his old employers before he was able to get another rucksack as they were almost sure to know where he had stayed. They would also know when he approached his bank in Geneva. He wondered how much head start he had. He needed money and his new identity documents as soon as possible.

Sleep still eluded him and he went over and over in his mind whether or not "The Firm" were party to Nikolai's actions. If it had been felt sufficiently important that he should die then once Nikolai failed to report back someone else would be on his trail. He again thought back to when he had met the man from "The Firm" and how much his life had changed since then.

He recalled how his curiosity had been roused and how he'd been unable to resist a second meeting with the man he had named The Suit.

Again this took place at the camp. Alan had learned little more before having to sign the Official Secrets Act after which he felt he was then committed to 'Service to the Nation'. In Alan's mind it was simply moving from one Government body to another. With the move his new employers had insisted that he use his mother's surname in future and that all references with his new employers would be amended accordingly.

Things had moved swiftly after that. He had to move off the base to a small flat in London's Kings Cross area, provided by his new employers. It was on the first floor of a converted Victorian terraced house. He didn't get a car however as public transport to his new office at Vauxhall Cross was plentiful.

He recalled that at the beginning all he did was to escort minor envoys on Government business around Europe and the Middle East. It had seemed like he had been taken on as minder and had spent a lot of time waiting while any business was conducted behind closed doors. Gradually however, as it seemed he became a little more trusted, he joined his envoys as an interpreter. This of course had revealed the nature of these meetings and had introduced him to many of the international minor government players.

It was during this period of his life that he met Marie.

It was his practice to arrive close to his office an hour before he was due to commence work and take breakfast at the nearest coffee bar or cafe. This would usually consist of one or two cups of coffee accompanied by croissants. He would either buy a paper at the station or carry a paperback. This interruption in the morning served as break between what passed for home and work.

He was not the only business executive who did this and he began to recognise a regular group of occupants to the cafe. After a while some would nod a recognition although it seemed the unspoken rule was that you did not converse. This suited Alan until one morning when he had not been able to get into his

In Pursuit of the Red Kite

novel and had not purchased a paper. He found his attention kept returning to a young woman who was a regular customer. This morning he had time on his hands and it must have become obvious to her that she had attracted his attention. As she got up to leave she gave him a small smile as she passed his table. Before he could respond she was gone.

Over the following week the smiles of recognition moved on to Alan asking whether he could join her at her table and to his surprise and against the code of the early morning set, she said yes.

Marie was not a conventional beauty; she had a thin face which when not relaxed or smiling made her look somewhat forbidding and unapproachable. It was the blue eyes set within a pageboy haircut that Alan had been most attracted to.

The relationship developed slowly mainly due to Alan's lack of experience with women. While tied to the army life there had not seemed much time for meeting up with girls. Alan had been more obsessed with his academic and physical development and, encouraged by his father, striving for his ultimate entry into the SAS.

Marie unlike Alan commuted into London from Hertford and it was only thanks to the railways cancellation of the last train that she finished up at Alan's flat. Having been out for a meal in Convent Garden neither had noticed the passage of time. Unable to get a cab to Liverpool Street station Marie realised she was stranded in London.

Alan had offered to sleep in a chair but whether or not the wine had anything to do with it,

In Pursuit of the Red Kite

Marie had insisted they share the small bed.

Over the course of the next few weeks Alan's inexperience with women was gradually eroded as Marie spent more time in London although Alan's frequent trips abroad meant that they were not together as much as they would have liked.

The one subject that became increasingly more difficult was what each did for a living. Whereas Marie was happy to talk about her career and the office where she worked as a seller of rare books Alan played down his occupation. He had told Marie that he worked for a Travel Agency which explained his frequent trips abroad.

For a while she had seemed happy with this explanation but as their relationship developed had begun to ask whether Alan's life would always be like this. Despite his inexperience of women Alan realised Marie was beginning to seek some form of commitment from him and was unsure how to respond to the situation.

He did not have to wonder for long. It was one morning in the middle of the week when they had met up in the cafe as usual that Alan saw that Marie seemed to be in an odd mood. Generally she had a happy disposition. This particular day she was quiet.

He asked her what was up and after some deliberation she told him that she had followed him to his office out of curiosity one morning. She hastened to add she was not spying on him. She had seen the building he entered and realised who his employers were. There were no secrets as to where the Secret Services operated from. Alan recalled that whereas he had known how to respond, knew that his response would need to be limited and to Marie, unsatisfactory. As proved to be the case.

That morning when they parted it seemed to be understood that their relationship would not develop much further.

That proved to be the case and it was only a week later that Marie told Alan that she understood

his position but that she could not live with someone who was unable to fully share their life with her.

Alan never saw her again. The morning rendezvous was over as were the nights at his flat.

As he sat in the cave in the approaching dusk Alan wondered, not for the first time, if he had not signed up with "The Firm" would he by now be a happily married man with children of his own living out in suburbia. In reality he knew it would not have satisfied him.

He remembered that following Marie's leaving he had become generally unsettled and had spent a lot of time at the gym, the workouts devised to stretch himself to exhaustion. He also realised that whereas his work was partially fulfilling it presented no excitement and increasingly he became dissatisfied with his life. This may have been noticed at work or may have been mere coincidence but several weeks after Marie's departure he was summoned to a late evening meeting at the office. He had been told that a special operation had come up for which his particular talents were required. It would take him out of the UK for some time. The operation had resulted in his current plight.

CHAPTER 5

October 1993

During the night Alan made his way down the valley maintaining a wide berth around any villages and had raised no unwanted alarms. It was a good time to make the journey as the days were still quite hot and humid but at night this dispersed and the temperature became much cooler. Since leaving the Friary, with the exception of Nikolai, he had not seen another person.

As the sun rose the following morning Alan reassessed his position. His aim was to make it to Forcalquier by lunchtime and hopefully catch a bus into Aix-en-Provence. Despite having some money he needed to get to his Swiss Bank in Geneva. It would be at the bank that he risked leaving the first indication of his re-emergence from hiding. It was a risk that someone might pick up the trail but he knew he had no option. Following the attack by the Russian there could be danger from his own side especially if they had sanctioned the action. They would almost certainly keep an eye on his bank. He could only hope that the Russian would not be missed for a while or that MI6 were not involved. Still whichever way you looked at it the sooner he got to Geneva and sorted out his identity and finances the better. It was also at the bank he had a new identity obtained by himself and deposited in his strong box.

In the deposit box in the bank's vault he had the new identity provided by "The Firm" which was no longer one that he could rely on. Fortunately some

In Pursuit of the Red Kite

sixth sense had made him obtain a separate identity before his self-imposed exile.

It was through a contact at the German Embassy that he had managed to obtain a German passport. At the time he was amused at the thought of having a secret identity and for not an inconsiderable cost had bought one. But to get it he had to use the one in the name of Alan Marks.

It took him much of the day to reach the bus station at Forcalquier. At the ticket office he bought a single ticket and learned that he had a quarter of an hour's wait before the next bus to Aix-en-Provence. It was in Aix that he would get rid of his rucksack and buy himself a hold-all for the small amount of luggage that he possessed.

He bought a copy of 'Aujourdhui' and strolled onto the concourse where he perched on a bench seat and scanned the paper for any mention of either himself or Nikolai, not that he expected anything to appear so soon. It would have been extremely bad luck if Nikolai's body had been discovered. He had disposed of both of the pistols into a small hole in the cave where he had disposed of Nikolai's body by having first rendered them unusable.

The trip to Aix was slow and from there he would have to get to Geneva. From Aix he would take a train to Marseilles, fly to Paris and take a connecting flight to Geneva a partly necessary detour as there was no direct link from Aix and partly to confuse any possible follower. Before that however he would spend a day in Aix.

His first priority was to visit a cash point, which was necessary but traceable, then to a local barber's shop where he had his hair trimmed and the beard removed. Too late he realised that he was left with part of his face paler where the sun had not penetrated. There was nothing he could do about this now. He had wanted to ensure that his appearance loosely matched that of his current identification documents and he would have to live with it.

He found himself a small hotel, Les Quatre Dauphins in Rue Cardinale, not far from the Cours Mirabeau, the main street of this attractive French town. Having checked in to the hotel Alan decide to go for a walk and headed back towards the Cours Mirabeau, a beautifully wide street lined with large Plane trees through which dappled sunlight passed down to the broad pavements below.

It was along this street that he decided to sit and have a coffee while relaxing and taking part in one of his favourite pursuits, people watching. The Café he chose was 'Les Deux Garcons' and he learned from the waiter that served him that it had been there since 1792, had been purchased by two waiters and had been a favourite watering hole for Paul Cezanne and Emil Zola who had been close friends. A fact he appreciated as you couldn't go far in this town without being reminded of Cezanne.

That evening he decided to have his dinner at the Café and took a table in the heavily gilded interior. Having obtained some money on his credit card, he had gone to the station only to discover he would have to wait till the following day before he could get a train to Marseilles. The cafe filled up with

In Pursuit of the Red Kite

groups of tourists and parties of locals and he soon found he could barely hear himself think as the decor was fairly reflective and everybody seemed to be in party mood. He had arrived earlier than the majority of patrons and had established himself at a small table for two near the window. This had been left open and he was assailed by street noise as well. He reminded himself of his time at the Friary where he had become used to a quiet existence, especially at meal times that were conducted in silence. It was with some relief that he finished his meal, paid the bill and left the restaurant. This was followed by a quick stroll before returning to his hotel and a fairly early night.

The following morning, having checked out, he took the train to Marseilles and began his journey to Switzerland, arriving in Geneva later that evening where, tired from his trip, he booked into the hotel nearest the station having taken the train from the airport.

The next day, after a small breakfast, Alan packed and left the hotel and took a cab to the Merchant Bank where his money and new documents awaited him.

At the bank he asked the teller if he could speak with the assistant manager, M'sieu Dubois. She smiled and asked him to take a seat.

The assistant manager arrived ten minutes later apologising for keeping him waiting. Alan saw that the man recognised him even though it had been two years since he had last visited the building. Before that there had only been a couple of meetings, sufficient to set up the account, collect his credit cards

In Pursuit of the Red Kite

and a small amount of money.

The manager scanned Alan's passport and handed it back.

M'sieu Dubois was friendly and was only too happy to assist. He led him through the security pass door into the rear of the premises and down a short flight of stairs to the basement strong room. Alan was shown into a small adjoining room and his box was brought to him. The manager explained he would be locked in and when he had finished his business he should ring the internal 'phone. The operator would inform M'sieu Dubois and Alan would be let out and his box returned to the vault.

As the door closed behind the manager Alan leant down and using his knife opened the seam in his jeans zip and pulled out the key to his box. He took out a German passport in the name of Paul Gerhardt and a roll of large denomination French and German currency which– amounted to about £10,000.00 of each. The documents he took were those given him by his employers together with those he had obtained himself. It would be sufficient for his immediate needs. However Alan had not created a history for the new character he was to become and that could become a problem if his new identity ever came under scrutiny. He was also very aware that any further use of his credit cards provided by "The Firm" would be traceable and lead to his whereabouts.

It was as Alan Marks that he had set up his account with the Swiss Bank and where the considerable fortune he'd made before retiring to the Friary had been invested.

In Pursuit of the Red Kite

At the outset of the operation for "The Firm" he had been given sufficient funds to ensure its success. Following a satisfactory outcome of the operation he had been told that should he be able to make any additional money he would be allowed to keep it. He was advised to be discreet about it, from which Alan understood they did not want to know, provided the money stayed offshore.

Alan picked up the 'phone and dialled the operator.

To his surprise it was not the manager who returned to let him out, but the clerk he had spoken to on his arrival, the attractive brunette who had dealt with his request at the counter.

Then she had smiled at him and he thought he had read an invitation in her sparkling eyes.

He tried to engage her in small talk but she made it quite clear that she was busy and needed to get back to her desk. The smile he realised came with the job. He was certainly rusty in that quarter and two years of celibacy had not helped.

He spent the afternoon purchasing a small wardrobe of clothes that would fit into the new holdall purchased in Aix and a briefcase which he decided was necessary to make him appear as the German businessman his new persona demanded. Having got himself kitted out he returned to the centre of town where he looked for another hotel.

On entering a small square he saw what he was looking for. The front could do with some serious redecoration he thought to himself as he pushed through the door into a comfortable but tired looking reception area.

"I need a room for a few days" he explained to the middle aged woman who had looked up from her seat behind the wooden reception desk as he entered.

"We have a large room overlooking the square." She replied. "That will be fifty francs including breakfast or there's a smaller room at the back for forty-five" she looked questioningly at him as she waited for his decision.

He went for the room at the back. He didn't need the view and maybe the front could get noisy later when the restaurants emptied out in the evening.

"I'll take the one at the back" said Alan reaching into his inside pocket in anticipation of her request for his papers.

"Passport?"

He handed her his new German passport.

She handled it with distaste and her expression became more hostile.

It was not the first time Alan had witnessed this reaction in the presence of Germans. Many people had long memories and bore grudges. Most he'd noticed did not allow their personal views to affect their judgement. The receptionist did not seem to mind who knew how she felt, an attitude Alan knew would not be tolerated in a more upmarket establishment.

She put the key on the desk as she said

In Pursuit of the Red Kite

"second floor, stairs are over there." She waved in the general direction of the small central staircase that would have been impossible to miss.

Alan picked up his bags and took the stairs to the second floor. The room he entered was not as small as he had at first feared. The layout common to most hotels, you passed the bathroom before entering the body of the room. There was a single bed with a low table on which were local guides and a tariff. A semi comfortable chair positioned opposite a table with a television on top and a mini-bar underneath. A wardrobe and a case rack completed the furnishings. The window in the far wall currently with curtains drawn completed the layout. Still he had a roof over his head and somewhere he could stay while he decided what direction his future would take added to which he did not plan to spend a lot of time in the room.

As he had planned to familiarise himself with Geneva he thought he would rest up during the afternoon and then take a stroll around the town during the evening. He'd bought himself a copy of an old Frederick Forsyth novel and started to read it. It was dusk when he woke up, the book had fallen to the floor. His mouth was dry and he got up and made himself a coffee from the room tray; he ignored the mini-bar.

On waking his mind had returned to the problem of his future and how it was no longer one of endless options. When he had entered the Friary his future had seemed relatively clear. He would return to England after two years and possibly seek further employment with "The Firm". He recalled that continued employment had not been guaranteed when he had accepted the original operation but he had assumed that with a successful mission behind him he would be of use. There was no reason to assume that his presence may have become an embarrassment to his employers.

It was difficult to believe that both the Russian and UK governments had agreed that he needed to be silenced if indeed that was the case. The more he had thought of it over the past couple of days he found that he became increasingly angry at his plight. The anger had fed a determination not only to survive but to fight back.

Simply to survive was not enough, he knew that way he would spend forever looking over his shoulder and wondering whether he was in someone's sights. He had to find a way of removing the threat.

As he stood at the window overlooking a small backyard and the flank wall of an even more uncared for facade to that of his own hotel, the solution to his problem came to mind. Not so much an inspiration but an acceptance of "the bleeding obvious" he said aloud.

He was pleased that he had had the foresight to make a report of his mission. The decision he needed to make was should he let "The Firm" know of its existence or not. One copy still remained in his strong box at the bank. Would they call off the search if he warned them of its existence. Would that be enough or would it simply increase their determination to silence him. He had to assume the latter.

In Pursuit of the Red Kite

He left the hotel and strolled across the square to a restaurant where he would take an early evening meal, then go for a walk afterwards to develop a strategy before returning to his room for the night.

As he waited for the food he found himself scrutinising everybody in the square outside; was he beginning to feel the paranoia of the hunted he wondered. He stopped himself and then reasoned it was, nevertheless, no bad thing to stay alert.

He barely tasted the food as he mulled over the task in front of him. He heard the door open and a warm draught of air hit him as he looked up to see a man in a business suit come in. Alan caught his gaze and the man quickly looked away seeking a waiter. Did he look away too rapidly he found himself thinking. He returned to the menu.

He became aware of the waiter addressing him.

"I wonder M'sieu would you mind sharing your table?" His face was apologetic as he posed the question.

"We are very full this evening" he added as the question hung between them.

Alan realised he should respond and rather hastily said "No, of course I don't mind", a reaction he realised as typically British, on reflection a German would probably have been more direct.

The waiter led the businessman over. He shrugged as he said "I hope you don't mind" in an American accent, whilst pulling out the chair and sitting opposite Alan. The waiter handed him a menu.

"No not at all" Alan replied.

"English?"

Alan caught himself

"No, German" he said.

"You speak English well" the American said as he put his hand across the table for Alan to shake.

"Jake Gregson" he announced.

"Paul Gerhardt", Alan briefly shook the hand.

"What's the food like here?"

"I don't know, it's the first time I've been here."

"How did you hear of the place?"

"I didn't, I took a chance."

"Me too" the American chuckled. He looked round for the waiter and ordered a beer.

"Can I offer you a beer?" he asked Alan.

"That's kind" Alan said. He felt the quiet meal slipping away. This man wanted someone to talk to and probably drink with. He sighed inwardly.

As the meal progressed he found himself relaxing and even enjoying the company of this outgoing American who seemed to have an endless stream of anecdotes relating to his business as an engineer for Hewlett Packard, Europe.

It was a life that Alan had no desire to emulate. Endless travel between Boston and the Paris headquarters before roaming around most of the larger towns and cities of Western Europe finding ways of killing time between meetings.

Alan could not remember who suggested going for a beer after the meal, but they found themselves in a 'Tabac' in a seedier part of town. It was crowded, noisy and smoke filled with the strong smell of 'Gauloises.' They sat at the bar and ordered beer and cognac from the patron. The locals after a cursory look resumed their own conversations.

At around 11.00pm they were both the worse for wear but Alan seemed to be holding up better despite his two years of abstinence. He decided to quit.

"Got to go Jake."

"Already?" said the American.

"Got an early start" Alan lied.

As they more or less fell off their bar stools Jake turned and lurched off. Despite having had a lot to drink, unlike Jake, Alan felt both fairly sober and wide awake. They parted outside the Tabac and Alan's last view of Jake was to witness him staggering off in the opposite direction.

He decided to make his way down to the lake around which were where some of the priciest hotels in Geneva were located. When he arrived at the Quai du Mont Blanc he was pleased to see that the fountain 'Jet L' Eau' in the centre of the lake was in full force. He crossed to the waterside and for some time simply watched the display of power as the jet shot up into the night sky illuminated by the lights set into the lake.

In Pursuit of the Red Kite

There was however, another reason Alan had chosen to come to this part of Geneva. He remembered, while on one of his many trips in support of some junior envoy for the British Government that one of them had brought him here. His colleague's purpose had been to find what he had quaintly called, at the time, a 'lady of the night'. Then, Alan had not followed suit, but recalled how the man had not stopped talking about it the next morning.

Maybe it was the drink or maybe the way the bank teller had not risen to his charms that he felt a need to do some research of his own. Or could it simply have been two years of enforced abstinence.

Most of the more expensive hotels had bars where a piano player provided background music for their guests to listen or dance to. It was also an area where executives staying in Geneva on expenses tended to frequent. Two of the more popular were 'Hotel de la Paix' and 'Hotel Beau Rivage'.

In this part of town the prostitutes were reputedly the best and also the most expensive. With the amount of money now at his disposal Alan reasoned if this was the way to round off the evening then he could afford the best.

He entered the first hotel he came to. As expected, just off the reception area was a bar from which he could hear the muted music of a piano. He crossed reception and entered the dimly lit space and took a seat at the bar. He told the barman to make him a tab and ordered a sparkling water. Obviously puzzled the barman produced the drink and placed it

In Pursuit of the Red Kite

in front of him.

"Will there be anything else sir?" he asked.

"No that's fine for now" Alan thanked him and turned to inspect the room.

There were quite a few patrons plus several girls and men, apparently on their own, both at the small tables around the room or sitting, as he was, at the bar.

He knew he had come to right place as he noticed some of the single girls either surreptitiously or overtly giving him a look over. The choice would be his however. None approached him. He settled back against the bar and studied the room. It seemed the form was having selected a girl you then asked them to dance and on the dance floor, negotiations took place.

Some couples seemed to make a quick decision, others took longer or parted to renegotiate with another customer. Alan realised that if he left it too long the choices would seriously diminish.

There had been one girl in particular, sitting at the bar who he had found his attention returning to. As he looked again he saw that she was watching him. He smiled and raised his glass. She returned the greeting but remained seated. He got up and made his way to where she sat.

She smiled as he approached.

She was slim and probably fairly tall. Sitting it was impossible to tell. She had shoulder length dark brown hair and her face was fine boned without looking too hard. Brown eyes and a nicely proportioned mouth completed an attractive face.

She was wearing a business suit of a dark navy material under which a white high necked blouse covered her small breasts. Black nylons and black high heeled shoes completed Alan's inspection of the girl who could be his companion for the night.

"Hi" he greeted her in English

"Hi yourself." She responded with a strong French accent." Would you like to dance?" "I'd rather not" said Alan who had never taken to the noble art in any of its many forms. "But may I buy you a drink?"

In answer she showed him a glass that was already full.

"Perhaps later" she paused "What is your name and what do you do?"

"The name's Paul and at the moment I do not need to work" he replied at which her interest seemed to take on a new level.

She stretched out her hand and pulled him a little closer.

"Well Paul perhaps we should get to know each other a little better"

Alan smiled inwardly, so much for the preliminaries.

She studied his face as she asked "You know what it is that I do?"

"I do"

"And you would like it to be for the whole night?"

"I would" he replied.

She took a moment before responding. No doubt assessing just how much she could expect to get away with.

Alan remained silent. He had a maximum figure in mind having heard from his colleague some years ago that the girls here were very expensive but well worth the price.

"One thousand English pounds" she said watching his face.

After taking some time to respond, during which there had been no offer of a reduction he finally agreed. Her smile seemed to contain a look of relief.

"That does include a Continental breakfast" She had the grace to laugh as she added this.

"Good. I would hate to go away and have to tell my friends of poor service" he joked back. He called for the bar bill and was not surprised to see that it included her drink as well as his own.

She turned and picked up her hand bag before sliding off the stool. The top of her head reached his nose. She was not as tall as he had at first thought.

"Do you have a coat?" he asked.

"No I have a room here" she replied. Then sensing the unspoken question in his eyes said "It is included in the price." On leaving the bar they returned to the reception area and took the lift to the fourth floor, then along a long corridor before stopping outside her room. They had not seen another person since leaving reception.

The room they entered could not have been more different from the one at his hotel. Whereas the layout was similar, that's where the likeness ended. The bathroom was lined in marble. As well as a bath there was a shower large enough for two. The room was spacious and square with a large bed in the centre of a long wall. The room lighting was subtle and the decorations and décor had been 'designed'. The far wall was covered by floor to ceiling curtains and Alan imagined that they hid a view to the lake.

He realised that he did not know how to proceed. There had been no passionate build-up to this moment and he briefly wondered if this was such a good idea. He was here now and being British he would endure the consequences.

He looked up to see her looking amusedly at him.

"What?" He asked.

"You have not even asked my name"

At this Alan felt himself redden. He had been too immersed in his own deliberations.

"I am so sorry that is very rude of me. Will you please tell me?"

"Nicole" she replied. Then added "I think this is the first time you have paid to have sex *n'est pas.*"

Alan had to admit it was.

Tant pis, if you think of it as pleasurable exercise then you will enjoy it" then added "but if you try and believe it has to be romantic then you will not."

Alan stood there, if anything feeling even more inadequate.

She took pity and gave him a hug.

"Go into the bathroom and take all your clothes off and take a shower. Put on the gown you see hanging there and come back to me."

Alan did as instructed. Suddenly his brain took over and for the first time he considered his potential vulnerability at the hands of Nicole. Would she rob him, steal his credit cards, video and try to blackmail him. No he told himself, it would be bad for business. And with that thought he climbed into the shower. He towelled himself dry, tied the robe and went back into the bedroom.

The sight that awaited him drove any further hesitation from his mind.

Nicole with little on was standing in front of a full length mirror allowing him to get a complete all round view. There was no spare fat on her well proportioned body. Nor was it too thin. He just stood there and took in the beauty of this woman's until she said

"Come over to me Paul. But do not touch me"

Alan did as he was told. He noticed that Nicole's expression had now become serious.

He stood in front of her as she raised her arms, undid his bathrobe and dropped it around his feet. She then placed both hands on his chest before slowly lowering herself in front of him. This was the introduction to a night Alan was to remember for the rest of his life.

Nicole pushed him gently back to the bed where he laid back with his legs over the end. She got up and sat on him then began a slow gyration with her hips. By raising himself on his elbows Alan was able to watch in the mirror opposite as she began to caress herself. This proved too much for him and was unable to prevent a premature conclusion so early in the night.

At that Nicole dismounted and with a smile said "do not worry that was only the beginning" and so it proved to be.

As the night wore on he could not believe the way pleasure could be transmitted between two bodies in so many different ways. It also became evident that Nicole was using his body as a love toy. At first he was not sure how to take this but soon realised it only heightened his own pleasure.

Between each act Nicole insisted that they wash and cover each other with a variety of body oils set out on the bedside table. This only added more sensuality to the next session the number of which Alan lost count.

He awoke to find Nicole gone but heard the shower. He was still wearing his watch and discovered that it was just gone 8.00am. He laid back. What was the form for the morning after. The shower was turned off and minutes later Nicole returned wearing nothing but a smile.

" Breakfast will be here at 8.30" she said "so how about one last time?"

Afterwards as they lay there Nicole said "we should get dressed before it arrives" She got up.

Alan watched her. As she dressed she said to him

"You do realise that some of the things we did last night may not be good to do in a more romantic situation. In fact they could result in a not so liberated woman seeing them as perverted acts. Just be careful for your own sake" This was delivered as a friendly warning and Alan realised he was being given good advice.

Breakfast was an almost silent affair after which Nicole hastened his departure with a smile and wave at the room door.

Back at his hotel 'the dragon' was at reception and when he asked for his key handed it over with a disapproving look. Alan winked at her and held onto her hand longer than necessary which only caused the look to change to one of anger.

Pleased by this reaction, he walked over to the lift and returned to a room that looked even cheaper

by comparison to the one in which he had spent the previous night.

CHAPTER 6

November 1993

Sir Ian Rush was unable to return to the "Red Kite" file the following day. There had been a lot of activity among government organisations following the IRA bombing at Canary Wharf and he'd spent the whole day attending meetings.

As a result of the search for the terrorists a small bomb factory had been found in Islington and two men were being sought in connection with the event. What was more disturbing was a list of new IRA targets found on the premises. The new campaign was to be aimed at individuals rather than property, and in view of this find, the general feeling was that Canary Wharf was a one off, a fitting opener to the end of the ceasefire and the beginning of a new era.

It was therefore Wednesday morning when Sir Ian called Amanda in and asked her to bring him the file.

As before, she and the Security Clerk arrived together. He carried the file and Amanda carried an expression of frustration. Sir Ian signed for the document. The Clerk left as he looked up at Amanda.

"I would appreciate a cup of Earl Grey Amanda" he said.

"Yes sir" she replied tightly as she turned and left his office.

He allowed himself a smile. He scanned the first part of the file to refresh his memory until he arrived at the section where it had been reported that both the British and Russian services would provide their own "discredited" agent as part of the operation. The file went on to tell him that the man selected to act for MI6 had not been chosen from within the Service. As he turned the page he was faced with a poorly copied photograph of Alan Marks from 22 Squadron SAS. He noted the change of surname from his father's to his mother's. No doubt the reason for the change would become clear.

"I wonder what you did to earn the title "Red Kite", he said aloud. He looked up to see whether anybody had heard him. His office door was closed. His habit of thinking aloud had not been spotted by anyone in the department. It did however cause his wife to become irritated with him from time to time.

Stapled to the back of the photograph was a single page of text that said Alan Marks had been forced to resign from the SAS. Of this Alan was unaware. It had been inserted into his service record by his new employers in case there were to be any future investigation into his past. It stated that, because of an alleged act of cowardice on his part, during his involvement in the Gulf War, he had left the Squadron. Now the name change had become clear. It would not look good for the department to have recruited someone with a dubious track record. Sir Ian put the file down and stood up. Where was his "Earl Grey." He opened his office door, which fortunately opened inwards otherwise there may have well been a collision with Amanda who stood there with one hand out reaching for the door knob that had eluded her and in the other the long awaited tea.

"Sorry Sir" she said "I got slightly sidetracked".

He took the cup from her.

"That's OK." He smiled, not wishing to seem impatient.

"Was there anything else?" she asked.

"Er no, that's all" he replied realising as soon as he'd said it he had confirmed that he had come hunting the missing tea.

He closed the door and sat down again at his desk. He turned back to the photograph and studied the clean cut serious looking young man of slightly Latin appearance. Somehow he did not look a coward Sir Ian thought. He returned to reading the file.

There followed a separate paper on Alan's life before and after he had joined MI6 as an employee. It was noted that Alan had achieved a reasonable academic success and that he had no living relatives. He had made few friends, preferring to live a solitary existence. There was no record of regular girlfriends, though it seemed women found him superficially attractive. Once they got to know him however they soon found that he was not ready for a serious commitment.

"No close ties." Sir Ian noted.

It was at the end of 1991 that the plot to hoax Saddam was devised by MI6 and with the complicity of the KGB and the search for suitable agents began.

Sir Ian's predecessor had approached both military and civil security forces for a likely candidate culminating in the selection of Alan Marks. He surmised that Alan had been selected not only for his fluency in languages but for having no attachments.

Sir Ian knew only too well the approach that would have been adopted by his predecessor to recruit Alan. A period of watching and grooming would then follow before putting him into the field.

He put the file down and asked Amanda for another cup of tea before reading the details of how the operation had been prepared. It was absolutely paramount that neither government could be implicated if anything went wrong with the operation and more importantly if it were successful.

His predecessor had pulled no punches with Alan. He was told he was on his own if the operation was blown and he was captured. There was no question of H M Government coming to his aid or seeking his release.

Sir Ian wondered, not for the first time, why anybody took on such a task.

Alan was told he would be given a new identity on completion of the operation but it was vital that in order to maintain credibility of his cover, any investigation into his background by the Iraqis it would reveal had been made to resign from the SAS, thereby providing a reason as to why he had no love or loyalty for his country. At first Alan did not take kindly to the way he had been set up. However the previous administration had obviously finally sold the project. The telephone rang. "Front desk Sir. DCI

In Pursuit of the Red Kite

McCullock on the line."

Sir Ian looked at his watch . Just after 11.00am. He frowned.

"What does the bloody man want now" he thought.

"Put him through."

"Yes Sir."

"Morning McCullock, what's the problem?" he asked.

"I thought you would like to be the first to know Sir Ian" the sarcasm in his voice thinly veiled "We've had another bomb go off."

"Where?"

"The Aldwych. On a bus."

"Casualties?"

"One dead and one seriously injured."

"Why on earth do they want to blow a bus up at this time of day?"

"Agreed, it does seem odd. I could understand it in the rush hour" said McCullock "although I never saw the IRA following the Hammas."

"What?"

"Suicide bomber, Sir."

"Really?"

"No, we think it may have been a faulty device on its way to another target. It's probable the

In Pursuit of the Red Kite

IRA scored an own goal. It is, however, essential that the casualties are ID'd as soon as possible as they could be the perpetrators."

"Maybe there is some justice then!" Sir Ian said more to himself than the inspector.

"Maybe Sir" McCullock was noncommittal.

"Thank you McCullock. I take it you have it under control, area cordoned off etc."

"Yes, this morning will be chaotic until we are sure there are no more devices and have got the debris removed. I'll talk to your liaison officer later. With respect we don't need any more Scene of Crime experts right now."

The DG got up from his desk his conversation with the Inspector ended. He went over to the window and again looked down on the silent image of the river below, his mind only partly on what McCullock had reported. The scene was one of complete normality, river buses and barges made their way back and forth on the Thames, their wakes glittering in the sunlight. He raised his eyes. The traffic along Millbank still seemed to be running.

"No jams yet" he thought.

The intercom rang. It was Amanda reminding him of his midday appointment with the Prime Minister's Private Secretary.

"Thank you. Yes."

He sat down and closed the file. When he returned to his office he would telephone his opposite number in the KGB, Yuri Goroshenko. On reflection he thought he should complete his reading and find out how successful the operation had been.

He would ask Harry whether they had received any contact from their man as the two years of lying low had been completed and in theory he could re-surface at any time. As he picked up his briefcase to leave for his meeting he wondered whether the current administration would welcome the reminder about the operation. No doubt the PPS would have a view on the subject.

CHAPTER 7

October 1993

Alan had spent the afternoon exploring the town. From his hotel he had taken a route that took him to the town's main thoroughfare where he had selected a small cafe.

He had sat at a pavement table for two and ordered a cognac and cafe noir. For a while he had just sat and people watched. It was a warm day despite the time of year and he found his attention wandering from the task. His table was in the shade, the buildings opposite bathed in strong sunlight. It was after his second coffee that he pulled out a small notebook and pen. These he had purchased earlier with the aim of jotting down ideas from which to form a strategy for a new life ahead. It would seem he could no longer rely on his past.

From his school days he had remembered being told it is important to have a plan in principle as to how the task was to be set out. You will change it often his tutor had said, but mostly in sequence not in the main direction you are aiming for.

He smiled to himself at remembering this detail. It had not served him too well at school although he appreciated the basic wisdom of creating ordered thought.

For the remainder of that day and the next he had tried to get to grips with the problem. He was distracted by the town and he spent a lot of his time taking long walks visiting museums, historic and religious buildings. During his walkabout he had realised the size of the task he had to deal with. It was no longer possible for a reintroduction into his past career with "The Firm". It was a new whole life plan he had to map out. He also realised that staying so long in Geneva was a bit of a luxury and that he should move on. He decided that one more day and he would leave Switzerland.

It was on the third morning of his stay in Geneva that he decided to continue his quest for inspiration and breakfast at the café not too far from his bank. Every day he had purchased a French paper with the purpose of seeing whether Nikolai's body had been discovered. Nothing had been reported and he wondered if it was of sufficient import to appear in a Swiss newspaper.

It was another beautiful morning, the sky a pale blue with a chill breeze that decided him to sit inside instead of taking an outside table.

Having ordered he took out the pad and pen, read through his previous efforts and with a sigh crossed them out. He would need to begin again. The only conclusion so far was that it had to be somewhere far from Geneva where he would begin his new life.

As the waiter arrived with his coffee he looked up and noticed the bank clerk with the welcoming smile entering the cafe. Instead of simply smiling or nodding in recognition, he stood up and assumed what he thought was a welcoming smile of invitation.

Without being rude to a company customer she could not ignore the implicit request to join him.

In Pursuit of the Red Kite

Catharine De Farge recognised the man standing and smiling at her from his table. She remembered him coming into the bank a few days earlier and thinking he had seemed nice but recalled she had been a little short with him as she showed him out.

"Damn" she said to herself as she saw the position she was in. She liked to take her coffee alone before going into the office, she found it set her up nicely after her drive into Geneva, especially after dealing with the morning rush hour. She wondered what he was still doing here. For some reason she'd had the impression he was passing through.

Alan could not help but notice the slight look of irritation on her face before professionalism took over and she rearranged her expression into a smile and came over to his table.

"Would you care to join me for breakfast?" he asked.

"I will not eat thank you" she replied "but a coffee would be most welcome."

He watched her sit before sitting down himself. The waiter looked amused, whether at his approach or at some private joke, Alan would never know.

"M'sieu?"

"A coffee for Madame" he looked at her "Black or white?"

"White, please."

Neither seemed inclined to be the first to

make conversation. Alan gave in as the silence extended.

"I hope you didn't mind me asking you to join me?"

"It's OK." she said and this time the smile looked genuine.

"I don't even know your name?"

"It is Catharine De Farge." She offered her hand across the table.

Alan took it. It was dry and smooth, the fingers long and slender. "Thank you" he smiled at the banality of his next remark "Do you always take coffee here?"

She smiled showing almost perfect teeth. He decided that, as he watched her, it was the imperfection that made her more attractive.

Catharine having found herself with this man decided she would get to know a little more about him. She had often been told that she was too direct when conversing with new acquaintances. Her friends were less polite, they told her she was nosey. Of course it made no difference, she told them, people could take her as she was or not at all. Being young and attractive, most tolerated her.

"What are you doing here anyway?" she asked him.

"Seeking inspiration for a report I have to write" he replied.

"A company report?"

"Yes, in a way."

"Can you not do it at the office?" Catharine enquired.

"My office is in Berlin" Alan replied realising that now he would have to begin using his new identity as Paul Gerhardt whilst sticking to the name known at the bank.

"So what is it you are doing in Geneva?"

"Well, I'm sort of relaxing before I go back to Berlin."

"Relaxing?"

Under this gentle interrogation Alan began to flounder, remembering his night with Nicole. Catharine noticed his embarrassment.

"I'm sorry, I didn't mean to intrude" she said looking concerned.

"No it's OK" he paused. He was having to make it up on the spot. "Well for a while I have been convalescing." another lie.

She raised an eyebrow in question.

He went on "Well I suppose the pressure of my work began to have an effect on my performance and it was decided that I should take a break."

"For how long?"

"Oh" he mumbled "about six months." As he said it he was not sure but something in Catharine's eyes seemed to reflect an inner reaction. It was gone as soon as it appeared and her look of polite interest was back in place.

"Anyway that is enough about me, what about you?" Alan grinned.

"What is it you want to know?" Catharine asked.

"Oh, how long have you worked at the bank, do you breakfast here everyday, do you live in Geneva.......?"

"Hold it! One at a time." She took a sip of her coffee and eyed him over the rim of her cup. She put it down.

"Five years, yes and in a little village about 20 kilometres from here. Now what?" There was now merriment in her eyes.

Alan put his hands up in surrender.

Before he could reply she glanced down at her watch.

"Oh dear!" she exclaimed "Now I'm late." She stood up and called the waiter.

"I'll get this one" said Alan.

She paused before saying "OK, but the next time is on me."

"Tomorrow?"

She paused, no longer smiling.

"Perhaps. Thank you again" she turned and left as the waiter arrived.

As she walked out of the cafe she turned

briefly at the door and waved. She smiled to herself as she walked off to work.

Alan contemplated. Maybe he would stay in Geneva a little longer, his earlier resolve to leave the next day already beginning to weaken. What was one more day after all.

"I will pay for madam. Put it on my bill" said Alan. The encounter seemed to have provided the necessary inspiration to Alan to continue with the task of mapping out a future and before long a loose plan in constructing a past history, linking all the main points together, covered the first pages of the pad. As he continued Alan was reminded that the new report needed to be lodged with his solicitor. It would contain a list of all the people he had been involved with at 'The Firm,' together with any details of their status that he could remember and, he asked himself, should he continue in keeping a diary on how his future developed in case it later helped him to stay alive?

The original list, attached to the report he had taken from his strongbox, contained many innocent academics who had provided him and Nikolai with the realistic and factual background material necessary to convince the Iraqi leaders' scientific advisers that the product they were being offered was genuine.

Of all the people he had met there was one man that he would never forget. Aziz Ruboek. A colonel in the Iraqi army, diplomat and probably a spy as well Alan had thought at the time. Ruboek, a lean aquiline featured man, was tall for an Iraqi. His eyes, so dark brown that had they appeared almost black, seemed as if they could see right into your soul. At no time, in their many encounters had he seen Aziz smile, he had wondered if the man had any sense of humour at all and imagined that he would make the perfect interrogator.

Alan remembered that Russia, Germany, Austria and South Africa had been the sources of the scientific information supplied to the Iraqis; neither the UK (excluding himself) nor America had been involved. On reflection it was natural to assume that the latter would have stretched the credibility of the exercise. It also successfully distanced those countries from any media backlash if the whole thing had come apart.

Alan sat back in his chair and stretched. Enough writing for now he told himself.

He recalled the waiter and ordered a last coffee and the bill.

As he drank he reconsidered his position. Presently there was no reason to feel in danger. Nikolai may have been able to inform the KGB that he had broken cover. He couldn't, however, have reported that he had failed in his attempt on Alan's life. Nikolai had been informed of his whereabouts when he had been instructed to remove Alan. So the Russians had been able to track him down using the tracking device concealed in his hold- tracked and then waited him out.

He realised that the KGB would begin to suspect something was wrong when Nikolai had not reported in within three or four weeks of sending him to eliminate Alan. Even then they would probably make some allowances. At the moment he felt he still had a little time on his side.

He paid and left the cafe and continued what had become a habit over the last teo days. He had planned to again visit the old town before lunch. He would then return to his hotel and work studiously till he decided it was time to eat. A meal on his own, by preference. He also thought that maybe another night with Nicole would be something to look forward to.

As he strolled along he removed his jacket. It was becoming hot and with the sun almost directly overhead the shade on the streets was becoming scarce.

Since he'd been here he had already grown to like Geneva and the routine he'd established of mixing working on his plan for the future and getting to know its history and visiting its ancient monuments he'd found enjoyable.

His day worked out as planned but by ten that evening he decided enough was enough, his mind becoming distracted by the possibility of seeing Nicole again. He washed before leaving his hotel and made his way down to the lakeside and the hotel in which he had previously found her.

He pushed his way into reception and began to cross to the bar only to see Nicole coming out with a large elderly man on her arm. As she saw Alan an expression of disappointment crossed her face. As they passed she looked at Alan and shrugged. There was nothing she could do as the pair crossed reception to the lifts.

In Pursuit of the Red Kite

Suddenly Alan's night of pleasure had vanished and he found he had no desire to go into the bar and find himself another companion.

He turned and made his way back to his hotel for an early night. One in which he found it difficult to sleep.

Before turning out the bedside light he checked that he had a pen and his writing pad to hand. It was again something he had been advised in his late youth and had become a deeply ingrained habit. Rather than lying awake worrying as to whether he would remember important issues the following morning, record them at the time and disrupt sleep as little as possible. Not that he got much that night anyway.

It was around seven the next morning before he surfaced.

His first thoughts on waking were no longer of last night's missed opportunities but the possibility of meeting Catharine for breakfast.

Whereas at the Friary there had been some restriction as to the nature of keep fit Alan had resumed an exercise programme begun during his service in the SAS and maintained it whenever possible. His day would begin with half an hour's jogging through the streets around the town followed by a shower on his return to the hotel.

At her cottage Catharine also was awake early but unlike Alan she was not into keep fit. She lay and contemplated her meeting with Alan at breakfast the previous day. There had been no doubt in her mind that she would see him again. She was physically attracted to him and from their short acquaintance thought that his personality was likeable. It had been some time since she had been this attracted to another man.

She spent a long time on her appearance as the clothes she would be wearing would be limited to the conservative requirements of the bank whilst making her look as appealing as possible.

Alan had resisted the impulse to get there too early as it was unlikely that Catharine would alter her timetable, that is if she turned up at all, he reminded himself. As it turned out he needn't have worried. He saw her approach the cafe from the opposite side of the street, giving him the opportunity to observe her form and movement as Catharine had intended he should.

After an initial awkwardness the conversation became more relaxed as they got to know each other better and by the time Catharine had to leave for work she had manoeuvred Alan, with the right amount of hesitancy, into inviting her to dinner that evening. She had agreed to meet him at the cafe and they would take it from there.

Alan tried to follow his normal pattern for the day but his attempts on the report proved to be a waste. Catharine occupied most of his thinking time. He was unable to decide whether his feelings went beyond physical attraction. It was over two years since he'd had any contact with women other than Nicole and he was having trouble convincing himself that he would succeed with Catharine.

In Pursuit of the Red Kite

That evening Catharine took Alan towards the south of the lake. Here she told him was a small restaurant known for its typically Swiss cuisine.

It was indeed a small restaurant, crammed between shops. There were only about ten tables and the Maitre'd seemed to know Catharine and showed her to a discreet corner where there was a table for two. Alan wondered if it had been pre-arranged. Not that that mattered.

The ambience and the food seemed conducive to the mood both were anxious to cultivate. However there were times when the conversation lapsed as Alan found he had no credible current history on which he could draw so he would revert to his earlier life before joining "The Firm" as a source of conversation. Despite that the evening was a success and it was over the coffee that Alan found himself reaching out and taking Catharine's hand. As he did so her feet touched his and something passed between them.

"Shall I get the bill?" he asked.

"Why not?" Catharine answered looking down at her watch.

"Have I kept you out too late?"

"No, not at all, I've had a lovely evening."

"Well thank you for bringing me here" was all Alan could think to say realising how formal it sounded.

Catharine laughed and squeezed his hand.

As they left the restaurant Alan asked her how

In Pursuit of the Red Kite

she would get home.

"I have my car."

"Oh, then I suppose I'd better take you to it?"

"Yes, I suppose you should"

Catharine was walking alongside him, head down and he was unable to judge her mood. He took her hand. She didn't resist as they walked on in silence.

It was at the car, a Renault Clio, that they stopped and she turned to look up at Alan, he decided it was now or never. He put his hands on her shoulders and Catharine turned her face up to him, her eyes closed, Alan kissed her gently. She pulled back and looked at him as if coming to an important decision.

He waited wondering if he'd got it totally wrong and misjudged the situation.

"I want you to take me back to your hotel." said Catharine.

Her words stunned him.

Catharine laughed at his expression. "Well?"

"Anything to please you" he joked back, surprised at the transition from gentle romance to physical attraction. He couldn't help but notice that their pace increased as they walked back towards his hotel.

The night porter barely looked up as he reached for his key and they took the lift to his floor.

In Pursuit of the Red Kite

Alan had at no time considered this outcome to the evening.

Had his night with Nicole helped him prepare for this? He kept in mind her words that not everything they had done would be appreciated by a new lover.

Later, in bed, the thought came to him again and he must have smiled as Catharine asked what he was thinking.

"I was thinking that was great" he replied turning on his side to look at her.

The next morning Alan asked Catharine would they meet up again after she finished work. After some deliberation she said she would meet him at his hotel and they would go out for dinner. Catharine would return to her cottage for a change of clothes after work. Alan was not invited and he wondered, not too deeply, about this.

It was on the following morning he awoke to find Catharine sitting up just looking at him, no expression giving away her thoughts.

"Are you Ok?" he asked her.

"Has anyone told you that you talk in your sleep?"

Oh Christ what had he given away. Was it about Nikolai.

"No, I didn't know I did. What did I say?"

"You seemed to be talking about the army. Did you serve in the Gulf?"

"Yes."

"Well, I couldn't make sense of it, but why I asked you is because you were talking in Italian and I always believed that one thinks and talks subconsciously in their native tongue."

"My father was Italian." He told by way of an explanation

Alan felt only slightly relieved as he tried to sound convincing.

"I see" said Catharine. Alan added no more explanation.

She didn't know how far to push it. She didn't believe him but why make an issue of it. She liked him but since there was no possibility of a permanent relationship, let him keep his secrets. She sighed and got up off the bed and made her way naked to the bathroom for her shower.

Alan watched as the strong daylight from the window illuminated her. He heard her turn on the shower and laid back on the pillow and gave himself a mental dressing down. His defences had been so easily penetrated by this stranger, if he was to survive he was going to have to sharpen up and be more careful. He would have to leave Geneva where his old personality would now be remembered by two people, Catharine and the assistant manager of the bank. He realised that his first thoughts were not that he would have to leave Catharine, much as he liked her, but that his own self-preservation came first.

Did he just pack and go. Say nothing. No, that was cowardly as well as adding more suspicion as to who or what he was in Catharine's mind. He wanted to be forgotten or at best fleetingly remembered as a notch on Catharine's belt.

As he lay there, she came out of the bathroom, sat on the edge of the bed and took him by the hand. She seemed serious again.

"Alan, there's something I think you should know and now seems to be appropriate."

Alan just looked at her and waited.

She looked down avoiding his gaze. "My husband returns home tomorrow, so I can't see you anymore."

Alan was not sure how he felt. She had kept it from him although he wasn't particularly surprised. He would miss her but it would certainly solve the problems that he saw would arise out of anything more permanent.

He put his hand up and stroked her hair.

"Hold me" she said her eyes glistening.

He pulled her to him and put his arms around her. They sat entwined for some time. There was no point in words, a genuine affection was the best either would walk away with and neither wished to spoil it.

Eventually Catharine pulled away. "I will pack now. I won't have breakfast with you, I will just go to the office."

By the time she was ready to leave Alan was up and dressed. At the door to the room she kissed and quickly hugged him.

"Good luck, whatever your story is" she said and turned and walked in a businesslike way down the corridor. She did not look back and Alan watched her until she entered the lift.

Back in his room he decided that it was definitely time to leave Geneva. He'd probably stayed too long anyway he thought. He had, possibly thanks to Catharine, made a plan.

CHAPTER 8

October 1993

Alan had been able to obtain as much money as he needed for the foreseeable future from his Swiss Bank accounts, none of which were known to anybody but himself except for the one that his former employers had paid his salary into. His new identity would make it impossible to trace his movements through the credit cards and cheque book that he had already set up.

There was one area of risk that Alan knew he would have to expose himself to and no matter which way he looked at it there was little alternative. To make his warning of publication of his report on his death a real threat he had to leave instructions for this to be effected and that had meant using someone he could trust and rely on to carry out his instructions and to Alan that had left only one man.

The solicitors who had acted for his family for many years and had their practice in Colchester in Essex. Although most business had been between his father and the senior partner George Treadwell, Alan had met and had some dealings with his son Tony. It was to Tony that he would now turn to for assistance.

Alan returned to the café for the last time for coffee and breakfast. The morning which had begun cloudy and was, according to the waiter, to result in some rain, had in fact turned pleasantly sunny and cooler. His mind however, was no longer on the weather. He had formulated a plan to make contact with Tony Treadwell. He would put his new identity as Paul Gerhardt to the test. He would fly to England

and communicate with Tony personally.

That decided he called in at the first travel agents that he came to on leaving the café. From Geneva he would fly to London Heathrow where he would pick up a rental car and drive to the Essex/Suffolk borders. The earliest flight he could book was at noon the following day and he spent the remainder of his time in Geneva refining his plan for when he arrived in England.

Next morning he settled his account at the hotel and took a cab to the station. The concierge did not hide her expression of approval that he was leaving

The flight produced a synthetic lunch and as much wine as you liked. Alan was taking no risks with alcohol. The last thing he wanted was to be picked up for drunk-driving. It was two years since he had driven a car and even longer since he had driven on the left. He had kept his British driving licence in Geneva along with one in the name of Paul Gerhardt.

Having taken off in sunshine, the plane had to break through heavy clouds on its descent and Alan could see through a murky sky the suburbs of East London rising to meet him as they circled for the landing approach to Heathrow.

He went through the green channel without incident and made for the Hertz desk where he booked out a Vauxhall Cavalier. He took out the necessary insurances, was given a set of keys, a bright smile and directed to the collection compound.

In Pursuit of the Red Kite

He had bought a collapsible umbrella in Geneva, almost as an afterthought. He was glad of it now and wished he'd had the foresight to buy a light mac as well. He turned up his collar as he hauled his luggage to the car.

So far so good, both the passport and his forged driving licence had been accepted without question.

Having stowed his luggage in the boot he sat for several minutes familiarising himself with the controls before starting up the engine and heading for signs directing him to the M25 which would take him on to the A12 then across Essex to Suffolk.

The weather did not improve and by the time he reached the outskirts of Colchester he was driving through a steady downpour. He had already decided where he would stay. He had been in the area before and if there was a room available he would stay at the Dedham Vale Hotel. An expensive hotel with a very pleasant refurbished Georgian interior, at least it had been when he had last stayed there some years earlier.

There was no problem in booking in and having unpacked and settled himself into a double room to the rear of the hotel he sat down to write a note to his solicitor. He used the hotel stationery.

In it he simply asked Tony to contact him as soon as he could at the hotel. Alan hoped that Tony was not on holiday otherwise he may have to remain in the area longer than planned. Whereas he had no reason to believe the service was aware of Nikolai's failed attempt on his life, he already felt unsafe being so close to an area where just possibly MI6 could already be maintaining surveillance on his few links with the past.

Hence the note, which was hand delivered and not a telephone call.

He would leave it until the early evening. He would park near to the solicitor's office and walk the remaining distance before pushing his note through the letter box. He had addressed it to A. Treadwell, to be opened by addressee only. He was sure solicitors secretaries were used to receiving this type of mail and would do as requested.

Alan had made slight alterations to his appearance before arriving at the hotel. He had stopped at a Pub on the A12 and after a snack had gone into the toilet where he had inserted some cotton wool into his cheeks, combed his hair straight back and put on a pair of plain glasses, purchased in Boots the Chemist. He checked it out in the mirror and barely recognised the face looking back at him. It would do. Even if there was a watch on the offices he should not be recognised. The poor light of an early dusk made worse by the rain was also in his favour as he parked in a side street.

He walked purposefully to the office, which from checking the directory at the hotel, he confirmed was still situated at the same address. Having delivered the note he did not hang about, but while he was in town he went to the cinema rather than being shut in his room watching television before returning to the hotel for a late dinner.

With little to do and short of inspiration he was unable to concentrate further effort on the report

In Pursuit of the Red Kite

the following morning. As the day wore on Alan found himself becoming frustrated waiting for the call. He could not leave the hotel. His luck held up and at around 11.00am, his room 'phone rang.

"Mr Tony Treadwell for you sir?" announced the receptionist.

"Thanks. Put him through" said Alan.

"Mr. Gerhardt?"

"Tony it's Alan Marks." There was a short silence at the other end of the 'phone.

"Alan, what are you doing here?" queried Tony.

"It's a long story. I was hoping to tell you over dinner" said Alan. "How are you fixed?"

"Sorry, can't do this evening at such short notice, but I could do lunch today if you like?"

"Fine, even better" said Alan "about what time and where?"

"Well, why don't we meet at the Maison Talbooth."

"Where's that?"

"It belongs to the owner of the hotel you're in and it's a short stroll down the road, or an even shorter drive. How about seeing you in there, at about half twelve?"

"Good, see you then. Thanks Tony."

"OK see you later."

In Pursuit of the Red Kite

Alan hung up and looked at his watch. He still had over an hour. Having first resumed his disguise he went down to the lounge and ordered coffee. When it came he asked the girl directions to the restaurant.

"As you leave the hotel turn left, it's not far, just follow the road. It's on the left." she added.

Alan thanked her. As he drank his coffee he reviewed what he was about to ask Tony to do for him and for the first time he felt a pang of worry. What if Tony thought it all too risky. Would he believe him, would Tony think he was insane. At around twelve thirty he would find out.

The weather was marginally better than when he'd arrived in England. It wasn't raining so he decided to walk. He had put his smartest clothes on for the meeting to make it appear a business arrangement. He took his umbrella.

Alan arrived before Tony and had begun his first whisky and soda. When the solicitor arrived he looked around the restaurant. He did not recognise Alan who offered no help. Alan wanted to see how his disguise would hold up. Tony went over to reception and was led over to Alan's table where he asked

"Alan.?"

"Yes, Tony it is," Alan got up and shook hands as the waiter stood back.

"Will you have a seat" said Alan waving his hand towards the opposite chair.

In Pursuit of the Red Kite

"Thank you." The solicitor sat down and studied Alan more closely.

"Can I get you a drink sir?" the waiter broke in.

"A small gin and tonic please."

"Shall I leave the menu and wine list?"

"Please do," said Alan. The waiter moved away to get the drink.

"I wouldn't have recognised you" said Tony.

"Good. It's important that you're not seen with the real me" Alan told him.

"Are you going to tell me what the big mystery is all about?" Tony had the smile of a man prepared to humour his companion.

Alan looked out of the window down to the river bank at the far side of the garden. The river was a dirty grey and moving fast with strong currents distorting the surface. He turned back to Tony knowing that he may have a problem convincing him of the seriousness of his predicament.

"Well" Alan began "perhaps I should say that under the official secrets act I shouldn't be telling you the full story, but I think it's necessary in order to convince you."

Just then the waiter came back with their drinks and to take the order. When he had left, Alan told Tony of the time he had spent in the SAS and then without going into too much detail he outlined how he had been recruited by MI6 to carry out a hoax mission on Iraq.

Tony listened without interruption until Alan reached the part where Nikolai had tried to kill him and accidentally fallen on his own knife.

"Are you saying you believe your death was sanctioned by both Six and the Russians? Couldn't this have been simply a Russian initiative?"

"Who knows for sure, but it's not a risk I want to take in finding out."

Tony looked worried and was silent for a few moments before asking.

"Does this mean you can never reappear as Alan Marks?"

Alan shrugged by way of reply as the waiter appeared with the first course. He was followed by the wine waiter and Alan went through the ceremony of approving the wine, which was then poured and with a smile and a 'bon appetite' the wine waiter departed.

Tony looked at Alan

"What is it you want me to do?"

Alan smiled "Well, simple things first. I'd like you to prepare me a will in which I will leave everything to my wife or partner at time of death. If there is no-one then it is to be donated to the homeless. I'll leave that choice to you" he added.

"Right, but that assumes that I am told of your death" Tony told him.

"I have left instructions addressed to you with the SAS and MI6 to let you know as you are executor.

In Pursuit of the Red Kite

They may or may not of course. If I have a partner she will have your address" he paused. "That's the best I can do."

He stopped suddenly realising that he had put the solicitor at risk if his worst fears proved correct and MI6 also wanted him removed.

The solicitor saw the sudden change that had come over Alan.

"What? What else is there I should know about or you aren't telling me."

"I have written the whole matter down in a report and I'll let MI6 know that if anything happens to me instructions have been left for publication. You can only confirm to them that you are aware it exists."

"It can be suppressed, you know that?"

"Yes, I've thought of that. I have a numbered bank account in Geneva. I have a safety deposit box there also where there is a copy of the report. Those details will only be given to a third party. The documents will be deposited there. Anything I send to you is sure to be intercepted. I'm sure anyone MI6 believed to be connected with me will be under surveillance." He smiled. "Hence the cloak and dagger contact with you and our meeting here. I doubt whether I shall return to England again for some time, if ever."

"I sec." said Tony. "I'm only here to muddy the water" He smiled to show he was not offended.

"I expect your 'phones may be bugged. If they are after me they will almost undoubtedly put pressure on you to reveal where I am."

"Let them try" said the solicitor, but not sounding entirely convincing.

"The bigger problem to resolve is actual publication of my story."

"Yes" said Tony. "Maybe a leak to the press?"

"D Notice" said Alan.

"Mm."

"I have not thought that one through other than perhaps an offshore publication from a country that is not particularly friendly towards Britain."

"Let me think about that and maybe we can talk about it some more when I bring the will for signature."

They continued their meal in silence, each reflecting on the conversation and its implications.

"One thing that could be difficult" said Tony breaking the silence "is how do we get access to the money in your Swiss account?"

"I've thought of that, but first I want no-one to know I have any other accounts than that one. There must be no written record. Anything associated with me from now on must be kept away from your office or home."

Tony frowned. "Are you serious?"

"Deadly." He saw Tony's expression of concern. "Look if it's all too heavy for you I can use

In Pursuit of the Red Kite

another solicitor."

"No, no that's OK, it just is taking me a while to adjust. We do have one or two of our clients whose way of life is perhaps questionable but this is new to me."

Alan looked at Tony. "I wouldn't want you to feel I'm putting you at risk." he said.

"Let me think about it and we'll talk again when I meet you with the will. I will take the precaution of dating it three years ago so it will not seem as if I have seen you recently" he paused "anyway you were going to tell me how we will arrange the matter of access to the money in your account in the event of your death."

"Yes I was but first let's get some more coffee." He looked at his watch "By the way it's now getting on for 2.00pm, how long have you got?"

"Oh, another half hour if necessary. I have a client coming in at three." Tony replied.

Alan called the waiter over and coffee was ordered.

That done Alan set out his idea for arranging access to his account. "Firstly, you will need the Death Certificate and letter of administration, as I have no need to tell you. My idea was this; I was to have a photograph taken of the two of us together holding a newspaper clearly showing the date."

The coffee arrived.

Then he continued. "I will have two copies made of the photo and sign the back of each. You keep one copy, securely hidden and the other copy plus the negative will be deposited with the bank who will be instructed by me that the bearer, having presented the newspaper and photo, are acting with my consent and have sole discretion as to how the money and anything deposited with it is to be dealt with. At that time you should be notified."

Tony nodded then added, "What if something were to happen to me before you?" He thought for a moment. "I will let my father know of the arrangement if you have no objection?"

"None at all" Alan replied "but only sufficient detail to administer the will."

"OK. What do I do if there is no body and therefore no death certificate" Tony asked, more to himself than Alan.

Alan shrugged. "I've no idea. I leave that to you to do what you can. Still no body, no proof of death therefore you will not be able to accept any claim."

"True." Tony looked at his watch. "I must go." he got up, leaned across the table and shook Alan's hand. "Good luck."

When Tony had gone Alan decided to walk along the river Stour before returning for his evening meal and an evening of planning how he would continue with the writing of his story. Also to try and decide who he might persuade to ratify it.

It had become a lovely day and the walk along the Stour was a pleasant diversion and just for a short while he was able to put his future behind him.

In Pursuit of the Red Kite

The following morning he received a call from Tony and they arranged to meet for lunch in Colchester's central shopping area after first visiting the castle where they persuaded a tourist to take a photograph. That done, they took the film in for a 'rapid processing' while they had lunch.

Whilst waiting for coffee, Tony collected the prints and brought them back to their table in the restaurant where the two identical photos were signed and dated by each of them.

That out of the way Tony asked "Do you want to go through the will here or at my office?"

"I'll not come to the office", Alan looked around at the adjacent tables. Most were empty

"We'll go through it here" he said.

It was a simple straight forward document comprising no more than four pages of foolscap paper.

Alan signed in his real name and the signature was witnessed by the proprietor and waitress. It was a chance he had to take that any future search for him by MI6 would be kept out of media reach and the couple would not remember him.

When they had concluded the business it had been agreed that there would be no record of their meeting, at Tony's office. Tony was paid in cash.

"What if I need to contact you?" Tony had asked before his departure.

"You can't, I'm afraid." Alan had replied. "I will get in touch with you from time to time if I have to. It's better for both of us if there appears to have been no contact at all for the last few years."

"OK." Tony agreed. "Good luck and I hope you are wrong about your situation and are merely suffering from an overdose of paranoia" he smiled as they shook hands.

That evening Alan booked a flight out of the

London City Airport destined for Paris. He would book onward from there.

Leaving the UK was about as exciting as his entry and as he looked down on the City of London he could not help wondering when or if he would see it again.

CHAPTER 9

November 1993

Sir Ian Rush arrived at No. 10. He had requested five minutes of the Private Secretary's time before Prime Minister's briefing on events of the night before.

"Come in, Sir Ian."

John Harding, the present Private Secretary, came to the door of his office and invited Sir Ian Rush to enter.

"What is it, more cloak and dagger?" His eyes sparkled along with the grin on his face and, despite the deeply etched care lines, his pleasant visage encouraged an air of camaraderie. Some had mistaken his apparently easy going manner to their cost. Sir Ian was not one of them however.

"Something has surfaced which was put into action before my time" he began " and from my reading of the file, which is yet incomplete thanks to the IRA, is a subject I feel the PM should be reminded of."

"And what's that? Sit down Sir Ian" he gestured towards the wing backed leather chair in front of his desk. The men had begun their meeting as they entered the office.

"Tea or coffee?" the PPS enquired.

"Coffee, please."

John Harding spoke briefly into the intercom.

"Right, what is it the PM needs to know?"

"The subject was code named 'Red Kite'."

"Oh yes, I do remember this one" he looked at Sir Ian waiting for him to continue.

"Well, according to the file our man was instructed to go to ground for two years. That time is up and no doubt as a member of MI6 he is likely to reappear on our doorstep in the near future."

"H'm." the PPS looked into space.

Sir Ian allowed him to ponder.

"We don't want another Bravo Two Zero do we" the PPS said more to himself than to his guest. He turned back to Sir Ian "I will have a word with the PM and get back to you sometime before the close of play." He looked at his watch. "Forgive me but I think we are both due in the next office about now."

They rose together as the door opened and their drinks appeared. Both seemed unsure and the long suffering PA resolved the problem with a shrug and about turn. The PPS smiled at Sir Ian as they headed for the Prime Minister's office.

That evening at around eight thirty the call Sir Ian had been expecting came through. Amanda had long since departed.

"John Harding, Sir Ian."

"Thanks, put him through."

"Your question on ornithology this morning was discussed with the PM."

"And?"

"This administration, as the Yanks would say, has enough problems already. You must ensure the lid is kept firmly in place on this one Sir Ian."

"I thought you might say something like that. Did you discuss the fact that if it were to be made public it could make the present incumbent look good in the eyes of the electorate?" He paused.

"We did" replied the PPS "however on balance it was decided we did not wish to upset the Russians."

"Any useful suggestions as to how this might be achieved?"

"Leave that to you Sir Ian, after all you're the expert in matters covert, are you not?"

Sir Ian sighed, he really wanted no part in sweeping up somebody else's mess, but of course that came with the territory.

"Flattery will get you everywhere" was all he could think to reply before he hung up.

He would finish with the 'Red Kite' file before he made his way to the club for another late night and then tomorrow he would ring his opposite number in Moscow's KGB headquarters, The Kremlin in Red Square.

Despite standing orders on security Sir Ian

had locked the file in his desk and the records clerk had not chased it up. He took it from his desk drawer and in getting it out caught it on the edge of his desk and dropped it. "Damn" he cursed aloud. As he picked it up there was a photo left lying on the carpet, it showed the second member of the team, Nikolai, the Russian.

The final pages of the file only gave the briefest detail of the 'Red Kite' story. There was a departmental cross reference to all details of the operation its progress and conclusion. The note inferred that the operation had been most successful but there was no record of where the two principal players had secreted themselves. Just how much money had been taken from Saddam's purse was not recorded.

He sat back and pondered just what the Russian would say when he rang. That could now wait till the following morning. It had been a long and tiresome day. He picked up the phone and ordered his car.

The following morning, once settled behind his desk, and having read the overnight reports, he asked Amanda to put a call through to the KGB.

For once there were no problems in making a connection and his phone rang almost immediately.

"Your call to Moscow Sir" said Amanda.

"Thank you. Good morning Yuri."

"Good morning Sir Ian" replied Yuri Gorushenko from his office in the Kremlin.

They had met only once at a business initiative held in the British Embassy in Moscow.

In Pursuit of the Red Kite

Yuri had known his predecessor well and they had apparently had an understanding. Sir Ian however had not taken to the leader of the KGB, a short stocky man with fierce sparkling brown eyes in a face that showed a brush with the Tartars in his heritage.

Sir Ian remembered their conversation. He spoke no Russian and Yuri's English was execrable. The Russian Military Intelligence leader had cornered him and asked a lot of questions on issues that hung over from the previous administration, the details of which he knew little about. His lack of knowledge irritated the Russian and Sir Ian was left with the distinct impression that he had not done well. This angered him in turn as he did not appreciate the interrogation by a Russian peasant at what was supposed to have been a relaxing getting to know you affair.

Since then personal communications were avoided wherever possible. On the matter of "Red Kite" there was no other way but to speak to the man. The PM would be looking for some answers now that the issue had been re-opened. He was also uncomfortable with the instruction to "keep a lid" on the subject. He was to have his agent eliminated. Versed in the "double entendre" of politics any other interpretation was unlikely. He sighed.

"The PM thought I should have a word with you about an operation carried out by our two countries a couple of years ago" he began.

"And what is that?"

"Red Kite?"

"H'm, yes I remember it" acknowledged Yuri. "What is it you want to discuss?"

"I'm sure you are aware the time is about right for our operatives to reappear."

"That's right" responded the Russian, but not helping the conversation along.

Sir Ian continued "I don't know what, if any, action you now propose?" he let the question hang.

"Action? But it is all finished. What further action had you in mind?"

Why was it he wondered, did he feel he was being baited by the Russian.

"The PM feels that if the story were to now get out into the media it would not help international politics."

"Or his own political situation either." added the Russian with a laugh. Before Sir Ian could respond he continued, "For your information Sir Ian, but for different reasons I share his concern. It was something I discussed with your predecessor and we agreed that I would deal with it. Tell the PM not to worry, he will not see his man again

Once again Sir Ian found himself becoming angry at his predecessor for not making aware of the file or advising the PM's PPS of its circumstances, it highlighted his ignorance on the issue and causing him a certain loss of face with the Russian.

Sir Ian, now that he realised the clean-up was being dealt with by the Russian, allowed himself to indulge in a feeling of moral repugnance at the cold blooded elimination of an agent to satisfy political expediency.

As if reading his mind the Russian said "Why do you worry Sir Ian. My man is a rogue and before this operation he was wanted for murder. He believed he was buying his pardon" Yuri laughed "and your man I am sure knew the stakes."

There was a pause between the two leaders broken by Sir Ian.

"We would like to know when the matter is concluded."

"Of course Sir Ian." The head of MI6 could hear the contempt in the Russians reply.

"Thank you Yuri. I'm sure the PM will be most grateful."

"I'm sure your PM has much more to worry about with the IRA at present." The Russian prodded.

"That is so."

"Goodbye Sir Ian, I will be in touch."

"Thank you Yuri." Sir Ian Rush hung up.

To the outside world and his employers however Sir Ian had the reputation of being quite ruthless. But it still did not sit well on his conscience that he was now party to authorised dirty work.

CHAPTER 10

October 1993

As Alan flew towards Orly on Ryan Air flight RA 237 he went over in his mind the plan that he had begun to put together in Geneva. He was only too aware that for his report to have credibility it would be necessary for his account to be authenticated by reliable witnesses of some standing.

In view of the nature of an operation which had relied on lies, deception and half-truths for its success this would not be easy. He'd struggled with this for some time and in the end had decided that his only way forward was to use a similar route to that taken in planning the operation. It would get harder as his training had taken him underground and at the moment he had not reached any decision as to how he would deal with that aspect. He was aware that he must make a start and not believe the task was impossible.

His approach to the first section of the new report therefore was to try and speak to someone he could trust who had been involved in his training.

Because the operation had required a high degree of technical knowledge in the subject of Red Mercury and its known and suspected capabilities, both the KGB and MI6 had agreed that their agents would learn from academic sources the detail they would need to convince the target.

This had involved both Alan and Nikolai in attending seminars, lectures and becoming mature students at the University of Technology in

Karlsplatz, Vienna, under the tutelage of Doktor Hans Freiburg. Of all the people that Alan had been involved with he had come closest to a friendship with the Doktor and it was to him that Alan had decided to turn for help.

The flight was scheduled to land at Orly just after one o'clock in the afternoon. Alan went into the transit lounge to await his connecting flight with Austrian Airlines to Vienna's international airport, Flughofen Wien Schwechat. He had a couple of hours to kill and expected to arrive at the airport located on the east side of the city in the early evening.

From there he would take a cab into the centre where he would book into a room at the Hotel Pension Schneider.

He had never stayed at the hotel while he had attended the university course but he had seen it often and it came well recommended. It was located in Getreidemarkt near to Theatre an der Wien and its connection to the theatre could be seen around the foyer by the autographed photographs of the stars who had performed there.

As the cab approached the city centre Alan's thoughts turned again to the Doktor. Alan was aware that the Doktor could only validate his time as a student and the subject material but he had to begin somewhere if he were to try and prevent his own demise. Had the Doktor had any idea as to why he was teaching the two mature students in his subjects, Biomass Technology and Physics. Probably not, Alan thought, although it was not unusual for people to begin studying later in life, subjects in which they were patently ignorant. Maybe he would ask Hans if this were the case if it turned out that he was prepared to speak to him.

He sighed, it was the only option he'd got. Should he try to capture Hans' sympathy towards his plight? Perhaps an easier course would be to say that he had been asked to flesh out an internal report he had to prepare for his employers. Alan felt guilty. He did not like using people especially those he considered to be his friends, however he knew that the feeling of guilt wasn't so deep that it would prevent him at least approaching the Doktor. It was a risk he had to take and trust that if the Doktor could not be persuaded then at least he would keep whatever he learned from Alan to himself.

At the outset of the operation Alan's tuition fees had been paid through an English Metallurgy Company with Alan posing as one of their employees. His cover had been as a trainee salesman whose developing career required him to have a good background understanding of the basis of fusion physics. As he'd explained to the Doktor over a coffee break in the university canteen, he had to have sufficient knowledge on the subject of Red Mercury, its potential uses and the processes involved in its production. It was important that he could talk intelligently and with confidence in discussing its ability as a fusion accelerator.

The rain that had greeted him on landing seemed to have set in for the night. As the taxi neared the hotel visibility had deteriorated and lights were coming on. His return to Vienna was not marred by the weather. He had seen the city in all its moods none of which had stopped his liking for the home of the Hapsburgs.

He paid off the driver and dashed across the pavement into reception where, having completed registration and handing over his passport, he was given a key to the second floor room and a porter stepped forward to carry the little luggage he had.

The room was comfortable and warm and he felt insulated from the weather. Before drawing the curtains he stood and watched the rain slashing across the street lights. He looked at his watch, 6.30 pm, too late to try and contact the Doktor this evening, he would try first thing in the morning. Tonight he would dine in the hotel and then have an early night. His appetite for nocturnal company had been sated by his experiences in Geneva.

The following morning he rang the University to be told that the Doktor was lecturing until midday but if he would like to telephone about 12.30 he should catch the Doktor before he went to lunch. Alan thanked the secretary having agreed to ring back later. He had left his name, Alan Marks, with her. Maybe the Doktor would remember him.

Despite the steady downpour the previous day, the storm had blown over. It was a lovely morning and Vienna was too attractive a city to stay inside. Alan decided he would pass the time doing a little sightseeing and a little shopping. His wardrobe was meagre and although he did not want to carry too much luggage around with him while his future was too unsettled there were a few basic items he had to buy, which were necessary for his comfort and appearance.

He had considered whether he should get himself a gun and on balance felt that it would do no harm and possibly some good. He had established a few connections in Europe and was sure he would be able to obtain arms if he felt endangered. At the moment, he reasoned, nobody knew that he was out and running although that thought could be a little optimistic he accepted.

He knew that the more people he contacted in verifying his story the more chance there was that somebody would mention having seen him to MI6 or the KGB. At present he was safe. Would he still be after speaking with the Doktor, he asked himself.

He returned to the hotel by 12.30. He didn't want to miss Hans. He picked up the phone and rang the University as Alan Marks and asked to be put through to Hans. He explained to the secretary that he was an ex-pupil of the Doktor's.

This time he was in luck. He was put through and the familiar sound of Hans' voice came on the line.

"Herr Marks. What can I do for you?"

"Hans, it is Alan Marks."

At the other end of the 'phone Hans paused. He remembered the voice and the name confirmed it.

"Look I need to speak to you on a private matter, face to face if that's possible?" Alan hesitated wondering how much to explain over the 'phone but not wishing to lose the chance of getting Hans' help.

"OK, I think I understand" said Hans his curiosity aroused. "Why don't we meet up and you can tell me all about it. I take it you are not too far away?"

Alan felt more relieved than he would have cared to admit.

"I'm in Vienna, staying at the Hotel Pension Schneider."

Hans vaguely knew the name.

"Not far from the Theatre an der Wien, in Getreidemakt" he added.

"Oh I know where you mean" Hans told him. "Why don't I come over this evening and you can buy me a drink."

"It'll be my pleasure" said Alan. "Why not come for dinner?"

"I can't make dinner but I could get there for about 8.30 if that's OK", Hans offered. He was eating at home with his daughter Anna and by now she would have bought the food. Although she would understand and say it was no trouble he was only too grateful for his daughter providing him with more than the occasional meal to put her to any trouble.

Besides, he thought as he hung up, just what was it that had made his former pupil contact him and then become evasive on the 'phone?

Having made contact Alan was at first pleased that at last he was about to make real

In Pursuit of the Red Kite

progress, then he again began to be assailed by doubt. Was the Doktor enough of a friend to be trusted; was Alan exposing him to unnecessary danger? He had little option, he would have to trust Hans and hope that he was willing to help him.

Alan had lunch in the hotel dining room which seemed to be doing a good trade in business lunches. It was a busy and noisy time and he was unable to concentrate on anything other than his food and the immediate environment.

He would spend the afternoon walking around the area and getting to know in more detail this section of the city centre. This seemed to be becoming a way of life since leaving the Friary.

He left his coat in the room. The weather looked good and despite a slight chill in the air he knew that in a short time he would be warm enough. He set out towards Karlsplatz. He knew he was in an area of traditional and Art Nouveau architecture but was surprised to see a Henry Moore sculpture in front of St Charles' Church in the south east corner of the park. He'd never been too sure about Moore and this exhibit did nothing to improve his opinion.

From there he headed north along Schwarzenbergplatz until he reached the Ring and the Cafe Schwarzenberg, a traditional coffee house. Despite the chill air there were several people sat at the outside tables. He joined them and spent an hour people watching and rehearsing what he would ask Hans when he met him later that evening.

The hotel dining room took on a different mood in the evening with the lights on and a pianist playing to the very few people eating there. By the time he had finished there were a few more but it seemed that at this time of year the Hotel relied more on business trade than tourists.

He looked at his watch, 8.20, Hans would be here shortly. He called for the bill and a second cup of coffee. He had agreed to meet Hans in reception.

Hans was standing with his back to Alan reading a hotel pamphlet. He was dressed casually in a high necked leather jacket and slacks. Alan smiled to himself, Hans liked to think he looked fashionable but never quite got it right.

As if sensing his approach Hans turned smiling and put out his hand to take Alan's.

"Alan. How nice to see you" Hans smiled as he said it.

"Hans, good to see you again" and indeed it was. Hans had not noticeably changed since Alan saw him last, some two and a half years ago. He had put on no extra weight nor apparently aged. The round face sporting a neat moustache under a button nose looked questioningly at Alan. Alan took him by the arm and led him into the hotel bar.

The room was comfortably furnished and there were few customers, so they chose a corner table away from the bar where they could talk without too much risk of being overheard.

As they sat down the waiter followed them over "Herren?"

"Your usual Hans?" asked Alan.

"Why not?"

"Two large scotches, no ice and would you bring us some water?"

"Certainly sir." The waiter headed for the bar.

"So what's it you want to discuss?"

"It could be a long story" began Alan.

"So, we may need plenty of time I suspect."

"OK, but first how are you, how's work and how's life treating you?"

"All is well, I'm fit and active still and there will always be another batch of students each year. The consultancy work is irregular. How is the use of Red Mercury and its possible applications going." He held Alan's gaze and watched for a reaction.

Since the call Hans had thought through his time with Alan and as he'd spent so much time explaining the detail of the red gel it was not too difficult to hazard a guess as to what the conversation was likely to be about.

Alan looked slightly uncomfortable and gazed around the bar to see if anybody was taking any interest in them.

Hans' smile increased at his ex-students' discomfort.

"So I have hit a target, eh?"

Alan did not respond to the smile, instead he

looked serious as he said to Hans.

"There is something I need to discuss with you but at the same time I am concerned that in doing so I may put you at some risk."

"Why not let me be the judge of that. Give me an outline and if I think it's getting too deep I will tell you so." Hans regarded Alan for a moment then continued "But why me?"

"Well I may be wrong but of everybody connected with this thing I feel I can trust you more than anyone else." Alan replied having decided to rely on the truth.

"I'm flattered. OK tell me then, in your own time, what this is all about. Oh, do you mind if I smoke?"

"I don't" smiled Alan, "but if you are still using that old pipe of yours I'm sure the rest of the customers here might object."

Hans ignored him and took out his pipe and made it up as Alan gave him an abbreviated account of what had happened since they last met.

Hans could not at first believe the story Alan told about a hoax arranged by the Western Powers on Iraq, although he could understand the reasoning behind it.

As Alan talked Hans puffed away on his pipe and wondered at the risks that had been taken by both the UK and Russia and their complicity in keeping the 'mad dog' down.

As Alan continued Hans found himself

thinking of the damage the story could do to the respective governments in the hands of a malicious media. He knew there were many organisations which would capitalise on the situation and exploit the threat of reprisals from a nation which would have no compunction in initiating a reign of terror on those they considered to be the enemy. In some respects he thought it would have been better for it to have become public knowledge two or three years ago when there would have been much more public sympathy. Now with the memory of the Gulf War faded the Humanists would make much of how Saddam's excessive spending would only have increased poverty amongst an already suppressed nation.

It came as less of a surprise to him than maybe Alan had expected when he told Hans of the attempt on his life.

Hans simply nodded in understanding "What are you going to do Alan?"

"The only thing I can do is to pose a threat of exposure and hope it's enough to keep me alive" was Alan's reply.

"But they could suppress the story and discredit you, surely?" Hans asked him.

"Depends where it was published" said Alan "and yes you're right about being discredited. How I plan to cover that point is to persuade established and believable experts to authenticate, in part at least, that the story is credible. That's where, I hope, you come in?"

In Pursuit of the Red Kite

Despite the fact that this was the point of the meeting, Hans was no longer smiling and looked as serious as Alan had ever seen him.

Alan went on to, he hoped, persuade Hans to aid him. "I know that no one person who helped knew the entire plan. I'm sure I can link each ones involvement to make it credible."

"Maybe" was Hans' contribution. He looked down and commenced restocking his pipe.

Throughout Alan relating his story to Hans over the course of the evening, the waiter had kept them well supplied with drinks.

Hans finally looked up with a smile "It's a good job I didn't bring the car" he said changing the subject and breaking the silence that had followed his previous remark. He looked at his watch with surprise "it's nearly 11.00. I have a day's work in front of me tomorrow. Not like you young man." He stood up and must have noticed the look of alarm on Alan's face. He leant across and patted him on the shoulder.

"Don't worry, I'm not running away, and you can trust me. Let me have some time to absorb what you've told me and let's see what we can come up with. Come over for lunch tomorrow."

"You may not know it but there is the Technical University Mensa in Resselgasse not far from here and very convenient for me. When you get inside, look for the yellow zone and go up to the first floor. They do a good lunch there between 11.00 and 2.30. If it's convenient I'll see you there just after 12.30?"

"Yes, no problem" said Alan, with an audible sigh of relief.

He helped Hans on with his coat and saw him out of the hotel where they made small talk until the cab, ordered by the hotel, arrived to take Hans home.

As Alan lay in bed that night he worried over the step he had now taken. Had he done the right thing? It was too late now and if he was honest with himself he felt slightly relieved to have somebody he was able to talk to. Hans, who was his senior by some twenty years, had assumed the role of father confessor.

CHAPTER 11

October 1993

Hans did not go straight to bed. He made himself a coffee, put on a CD and sank into his armchair. He was too alert to sleep. The cause - Alan's story. If it were to be believed.

He tried to recall how much time they had spent together at the University. Hans' role as lecturer had kept him at a distance from his students, including Alan. He had known very little about the man, any socialising that they had in that period had either been in the University canteen or in a local bar where it was all small talk. Hardly the basis for a deep and lasting friendship. He sensed that despite Alan's calm exterior he was in fact unsure what to do and understandably, not a little concerned about his life.

Still, Alan had sought him out, had trusted him with his life in fact. He had felt flattered at first but now as he went over the details of their conversation he had to admit to a little more than worry about possible consequences of becoming involved. And what would Anna, his daughter, say. He had to involve her in any decision that might affect her by association.

He was trying to convince himself he still had a choice. That when he saw Alan tomorrow he could tell him he had decided on balance, that he didn't

want to be involved but, of course, Alan's secret

would be safe with him.

How would Alan react?

By the time he decided to retire to his bed he had realised that really he had no choice but to help. Would he be breaking any Secrets Acts he wondered. He didn't think so. He had only lectured on a subject that was common knowledge to all his students. He had not been party as to how that knowledge had been used.

Hans had a bad night and was relieved when it was finally time to get up and get himself prepared for University.

On arriving at the Technical University in Resselgasse the next day Alan entered the building to discover that it was not too difficult to find his way to the Mensa on the first floor.

It was just after 12.30 and Hans was already seated at a table which, considering how busy the place was, he had somehow kept to himself - no doubt the privilege of being a lecturer. Hans stood up as he saw Alan cross the floor towards him.

"Have a seat Alan" he said with a smile, indicating the chair opposite. Alan was relieved and returned the smile and did as he was bid. "I will order for both of us." He offered Alan the printed menu of the day.

Alan chose and Hans went off for the food as Alan studied the room and the people around him. Most were students in their early twenties, there were a few older men and women who could have been mature students or lecturers.

As Hans put down the tray, Alan asked him had he decided whether help or not. His anxiety had made him forget his manners and he had prematurely gone straight to the point.

Hans shrugged and sat down. "As I said last night I will help all I can although I can only truly verify that you were a student here for a period of time and that as part of your course you studied Red Mercury and its properties."

"That will be a great help and the first step on the road" said Alan as he reached for his knife and fork. "Thank you Hans." he looked down at the food on the tray. "This looks good." He studied the small pork chop, a spoonful of apple sauce and a handful of chips with what he hoped was a look of relish for the feast to come.

The only conversation between the two men throughout the meal consisted of more about the University and Hans' role as a lecturer at various scientific venues. Mostly in Europe he told Alan but added with some pride that he once visited the USA and had given a lecture at MIT.

After lunch Alan followed Hans to his office in the physics department. He noted little had changed in the last two and a half years since he first enrolled at the University. On the way Hans told Alan he still found time to carry out some research work.

In his office, instead of sitting behind his desk, Hans took a position by the window while Alan moved some paper off a chair and waited for ~~the~~ him to speak.

Hans turned.

"Look," he began, "I've decided to help you within the limitations of the law and my reputation. Where that will get you I'm not sure. However, there is one condition - that my family aren't harmed in any way." He looked at Alan for some guarantee.

Alan sighed "I'm sorry Hans, that is something I can't promise" he looked Hans in the eyes as he continued "I can't see that you will put yourself in any real danger, after all your involvement is as you said earlier, a matter of record. The facts could almost be established without direct reference to yourself, from University records." he concluded.

"True. Maybe I'm over reacting" said Hans. He turned back to the window. "Then why come to me at all."

"I hoped that would have been obvious."

"Maybe, but I want to hear it from you."

"I need someone I can trust and rely on."

"H'm."

"Hans I don't want to make you do anything that goes against your professional ethics" Alan tried to keep the exasperation he felt from sounding, in his voice.

In Pursuit of the Red Kite

Hans looked at his watch. "Hell, I'm sorry Alan I hadn't noticed the time, I have a lecture in five minutes." He saw the look of frustration on Alan's face. "I truly am sorry." He pulled a chart across his desk. It was a timetable. "Tomorrow afternoon I only have one late lecture. Can we meet for lunch again and I promise we will conclude this business if that's OK, but come to my office first."

Alan stood up "That's fine Hans." as he turned to go he noticed Hans' still looked worried. "I'll see you same time here tomorrow then."

Hans saw him to the door and as he watched Alan walk back along the corridor he couldn't help but feel he must have seemed pretty ineffectual. It could not be helped. After all, he told himself, it was he who was doing the favour. He would talk with Anna and get her view. He would tell her that he'd been asked to authenticate certain facts and maybe help on editing a report on Alan's time at the University and the course details.

Alan had produced no further work on his own report by the time he set off to see Hans the following day. He had passed the intervening time re-acquainting himself with some of the older parts of the city. He wondered to himself as he wandered the streets through showers and sudden bursts of blue sky and sunshine, why he was always drawn to the architecture of towns, in particular their religious buildings. He found no reason he could justify and decided it must simply satisfy some emotional rather than academic part of himself.

At the University he went straight to the

second floor, turned left out of the lift and followed the signs to the Physics Department.

He entered the small outer office where Hans had a PA and secretary at his disposal to help him both run the department and organise his lectures. Alan was aware how important it was for Hans to maintain his reputation in the forefront of his subject, if he did not the up-and- coming geniuses would find places elsewhere. The University Board maintained a strict commercial view on how the Universities achievements were viewed by the outside world and by the competition.

As he entered the office he hadn't expected to see the dark haired girl who looked up at him. Hans' previous secretary had been more matronly. Good for Hans, he thought.

"Doktor Freiberg please."

"Is he expecting you?" she asked. Her voice had a warmth to it and her face gave a small professional smile of welcome.

The smile did not reach the dark brown eyes, he noticed. He also noticed the compact figure despite the fact that she was seated behind Frau Hecht's old oak desk.

"Yes."

"You have an appointment?"

"No. I'm a friend. He is expecting me. Paul Gerhardt." Alan had explained to Hans that he was using false documents which had made Hans feel a little more secure in deciding to assist.

"Oh yes." The warmth vaporised. "Please wait. I'll tell him you are here." She got up from her desk crossed the room and entered Hans' office. That's odd, Alan thought, why didn't she use the intercom? Was there some problem? Had Hans had second thoughts, he wondered with just a little alarm.

He looked at the closed door and heard the sound of muted voices. It was several minutes later before the secretary returned and Alan noted that the figure when seated had not done justice to the first impression. He realised she was taller than he had first imagined. She wore well-fitting jeans into which was tucked an open necked white blouse.

"Doktor Freiberg will see you now Herr Gerhardt." She stood to one side to allow Alan to pass. There was a look of animosity in her eyes which he noticed and was puzzled. He thought she must be a very protective PA or maybe Hans was having a relationship with the woman. If so he could not help but admire his taste.

Hans stood up as he entered; the old smile back in place. Alan felt relieved.

"Sit down" he indicated the chair in front of his desk where Alan had sat the day before, as he crossed to close the door to the outer office.

Alan sat.

"I see your taste in PA's has improved" he joked.

Hans grinned and said "I'm afraid Frau Hecht is off sick at the moment and my daughter Anna has kindly come in to cover for me."

"Oh, I'm sorry" Alan said alarmed at the faux pas.

"Don't be" laughed Hans "either way I'm flattered."

"No wonder she looked so protective. I thought maybe she was your mistress."

"Oh no" said Hans "I'm wedded to the job which has been a good wife to me since Anna's mother left fifteen years ago."

"I'm sorry, I didn't mean to pry."

"I know, dear boy, I'm fully over it now." he added "it happens to so many these days. Now how about lunch, we'll go out to a small wine bar I know which doesn't get too crowded at this time of year. I think it is better if we are to continue yesterday's conversation we don't do it here."

"Hans, I am in your debt" said Alan.

"Not yet, but who knows" grinned the now amiable friend he was beginning to believe he had been right in trusting.

As he left the office Hans introduced Alan to Anna as Paul Gerhardt. Anna politely told him she was pleased to meet him but this was belied by the look in her eyes.

Anna was an only child and had been the glue in an unsuccessful marriage that had finally terminated when her mother had left for a younger man. Her mother had met Hans when she was in early twenties and was more impressed by his academic qualifications than the person. She was extremely attractive and enjoyed the social life she believed his career would bring, something that Hans had no time for.

She had taken several jobs which involved her on the front line of the companies she had worked for as a receptionist. She was good at making people welcome and liked the flirtatious response she often got in return.

Eight years into the marriage she had decided that she was in a relationship that did not provide the life she wanted and when it came to it a six year old daughter was insufficient reason to live with a man who spent much of his time in pursuing his career.

At the time Hans was distraught as he had not seen it coming, added to which he found himself as a single parent.

Anna had seemed to deal with the situation better than her father and at six years old had a much older view on the world. She had been an average student at school and at upper school where she showed promise in languages and literature so it was no surprise to Hans when she announced that she wanted to become a freelance journalist when she had completed her schooling. Hans had insisted that she go onto university to which she had offered little resistance. His chosen career had ensured that they were financially comfortable and when Anna reached the age of twenty he had persuaded her that she should move out and begin a life of her own as he was quite capable of looking after himself.

To his surprise there was a determined resistance to the proposal but he had won at the end on the compromise that she found herself an apartment not too far from the family home.

Anna was now a writer for several national magazines and was sometimes asked her views on articles written by others. The advantage in being freelance enabled Anna to step in and help her father out in the current circumstances or when Frau Hecht was on holiday or as now, off sick.

There was no serious man in Anna's life. There had been a regular supply of boyfriends during her time at university and since embarking on her chosen career but none had lasted or become serious. Mostly the relationships had foundered on the fact that the career had taken precedent over anything else in her life and the boyfriends had just drifted off.

Hans led Alan through the narrow back streets around the University until they arrived at the door of a narrow-fronted building where the sign said it was a wine bar, but Alan couldn't help feeling that several years earlier it had said it was a beer cellar and it would change again with the dictates of fashion. What he didn't doubt was that it would always sell food and alcoholic drink.

There were booths along one side of a long narrow room. These were faced across an aisle by a long narrow bar patrolled by a barman and maid. A dumb-waiter set into the back fitting would deliver food from some other part of the building.

Hans had been correct. It was not busy, they got a booth to themselves and ordered lunch and a bottle of Frascati.

Since meeting Anna, Alan had been puzzled by the apparent hostility he sensed in her when she had discovered who he was. He asked Hans whether he had discussed his situation with his daughter.

"Why?" Hans reddened.

"I just get the feeling I'm not too popular."

Hans smiled "I suspect it's the female mind at work. She knows I met with you a couple of times recently and since then I have been perhaps a little more introspective than usual. Then you come to lunch the following day. She sees you as the cause for my quiet mood and assumes you have caused me to worry over some matter."

"I see."

"I shouldn't worry."

"I don't want to put you or Anna in danger" Alan told him.

Hans felt a little guilty. He had spoken with Anna the previous night but he could not remember having said anything that should have caused her concern or explain the attitude Alan had picked up on.

"What is said can never be unsaid Alan, so I suggest we move forward. Anyway I could have stopped you if I had not wanted to help."

"OK and I know I have not asked your opinion, but if you were in my shoes what might you do?"

"Mainly be very careful. I think the more people you approach the easier it is going to be for somebody to realise what you are doing and trace you."

"Yes that thought has been uppermost in my mind too."

"I'm sure it has, but I do have an idea that may reduce some of the exposure."

"Good. I hoped you might."

"Now as I understand it I was not the only one who taught you on the subject of Red Mercury, academically I mean" he added.

"That is correct, I had to be seen to be widely versed in the detail and know where research was being carried out, where raw materials came from, who could manufacture Red Mercury and who would produce and deliver the product. Nobody knew the whole picture but I suspect there were several who were able to make a fairly intelligent guess."

"Where did you have to travel to as part of your education?" Hans asked.

"St Petersburg, Moscow, Irkutsk in Russia, Berlin and Frankfurt in Germany, Johannesburg and Stellenbosh in South Africa and of course Vienna and Graz in Austria."

"You didn't go to work in the States?"

"No in fact it was agreed that the Americans, although they knew about it, would not take part in this exercise." he added ironically.

"And there was only one other operative in the field you said, Nikolai?"

"That's right."

"And did he have a similar brief?"

"As I understand it we covered the same ground."

"I suppose the one point I find difficult to understand is how you were able to persuade the Iraqis to believe you. The Russians, yes I can understand. Russia did not involve herself in the Gulf War and if anything I remember made noises of support for the Iraqis. But you, a Brit, it must have stretched credibility to believe you were on their side." He looked to Alan for explanation.

"I relied on convincing them of my sincerity to their cause on two counts, one that I was in it for the money and secondly that I could prove I had a reason to resent my own country and wanted to harm it in some way. That," he added "was done for me by MI6. They inserted some damning reason for me having to leave the SAS and then the document with my service record was somehow mysteriously leaked."

Hans poured them both another glass of wine and before Alan had time to develop this point the waiter arrived with their lunch, a plate of garnished wholemeal sandwiches. They had a few mouthfuls before Alan continued.

"The money side was easy. Nikolai and I demanded a great deal to broker the arms they wanted. The amount was no problem but arranging for its payment between two parties who basically did not trust the integrity of the other took almost longer than convincing them to buy the weapons." He laughed at the memory and took a mouthful of wine.

"As I have already explained, MI6 had already thought of the Brit seeking revenge on his own country as the best aspect for my cover." He paused. Outside of the UK nobody seemed to know of his history with the SAS. Except the Iraqis, he reminded himself.

Hans was thoughtful for a while. He stoked his pipe and Alan sensed that Hans had come to some conclusion as to how he might proceed, and knowing Hans it would have been considered very thoroughly.

"I don't want to give the wrong impression or make you feel guilty by anything I have to say." He looked at Alan who returned his gaze but said nothing.

"Now" he continued "I think that should your theory be correct and there is a plan to remove you, then I think they will keep an eye on your family, friends and anyone you were connected with in the SAS, MI6 and those of us who provided you with the necessary background. I think this is something you believe also?" he asked Alan.

"Yes, that's true."

"Well then, once they are after you they will put a covert watch on anyone they believe you could be in contact with. They will also make discreet enquiries as to whether you have been seen with any of these people. Now the latter takes less manpower, but they will not know if anyone has decided to protect you. Therefore I imagine if they want you badly enough, they will use the former with your more intimate contacts and the latter with people like myself who only performed a service and who they believe will want to stay in the good books of the Security Services"

He smiled for the first time in a while as Alan looked a little concerned.

"To put your mind at rest, I support you and your endeavours. It is how we progress from here we need to discuss."

"Agreed. That is really very good of you Hans." Alan felt relieved.

"So I suggest you maintain a low profile while you are writing." As Alan was about to interject, he held up his hand "I know. "How will you get authentication?" Yes?"

"Well, yes."

"I am going to help you there."

"I appreciate you providing me with a shoulder to lean on, but as you know I don't want to put you in any danger."

"Do you think I am not in danger already" he joked.

"How?"

"By being seen with you, at the Hotel, here, at the University. Somebody will innocently say they have seen me with the man in the photographs MI6 produce. So there you are!" He spread his hands as if there were to be no further argument on that point.

"Now, as I have said I will help you. Every few months there are seminars around the world I am invited to attend. Next week there is one in Moscow which I had not made up my mind about. Now I have I will go. It coincides with half term here at the university. I may see the men you wanted to meet. If not, as it is easier to move round as a tourist now in Russia, I will simply visit these men."

"But if you specifically discuss 'Red Mercury' they will be suspicious."

"Why should they be? It is still a topic of great interest. For your information development has continued with it over the past two years. Outwardly as a more efficient energy fusion source, but we all know that its military capabilities are really of more interest."

"H'm, but I don't see how you will get them to authenticate their involvement with Nikolai and myself."

"I will not ask them to."

"Then how?" said Alan with a note of desperation in his voice.

"As the Americans would put it, I'll wear a wire. Then if they bring up the subject themselves I will have it on record. If they don't mention the Saddam issue then we are out of luck"

"You will tape the conversation and use the tape as evidence?"

"But only if it becomes an issue. That's it! Now," he said looking at his watch "I must get back to work. Anna will give me a bad time if I'm late for a lecture."

At the mention of Anna's name, Alan asked how she was. Hans told him that she was OK and sensed there was more to come. He waited.

"Are you her only family?"

Hans smiled at the transparency of the question.

"Yes. She was married but got divorced about a year ago. Fortunately there were no children."

"I didn't mean to pry" said Alan realising it was not the first time he had said this.

"Yes you did; and I don't mind and before you ask, she lives and works here in Vienna. She has her own apartment. Shall I tell her you enquired?"

"Oh no" Alan looked embarrassed "I don't think she would appreciate that" he added.

"Just because she is a bit protective towards me, don't let that put you off" said Hans deciding he had teased Alan enough. "I really must go. I will leave you to consider what I have suggested but will not be able to see you for a couple of days. We'll have dinner, OK! I'll ring you once I've checked my diary."

As he was leaving, he turned and said "I suggest you start looking for somewhere to live in the near future. I will think about that too unless of course you want to stay at the hotel" and with that he was gone leaving Alan to ponder and wonder what he would do for the next couple of days. He sensed if he followed Hans' suggestion that he kept out of sight he would have to get used to the boredom of inactivity.

The weather was cloudy but dry and Alan decided to ponder the subject on foot.

CHAPTER 12

October 1993

Over the next two days Alan did his best at producing his 'memoirs' as he had dubbed the report.

That he was not a writer by choice was patently obvious by the slow progress he made. His spelling was poor and the grammar appalling he realised each time he re-read his efforts. He reckoned that if he had been a smoker he would by now be on several packs a day. As it was he distracted himself from the task by finding spurious reasons to leave the hotel and go for walks.

Should he ever have to seriously maintain his threat and have the report published it would need some serious editing by someone much more experienced than himself.

He had not heard again from Hans and was beginning to wonder whether the Doktor was having second thoughts. His uncertain mood lifted when, on his return from a visit to the Upper Belvedere Museum, he found a message to call Hans.

It had not been Alan's first visit to the Belvedere with its aim in providing the background to the more popular works of Gustav Klimt and Egon Schiele. He had visited the Gallery when he was studying in Vienna and was pleased to find that it had not been rearranged. Each of his favourite paintings were to be found where he first saw them.

The message simply said to call back if dinner that evening was still convenient, with a suitable time and place. When he telephoned the University he was put through to Frau Hecht who had returned from her sick leave and he had to be satisfied with giving her the details as the Doktor could not under any circumstances be disturbed.

He told her he had booked a table for himself and the Doktor at the Restaurant Smutny in Elisabethstrasse for eight thirty and asked her to extend the invitation to Anna if she were also available. From their last meeting his expectations were not high. Was she now against any relationship she saw forming between himself and her father?

Alan had chosen the Restaurant Smutny for two reasons, the first that he could walk to it from his hotel and the second because it served typical Viennese food. He arrived ten minutes early and waited at the bar where he bought himself a whisky. He perched on a bar stool watching the door. His guests were on time and to his surprise and pleasure Anna preceded her father through the door. She was wearing a long black coat under which she wore a black dress showing her slim figure to advantage. She wore a thin gold choker around her neck and her hair fell loosely around her shoulders. Her father was dressed in a black leather jacket and brown slacks. Alan thought that if only both were either brown or black Hans would have looked casually smart. He was not a natural dresser. The waiter led them over to the bar. He held out his hand to Anna who took it briefly, a small smile at the corners of her mouth.

"Good evening Herr Gerhardt."

Alan nearly forgot himself as he replied "Call me Paul. Please."

Anna stood aside as her father joined her and said "Evening, Paul."

"What would you like to drink?" Alan asked. It seemed he was to be known as Paul in front of Anna.

"Shall we drink at the table?" It was not really a question as Anna looked towards the dining area.

"Certainly" Alan turned and the waiter who had not moved far away came and led them to their table.

Alan sat facing Anna and when she had settled herself he asked the waiter to take their drinks orders. To Hans' amusement there was an air of tension between his two companions. He had no intention of easing the situation, he was old enough to know that he wouldn't have been thanked by either party if he had.

Later, back in his hotel room Alan went over the evening and thought that it went as well as he could have hoped. The ice had been broken even if it hadn't been melted. There were a couple of times when Anna had seemed to be genuinely amused by his company and the conversation. Both he and Hans had refrained from discussing the reason for Alan being in Vienna and he wondered just what explanation Hans had given her. Was she still thinking of him simply as an ex-student.

Hans had mentioned that Alan needed somewhere more permanent to stay in the city and Anna had offered to help him should he wish to find an apartment.

On parting no firm arrangements had been made. Hans had vaguely said they should meet again next week sometime after he had made his travel arrangements for the seminar in Moscow. Alan had noticed the questioning look that had passed from Anna to her father but Hans did not elaborate in front of Alan.

The next two days were the weekend but neither Anna nor her father suggested he might like to spend part of it with them. In fact they had not asked him what he would be doing probably in fear he might invite himself into their company. Alan decided that if he were to be accepted on a more regular basis the moves now had to come from them.

He spent the next four days working, visiting museums and on Sunday had hired a car and driven out into the Vienna Woods before remembering that a large number of the Viennese would do the same. In the evenings he had visited cinemas and clubs but not being a gambler by nature, this had held little interest for him.

It was beginning to dawn on Alan that for the first time in his life he lead a lonely existence and was no longer enjoying it. Apart from Hans, Anna and the hotel staff there was no one he could have a conversation with and even the hotel staff had a limited interest in their client.

Lying in bed the following morning he remembered part of their conversation the night before. Why not take up Hans' suggestion and get an apartment. He was becoming bored with hotel life and it was not the cheapest way to live if he were planning to spend the immediate future here as Paul Gerhardt. Not only were there the economics in favour of the suggestion but it might also provide him with an opportunity of getting Anna on her own. His only concern was that the way events were turning out meant that he was spending more time in one place than might be safe but realised that he had no real choice in the matter.

He visited several estates agents and eventually he found an apartment that he liked the sound of and telephoned Anna to tell her. Anna remembering the promise she had made over dinner, offered to go with him to look at it.

He rang the agency and an appointment was made for late that afternoon. He arranged to meet Anna outside the apartment.

The agent was there waiting for them and by the look on his face Alan guessed he thought they were taking the place together. Fortunately Anna hadn't noticed and had passed into the apartment ahead of them.

The apartment was on the fourth floor of an old stone building and most of the windows overlooked similar period structures on the opposite side of the street. The exception was the dining area which had a corner aspect that looked out onto a small public garden.

Alan liked it and Anna gave it her seal of approval.

The agent, pleased to have made such an easy sale, opened his briefcase and took out a form to take down details. There was a little embarrassment as it was made clear to him that the flat was for Alan only.

Throughout the tour of the apartment Anna had seemed distant to Alan. Maybe she regretted having volunteered to help him. It was only after Alan had agreed to telephone the agent and he had left to return to his office that an angry Anna turned on him.

"Why is my father taking this trip to Russia?" she demanded.

Alan did not reply and ignoring his puzzled look she ploughed on.

"Before you arrived he had said there was no way he was going back to Moscow. He doesn't like the place or the Muscovites. Now he has arranged to go to the seminar and he will not discuss the reasons for this change of heart."

He knew it was the wrong thing to say almost before it was out "Why should it be anything to do with me?"

Anna looked at him in disgust. "I know my father and the only recent influence on his life has been your appearance here in Vienna. I'm not a fool you know."

Alan found his temper rising and couldn't back off. "If you know him so well then why don't you ask him?" he shot back.

Despite her anger he noticed the sparkle of tears in her eyes as she replied "I have, but he won't tell me. He won't lie to me and say he's changed his view. He simply refuses to discuss it with me." She turned and took the stairs that led down to the entrance of the apartments.

No more was said as Alan closed the door and followed her out of the building. She strode off and didn't look back.

After a moment's hesitation he took a cab to the hotel and tried to telephone Hans to warn him of Anna's reaction. He got through to him at his apartment and briefly explained what had happened.

"Oh dear" said Hans "I should have foreseen this. Never mind Alan I will have to deal with it in my own way. I'm sorry to have put you in that position."

"Don't apologise, I feel bad enough as it is."

"I will ring you after I've spoken with Anna. It would be a good idea if you didn't try and make

In Pursuit of the Red Kite

contact until I give you the all clear."

Alan couldn't help but smile at Hans' last comment, the last time he'd heard that expression had been from a bomb disposal expert in Kuwait.

"OK, I look forward to hearing from you soon" said Alan as he hung up. He was sure that Hans was beginning to wish he hadn't offered to help out with his problem.

It was mid-morning the next day when Hans rang Alan as he was working in his room at the hotel. His move to the new apartment was not until tomorrow.

"Could we meet for lunch?" He sounded serious.

"Yes of course. Where?"

"Here at the University is probably the best place. Come to my office." said Hans.

"Alan."

"Yes."

"Please follow my lead and trust me, OK."

"Right" said Alan not quite knowing what he would be letting himself in for. In an hour's time he would know.

At the University he went straight to the Doktor's office. He hesitated momentarily at reception.

"Please go in" said Frau Hecht a little sharply

In Pursuit of the Red Kite

and from her expression he knew that she was aware of some problem between him and the Freibergs.

The women are closing ranks thought Alan as he knocked on the Doktor's door.

"Come."

He entered. Anna sat at the end of her fathers' desk. Hans sitting more erect than usual sat in his chair.

"Please sit down Alan."

Not Paul this time. Alan now knew something was up.

The room has an atmosphere that you could cut with a knife he thought as he sat. Anna had not looked at him since he had entered. Hans had called him Alan in front of Anna and she had not reacted. Again he wondered what had taken place between father and daughter.

"Alan, I have had a long discussion with Anna, in fact" he said ruefully "we spent most of yesterday evening talking about you and why you're here."

Alan looked alarmed. "Do you think that was wise?"

Hans raised his hand. He was going to maintain control of this meeting. Anna turned and gave Alan a venomous look.

"Maybe I should have asked your permission before doing so but I decided to let Anna know what is happening especially as it may well have an effect on her."

Anna looked at her father angrily but said nothing.

"I have explained why I have offered to help and that I'm going to Moscow at the end of next week to make a start on collecting the proof you need" he said addressing Alan.

"I think it's insane" said Anna as she glared at Alan raising her hand to make the point.

"Come on Anna" her father interjected "we agreed we would help Alan."

"Yes, that's true, but you know I don't like the danger he has placed you, in fact both of us in."

"There is little point going over that again" said her father. "What is done is done. Let us move on."

"I said I would help" flared Anna.

"OK, OK" said Hans exasperatedly.

Anna leapt to her feet and left the office slamming the door behind her. The silence that followed was broken by Alan who looked at Hans and said "I think that went rather well, don't you. I think she's with us." It was a successful attempt at diffusing the tension and both began to laugh. With deference to Anna they tried to keep the noise down, but the more they tried the worse it became.

Suddenly the door opened and Frau Hecht

entered carrying a pot of coffee and some sandwiches on a tray. The men stopped, frozen like schoolboys caught out by the teacher. As she put the tray down, she gave each of them a glower and turned and stalked out of the room.

Both men collapsed again.

When they had managed to pull themselves together they ate their lunch more or less in silence. As he got up to leave Alan, with a smile on his face said to the Doktor.

"Sorry about this Hans, but you are an experienced man of the world and I'm an abject coward. I'm going to have to leave you to placate the women. I'll call you later."

The Doktor and Alan had dinner together the evening before Hans flew out for his conference at the Moscow Institute of Energetics. It was agreed that Alan would not make contact with Hans during his stay. In an emergency Anna would be the link between the two of them.

Later, that same evening, while he was drinking his nightcap of a weak coffee, Hans realised that the whole issue they had been wrestling with for the last few days could be simplified and reduce any risk to either himself or his daughter.

All he needed to do is make out a reference for Alan covering his time at the institute and with an indication of his abilities and his general attitude to taking up a scientific career. It was something he did all the time for students who had left the university and were looking for employment. He sighed, why hadn't he come to this simple conclusion earlier. "I must be getting old" he told himself. That would then go into university record for anyone to see.

He would not go back on his promise to Alan and would produce a more detailed document but that would be made at home.

CHAPTER 13

October 1993

If he were honest with himself Alan would admit to being totally bored. Since Hans had left for Moscow there had been no one to talk to.

The apartment he had moved into in Richtergasse Strasse was on the fourth floor of a brick and stone monolith. It was furnished in what could at best be described as unassuming taste.

Alan had wondered what to do to personalise the place but had only got as far as leaving magazines and papers he had bought strewn about the living room and bedroom. He was reluctant to go any further with his future movements so uncertain. He may even have to get out quickly if the Freiberg's warned him of any approaches by the security services.

He had moved the dining table into the large bay window at the front of the house which now formed his writing desk. All his efforts to date were hand written, he could not type although trying to interpret his notes had more or less decided him to buy a typewriter and use two fingers.

Yesterday's coffee mugs still stood like a row of soldiers along the window ledge, he gathered them together and took them into the small galley kitchen, put the kettle on and made his first cup of the day.

He stared out of the window at the building opposite - it could have been a reflection of the one he was in. He had never seen anyone moving about opposite despite the fact that the curtains were drawn at night and lights would go on. People obviously lived there, but who, was still a mystery. Not that Alan had any great desire to make acquaintanceships with the locals or anybody in his own building for that matter. The fewer who knew him the better. Vienna, like any large city, had a population that did not communicate with its immediate neighbours nor was it thought odd for you to maintain a solitary existence.

Down at street level the commuter population was underway. Above them the sky promised more rain. That he didn't mind at first. It had reduced the temptation to go out and would help him concentrate on his task. Much of the time as he sat there staring out of the window for inspiration he again wondered whether it would all be worth it. But then he would remind himself that he did not want to be on the run forever or be unable to put down roots or normalise his life. Usually at this point he felt guilty about his association with Hans and Anna and at the danger he may have placed them in.

However once Anna came into his thoughts he would again he wondered how to find a way to get back into her favour. Since their first meeting he had been attracted to her but so far had only managed to annoy her. How could he remedy that?

Coffee made he returned to the living room. By 11.00am he had made a perfunctory effort at working but crossed out more than he produced. He had reached a decision regarding Anna. Using Hans as the excuse for the call he would ask if she had heard from her father. He picked up the phone and dialled the University where Hans' secretary told him that Anna was not there and she wasn't sure what her movements were. The frosty atmosphere of Alan's last visit had not melted. He tried Anna's home number, more for something to do than because he expected an answer, therefore he was slightly taken aback when he heard Anna's voice.

"Hello?"

"It's Alan."

"Oh" there followed a silence, waiting for Alan to explain the purpose of his call.

"Have you heard anything from Hans.......your father?"

"No, but then I don't really expect to, he's only away for a few days and he would not normally telephone me from a conference unless of course there was good reason." Her tone was abrupt and Alan's disappointed "Oh" of acceptance made her relent a little.

"I will telephone you if I hear anything." she added.

"Sorry to bother you, I guess I'm just feeling a bit frustrated with the writing and needed to hear another human voice." Alan explained trying for the sympathy vote.

Anna could not have explained to herself later why she responded with "Well, if you're really frustrated you could buy me lunch."

Alan couldn't believe his luck and tried not to sound too eager.

"Sure, that would be nice."

They agreed to meet at the Cafe Schwarzenberg at midday.

Anna swore at herself as she replaced the receiver. She was having a lazy day at home while her father was away and had enjoyed fiddling about with some minor chores.

"Now I have to get dressed up for lunch" she told the room.

Anna was basically an optimist with a usually cheerful disposition which could not be dampened for long by circumstances beyond her control. She had to admit that with or without her permission her father had entered on a course of action, which if she had been consulted first, she would probably have vetoed. As she loved him deeply she had known she would go along with it in the end.

Having heard Alan's voice again after making that decision she no longer felt able to maintain her anger with him. As she looked at herself in the little mirror on the kitchen shelf she remembered that when they had dined with her father she had enjoyed his company, although she had not made it too obvious. Also she reflected , it had been some time since she had had any sort of a relationship with men and whereas Alan seemed OK, she supposed it would take more than a couple of meetings to form any strong opinions as to what type of character he was. She admitted to herself though, that if she was honest, she was attracted to him.

Alan spent the rest of the morning smartening

his appearance and generally tinkering with the report. His mind wasn't on it and most of what he produced he knew was destined for the waste paper basket.

He arrived at the cafe first and as it was still relatively early for the lunchtime population, was able to choose a table that was a little apart from its neighbours, would only sit two people and had a view onto the busy pavements outside.

He almost missed the smart young woman walking towards the cafe. Anna was on the opposite pavement and as she crossed the road she caught sight of him and smiled. She was wearing a simple two piece beige suit with a white open necked blouse. She carried a folded umbrella and wore a beige leather handbag that matched the medium height heeled shoes.

Alan's successes with women in the past had been unspectacular although the recent episodes in Geneva would not be quickly forgotten. Somehow he hoped he would fare better with Anna.

The waiter showed her to the table as Alan rose to meet her. He was unsure how to welcome her, a decision she took for him by holding out her hand which he took briefly. They ordered drinks and as the waiter left Anna said,

"Before we go any further, I want to say I'm sorry about how I reacted to you and my father at the University last week"

"Don't apologise" began Alan as she held up her hand to continue.

In Pursuit of the Red Kite

"And if I can help in any way let me know." she smiled to emphasise the offer.

"Well, thanks." He didn't know quite how to react to this new Anna.

Fortunately the drinks arrived and the next half hour was spent attending to their appetites and making small talk. With coffee, the conversation drifted back to what Alan was trying to achieve. Not too successfully he admitted.

Anna thought for a moment. "With Dad away I don't have too much work on at the moment and to be truthful I think when he's here he is trying to create a job for me. I'm sure he could make do with his secretary and the occasional temp."

She became quiet for a moment. "I know Dad's told you of my divorce and since then we have become very close. He has become very protective towards me" she looked at Alan who said nothing and waited for her to continue "I suppose that's why I got angry with him when I learned what it was he was helping you with, it seemed he was placing us both in unnecessary danger. I realise I was being selfish and acting a bit like a spoilt child."

"Anna, believe me, I don't want anything to happen to either of you and it wasn't my intention to put either of you in any danger. From talking to your father it just developed this way and I'm truly sorry."

She reached across the table and squeezed his hand. "Right, that's enough true confessions, let's go forward. It would seem the best thing is to complete your report with as much authentication as possible.

Once it is in place you have some Life Insurance."

Alan, who was much slower in his mood swings realised he was going to have to get used to these seemingly rapid changes in Anna.

"That's the way it seemed to me" her hand was still on his and Alan did not want to make the move that might cause it to be withdrawn. "I'm making quite good progress" he lied "It's the authentication that won't be so easy. First the people we approach have to be sympathetic and be prepared to stand up and be counted if called upon."

"What I was going to say to you, before the personal confessions, was that I could take down the story and type it up for you on the Word Processor. That way when it's finished you can have it on disc which is so much easier to transport and you can run off hard copies any time you want.

"That would be great" he said "but are you sure. I can't dictate, I've never done it before."

"Well give it a try and if that doesn't work I'll get you to tell me the basic details and I'll draft something up for you and then you can correct it before we make a disc."

He looked at her and shrugged "What can I say, I'll be forever in your debt and it will certainly save a lot of time. Thanks."

They finished the meal and Alan paid the bill. It was agreed they would make the first attempt the following morning with dictation at Alan's apartment. When they had got sufficient down Anna would use the University equipment to put down the text. Alan could then edit it.

As they got up to leave Alan said "I don't suppose you'd care for dinner this evening?"

Anna looked away which Alan read as a sign that either he was pushing his luck too far or that maybe she already had plans.

Sensing his confusion Anna said "If you're sure, only going from hardly speaking to each other ----" she looked at him for assistance "would it be a bit too much."

He smiled with obvious relief "Corny as it might sound, it won't be too much for me."

Anna laughed "OK where?"

"Where we had dinner with your father, if that's acceptable?"

"Fine, I'll see you there at eight. OK?"

It was agreed. They departed; Anna for her apartment and Alan, who could not face another afternoon trying to write, for the Belvedere Palace.

Dinner that evening went well although it began with each of them being a little reserved. Each felt that maybe their lunch had taken them rather suddenly into the beginnings of a relationship. At least that was what Alan hoped.

CHAPTER 14

October 1993

In Moscow Hans was attending a welcome reception in the University main hall having first settled himself into the Intourist Hotel. Although tourism was encouraged to bring in revenue, Moscow seemed to present visitors with an uncomfortable mixture of grandeur and dilapidation. The flight with Aeroflot had been predictably basic with threadbare carpeting and a brusque offering of a lukewarm fruit drink – no cup or glass was forthcoming so Hans drank from the bottle. The taste left him unable to determine what, if any, fruit it contained. Thankfully the University appeared more welcoming than his hotel. With its worn furnishings, grubby windows and rather intimidating concierges ensconced on every floor, Hans hoped to be spending the minimum of time there.

Despite the academic setting there were reputedly many of the Moscow Political elite present as well as the inevitable Security presence of the KGB.

The day's lectures had been on the development of nuclear fusion for peaceful purposes using different accelerators. Red Mercury still featured highly on the agenda although Hans noted there was no noteworthy advancement in the use of the material. He had a strong feeling that there had been advances made both in South Africa and Russia but neither wanted to share their knowledge with the other nations present. It could only mean one thing and that was that developments were all in the arena of Military use.

Hans was not alone in his concern over the miniaturisation of nuclear fusion. It made it even more attractive to the less scrupulous warmongering nations of the world. It was the terrorist groups which posed the most serious threat to the West and Europe. Small devices would be readily transportable and it would no longer be necessary to develop a national nuclear programme to become a nuclear power in the world. The lid was coming off Pandora's Box thought Hans.

Like many scientists however his desire to advance science and technology would always take precedent over how that advance might be later deployed.

Hans was sitting with an old friend from Frankfurt, Carl Muller. They had both passed their degree courses and got their doctorates at the Johann Wolfgang Goethe University of Frankfurt where Carl was still a part time lecturer and technical adviser to the British owned Thor Chemical Company at Speyer near Manheim in Germany.

Hans had been pleased to learn that Carl was going to be at the seminar and they had arranged adjoining rooms at Moscow's Intourist Hotel.

Before leaving Austria, Alan had given Hans a list of the Russian and other scientists he had met and had provided him both with technical advice and background information on Red Mercury. This was to ensure credibility to his and Nikolai's cover story as agents for illegal dealing in the supposed fusion bombs which Saddam Hussein had been so eager to get his hands on once he had been led to believe in their existence.

There had been three Russian professors on the list, one from St Petersburg, one from Irkutsk and one from the University hosting the conference.

Professor Ivan Kolmsky from Irkutsk was not on the attendance lists. Hans knew Professor Yuri Nikitin of the host University and had already spoken to him briefly on the first day of his arrival in Moscow. The third name, the Doktor from St Petersburg, Vasily Radishchev, he did not know. Carl however had met Vasily and was able to point him out to Hans. Vasily had a reputation of using other people's research and claiming the results as his own; many a bright student had suffered at his hands where, due to his position and influence, he had been able to deny the student any credit. Hans noted the warning from his friend.

He had therefore watched the man at the seminar. He did not appear too popular with his contemporaries but, as many of his type, this seemed not to worry the Doktor. He had an arrogance that would allow him to join groups and interrupt others as he saw fit. He was a large overweight man with thin red hair and a pale complexion. The most off-putting feature was his blue eyes which sparkled like ice from between puffy lids. His mouth was small and the corners turned down as though it was a face not much used to smiling. Despite his unsavoury visage he dressed well for a large man. Hans got the impression that the Doktor was capable of anything at the right price. He wondered if the Iraqis had met him and what they thought. No doubt he looked purchasable to them also. Was it a clever twist in the original plan to introduce such an unsavoury character into the plot. Hans stopped himself as he realised he was performing a character assassination on a man he had not even spoken to. His view was based on what he had heard from Carl and what he could see. "Still, I'll trust my first impressions until he proves me wrong" he said to himself.

After a lengthy meal heavy with speeches and vodka, the dinner finally ended with the delegates drifting through to the bar to spend what was left of the evening drinking and discussing the day's lectures. Some would leave for more private parties and some would return to the Intourist or Rossaya Hotels for an early night.

Hans had two more days to go and was aware he had not yet been able to get into a private conversation with either of the two scientists Yuri Nikitin or Vasily Radishchev.

Neither he nor Carl were ready to retire so they searched the smoky atmosphere of the bar for a table. It was then the Gods took a hand in matters.

At a corner table with plush banquette seating on two sides and two leather wing chairs facing inwards sat Yuri with another delegate. Hans took Carl's elbow and pushed him towards the table muttering "We should talk to our hosts" in Carl's ear.

Yuri looked up in surprise at the invasion and then recognised Hans, smiled and waved his hand at the other chair.

In Pursuit of the Red Kite

"Hans my friend, come and join us."

Carl found a chair and brought it over to the table, once Hans had introduced him. In turn Yuri introduced them to the other delegate who was a South African named Piet de Vries, a professor from the University of Witwatersrand in Johannesburg. He was a small bespectacled man with long wispy hair. The archetypal absent-minded professor.

He half raised himself from his seat and offered his hand to Carl and Hans.

"Pleased to meet you gentlemen." His voice was deep and warm, strongly at odds with his appearance.

The group talked of their current projects but as with many others the mixture of alcohol and camaraderie soon had them putting the world to rights. Hans who could hold his drink well and who had resisted too much drink earlier in the evening saw an opportunity to get the conversation round to the topic he was assigned to investigate.

He excused himself and went to toilets at the far end of the bar. None of the cubicles were taken. He took the one farthest from the entrance and went in and closed the door. He checked the pocket recorder and mike connection to make sure there were no problems. He would switch the recorder on from his inside pocket. He rejoined the group at the end of a long Russian joke which from the expressions on Carls and Piets faces was not too good but they judged the moment and roared their applause. He sat down and rejoined the conversation at the point where the scientists were beginning on the "You wouldn't believe me if I told you stories."

After a couple of anecdotes from Carl and Piet, Hans switched the recorder on while Yuri's attention was diverted and then introduced his topic.

"I heard an unlikely story about Saddam following the Gulf War." No subtlety, straight in, he thought to himself.

"What was that?" obliged Piet.

"Well the story I heard had to do with the alleged traffic in arms from the dissolution of the old Soviet Union." He looked respectfully at Yuri who smiled and waved his hand. It was not a state secret, the world knew how the Russian Mafia and black marketers had got rich on selling off surplus arms to emergent nations and terrorist groups the world over. Joining the Czech's who had been selling Semtex and Kalashnikovs to anybody who could raise the cash, long before the break-up of the Soviet Union.

"Go on" encouraged Carl who was now looking a little flushed, his eyes sparkling.

"Well, in a nutshell, what I heard was that a complicated hoax was perpetrated on the Iraqis by the Russian Mafia. They knew how keen Saddam was to get his hands on weaponry, especially anything he felt would give him an opportunity to retaliate on the West after his loss of face in the Gulf War." He paused and took a drink.

"As we all know there were many rumours surrounding the development of Red Mercury in nuclear fission and the production of small but lethal weapons. Well as I heard it they managed to convince Saddam that these weapons existed together with the necessary launchers. The whole package could be carried manually by units of no more than two soldiers on foot."

Hans paused and looked around, his audience waited in silence for him to continue. It seemed he certainly had their attention.

"There was also supposed to be a smaller hand held version that could be triggered by radio signal over fairly long distances. The idea being that this device could be taken anywhere by the terrorist who could then get well away from the danger zone before it was set off. You can imagine a circle of these devices could be left around the centre of any city and could be triggered as one or in series dependant on the whim of the operator. You can also imagine how attractive the concept must have been to Saddam. How they then convinced him of its plausibility must have called for some well staged theatre, if" he paused "the story is true?"

He sat back, his tale of the rumour complete. A stone had been cast into the pool - would the ripples produce anything? It was Carl who reacted first.

"I have to admit that I'd heard a story not dissimilar to that a few years ago. Yes" he mused "I'd forgotten about it. I wonder what happened?"

"No idea" said Hans. "As I said it was only a rumour."

Yuri who had sat silently through the discourse looked conspiratorially around the bar before leaning forward.

"I wouldn't dismiss it as a rumour. I can tell you there is a lot more truth in the story than most of us get to hear about. Take it from me."

All three looked at him and waited for him to continue, but he wanted more encouragement. Piet obliged.

"Come on Yuri, you can't leave it there. What do you know?"

"I understand certain members of the Military were also involved in creating the hoax. And I heard on reasonably good authority from a contact in the KGB that the whole matter was encouraged by certain Government Ministers. When Saddam discovered he'd been conned the Iraqis made a protest to Gorbachev through the embassy, but as you can imagine any possible link between the mafia and government was most strongly denied."

"How did it end?" asked Hans.

"Well, it subsided rather than ended" said Yuri. "The Iraqis are still deeply suspicious that they were hoaxed by our government and one or two of the other nations involved in the Gulf such as the USA, France and the UK."

"Thank God those weapons don't exist" said Carl who seemed to have sobered up as the realisation of the potential such an instrument of death would give to an unstable leader.

"They don't?" asked Vasily cryptically. Hans turned to see the Russian standing behind him. How long had he been there?

In Pursuit of the Red Kite

Hans looked questioningly at him but he would say no more, he just stared at Hans in a totally dispassionate way. Was there more behind that look? Hans shivered inwardly, had he gone too far already with his mission? He was well aware of Russia's interest and development in 'ballotechnic' weapons. He knew the theory that Red Mercury gel had a possible contribution to fusion weapons and when fused with tritium atoms could produce a thermonuclear explosion. Some experts outside the old Soviet Union believed that it was already contained in Russian neutron weapons and could be used with the M-1975 240mm mortar.

"Another round of drinks" said Carl who, despite his advanced state of inebriation, had noted the mood change of the party. Yuri looked relieved and readily agreed. Piet used the moment as an excuse to leave and Hans who felt he needed to keep an eye on Carl's condition, also said he would enjoy another vodka, heavily laced with tonic. Vasily declined and nodded to the group moved off to re-join a companion at the bar.

It was 12.30am before Hans was able to drag Carl into a cab and return to the Intourist where he delivered him to his room, saw him inside and then made his own way to bed. Despite the lateness of the hour the streets of Moscow were still heavily populated and the Intourist Hotel was as busy as a hive.

Hans did not sleep well. He had the suspicion of a hangover and his mind had been stimulated by his conversation with Yuri. He played the tape several times as he lay in bed checking, not only for the sound clarity but that each of the scientists present had been named clearly in the text.

As a result of a restless night and the fact that the first lecture of the day did not begin until 10am, he decided to take an early morning walk.

There were few people about in the hotel lobby. He made his way out onto the Lenina Prospekt and headed for Red Square, his destination, the Kremlin. He wanted to visit some of the buildings while in Moscow and he should be able to visit the Cathedral of the Assumption without the need or desire for a guide.

It was a chill morning with the makings of a good day ahead as a few wispy white clouds scudding across the blue sky indicated a breeze. At street level he was well protected, it would be in Red Square where he would be more exposed.

He entered the Kremlin by the Nickolaskaya Tower entrance and slowed his pace to a stroll as he walked among some of the more renowned buildings of the Old City.

The Cathedral was open and as he entered, due to the darkness inside it took a moment for his vision to adjust. Daylight filtered down from above to mingle with the weak light of thousands of candles.

Hans was not a religious man but he was always conscious of the atmosphere that seemed to pervade religious buildings. He walked around the inside inspecting the artefacts and icons. His head was beginning to clear and he sat in one of the pews facing the altar thinking again of the previous

In Pursuit of the Red Kite

evening.

As he sat there people came into the church and paid their respects before beginning the day's work. Most were poor workers at this hour of the day, he noticed, the clothes drab browns and greys, the women their heads covered with scarves.

He had probably been sitting there for fifteen minutes when one of the figures approaching the altar seemed familiar as it approached, genuflected and crossed himself. The man turned and Hans recognised Vasily Radishchev the scientist from St Petersburg. He was surprised, he would not have believed the man to have any religious inclinations.

Hans got to his feet and contrived to meet the man before he left the church although unsure as to what he would say when he did. Vasily was walking more quickly than Hans had guessed and it was only at the main entrance that they met up.

"Excuse me Professor Radishchev?" Hans began.

The Professor stopped and turned to look at Hans through cold blue eyes from the puffy face that showed no more emotion than if he were a specimen under a microscope.

"Yes?" Vasily replied.

"I am at the conference at the University, we had a drink last night?" Hans explained.

"Ah, so where are you from?" he asked Hans

"Vienna."

"You are Austrian?"

"That's right" he paused "and you Professor are from Moscow?"

"No, St Petersburg."

They were walking away from the Cathedral towards Ivan the Greats Bell Tower.

"So you are taking in the sights?" continued Hans.

"No. I have been here many times. Today I come to the Cathedral. I always come here when I am in Moscow." He looked at his watch.

"I am going back to Hotel Rossaya for breakfast, are you staying there?" He raised one eye to emphasise the question.

"No, I am at the Intourist" replied Hans seeing his opportunity slipping. In desperation he added "Maybe we can have a drink or dinner this evening, I'm doing a paper on Red Mercury and I understand you to have specialised in its development?"

Vasily stopped and stared at Hans before replying.

"Yes, that is so, but why me?"

"Oh, because I'm writing on both the Military as well as its peaceful application and I believe you were involved in its weapons capabilities."

"Yes, but that is an aspect I am not sure I should discuss now that it is the peaceful use of the chemical we are developing."

Hans felt himself tense, had he made the Professor more suspicious. He had prepared a plausible explanation and hoped it would suffice.

"I'm trying to prepare a thorough history of its development since it was first produced in 1965 at the research centre at Dubna."

"Well maybe we will meet. I will talk with you after the afternoon session is over. Goodbye Doktor" he made no attempt to shake hands but turned and strode towards the Saviour Tower exit from the Kremlin.

Hans stood and watched him go, wondering whether he had done the right thing. "Too late now, the die is cast," he told himself. He looked at his watch. There was just time for him to get back to the hotel, have breakfast, and get to the University for ten o'clock and the start of the day's lectures.

CHAPTER 15

November 1993

In Aix Inspector Renard was seated at his desk feeling frustrated. He still had not heard from Marie Lemerle. In his opinion the forensic pathologist had had plenty of time to come up with some evidence as to how they might identify their mystery corpse.

The sunlight streaming in from the window behind him illustrated his frustration by showing the shadow of a dancing finger on the desk top. Seeing it he immediately stopped. He called out to Annie.

"Can you chase up that pathologist for me?"

"Poor woman," Annie thought as she replied "Right away sir" with just the right amount of irony in her voice.

As she began to dial the number a motor cyclist entered wielding a folder "I believe you're waiting for this," he said as he stopped in front of Annie's desk.

"You wouldn't believe it," as she got up and took it from him, signed where he indicated on his pad, crossed over to Pierre Renard's office, rapping on the open door and entered uninvited before placing the document case on his desk.

"Is this what you were after sir?"

"About time!" the inspector replied before

taking it and studying the package. "Thank you Annie. Quick work" he told her with a smile.

"Always pleased to oblige." she dropped a curtsy before turning and leaving Pierre to continue with his scrutiny.

He picked up a paperknife and slit open the seal. He pulled out a standard form attached to a bound report. He leaned back in his chair, leafed through the technical pages and went straight to the conclusion.

Unsurprisingly there was no positive ID however he learned that the victim was in his mid-thirties, there were usable fingerprints and it was the fact that his dental work appeared to have been carried out in Eastern Europe confirmed he would need the assistance of Europol in tracing this man. The report confirmed that it was the knife wound that had killed the victim and that the corpse had died approximately four weeks before discovery.

The dried blood which had been discovered near to the top of the fissure into which the body had been dropped was confirmed as B RhD positive and matched that of the victim. The only other piece of information contained in the report which the inspector found useful was that most of the clothing had tags in Cyrillic text which further indicated that their victim came from an Eastern Bloc country.

He put the report down, put his hands behind his head and considered what the report had added to the investigation.

In Pursuit of the Red Kite

Little had come from the local and national press when the crime had first been discovered. The local paper gave it front page, the 'Aujourd Hui' assigned it to page five and as there was no information, or a photograph of the victim it received no further coverage in either paper. The world had much more important matters to worry about.

What had they missed?

He tried putting himself into the mind-set of the murderer. Hide the corpse but don't leave anything on it that may identify it. There must have been some documents in the rucksack originally. So the murderer would either have taken them away or thrown them away. How large an area did the team cover in its search for evidence. The more he thought about it the more he felt that another visit to the scene of the crime was called for.

He called to Annie "Is Maurice in?"

"Yes he's in his office."

"Could you get him to come through?"

A couple of minutes later Maurice appeared in the doorway "You wanted to see me?"

"Yes. What have you got on this afternoon?"

"Nothing that I would greatly miss. Several reports on petty crimes that I'm a bit behind on. Nothing important. Why?"

"I want to go back to the crime scene of our murder. Just to check for myself that nothing has been missed." he nodded to the report on his desk "Our forensic report."

"Good reading?"

"Get your jacket. You can read it in the car as we go along."

Renard told Annie they would be out for the rest of the day as they made their way through the office to the yard at the rear where his car was parked.

The journey was uneventful. They parked the car as near as possible to the site, locked it and began the climb up to the footpath from which they would reach their objective.

On the way the inspector told of his frustration on lack of progress and that what was contained in the report was useful but did not lead them much further. What they needed was a picture of the victim and a name. That would enable them to discover whether he had recently entered the country as a tourist through one of the air ports or a at border crossing. Maurice added that of course the man may be an immigrant now living in France to which Renard only grunted by way of reply.

After half an hour's climb, most of which was conducted in silence, they found the spot they were looking for. Having become hot and tired from their walk, both sat down with their backs to the rock-face on one side of the path and looked out over the opposite edge at the distant forest beyond. Where it commenced, at the foot of the rock-face, could not be determined from their viewpoint.

It was after several minutes of silence Maurice asked "What now?"

"Imagine you were our man and you didn't want to be found what would you do?"

"Well much the same as what he did. If it was not for bad luck I believe he would have got away with it," replied Maurice.

"It's the fact that he took the precaution to remove any identifying documents that has got me wondering." Renard informed him.

"I would imagine he would have taken them with him and disposed of them somewhere else. Or simply have thrown them away." said Maurice

"Exactly what I have been thinking." he stood up "It could have been an instant reaction to the problem or a considered plan." He looked at Maurice. "Let's assume that it's the former. If the latter then we have little or no chance of ever making any progress with identification. Unless," he added," Interpol are approached by an Embassy looking for a missing National or someone comes forward through missing persons."

They both turned and looked at the opposite edge of the path. They crossed over, cautiously knelt down and leaned over. The drop down to what looked like a lower footpath was about two hundred feet. The rock face between was a myriad of ledges. Some with coarse vegetation and some simply narrow rock outcrops. The inspector had had the foresight to bring along with him a pair of bird-watching binoculars which he now used to study each ledge in turn upon which something could have lodged.

"We'll need to cover the whole length of the path that runs between here and the entrance to the fissure." Maurice told Renard, helpfully. He got a grunt for his efforts and thought he heard something about " ----the obvious."

It was as they got near to the end of their search area the inspector thought he could see something on one of the lower ledges. It appeared to be wedged between some loose rock and the base of a small shrub that hung off the cliff face. He handed the binoculars to Maurice and directed him where to look. After what seemed to the inspector too long a time, Maurice looked up and said.

"You could be right." He got up and handed the binoculars back to Renard. "We'll need someone to abseil down and check it out."

"Exactly." Renard pulled out his mobile phone and called Annie.

"Annie do we know any abseilers. I need someone to go down a cliff face." He paused before adding "I don't suppose we have anyone at the office who can help, but ask around anyway. If not, try that group of potholers. I'm sure they would be only too willing to assist us."

Having given his orders he told Maurice that

unless he had any further areas that might be further investigated then they would walk the scene once more and then head back down to the car.

On their return to the office they found that Annie had come up with someone who was willing to abseil down to investigate the object on the ledge. It was Leon De Clerk, leader of the potholing group who had discovered the victim.

He would come to the office the following morning and pick up the two policemen before driving up to the scene.

Next day they left the office in Leon's Landrover, squeezed in between all his climbing gear. They helped him carry all the necessary equipment up to the path and showed him where they wanted him to descend. Leon secured the ropes using pitons hammered into cracks in the rock face and then around a conveniently positioned trunk of a shrub. He tested the pull of his full weight several times before throwing the rope over the edge of the path.

It was then a matter of watch and wait for the two policemen. When he reached the ledge they saw him bend and release the object which he held up and waved.

"It's a hotel receipt." they heard him shout "

The inspector wondered how this might help. With the practice of passport ID when staying at any hotel in France there was a chance that with the help of Interpol they might trace the body.

"Was there anything else down there?" he queried, as Leon clambered back onto the path.

"Not that I could see. I did check down as far as the path below and I took a good look at any likely place on the way back up, which is why it took me so long." Leon replied.

"I suppose the only other thing we might have found would have been a driving licence. Any money would have been taken by the murderer."

They helped Leon gather up his equipment and pack it back into the car.

On the drive back to Aix, Renard considered what this information might produce. The press would certainly be more interested now and no doubt come up with some far-fetched theories about international spies falling out, or an agent being given a 'wet job' to carry out. His speculation was more or less spot on as the local papers used their front page for several days, coming up with wild and imaginative theories as to what had taken place. The 'Aujord Hui' even gave it second page prominence.

So, did the victim live in France? Not that they had discovered so far. Or had he arrived recently with a specific brief which had gone wrong?

He passed all that he had on to Interpol who got in touch with, among others Russian Embassy in Paris.

It was over a week later before the Embassy got back and simply confirmed that Nikolai was a

Russian National and they would arrange for the body to be repatriated. It was neither confirmed nor denied that their victim had a criminal record or was in a government organisation.

To Renard's frustration no further information was forthcoming. The trail had gone cold and the murderer was probably no longer in France. It would remain on their 'unsolved list' of cases.

CHAPTER 16

November 1993

When the D.G. arrived at his office he was met by an agitated Amanda "What's up?" he asked, before she had an opportunity to explain.

"Moscow's been on. Would you ring Yuri as soon as you arrive."

"Any idea what it's about?"

"They wouldn't tell me. I offered to put them through to Harry, but they insisted they speak to you."

Sir Ian sighed. There had been no let up on the IRA front over the past few weeks and he could do without another major problem right now he told himself.

"Ok, try and get him for me. You know I have to go out again in half an hour?"

"Yes sir" said Amanda as she left his office.

Within five minutes he was connected to Yuri.

"Late start, Sir Ian" teased the Russian.

"We're having to make substantial cuts to meet the budget, so I'm only part time" replied Sir Ian somewhat sarcastically.

The Russian chuckled and then became more serious.

"I think we have a problem, you and I" he began.

"We have?"

"Your agent Red Kite is on the loose."

"Oh?"

"My man Nikolai is dead and I believe that your man was responsible."

"Oh... Are you sure it was Red Kite?"

The Russian ignored the question and replied with one of his own.

"Has he been in contact?"

"No. But tell me what happened to Nikolai." The frustration was already beginning to show in Sir Ian's voice.

"His body was discovered in France about three days ago. From what we can make out he seems to have been dead about a month."

"Where was he found?"

"In a cave in the Montagne de Lure in Provence."

"Who found him?"

"A group of potholers."

"What was he doing in that part of the world?" Sir Ian queried, more to himself.

"We suspect that's where he hid, although exactly where, we do not know," lied the Russian.

In Pursuit of the Red Kite

"How did he die?"

"He was stabbed and tossed down a fissure. The body fell to a cave below and it was your man's bad luck that it was found at all" said the Russian.

"What have the French said?"

"Naturally they are suspicious but we have told them he was a University Professor on a walking holiday with no companion that we know of. We provided them with photographs and they are carrying out an investigation in the local towns and villages but somehow I don't think they'll come up with anything" he paused. "I think Sir Ian this Red Kite of yours needs to be found and stopped. Regrettably we have to assume he suspects it was not intended that he survive the operation and now no doubt he's on the run. Not only from us but I suspect you also."

"You have something in mind?" Sir Ian understood the Russian well enough to know that he would not have contacted him until he had devised some course of action.

"I think we need a small team, including someone who would recognise him despite any aliases he may use. Preferably someone who knows him well enough to have a good idea of what he might do. That particular person will have to be supplied from your end. However we will also have an asset involved."

Sir Ian smiled to himself. "To make sure he's not missed a second time?"

The Russian grunted, embarrassed at this reminder of their failure to silence the British agent"

"You have to understand Sir Ian" he continued "that the political situation has changed since our joint operation. It is becoming more evident that the USA will go into Iraq to confirm whether Saddam has a nuclear strike capability or not. The UK will be dragged along with them. On the other hand Russia will not get involved and will wish to remain impartial."

"And if this got out the Iraqis would not trust you?"

Sir Ian's sarcasm was not lost on the Russian.

"We will blame the mafia."

"And they will trust you?"

"When did a Russian or an Arab ever trust each other?" parried Yuri with a laugh.

"Leave it with me for a few hours and I'll see what we can come up with and contact you again this evening. Where can I get you?" Sir Ian asked.

"Through this office. If I'm not here they can reach me on my mobile."

Sir Ian put the receiver down and called Amanda.

She came in, a questioning look on her face.

"It's Red Kite. Apparently he's flown the coop and his partner's turned up dead. The Russians think our man killed him. First get me the P.P.S. I'll need to be excused for an hour or two today, then get me Harry."

In Pursuit of the Red Kite

"But Sir, Harry?"

"I think regrettably we have to involve more people in this. We have to track him down before they do otherwise we will lose an agent. We have to prepare a damage limitation exercise rather quickly to prevent unnecessary speculation as to whether our man is a killer or, as I suspect, the Russians set out to silence him and somehow it went wrong. Harry is just the man we want on the team." Sir Ian was decided.

Amanda looked doubtful but said nothing as she hurried off. She stuck her head into Harry's office. "Sir Ian wants you" she said. Harry looked up from writing one of his interminable reports. "Now" she added grinning and rushing back to her office to telephone the Prime Ministers Personal Secretary.

Harry, more out of habit than suspicion locked up his papers before getting up, straightening his tie and heading for the D. G's office. The door was open; he went through the motions of knocking on the frame.

Sir Ian watched, steely eyed. "Come in and have a seat" he indicated a chair in

front of the desk.

"Oh and you had better close the door." The phone rang.

"Yes?....good" he put it down. He'd been given the morning off from the bloody IRA. He looked at Harry as he marshalled his thoughts. "We have a bit of a delicate problem. I need to discuss it at least in part with you.....there are issues I cannot mention and therefore you will be working blind at times. Regrettably that's the way it is."

"OK Sir" said Harry "What do you need?"

"One of our agents seems to have decided to go AWOL. He needs to be found and brought back in." Sir Ian stood up and began walking around the office as he told Harry those elements of the "Red Kite" operation necessary to make sense of the task he was setting him. It also helped in that he could look out of the window during his perambulations and avoid unnecessary eye contact with his deputy.

"Just over two and a half years ago we recruited an SAS officer to MI6 to assist with a very complicated operation, a joint venture with the Russians. He spent a few months learning the ropes before being sent out on a mission. At the end of the operation the agents were to go to ground for a couple of years to avoid certain political fallout and protect themselves from possible reprisals from the injured party."

Harry thought that it had all the hallmarks of the previous administration but kept his opinion to himself as Sir Ian continued.

"We had a call from Moscow this morning to say that their half of the act has been discovered dead somewhere in Provence in Southern France. He had been stabbed. It looks like our man did it although we have to find him to be sure of the facts." He stopped in his pacing and fixed Harry with a stare. "That's your job" he announced.

"We have to put a small unit together, one of

theirs and one of ours to trace him and bring him in for questioning." Sir Ian repeated his earlier statement to give it additional emphasis. Harry simply nodded as the DG continued.

"Now we need someone who knows Alan Marks, his ways, habits and can out-think him. Ideas?" he fired the question at Harry.

"You said he was SAS trained, why don't we get hold of his unit commander and enlist his aid?"

"Ah, yes, good idea, however that may not be so easy. It seems Alan Marks was

drummed out of the squadron in disgrace, I doubt he has too many friends." He continued " From my reading of the file it is evident that he was set up to give credence to his character." "Surely that's to the good. We don't want him hunted by a friend, do we?" The irony was not lost on Sir Ian who peered quizzically at Harry, but Harry kept his face expressionless.

"I'll need to know a little bit about this character" said Harry.

"Yes, well I'll let you have what little personal history we have from the file. It's the operation that's hush-hush, you understand."

Harry caught Sir Ian's eye as he emphasised the need for secrecy.

"Just what I need to know will do at this stage" said Harry. Sir Ian looked relieved.

"I will need to know where he was last seen and get the facts on the death of the Russian, Nikolai

Pietrofka. Are we sharing information with the Russians?"

"Of course" said Sir Ian looking offended.

"And are they sharing with us?"

"I will speak to them and get everything directed to you." He looked pointedly at his watch.

Harry stood. "The file?"

"I'll have security bring it in" said Sir Ian as Harry turned to leave.

Back in his own office Harry sat down at his desk and smiled. Something of interest and, if he was not mistaken, politically embarrassing at least to the Russians. It could be fun. Not of course for the poor sod if they catch him first. He pondered the reasons why an agent might want to kill his fellow agent. An argument, an accident or maybe he was instructed to. Amanda broke in on his reverie and handed him a buff folder with the name Alan Marks on the front. Harry smiled his thanks and settled down in his chair to read Alan's abbreviated life story. It was obvious the file had been vetted. It did little more than describe Alan and included a photo taken at least two years ago. When he'd finished he wondered why a man who had met with disgrace had been enlisted. Why not a 'Six' regular? Then he told himself not to be so naive, Alan had all the requirements for a good deep cover man and only a doctored service record with MI6.

While he had been reading the report Amanda had bustled in and out of his office with faxes, maps and photographs. He picked up the photographs, the first was another of Alan, the second, Nikolai the dead agent and the third showing Nikolai very dead. He winced at the picture of the badly decomposed body, which had been provided by Interpol.

The faxes told him of the time, date and place where the body had been found together with a list of contents of Nikolai's clothing and rucksack.

He put those aside and opened a large scale map of Provence and studied the Montagne de Lure area and the surrounding villages and towns. He tried to put himself into the minds of both Alan and Nikolai. Had they spent two years in this area, or were they just passing through, fallen out and Alan had simply hidden the body. As he looked at the map he realised his last idea was impractical. The area where the body was found was inaccessible to traffic and to carry a body that far was not on. Maybe they had already gone their separate ways from some other part of Europe and the Russian had got himself killed by somebody else. In fact, Harry thought, it was likely it was an elaborate smoke screen put up by the Russians themselves that had gone wrong.

"Keep it simple, at least to start with," he told himself "let's assume they have come out of hiding together and one or maybe both have been instructed to kill the other by their respective controls. If that were the case our man would most likely have reported in and I wouldn't be sitting here. Sir Ian would have kept it to himself. So, that scenario is unlikely. If both had been eliminated to order, there's another body to be found and why would the KGB be speaking to us if it had been planned that way. No" he was prepared to convince himself at least for the time being. "something went wrong with the final stages of the operation, as a result their man's dead and ours is on the run believing he is a marked man."

He went back to the maps. It seemed the police so far had come up with nothing but it was still early days. Assuming they had stayed in the region for two years where could they possibly have stayed untraced for so long and was it relevant.

The maps of France held in the office were good but Harry thought he would see

if he could improve on the scale and therefore the detail. He remembered from walking holidays in France that you could get the French equivalent of Ordnance Surveys. He racked his brain but could not remember what the series was called, but every area had its own reference number. He would go down to Longacre at lunchtime and see what he could find in Stanfords.

Having gone as far as he could down that avenue his next move was to arrange a visit to Alan's old unit. Records told him the commander was still the same and some of the training team who had trained Alan were still there.

He dialled and with little trouble was connected to Commander James Morris.

"Morning Commander. I would like to make an appointment to come down and see you."

"May I ask why?"

As an invitation was not immediately forthcoming Harry continued "It's a somewhat

In Pursuit of the Red Kite

delicate matter. We need to talk to you about Alan Marks, he was in your unit during the Gulf War."

"That's correct. What's he done?" the commander replied guardedly.

"We're not sure and that's why I need to see you and maybe if you have anybody there who knew well him I would like to speak with them too."

He waited as the commander deliberated on the request.

"You know he left us under a bit of a cloud, don't you?"

"Is that so?" said Harry. The question however brought out no further information.

"When had you in mind?"

"Would tomorrow be convenient?"

"Certainly, around eleven hundred hours would suit my diary" said the commander.

"Good, I'll see you then and I'll bring my security clearances with me." he added.

The short exchange over, Harry had learned nothing more about the missing soldier, not that he had expected to. Perhaps tomorrow would be more productive he thought to himself.

At lunchtime he went to Stanfords and without too much trouble found a map of

the type he was looking for. As is usually the case when buying large scale maps he had to obtain three different sections to cover what he considered to be an adequate area for investigation.

He'd worked on the premise that if the body were to be at the centre of a circle he would work on an approximate two days hike from the most likely directions.

Back at the office he indulged in pouring over the maps having first made himself some coffee. "Somewhere" he thought "we have a magnifying glass." He got up and called to Amanda through the door.

"Seen the magnifying glass anywhere?"

"Yes it's here" she called. "Why, have you had a pay rise."

Harry grinned, it was the sort of humour he appreciated and Amanda knew it.

"Just give me the bloody thing, and less of the cheek" he replied, then added, "Well yes I have, haven't you?"

Amanda placed the object of his desire on the desk in front of her and said "No! And in that case you can afford to come and get it yourself."

Back with his maps Harry settled down once more to a serious study of the area.

Apart from the towns and villages which the police were already covering, there were farms and the larger estates to consider.

The only other object that came to his attention was what he assumed to be a monastery. There was a symbol indicating a religious building on

In Pursuit of the Red Kite

the lower slopes of the Montagne de Lure, close to Saumane. He checked further but there was no other village marked and therefore it was unlikely to be a church. It was within the radius he had ringed on the map from where the body had been discovered. It was worth a try although he was sure the police would have thought about it already.

Harry looked at his watch, he could telephone the French Police, but they would no doubt be curious as to why M16 were taking an interest in the case. The only solution, on reflection, was to send in an independent investigator, assuming of course that nothing came up on any reports being processed via the Russians. Was it all a waste of time? Harry knew that it was more than likely that their man was now well away from the area and he could not, on reflection, see any point in finding out where Alan had stayed.

He picked up the phone and dialled records on the internal system.

"Who do we have in Southern France. In the Provence area?"

"We only have a retired man down there. He lives in Aix with his wife," came the response after a moment's silence waiting on the computer. "Children left home; just the pair of them."

"How old?"

"Mid-fifties."

"Will he still do the odd job?"

"Depends how odd."

"I'm trying to trace one of our agents who disappeared recently and we believe he may have been in the region. We need a discreet enquiry. Something the police need not know about," stated Harry.

"OK thanks. Let me think about it and come back to you." As he had been talking it had occurred to Harry that maybe it would be better to send in someone from the SAS. The man they hoped to recruit to track Alan Marks down was a natural candidate. If there was a trail to follow he should be in at the beginning. If they drew a blank nothing was lost, at the moment they had no leads to follow.

That decided, Harry would meet the Commander tomorrow and take it from there. Sir Ian may have to apply the necessary pressure to get a man prised from the Commander's unit.

CHAPTER 17

October 1993

Hans pulled together his notes as the afternoon seminar drew to a close. It was the last formal day. Tomorrow was a day where the University facilities were put at the disposal of the delegates as an informal forum in which to meet and discuss any topics of mutual interest. In the evening there would be a large formal dinner with more interminable speeches about goodwill, collaboration and unity which were par for the course in any international conference. The Russians and Eastern Bloc countries always seemed to make a big event out of these occasions. If he could he would find some way to get out of it.

Hans had decided he would stay till the end of the conference instead of slipping off a day earlier, his decision being based on the fact that he'd made little progress on Alan's behalf.

As he sat there putting the papers back in the folder provided for him he was aware of someone standing in front of him. He looked up to see Vasily Radishchev.

"Herr Doktor, I am able to have dinner with you tonight" stated the Russian.

"Oh, that's good" said Hans smiling up at the large man "Can you recommend somewhere. You know Moscow considerably better than I do and it would be nice to get away from the University for a while."

"Certainly. Do you know the Arbat at all?"

"No, but I'm sure I can find it if you let me know the name of the restaurant. I will take a cab from the hotel" he explained.

"Good. In that case I suggest we meet at eight at the "Prague Restaurant, I will book a table for two." He paused, studying Hans like a doctor looking at a specimen through eyes that mouth went through the motions of smiling although the attempt did not reach his eyes.

Hans could not help but feel the Russian was suspicious of him. He knew he was not good at deception and his direct approach to life did not suit the role of spy and investigator he now found himself in. Not for the first time he wondered whether he had been a wise choice on Alan's part.

"I look forward to it." You liar, thought Hans to the retreating figure of the Professor from St Petersburg.

Hans put on a suit for his dinner that evening. The casual approach among business men had not become the fashion in Moscow and, being of the old school, Hans preferred the more traditional approach. It saved him to having to make appropriate dress decisions for himself. He fitted and tested the tape recorder, then rang down to reception to book a cab only to be told that there were always plenty waiting outside the hotel.

He took one last look around the room trying

to memorise where everything was, locked the door and left his key at reception before going out to the waiting rank of taxis. The night was chilly and he pulled his overcoat closer round him. His cab was an old Zil. He told the driver his destination and sat back for what turned out to be a short ride.

'The Prague Restaurant' marks the entrance to the Arbat. Arbat Street is a cobbled pedestrianised street that is a popular shopping and meeting place in Moscow. There are many shops, cafes and galleries and most tourists make for the area at some stage during their visit. The street was teeming with early evening promenaders and Hans found the atmosphere here pleasant despite the chill night air. He stood for a moment studying the old buildings before turning and entering the restaurant where he was immediately met by a waiter who relieved him of his coat and led him to a corner table at which Vasily was already seated drinking what looked to Hans to be Vodka.

Vasily half stood as Hans reached the table. He did not attempt to shake hands but gestured for Hans to sit. The waiter pulled out the seat and Hans did their bidding.

"A drink Sir?"

"Whisky with ice" said Hans.

"Well Doktor do you like the restaurant?"

"Yes it is most attractive" said Hans looking round the room where most of the tables were already taken by well-dressed couples or business men. The decor was plush and Hans thought that if the food was good and he was in more personable company it

In Pursuit of the Red Kite

would make for a most pleasant evening. With that thought he reminded himself of Anna and felt slightly guilty for not having made contact over the last few days.

He wondered how she and Alan were getting on. So far it had been a rather tense relationship hardly likely to develop into anything more meaningful he mused. He was aware that Vasily was waiting for him to respond more fully.

"I do not know the Arbat at all he confessed, but from the little I have seen in coming here it seems an attractive area."

"It certainly draws the tourists" remarked Vasily dryly. He beckoned the waiter over.

"May we have the menu please?"

"Certainly sir" said the waiter looking somewhat flushed at not having already judged the correct moment at which to attend to his customers.

Vasily had a smirk on his face, having put the waiter at a disadvantage so early in the evening.

There followed a silence between the two men as if each were weighing up the other but neither wished to declare his hand.

Hans felt on edge, he was entering a world he felt was completely unfamiliar to him. The Political arena of lies and deceit. He decided to take the initiative and break the silence.

"What is it that you do Professor?" he asked.

"I mainly lecture at St Petersburg" said

Vasily. "Sometimes I advise the government and as you may know I was involved in the military development of fusion weapons."

Hans feigned denial of any knowledge of Vasily's career. He suspected a trap in admitting he knew anything at all of the Professors life or work. He had not switched on the recorder as he had not expected to get to the main subject of his interest so soon.

He was saved from taking the matter any further by the waiter enquiring as to their choice of food and for the next three quarters of an hour, while they ate and drank, the conversation was kept to more domestic issues.

Hans discovered that Vasily had once been married but now seemed to keep himself amused by a succession of female students though how he managed it stretched Hans' imagination and credibility. The Professor seemed to be singularly lacking in any charm or charisma.

At the end of their meal Vasily produced cigars which Hans declined but the Professor lit his and relished the pleasure it gave him. Hans eyed him through the smoke and Vasily catching his eye, turned his attention to the purpose of the meal. Hans flicked the record switch with his finger, his hand having been in his pocket for the last five minutes waiting for this moment to arrive.

"Well you are writing a paper on Red Mercury Herr Doktor. May I ask why?"

"Of course you may and I hope you will be

able to contribute" said Hans attempting to appeal to Vasily's ego.

Vasily smiled and shrugged deprecatingly. "I would be delighted to be of assistance" he replied. "How may I help?"

"Well," Hans began "much of the technical development is now a matter of record and I am generally aware of most of the research projects currently in hand" he paused. "No, my paper is as much about the mystery and rumour surrounding Red Mercury since it was first produced here in Dubna in 1965."

"You interest me Herr Doktor. What do you mean by mystery?"

"Well I am sure little of what I have to say is not a mystery to you Professor but since its inception there was and still is a lot of speculation as to its capabilities as was discussed last night. Now whether it deserves the reputation that has been built up in scientific circles and has been picked up by the press is really a matter of personal opinion. Vasily waved a hand that may have said yes to the question or simply "get on with it." Hans continued

"I suspect that this was therefore the reason that actually drew the existence of Red Mercury to the eye of the general public." Again he paused. This time Vasily simply stared at him and waited for Hans to recommence his narrative.

"It was such an article that gave me the idea for producing a paper on the subject."

"So your paper will be a publicity seeking

piece of fiction with just a touch of fact" said Vasily in a contemptuous tone.

Hans decided that maybe this would be the best route to pursue and grinned weakly.

"Well you have to admit that if in pursuit of its rumoured potential and added to what I have recently read in 'The New Scientist', a man associated with it has been murdered, although it was unclear as to exactly what his involvement was." Hans paused before continuing. "Although it could make an otherwise dull paper more sensational by speculating that there is a link between the two. Many papers written may be well documented pieces of academic work but I want my paper to be an interesting read as well."

"So you will spice it up no doubt with over dramatisation" sneered Vasily "and what else will make your article so interesting?"

Hans paused and looked at Vasily as if trying to consider whether it were worth continuing against so much scepticism. He decided he would.

"The same article talked about hoax claims of the capabilities of Red Mercury and that its development to form fusion weapons was perhaps exaggerated if indeed they were true at all."

Vasily suddenly seemed to take more interest in the direction the conversation was going.

"What claims?" he asked.

Hans would now improvise the facts to see what response he could obtain from the Professor.

"Claims that fusion weapons and material were available and that for the right price could be obtained by parties who did not themselves have the capability of producing their own." Hans looked at Vasily whose attention seemed to be focused on his coffee cup. "It's my opinion that the man who was murdered was involved in such a deception."

"I see" said a very thoughtful Vasily. "So how can I help you Doktor?"

"I am not sure." said Hans pretending to give the question consideration for the first time. "Maybe you can verify some of the rumours?"

Vasily looked up. "Rumours. Are there more?"

"I don't know. Are there?" Hans countered.

Vasily weighed his thoughts before replying. "Maybe there are Herr Doktor."

"What do you know then Professor."

"Let me ask you a question first. Do I get credit or better still some financial inducement by contributing to your paper?" he asked.

"Well, that depends" said Hans "on whether it was of interest and of course if it could be attributable."

"What do you mean?"

"If you can prove or at least put your name to any story that might give validity to its potential then that would increase its interest and of course its value." Hans felt he was getting somewhere at last and if he continued appealing to greed and ego he could do very well from this source. But Vasily was wary.

"Have you heard of any other rumours Herr Doktor?"

"Well I was drinking with Yuri Nikitin and Piet De Vries last night, and there was indication of an international plot to hoax a certain Middle Eastern war monger. But of course you were there too."

"So now you have heard also." It was more of a statement than a question.

"Yes" said Hans and waited for Vasily to go on.

"But this is no surprise to you, is it Herr Doktor?" challenged Vasily. "Because you were involved."

"Me?" said Hans looking indignant. "Please explain."

Vasily did not know whether to trust Hans or whether he was being set up. Hans waited hardly daring to breathe.

"Are you telling me that when you were asked to teach that certain individuals about Red Mercury, some years back, that you did not know why?"

Hans felt himself go cold. The Russian obviously knew the whole plot and maybe could name some of the other players.

"I had my suspicions" he countered." that

there was something more than an academic reason for their education."

"And you need me to verify that. Isn't that why we're having this conversation?"

Hans shrugged.

"You know that this rumour must never be allowed to be confirmed and become public knowledge. You were made aware of the repercussions" stated Vasily.

Hans said nothing but he was beginning to become angry at the thought that the Russian appeared to have been told what he was getting himself involved in some years ago and Hans had only been given some cock and bull story by his government when asked to provide background information for Alan and Nikolai.

It would seem, he thought bitterly, he'd been told all he needed to know.

"Of course" he snapped back angrily at Vasily, attack being the best form of defense.

Both men sat there in silence. Vasily waved the waiter over and indicated the coffee cups. "More coffee" he demanded "and I will have a Vodka. Herr Doktor?"

"Yes, Vodka for me too" said Hans. He knew that now was the moment when either they would become collaborators or Vasily would drop the subject entirely and say no more. His next question took Hans by surprise.

"Is this why you were talking to Piet last

night?"

Hans simply looked at Vasily noncommittally.

"Because he still works on the military aspects of this?"

Hans who had had no idea of what Piet was now involved with simply replied   "Maybe."

"You know that they reckon they have done it. The South Africans?"

"I had heard" lied Hans, not sure what it was the South Africans were supposed to have done but Vasilys' next comment confirmed his worst fear

"They're mad bastards down there you know. They would use it too" he concluded. He seemed drained of energy and Hans left him to his thoughts as he considered what he'd heard. He felt if he pushed too hard for a categorical statement Vasily would clam up. He called for the bill.

When it arrived he went to pay but Vasily stopped him. "No my friend, in Russia hospitality is very important to us. You are my guest."

"Then you must come to Vienna and allow me to repay the hospitality" said Hans.

"Of course Herr Doktor. I look forward to it."

Both knew that neither meant the invitation to be accepted.

Was there a hint of menace in the Russians reply, Hans wondered. It is late he thought. It's just my over worked imagination.

It was agreed that Hans would contact the Professor again once the outline of his paper was settled. He would set out what information he would require and how it might be substantiated.

As they got up to leave Vasily and Hans exchanged business cards.

They said their farewells outside the restaurant where Vasily managed to secure a cab for Hans. As the cab drove away Hans turned to see the Russian staring after him.

CHAPTER 18

November 1993

Yuri Gorushenko was not in the best of moods. He had lost an agent and it seemed the Englishman was still alive.

He'd already bitten his secretary's head off that morning and word had got around the department that it would be a good day to get an assignment outside the office.

He strode to his door and yelled for his aide Andrei Petrov to get into his office. He did not like Andrei and he was sure the feeling was mutual. He was also unsure of the man's sexuality and this made him feel uncomfortable. These were however, insufficient grounds for getting rid of him he reminded himself

"Oh, for the good old days" he sighed.

Andrei came in almost at the double.

"Comrade?"

"Come in and sit down, we have work to do."

Andrei knew he would be the one doing it and waited in silence as Yuri strode up and down behind his large battered timber desk. He did not look at Andrei as he began.

"As you know we have lost an important agent and we suspect the Englishman killed him.

"What progress?" demanded Yuri.

Andrei squirmed in the chair. There was nothing to report. The French had so far drawn a blank and a diplomatic note from the French Ambassador to his Russian counterpart had ensured that the area had not been flooded by Russian heavies masquerading as tourists.

"As you know the French won't let us in. We still have some sympathisers in the Socialist party who are keeping their eyes open for us, but they're not professionals," he concluded.

"So nothing! You sit there and tell me you have achieved nothing," Yuri snarled getting into his stride. "What other avenues have you tried? What about the Englishman's family in the UK, is anybody watching them?"

"There is no family in the UK. Both his mother and father are dead and there are no siblings" replied Andrei. "How about the Brits. Have you spoken with your opposite number? Have they made contact with him?"

"That's hardly likely seeing he's now been warned that somebody's out to get him" said Yuri sarcastically, he paused, "unless those duplicitous Brits had him kill Nikolai and are now hiding him themselves."

Andrei let him talk on. If he could get some clue as to what his boss was thinking he might be able to precipitate some ideas of his own.

"Unlikely," Yuri continued, "they seem as embarrassed and concerned as we are if it gets out that we deliberately shafted the Iraqis albeit even in what at that time was believed to be the right course of action."

He turned to Andrei "What about the others?"

Does he mean the other case officers, thought Andrei "They have had no further leads either."

"Do you know what I'm talking about, you idiot?" The old KGB ways still hung on in Yuri despite the new enlightened establishment.

"Obviously not," said Andrei flushing, an angry sparkle lighting up his dark brown eyes.

Yuri breathed deeply. "Perhaps you are not the one to handle this investigation anyway. It requires tact and careful handling. What I am referring to" he glared down on his subordinate "is, has anyone spoken to those other people involved in the plot? Have they seen the Englishman? Has he approached them? If he does they should let us know without raising his suspicions." He could see from Andrei's expression that this line of investigation had not been followed up. "That is what I'm on about Andrei. Now do you think you and your team could handle that?"

"Yes comrade, of course." The anger still showed in Andrei's eyes. "But I do have a request to make."

"What's that?" snapped Yuri, who would have liked to have beaten some sense into the little shit's head. "That you authorise my access to the necessary case files." said Andrei smirking.

Yuri did not know how he managed to control

himself but realised he had left himself open to this one. Through tightening lips he replied. "Come back in half an hour and the necessary paperwork will be in place."

Andrei stood up "Thank you comrade." He turned and walked out of Yuri's office.

Yuri wondered whether it would be worth his position to put his boot up the little bastard's arse. The moment was lost and Andrei kept his job. He got up and walked to the window. "Why are the French always so bloody difficult?" He stood looking down on the courtyard which at this time of day showed little signs of activity. There was a light drizzle of rain in the air and as he looked up at the heavy sky could see that this was probably the best the day would get.

"Stop depressing yourself," he admonished "and set up the hunter." He reached for the 'phone and asked to be connected to General Dimitri Alexandrov. He had just the man in mind.

He continued to gaze out at the rain that from time to time was hitting his window depending on the wind's caprice.

The 'phone rang and he was through to the General.

"Dimitri, how goes the war?"

"The war? Dear Yuri, do not dignify the Chechens with such an accomplishment. Mindless rabble," he chuckled, "a bit of a thorn in our dear comrades' sides." The General was not known for his political sympathies and was pleased to tell his friends, when they would listen, that he was glad he was soon due for retirement. "What is it you want?"

"Your namesake!"

"Ah, you have some dirty work in mind comrade?"

"Is he available?"

"Dimitri Vorschek? Yes, I can release him for a while. When do you want him?"

"Is tomorrow morning too soon?"

"For you Yuri, of course not. He'll be at your office at 9 o'clock."

The man they were discussing was a unit commander on the General's own staff. A Georgian by birth, his records stated. He originally came to the Red Army from an orphanage. He had one talent and was one of the most emotionally dead people the General had ever encountered. His talent was killing. He was good at what he did and with the army training he had received had been honed into a most dangerous weapon. He had a reputation that the General had described to Yuri as quaint. He always made a clean kill. He would not become involved in torture or baiting his victim.

Dimitri was stocky with the high cheek bones of the Mongols predominant in his saturnine features. He had a mass of black hair that to the General seemed always too long.

The General knew Dimitri would be pleased at the chance of some action. With the breakup of the USSR and end of the cold war there had been less and less use for men of Dimitri's talents and the General had not allowed him to become involved in the Chechnia debacle. That would be too much a waste of such a good man.

Dimitri received his orders from the General at midday and by the appointed hour the following morning found himself sitting outside the KGB leader's office and being eyed surreptitiously by Andrei from behind a file he appeared to be reading.

After he had been kept waiting only half an hour Dimitri was summoned into Yuri's office where he was invited to take a seat while Yuri stood with his back to the window. He had used Dimitri before and knew that he would not need to go into a lot of detail with him. He would provide as much information as was available on the target and as soon as a lead came up or the Brits had their man in sight he would slip his leash.

Dimitri also knew from past experience that Yuri like all men of power in Russia would work on the 'need to know' principle and, in a country where secrecy formed part of the national characteristic, the information was likely to prove sparse indeed.

Yuri began. "We have a small security problem and there is the need to stop a potential leak that could damage our credibility with some of our new found friends."

Dimitri was surprised at the candour and directness of Yuri's opening comments. It must be truly serious he thought.

"You are to be part of a two man team whose aim is to stop a renegade agent from exposing what he believes to the media" he paused but Dimitri was not ready to ask questions.

"This man was working with one of our top agents, something obviously went wrong and from what we now know he killed our man."

"What or who is this agent?" Dimitri spoke for the first time since entering the KGB leader's office.

"He is an Englishman. He was chosen to work with our man Nikolai in a joint operation. They trained together and carried off a most successful operation." He stared at Dimitri for some seconds before deciding to part with the few remaining facts he had. "Nikolai's body was recovered a week ago in Provence." He saw Dimitri's blank look and added "in Southern France. He had been stabbed and dropped into a rock fissure where he was discovered by some potholers."

"And what of the French police. Have they found out anything?"

"No, absolutely nothing and what's more we have been told to keep out....So that

will require a degree of care and tact when you go in."

Dimitri sensed there was more to come.

"The other problem is that this is to remain a joint operation, there will be a man from the British SAS with you. You are to work closely with him. I believe his brief is to take the Englishman back alive. Your job is to see that does not happen; you are to make sure he dies. We use their agent to point out the quarry!"

"When do I start comrade?"

"As soon as we get some clear indication as to where we might start the hunt and as soon as the English select their man....In the meantime Andrei will let you have as much information as we have, including photos of the target. They were taken over two years ago and no doubt he will have altered his appearance as well as his name, but they might be of some use, who knows?" he concluded as he reached for his phone to summon Andrei.

"In the meantime return to your unit until I contact you."

Andrei knocked and entered carrying a thin brown envelope which he handed to Dimitri.

Dimitri, knowing the meeting was over, stood up and took the envelope before following Andrei from Yuri's office.

As the door closed Yuri sighed. He felt at least something was being done and he could trust Dimitri to deliver once he was locked onto his target.

The previous evening his long suffering wife Vanya had complained of his mood, which on reflection had not been good for many days. He had taken her by surprise by apologising, something which he was not renowned for and had then taken her out to dinner.

CHAPTER 19

October 1993

After a couple of days trying to help Alan get his report together Anna realised the way it was headed wasn't working. His notes and the work he had produced so far were a mess and she'd become sufficiently frustrated by it that she decided that she would have to tell him this morning. They would either work out a new approach or she would let him get on with it by himself. She phoned him to see if he was in and if so she was coming over.

He was and seemed pleased to hear from her.

She completed her makeup before checking around the flat and leaving for Alan's apartment. She left by the back exit which led onto an internal courtyard where she parked her Renault. She disabled the alarm, put her bag on the back seat, started the engine and pulled out between the buildings onto the street. Traffic was not too bad, the early morning rush hour had cleared. It took her only ten minutes to get to Alan's apartment. As he had no car she was able to use his parking bay in the underground car park beneath his block.

She locked the car and crossed over to the lift. There was nobody else around. At the fourth floor she got out of the lift which returned to ground level.

She crossed the landing and stopped at his door. She hesitated a moment before ringing the bell.

Right, she decided she would come straight to the point. In the nicest possible way of course, she didn't want to hurt his feelings.

He opened the door almost before the ringing echo had died. She smiled.

"Come in, I've just put the kettle on. What would you like?"

He followed her into the living room.

"Coffee please."

Alan went through to the kitchen as Anna crossed to the window and looked down onto the street below where some sunlight had made its way down between the buildings, giving deep patches of shadow at street level while flooding the buildings opposite.

"Alan, I've been thinking about this report of yours" she didn't turn.

"What have you been thinking?" he called from the kitchen.

"Well, I'm not sure how to put this without offending you, but I really think we have to come up with a different method of working."

"Go on."

"Well when I read through the notes and try to type them up, I'm getting totally lost.

Chronologically I mean. It's only when I've got so far with a section that some other point will come up that really should have been recorded earlier." She stopped and turned to look at him.

He was standing there grinning, holding two cups of coffee, and for a moment she had a fleeting suspicion that he had hoped she would come to this decision at some time. She didn't know whether to be annoyed or flattered. She let it pass and took the coffee.

"OK. I'm only too willing to be guided by you. You've discovered I'm no literary genius. What do you suggest?" He paused and looked concerned as he added, "other than to forget the whole thing."

"No, I'm not suggesting that." It was her turn to smile. She collected her thoughts for a moment.

"I know it might be a pain but I'd like you to tell me the story from the beginning, whenever you feel that to be. I'll make notes as you go and type them up into a precis as I see it. You vet them and then I fill them out."

Having agreed what they were going to do it took a little coaxing and a couple of false starts before Anna had Alan sufficiently relaxed to make any real progress. The biggest decision was from where to start. He wanted to begin with when he'd been recruited by MI6. Anna disagreed on the basis that there would be more impact if it were demonstrated that he had been the victim. He told her that he had never told anyone the full details of what had happened to him before being recruited by MI6. It was only now, he said, that he felt used and was, supposedly, to be eliminated by his own government.

Still he was not sure at first, but Anna argued her case well, and with little pressure he agreed.

A day later she finished the draft precis of his time from joining the army to being recruited by MI6 for him to read and correct. Alan told Anna he had joined the regular army on leaving the army school where he had been in the cadet corps. He said he'd had no firm objective or career in mind and it pleased his father who was a regular himself. He liked the ordered life. He liked the simplicity of a predominantly male environment and he was a fanatic when it came to physical exercise.

He had progressed easily and rapidly through the lower ranks to achieve officer status, at which point he felt he was moving into a career that did not fulfil him. He wanted a more active life and the SAS was the next logical step towards that.

His commanding officer was sympathetic when he approached him on the subject and wrote to the Herefordshire Training Centre in support of his application.

To his surprise he was given an opportunity to prove himself and after several weeks of gruelling training he was considered suitable material to be accepted in 22 Squadron and then his instruction began in earnest.

In Pursuit of the Red Kite

Looking back he could not admit to having fully enjoyed the experience but it had moved him on physically and mentally from a competent soldier to a more sophisticated military machine. He was trained to act either alone or as a member of a small insurgency unit.

His trainers had discovered that he had an aptitude for languages which was encouraged and developed as his course progressed. And it was later at MI6 that he was to use his knowledge of Russian and Iraqi Arabic learned for the operation he was to undertake in the SAS. The first as there remained some distrust between Russia and the Western Powers. And the second language might be an asset as it seemed that Saddam Hussein's posturing was becoming an increasing threat to peace in the Middle East.

Within nine months of enlisting he had become a Sergeant and the Gulf War had become a reality. It was in a joint operation with the Para's that he was to see his first real hostile action as part of an insurgency unit.

He learned that he had been selected because of his ability to speak Iraqi and for his physical appearance. He had inherited his father's dark hair, Mediterranean skin tone and looks.

He explained to Anna that the unit's objective was to report on troop movements and military installations and strengths to the Western forces. They would also carry out sabotage wherever possible but it was impressed on each member of the unit that this was of secondary importance. They must not jeopardise any cover they established for a brief moment of glory. The Western forces were seriously short of good intelligence information on the Iraq interior.

For the two weeks preceding their drop inside the borders of Iraq the five man unit trained together and lived together in order to assess each other's strengths and weaknesses. As in all infiltration units there would be a radio operator, a medic and a bomb maker. The unit would carry a limited amount of arms and explosives in with them. Additional equipment would be dropped as and when called for so that they could establish a cache of material and equipment that would, initially be impractical to carry with them.

There had been no reliable networks established within Iraq and they would have little knowledge of the terrain and forces disposition in the drop zone.

Looking back now at the plan of entry devised for the group he had, he recollected, misgivings as to its practicability or chances of success even then. However, desperate times had called for desperate measures and wasn't this what he had trained for.

He remembered the briefing well. They had travelled to a training centre in the Brecons. His companion was John Madely, also from his unit. John would lead the team. The third SAS man was

Leonard James from 16 Unit. The two Para's, Mike Thake and Gerry Brown, were from 12 Squadron.

The method of entry was to be a drop from an active bombing run close to the Kuwait border. The unit would be provided with captured Iraqi military uniforms and, as it transpired, badly forged papers. They would be armed with captured Iraqi hardware, manufactured in the Soviet Union and Czechoslovakia. They would also be carrying PE4 explosive with up to 2 hour timer detonators.

Alan said he remembered the expressions on the faces of the rest of the unit, they too seemed unable to believe what they were hearing. It seemed that the whole operation had been thrown together in haste. They were to be dropped behind enemy lines in an active war zone which gave them an additional hazard of exposure to friendly fire. They listened as the major, who had noted and expected some sort of reaction to this news, explained the thinking behind this method of entry was that their plane, which would be on the final bomb run, should not attract too much attention. They were to be dropped on the return leg of the raid so danger from "friendly fire" that night would be minimised. This assurance had given them small comfort. In discussing it later they had all felt that their chances of success would be improved by being dropped on the outer run as there would be less time spent over enemy territory before deployment.

The briefing continued as the major highlighted the towns and villages between Baghdad and the Kuwaiti border where it was believed ordnance and troops were stationed to service the front lines and hold the occupation of Kuwait City.

They would be provided with relatively accurate maps of the area, money and Iraqi survival rations to see them through the first part of the operation. These had been obtained from captured prisoners. Once established they would need to "live off the land" the major informed them.

At the end of the briefing the major had departed, leaving them to study the map and discuss the operation in more detail amongst themselves. They had been told they would be departing within the next two days and should not discuss the operation with anyone else on the camp.

At this point Anna suggested they break for coffee, before continuing, to which Alan rapidly agreed.

Continuing later, Alan recalled that when the major had left the room Gerry voiced what they were all thinking. "What a load of crap, we'll never get to Baghdad that way!"

"Nobody said it would be easy" John had responded.

"He asked the rest of us if we had all got our affairs in order."

Alan told Anna he had made a will which was deposited with the family solicitor who had his offices in Colchester and he had left a letter with the unit commander to be sent in the event of his death to the solicitor.

He went on to say that chemistry between members of the unit was good. Either somebody had done their homework properly or it was just good fortune. The worst part of the training for Alan had been the night drops where they had to free fall to within 1500 ft. before releasing their black parachutes.

As it had got closer to departure time the men in the unit reacted in different ways. John and Mike became quieter and more introspective whilst Gerry got more irritable and seemed to want to pick a fight with anyone who might oblige.

When finally they approached the drop off zone Alan told how they could see the flashes of the loads from the preceding bomber hitting the deck. The main concern was ground to air missile attack. The Gods were with them, they were destined to reach their destination unscathed.

Having passed through the bombers target area the plane headed further into Iraq towards Basra. They were to be dropped at Az Zubayr before the plane turned and raced for home.

The fuselage door was opened as the jump master hooked the unit up in line. There was no eye contact, as if to make it would bring bad luck.

As they jumped the cold of the night air hit them. They were dressed in Iraqi uniforms together with parkas for added warmth. The most dangerous time, they had been told, was at the start of the mission while they were still in the air. They landed safely and regrouped without incident five kilometres to the west of Az Zubayr a town on the fertile plain of the Euphrates. More by luck than judgement they had landed in fields avoiding farms and settlements. They buried their chutes in the scrub beneath some hedges and headed for the highway. By dawn they were to be part of the military effort.

From over-flying spy satellites and high resolution photography it had been established that the highway into Basra was used continuously to take troops to and from the front line and all types of armoured personnel carriers, tanks and jeeps used it regularly.

Alan said the plan was to flag down an empty returning jeep or truck and make their way north.

It was agreed that John, who spoke Iraqi the most fluently, would sit alongside the driver and the rest would get in the back. Once they had learned sufficient information on its destination and purpose the driver would be despatched.

At around 6.00am a likely looking brown and tan troop lorry toiled its way towards them. Not before time, as farm labourers would soon be on the roads and in the fields. The unit did not want to get involved with any local civilians.

John stepped out into the road in his sergeant's uniform. The truck pulled over as they got up from the ground and walked to the rear with their baggage. The one fear was that there would be returning troops or wounded in the back, but once again their luck held. It was empty. The drivers regiment was from Karbala to the south of Baghdad and he was returning to his base.

Fortunately he had no desire to stop at Basra and the vehicle's travel documents and registration would take them further towards their destination.

Listening to the driver talk it appeared morale was high among the troops. Saddam's propaganda machine was convincing them that Iraq was in a strong position. Kuwait was now theirs and the Western powers were being given a well deserved lesson.

John told them later that he was not sure when it happened but he was aware that the driver was becoming increasingly suspicious of their true identity. As they were approaching a petrol station the driver suddenly turned off the road saying he needed petrol. John could see that the tank was still half full and pulled out his pistol forcing the soldier to drive on and it was only when they were well away from habitation that he made him stop the truck. As the driver got down from his cab with John on the far side and us in the rear, he decided make his break. Gerry leapt out and gave chase as the driver first ran back down the road and then off into the fields. Gerry did not seem to hurry to catch him and waited till they were well of the road before bringing the soldier down and killing him with a quick clean break of the neck. The soldier had been too terrified to even turn and fight which would have made the killing of him somehow more acceptable, but this was war.

Alan told how they had buried the Iraqi in a shallow scrape in the ground and covered the spot with rocks. They took his papers and documents to study and compare with their own, he recounted.

The day was becoming hotter and there was little or no shade on this section of road. There was very little conversation among the team, Alan told Anna. The killing of the driver had brought home the realities of their task.

Before driving on they held a council of war in the back of the truck. Alan, who had a vague resemblance to the soldier, would be the new driver and would present the documents at any road block. They studied the map of military sites en route to Baghdad to see whether there might be an opportunity to carry out some sabotage. From the map and documents they learned that the next large settlement was at Ur where there was a battalion headquarters as well as an ordnance depot. They had been told to avoid any arsenal that may hold chemical weapons as this would have a lethal effect on the civilian population.

"We'll head for Ur" John had told them "and make that our first stop over".

Len asked him what had spooked the driver.

"I'm not sure," replied John. "It may have been my accent," he paused, "more likely it was my lack of knowledge of the 'on ground' situation at the front. I think he was expecting me to deny Saddam was doing so well and discuss what Iraq's true chances were in all this. Who knows" he shrugged "it's too late now."

They passed little traffic on the road although the route south towards the battle front was becoming busier. Apart from an occasional farmer working the fields the only other signs of habitation on the road were shepherd boys watching the military convoys. The dark eyes in the deeply tanned faces were expressionless.

In Pursuit of the Red Kite

As they got closer to Ur they had looked out for somewhere they could get the truck off the road and out of sight while they waited for nightfall. They had finally found a dried out wadi that was screened from the road by a stand of scrub. They drove in. Mike and Len back-tracked and removed the tyre traces from the coarse soil.

At eight the next morning they broke camp and headed for Ur. They would need to fill up with petrol at the first opportunity.

They had crude maps of Ur on which the barracks and arsenal had been located. They would drive around and pass the camp before finding somewhere to park up the truck.

When they arrived in Ur it was dusk although still very busy. The streets were thronged with local inhabitants and there was a strong military presence. The soldiers carried arms with them at all times and Alan's unit would not look conspicuous on the streets.

The barracks was located between the town and the highway. There was a five metre high electrified perimeter fence and the only way in was through a gatehouse off the highway across open ground where guards seemed to be checking all vehicle and foot soldiers' documentation.

John had told Alan to drive round and make one more pass before they found somewhere to quarter themselves and the vehicle.

As they had driven through Ur Alan had noticed that many military trucks were parked in the squares and back streets and did not seem to be attended. Remembering the old saying "The best way to hide a tree is in the woods," he suggested they simply find a quiet back street and leave one of them on guard. John agreed but to Alan's disappointment he was, he told Anna, to be the one left in charge as he bore the closest resemblance to the truck's original driver and he spoke Iraqi fairly fluently, therefore if there were any military police checks he was the one most likely to avoid suspicion. Reluctantly he had to agree with John's logic. He would see action soon enough he had told himself.

Between the barracks and the town itself they had seen several roadside cafes. These were brightly lit from suspended naked bulbs over tables and chairs scattered loosely over compacted earth. Most had few occupants. The soldiers preferred the town centre.

They found one that appeared to have no customers and over glasses of the sickly sweet tea that was so popular in the Middle East they would decide whether or not to attempt a sabotage of the army camp.

The truck lurched off the road and parked. The owner of the cafe wearing a dirty white robe and an ingratiating smile that appeared before they had climbed out of the vehicle.

He ushered them towards the table nearest the road. They ignored him and chose a table away from the roadside and out of earshot of the cafe. He did not take it personally but continued to fuss around until Gerry threatened to kick him away at the same time demanding cups of tea with the typical arrogance of the military over the civilian.

They had discussed a potential strike on the camp and despite the fact that it was well guarded it was being used by various battalions travelling back and forth from the front. This would make it possible for them to walk in they had agreed.

"It's risky. Depends how alert they are on the gate and how good our documents are" John had said, but the mood of the unit was positive and he was finally swayed.

"We don't need heroics at this stage," he reminded them. "We've a long way to go and sabotage is not the main objective of this incursion. Remember, we are to provide intelligence information from Baghdad".

Mike who was a more cautious individual, Alan recalled, had begun to have second thoughts. "We don't know how well the arsenal is guarded or how to get in and where to place the PE4."

"Look" said Gerry, the other Para, exasperatedly, "why the fuck did we come into town, why didn't we continue onto Baghdad?" Not waiting for a reply he continued, "we came in to see if we could knock off the ammo dump," he looked around, "otherwise why are we sitting in this stinking cafe?"

John had stepped in. "Right, I hear what you both say and we'll do a further evaluation tonight and if all seems possible we'll go in tomorrow night."

"Good" said Gerry, grinning at all and sundry. "Now what?"

"Back into town" John had said. "Alan will stay with the truck and we'll split into two groups, one to check the perimeter to see if there is another way in, which I doubt" he added. "That will be Gerry and Mike. Len and I will test security and walk in the front door. If we don't get out, Alan takes charge and you head for Baghdad. No more sabotage attempts, is that clear?"

They all muttered their agreement.

"The front door approach will need to be early evening while soldiers are still coming and going otherwise whoever is inside later will need a legitimate bunk for the night and that will give us problems".

"The perimeter road is not a great distance to walk but two soldiers will be too obvious. There are cameras and guards. But not a soldier and his girlfriend," John looked wickedly at Gerry. "You're the smallest. You'll have to dress up."

"You must be joking."

"I've never been more serious," John retorted, "buy a black robe and yashmak in the market and trade those boots for sandals. You'll be perfect."

The laughter that followed Gerry's predicament released the tension that had gradually built during the discussion.

Alan said he had dozed in the truck which did not seem unusual in that part of the world and was woken by John and Mike sounding pleased with themselves. There had been no trouble at the gate and the security on the arsenal had seemed lax and undermanned. They were convinced they could place their charges without too much difficulty. Half an hour later a grumbling Gerry returned with Len who repeated that the fence was not an option unless there was a power shut down and the only way they could achieve their objective was from within the camp via the entry point.

It was agreed that the frontal approach was the only option and John and Mike would go in, followed fifteen minutes later by Gerry and Len as back-up in case it was needed. Having placed their charges they would leave with a five minute interval between them, return to the truck and would then put as much distance as possible between themselves and the dump in the following two hours.

While they had been discussing this, John had produced a quick sketch of the camp layout giving routes from the gate to the arsenal. This he handed to Gerry and Len for them to study.

The following day was spent at their hide planning and assembling the bombs. Each was made using just over a kilo of PE4 explosive. When assembled they could be carried in their rucksacks without raising suspicion. Strategically positioned this would start a chain reaction amongst the Iraqi ordnance and would conserve their reserves. Whereas the day began cool it soon heated up and much of the time was spent trying to find enough shade cover and getting some sleep before their attempt to sabotage the barracks. There was little small talk and they each retreated into their own worlds Alan recalled.

Alan went on to tell Anna he was to take the unit into town where they would divide into two groups, John and Mike, Gerry and Len.

John and Mike would go in first. Gerry and Len would follow and familiarise themselves with the layout of the camp. They would meet up half an hour after the first pair had entered, in the camp canteen. There the final entry into the armoury would be agreed.

The whole exercise had to be carried out before the camp curfew and in order to get well clear of the area before the bombs exploded.

"Alan, what you will do once we have all left the truck is to park up and wait. Do not leave the vehicle on any account, is that clear?"

"Sure."

"If there is a problem and you need to move, fall back to the cafe we were in last night. OK?"

"No problem." Alan remembered he had agreed.

"If we're not out by curfew which is around 11.00pm get yourself back here tomorrow. If we don't turn up then give us a day before you get out. The radio will stay in the truck and you will need to send a signal out to let control know the operation is blown. No heroics, just get out," he grinned to soften the command. "I know you're not stupid!"

"I remember how the day had dragged." Alan told Anna. The tension was much greater than the previous day. Now there was going to be some action. The unit was to be blooded. At around six they made a final run through of the equipment. Alan got a further lesson on using the high powered radio and coding of any messages. At the base outside

In Pursuit of the Red Kite

Kuwait there was a permanent radio listening post.

An hour later they drove back into Ur. Alan said he had parked in the same side street as on the previous night, killed the engine and switched off the lights. The unit made no special effort to be either quiet or discreet, they were soldiers in their home town and they were off duty.

They left in pairs and went in opposite directions. John and Mike headed for the barracks, Len and Gerry to arrive later, by a more circuitous route as planned.

"I settled down in the cab, pulled my cap down over my forehead so that I would appear to be sleeping but could keep an eye on the comings and goings in the street." he continued.

It must have been at least half an hour later when he had begun to feel drowsy. He checked his watch, shifted on the hard seat and again checked the street through the windscreen and driving mirrors. Nothing unusual. There was a steady stream of pedestrians.

He woke suddenly to the distant rattle of small arms fire. People had stopped in the street all looking in the general direction of the barracks. Everybody seemed to move at the same time. The most cautious, away from the sound: the more brave and curious, towards the Barracks.

Alan had no illusions. The unit was in trouble. He started the engine and let it idle in readiness for a quick departure if called upon.

The firing continued in intermittent bursts.

Within fifteen minutes it was all over. Around him army vehicles were on the move. Alan joined them and headed towards the Barracks and the roadside cafe where he was to spend a further agonizing fifteen minutes before deciding that it would be risking getting caught inside a military cordon.

As he pulled out from the cafe, two trucks came speeding up the road behind him. There was no room for them to overtake and they laid on their horns encouraging Alan to get a move on. As he cleared the town and Barracks the trucks behind him stopped. Troops poured out and began setting up a blockade. Luck was with him he recalled. He resisted the temptation to speed up and drove at around forty until he reached the Wadi. He had to be cautious and time it carefully.

"I could not risk being seen leaving the road." He told Anna as head down she continued to record his dictation

He had slowed as he reached the turn off and until an oncoming truck had passed him and disappeared around a bend in the road. He had seen nobody on foot in the headlights as he approached the hide out. He switched off the lights and used the moonlight to see his way into cover.

Alan did not sleep that night. Every small sound he imagined was a returning member of the unit. It was not to be. By dawn nobody had returned. He would wait another twenty four hours before moving out.

He was torn by conscience, should he go back and attempt a rescue although he knew it would be futile. The only use he could be was to follow orders, stay put, and be there should they return. They had debated as to whether one or two should remain with the truck but the decision to use two approaches to the arsenal had determined the outcome and Alan was to stay with the truck.

"A day later my worst fears were confirmed." he explained to Anna.

Not one member of the party had showed. He would follow orders and head for the border having sent a radio message and having decided that if there was to be any form of hunt for him he reasoned that it would create less suspicion to head naively into the trouble zone. Throughout the previous day there had been a lot of troop movement on the Highway which he had watched from the hide.

He also believed that as a common soldier he would be able to pick up the gossip and try to discover what had happened at the barracks.

He drove towards Ur and hit the first road block at the outskirts of the town. Most troop trucks were waved straight through. Private cars and farm carts seemed to be the targets of a more thorough search.

As he got to the blockade a sergeant asked for his papers and where he was headed. Alan told him and was given a signed slip of paper.

"That will get you out the other side" said the sergeant as he handed the paper to Alan. "What's going on, not expecting the Americans are you?" Alan remembered he had joked.

In Pursuit of the Red Kite

He could see a soldier in his driving mirror looking into the rear of the truck.

Alan was pleased he had taken the precaution to remove the remaining equipment left by the unit and that he had buried it at the wadi. He'd covered the newly dug soil with rocks. He had kept some spare ammunition, grenades, PE4, detonators and the radio. These he'd packed in the driver's bench seat and covered with rags and the truck maintenance equipment.

The soldier climbed inside and Alan could hear him poking around. After what seemed ages he jumped back onto the road and walked down to the next vehicle in line. Alan was signalled to move off, the Sergeant had ignored Alan's quip. He'd probably been getting similar comments all day.

He pulled into the main square, locked the truck and went and sat at one of the many cafe tables. His plan was to get into conversation with the soldiers and try to discover what had happened at the barracks.

He found a suitable cafe that seemed to be more popular with the soldiers. He chose a table in the shade, sat down and ordered tea.

It was not long before a nearby table was taken by two privates and an NCO with whom he struck up a conversation. One of the privates, whose name he discovered was Ali, was the most gregarious member of the party and he did most of the talking.

"What's the reason for the roadblocks" Alan had begun with.

"The camp was raided by commandos the night before last and we think there may be more around."

"What did they do?"

"Nothing" replied Ali.

"Nothing?" Alan had asked him, "then what's all the fuss about?"

"They may have been an advance party" said Ali, not sure how to take Alan's remark.

"What happened then?"

"We caught them before they could cause any damage", he paused looking at Alan "as they were about to go into the armoury."

"I suppose you've locked them up and given them a sample of Iraqi hospitality?" Alan laughed in what he felt to be the appropriate sign of camaraderie.

"No point," said Ali "they're all dead."

Alan was stunned "How many?"

"Four. Three were killed in the shoot out and the fourth, who was wounded, died under interrogation an hour later. We lost four killed outright and five wounded, one seriously. I doubt he'll live."

Alan remembered how he had silently hoped none of them would survive. He had somehow prevented any look of shock showing on his face, but his mind was in a turmoil as he tried to maintain an outward appearance of a soldier's curiosity in what was the local hot gossip.

"How were they discovered?"

At this point the head NCO, joined in. He had given the appearance of being bored with hearing about the whole incident.

"They were unlucky in choosing our barracks. We have good security surveillance throughout the camp and alert guards on the gate."

Alan had waited for him to expand and after a pause for effect the NCO continued.

"They had reconnoitred the camp the night before."

Alan inwardly froze. He became aware of the officer continuing. "....the papers the two showed the night before!"

"What?"

"They were for a battalion that no longer existed. It had been merged with another and lost its identity."

"Great intelligence," Alan had thought to himself.

"The guard on the gate had recorded their documents in and later out."

Alan looked puzzled.

"We checked the records and this was spotted when the lists were handed into the office the following morning. It was the clerk who spotted the battalion which he himself had been part of before its merger. He reported it to the camp commander." He laughed. "Needless to say the duty guard of the night before was in great trouble. Not that it was his fault, poor sod," sympathised the officer.

"So you picked them up when they returned the following night. That was stupid of them."

"Not really. They didn't know that they had been discovered."

"I suppose not" Alan said.

The NCOs eyes lit up and he smiled as he told Alan how clever the camp commander had been. He was an old soldier and wise to covert attacks and sabotage.

"We let them through as though nothing was wrong. We were to inform the commander and wait further instructions as they were watched on the security cameras. That was the first two," he added, "and then ten minutes or so later another two showed up with similar documents. We then watched them moving around the camp. Meeting up in our canteen where they obviously made their final plan of attack. They left the canteen singly and made their way to the armoury - which is when we pounced." He looked arrogantly at Alan "It was like target practice." He sat back in his seat.

It was, Alan recollected, all that he could do to keep himself in check and not launch himself across the table and throttle the smug bastard. Instead he said,

"And you think there are more of them?"

"I don't, but the commander won't take any chances and he is investigating how four soldiers with such badly forged documentation could get this far into Iraq without discovery. Also they had very little equipment so they must have had a base somewhere."

"Any luck?"

"No, I don't think there will be. I think they were parachuted in under cover of an air raid," said the NCO.

Not a bad guess, thought Alan.

"I suppose your papers are in order" joked Ali.

Alan told Anna how he had bluffed it out. "Would I be sitting here if they weren't?" He smiled more confidently than he had felt despite having the truck driver's identity in his inside pocket. "I got a thorough going over at the roadblock" he added.

"I bet you did" said the NCO. "Where are you from?"

"Baghdad but I'm on my way back from the front for more supplies. Still it could be worse."

"How's that?"

"Well sometimes I have to take semi-invalided troops back. It's a slow ride and they never stop complaining" he added unsympathetically.

The private who had not said anything raised his wrist and tapped his watch.

"Back to work" sighed Ali. He stood up. "See you mate."

"Yes. Thanks for the tea" Alan said to the NCO as they all followed the silent private across the square and into a side street.

Alan had decided he must get well away from Ur before nightfall and find somewhere to lay up before planning how to get out of Iraq. He'd had a narrow escape.

As he was getting up to leave the cafe an open top jeep raced into the square. The passenger, he noted, was a high ranking officer. Alan noted how distinctive the man seemed. A hard unsmiling face with a strong aquiline nose. It was a face that I was going to meet up with again while working for MI6 he told Anna.

Getting out of Ur was not difficult. The troops on the blockade seemed to think any problem would be incoming and not outgoing which, Alan recalled, was good for him.

He would head steadily for Al Hillah, nearly three hundred kilometres north.

At night he had found somewhere to hide the truck. He knew that heading deeper into Iraq was not what he should be doing but he also knew that to try and get out by heading South through Kuwait was likely to be more hazardous. He had to get within easy reach of the border in an area of low military concentration to improve the chances of a Chinook pick-up, he explained to Anna.

As he drove he had developed his exit plan. During the solitary trip he could not forget the loss of his four companions. Had they been naive; had they underestimated the difficulties of what they had taken on. If only the documents had held up to scrutiny, the outcome would have been totally different.

"My anger became focused on the powers that had sent the unit into Iraq with such lethal consequences. How could military intelligence have been so bad?" Alan queried while looking into Anna's eyes. She said nothing but held his gaze.

Alan continued with his recollections. That night he had pulled into a petrol refuelling station established for military use just outside Al Hillal, he again filled up with diesel and decided to sleep in the cab. The papers he had taken from the original driver of the truck were never questioned, nor was his dialect, for in a time of war soldiers were conscripted throughout the country and varying dialects were commonplace.

There was a cafe of sorts and Alan was able to get local food as an evening meal. After one or two short conversations with other drivers he went back to the cab of the truck and took out the map.

As part of the briefing they had been given a series of locations throughout Iraq, each with a coded reference. Having chosen his exit route he would send out a signal which would be acknowledged by a repeat of his call sign and location code. He would then have to lay up for possibly three nights at the site waiting for the pick-up. If the Chinook did not come he would have to move location and try again, repeating the process.

He had decided to head for the Saudi border. At Al Hillal he would take the road to An Najaf heading south west. From there the road heads into the desert lands of the Al Hijarah. The largest town on this bleak highway was Al Hammam approximately 150 kilometres from the border where a nervous peace existed between the Saudi and Iraqi border patrols. In order to not show an overt threat to her neighbours, Iraq had kept a small military presence stationed there. The pick-up point was approximately 30 kilometres inside Iraq and approximately 10 kilometres off the road. Depending on the terrain Alan would drive as close as was safe before trying to hide the truck although if it was a flat landscape this would not be easy.

He would have to disable the truck in a way that should he need to head for a second location he could fix it and still have transport.

With only himself for company, he remembered, the feeling of futility at the fate of the unit began to prey on his mind. He blamed himself for not having done something that may have saved his comrades and he blamed his superiors and the establishment for sending them into Iraq with such inadequate documents and intelligence.

What had seemed to make it worse was that, apart from the occasional roadblock checks, his evacuation from Iraq worked according to plan with no major or unexpected setbacks.

The Chinook had come in under cover of a ground attack on entering Iraqi air space, but according to the pilot it was generally a quiet night.

Alan told Anna how he had darted from cover to the helicopter which did not exactly settle on the ground. He had been battered by the downwash of the blades as he climbed aboard. For him it was the most hazardous time of the operation. He had barely seized a handhold before the Chinook took off like an elevator and headed fast and low across the countryside.

"How often have you done this?" he asked the pilot.

"We've made five search and rescue missions so far," the pilot yelled back at Alan. The co-pilot raised a hand in welcome. Fifteen minutes later they were in neutral air space.

"Here's a head set," yelled the co-pilot. Alan put it on; they could now talk. He remembered their conversation in detail.

"When did you go in?"

"About a week ago" Alan replied.

"Bad?"

"Bloody disaster."

In Pursuit of the Red Kite

"What happened?"

"The rest of the lads bought it," Alan replied bitterly.

"Sorry mate, must've been rough."

"It certainly was for them."

"You alright? I mean you're not wounded or anything?" the co-pilot asked. "I mean should we get them to lay on medical assistance at the base. We can radio in if you like."

"No, I'm not even scratched," Alan told him.

The two airmen were both combat veterans and they understood how he must be feeling. He was most likely experiencing guilt and anger that would merge into depression. They had known cases where survivors had needed counselling to get over these feelings, they said they had even heard that suicides had occurred as a result of post combat stress. At this point Alan remembered that he had not responded and the flight had continued in silence.

In the rear passenger seat Alan stared into the blackness of the landscape. He became angry as the distance between himself and Iraq increased and he swore that somehow he would avenge the unit given any opportunity.

The Chinook swept in and circled the base. It set down close to the airfield buildings and a group of two soldiers in desert uniform walked out to the helicopter.

Alan jumped down followed by the pilot and co-pilot.

"Thanks lads, you did a good job," he said to both men.

"That's OK mate, don't let it get to you. Saddam's on borrowed time, we'll get the bastard."

"Sure" Alan replied picking up his pack which he'd dropped out of the door onto the runway where two men stood waiting.

"Sergeant Marks?" The first soldier, a Para, stood in front of him.

"Yes?"

"You are to come with us for an initial debriefing."

"Now?"

"Yes, now. You'll spend a night on the base before being flown back home. There you'll be taken to HQ for a thorough debriefing. Oh and by the way, you talk to no one else on the subject, is that understood?"

"Yes sir" said Alan. "So much for the warm welcoming committee" he thought "and they don't know yet what a balls-up it was."

"So what happened next?" asked Anna, who felt that she should say something at this point.

"The following day as promised I was flown back to HQ and for the next week was subjected to constant debriefing, going over details time and again," he told her.

"It was not only full detail of the operation that was needed but also any intelligence information that I may have picked up during the time I was in Iraq. Particularly, what the state of morale was both from the military and civilian viewpoints."

Alan had spent a week at the camp and recalled how at first his debriefing had been over long periods usually terminating with him losing his temper. These tailed off as he guessed they began to give up on him. Finally he was told he would be sent up to Loch Maree in Scotland for what was termed "rest and relaxation."

He remembered the commanding officer telling him how it was for the best and when Alan had resisted he was told he had no choice, it was an order and he would be leaving the following day.

Alan had stormed out of the office and headed for the canteen. Fortunately there were few people around and he found himself a table in a corner with a view over the parade ground. He wondered whether he would be back after his trip to Scotland.

It must have been some minutes later when he was aware of someone standing in front of his table. He looked up but didn't recognise the Para who stood there.

"Alright mate?" the man said. He was wiry and mean-looking. Alan sensed the hostility in the question, but did not reply.

"How's the hero?" sneered the Para.

"What's your problem?" Alan asked quietly.

"My problem mate is seeing you sitting there in the pink while two of my unit are decomposing in fucking Iraq."

"You know all about it do you?"

"I know enough. Seeing you there is enough. Not even a scratch on you."

"Is that so?" said Alan. "Seen a lot of action yourself, have you?"

"More than you mate and I don't leave my mates in the shit."

Alan looked around the canteen. Two other Para's were standing holding trays of food at an adjacent table saying nothing, just watching.

Alan sighed, this was a problem that would not go away and may be just the beginning of a pattern for the future. Better get used to it he thought. He leaned back in the chair till he felt the solidity of the wall behind him as the Para continued to stare at him willing him to react.

Alan knew further talk would make no difference to the outcome of the conversation. He could now see the man's legs below the table, slightly apart, balanced for attack. He suddenly kicked his legs out straight below the table, pushing himself off the wall at the same time.

In Pursuit of the Red Kite

The Para yelled in pain as Alan's boots hit both kneecaps. He fell back as Alan continued the movement to a standing position throwing the table on top of the man who could no longer see Alan or the arrival of a well placed kick in the genitals.

Alan heard the crash of trays hitting the floor as the other two Para's leapt to help their friend. He knew his chances were poor against two trained men but he would go down fighting. He went for the one coming in on his right hand side and parried the first blow. He aimed for the solar plexus but it was anticipated as the Para turned his torso and caught the blow on his ribs with a grunt.

Alan told Anna he had recovered consciousness on the floor of the canteen to see a crowd of men around him and a sergeant trying to get details of the assault. Then a medical officer pushed through the throng as Alan had tried to sit up. Pain shot through his head and he decided to let the medic have a look before he was told he could get up and with assistance helped to his bed.

Later the sergeant came to take his account of the incident. The sergeant looked grim. This type of incident was taboo among special forces and could result in his being thrown out of the force and may cost him his rank.

"Fortunately for you Marks, there were witnesses around to support your version of the facts," the sergeant concluded at the end of the interview.

The following morning Alan was brought before the Commanding Officer where he received a severe dressing down before leaving for Scotland and rehabilitation.

"The matter did not rest there, Alan told Anna."

"So what happened then?"

"Three days later a leader in one of the more popular dailies reported an exclusive report (as did two others) on their version of how an SAS officer abandoned the remainder of his unit to escape from Iraq." The bitterness still in voice as he related this to Anna and recalled that the journalist, with the minimal amount of fact at his disposal, implied that a unit, dropped into Iraq, had run into trouble and, with the exception of one officer who had returned unscathed a few days later, had been wiped out. He even had Alan's name although he took care to state the name was unconfirmed.

"I was not allowed to contest the article." Alan explained.

There was no follow-up in the press and Alan told Anna he suspected that the matter had been suppressed. However the damage was done and to a man whose self esteem was already low, pushed him to feelings of depression the likes of which he admitted, he had never before experienced.

It was to take Anna the best part of two days to get it all down to her satisfaction but at the end

Alan was sure she had been right in insisting they record events this way.

Anna realised that most of what he had told her so far would be of little use in producing the kind of document he really needed. In her opinion it was what followed that was important but she appreciated that this was probably the first time Alan had told anyone his life story and she would have to include all of it in order to disclose his entrapment by MI6.

After he left she added some of the facts that had come from her father as to why he was helping out with the part that mattered; someway of protecting Alan by using the knowledge learned from his course at the University. She could understand also how his unit must have felt having seen the press reports and how Alan's commanding officer had readily agreed to MI6 taking him on for whatever nefarious purposes they had in mind.

Tomorrow she would tell Alan that she had some idea, from her more heated discussions with her father, what he had been involved with in Iraq and why maybe someone was out to silence him. She would get him to flesh out the detail which would then be subjected to any changes that were necessary following her father's trip to Moscow.

CHAPTER 20
November 1993

In Moscow Andrei was making his way home to his apartment in the New Arbat district. He was driving an ancient Zil that had been handed down with some embarrassment from his predecessor when he retired and Andrei moved one step closer to Yuri Gorushenko. The car was an unreliable mule but even in its present state of decay it gave him a degree of status which was very important to him as he took himself and his ambitions very seriously.

He was enough of a realist however to know he would get no higher while Yuri ruled the department.

At thirty-one Andrei had no really permanent partner in his life and he would be returning to an empty apartment and his Russian Blue neutered tom cat for the evening.

This evening he was depressed. He was making no progress with the case and Yuri was giving him a bad time. The French police had still got nowhere and many of the possible tenuous links with the scientists and military personnel involved in the case originally were not yielding any information due to absences at conferences or involvement in some state development that precluded them from talking to anybody. Of the two he had traced, neither had been of any help.

As he sat in the slow-moving traffic he hit the dashboard in frustration. He turned to find that this seemed to have caused the driver of an adjacent vehicle some amusement so Andrei treated her to a look of contempt.

His apartment was in the Prospekt Mira district in a Stalin-era refurbished six storey block. A stone clad building which provided one or two bedroom units for the up and coming executive market that despite the nation's financial crisis seemed to be on the increase.

What Andrei particularly liked about the block was its lack of children or the retired, both being classes of society he had no patience with. The block was mostly made up of single men and women and the occasional couple and whereas Andrei was convinced some of the occupants were on drugs, there were no all night raves to blight the usual tranquillity of his life.

He parked in the open surface car park at the rear of the block and crossed to the entrance carrying his briefcase and a white plastic bag in one hand, the latter containing the makings of his evening meal. He swiped his security card and the lobby door unlocked. Using his card again he called the lift which took him to the fourth floor landing off which there were six apartments.

As he was putting his key in the lock he noticed the edge of something white just visible beneath the door. He smiled; perhaps the evening would turn out a little better after all.

Pushkin came to greet him and he knew from the aroma that one of his first jobs would be to clean out the animal's litter tray and open some windows. If only he could leave the cat to roam safely, he thought, but even round here the cat could have provided someone who was not too particular with an evening meal.

He let the animal roam the landing while he cleaned up. He made himself a drink, sat down and opened the note that had been pushed under his door. As expected and hoped it was from Hussein, the Jordanian Embassy staffer who had an apartment on the floor above.

Hussein was the nearest he had to a permanent partner, however due to the sensitive nature of their respective jobs and the less than liberal view Russia had towards homosexuality, their growing relationship was a well guarded secret.

Andrei had had several other men in his life, but none quite like Hussein, who had the dark black shiny hair of many of the Arabs. He had a lean boyish body and soft brown eyes and Andrei knew it would be only too easy for him for the affair to get out of control.

Past lovers had been Russians, mostly brutish and not interested in understanding his needs. Fortunately, Hussein was a more sympathetic and accomplished lover.

The note simply invited him up for a late night coffee if he was free. They would seldom approach the other's apartments before ten in the evening and

they always left around three in the morning with

In Pursuit of the Red Kite

furtive lingering goodbyes before creeping as silently as possible back to their respective apartments.

The arrangement suited them both.

Hussein's posting would keep him in Moscow for the next three years before returning to Jordan or being moved on to some other Embassy. This was another reason why Andrei was resisting forming a permanent attachment to the man.

CHAPTER 21

October 1993

At the University the final informal dinner party was in full swing before the delegates headed home. Hans was sharing a table with Carl and another young couple who were really only interested in each other. Hans didn't mind. Carl was easy company and he didn't have to concentrate too deeply on the conversation.

The after-dinner speeches were lighter than those held previously and Hans found his attention wandering around the gathering.

Suddenly he noticed two men who seemed to be having a somewhat agitated conversation, if the body signals were anything to go by. He froze as the larger man turned and looked directly across at his table. It was Vasily and as he had leaned back, Hans was able to see that his companion was Piet, the South African scientist.

He quickly turned back not wishing to catch Vasily's eye. "I didn't think they knew each other," he thought to himself. "Right now they look like they're involved in some conspiracy and why should they be looking over here?" Hans managed to worry himself with his musings. Had he overdone it and exposed both himself and Alan to danger?

All of a sudden he lost his appetite. At the first opportunity he would leave the dinner party and

In Pursuit of the Red Kite

return to the hotel where he would sit and worry himself still further.

In Vienna, Alan, the object of Hans' concern, was finishing his evening meal as guest to his daughter.

"That was great" said Alan, "you are a very good cook."

Anna laughed. "I think you're just easy to please" she replied "but thank you, it is nice to be appreciated. Would you like coffee at the table or in a more comfortable chair?"

Alan elected to sit on Anna's couch where she handed him his coffee and a copy of the report she'd printed.

"There. Take a look at that while I clear up."

Alan looked surprised. He hadn't really expected her to complete the task quite so quickly.

"Thanks." He took the document and settled himself to read it as Anna busied herself.

Felling guilty he got up and went into the kitchen. Anna turned smiling and raised her hands to push him away. "I can manage."

On impulse Alan's reaction was to put his hands on her hips. Her expression became more serious and he felt he'd got it wrong. He stepped back.

"Slow down soldier." Her smile told him that she was not too upset.

The following morning Alan went back to Anna's where they picked up from where they had left off the night before which had concluded with him telling Anna that he had gone into hiding in the Friary

"One thing I don't understand?" Anna asked

"What's that?"

"The way the Iraqis got hold of the bombs. I know they were dummies, but even so?" She let the question hang.

"If it had been too easy they probably would have been suspicious. As it was I suppose it was the deviousness of the plot that appealed to them. You see, as they controlled the switch and timing of the operation it removed Nikolai and myself from the equation. They never trusted us. We were only the intermediaries, the messengers." He remembered the Iraqi's threat. Even if he got MI6 and the KGB off his back he would always have the possibility of danger around him. He had to accept it was a risk he couldn't avoid but what was now giving him real concern was the exposure of Anna and Hans to danger. He was saved from taking that line of thought any further as Anna came over and handed him a coffee.

"I have wondered ever since we went into hiding what happened, if and when the Iraqis ever tried out the devices. I can't imagine they didn't." Alan admitted.

"I'm fairly sure they did" said Anna.

Alan became alert.

"What makes you think that?"

"Well, while you were out of circulation there was further trouble in Iraq that made news for some time."

"Yes?"

"Well, it was assumed to be Saddam taking out his defeat by the West on the Kurds in North East Iraq. 'Ethnic cleansing' became the phrase that the media used."

"What happened?"

"Saddam began bombing the Kurds in North East Iraq and the Allies stepped in and created a flight exclusion zone to help stop him. I remember it was the first time the phrase "ethnic cleansing" was coined."

"And did it stop?"

"No, Saddam victimised the Kurds in other ways with land based attacks. Whole villages were massacred or starved and forced to move towards the border. But Iraq's neighbours didn't want them either. In the end the situation in Iraq became less newsworthy as problems flared in the Balkans where the Serbs and Croats began a civil war and the U.N. became more involved as the break up of Tito's

Yugoslavia. It became more high profile than the plight of the Kurds."

"I see, so you think maybe Saddam used the bombs he'd bought from Russia by testing them out on the Kurds?"

"Well, the timing seems to fit, now that I have learnt about those bombs of yours." She looked at Alan.

"Yes, it's certainly a possibility" he replied, then laughed "I bet old Aziz got into serious trouble over that. He'd be lucky to have kept his head in the circumstances" he mused.

Alan crossed to the window and looked down on the traffic passing below. He turned to Anna.

"Hans should be back tonight. Maybe we'll learn a little more then."

"Yes maybe?" she replied.

The man in question had taken the Intourist bus to Cheremetievo airport after an early breakfast at the hotel. He had not slept well. He had spent half the night convincing himself that the KGB were onto him and the other half convincing himself that he was just being paranoid.

He barely took in the inevitable frustration of checking in and then being told his aircraft was delayed by an hour and he should listen for further announcements. He wandered through the duty free kiosks and shops trying to find something to take back to Anna. Apart from an over-priced silver necklace, he saw nothing that he felt she would appreciate and finished up as usual buying her "Amarige" perfume. He had asked for a seat in the smoking section. Fortunately they still existed on Aeroflot. He knew he would be smoking throughout the journey as he mulled over the past few days. The morning was grey and overcast but there was no rain and his spirits lifted slightly for the first time in nearly fifteen hours as the plane broke through the clouds into a brilliant pale blue sky.

CHAPTER 22
October 1993

The following day having completed the section of Alan's report before his recruitment to MI6, Anna found herself becoming more sympathetic towards him. He seemed to be basically a good man who'd met with unfortunate circumstances which might well have justified, at least to him, the course of action which had led to his present predicament including seeking an opportunity to take revenge on the Iraqis.

On reading all the notes through what worried her most was that this man was a soldier. Had he the necessary skills to evade capture from the politically motivated professionals? The cause of her concern had been aroused from her love of crime and spy novels. Was he sufficiently devious to elude his pursuers?

She re-read over what she had typed and decided that maybe she had put down the story too literally. She would need to be more succinct for the remainder.

She broke for a light lunch. Alan had wanted to join her but she insisted she had a day to herself if she was to break the back of the task. They had agreed to meet up again for dinner that evening. She would cook a meal at her apartment

As she sat over her lunch she wondered how her father was getting on in Moscow. Whereas he was a good scientist, recognised by the establishment for his contribution to their work, she could not help thinking that maybe he was not the right man to send on a mission amongst professional spies and politicians.

The more she thought about it the more uneasy she became. It would not take much she believed, to start a trail to Alan.

She tried to put these concerns to one side as she began the next section of the report.

"I was recruited by MI6 which wasn't difficult for them as, despite assurances to the contrary, the records indicated that I had let the regiment down." Alan had told her. "In the time I spent afterwards at the Friary in Provence I realised of course that I'd been set up, which is why I have no compunction about writing this report for publication."

He told her how he was sent to Vienna to attend the course at the University where he had met Hans. Following this MI6 flew him to Moscow where he was taken to KGB headquarters and introduced to Nikolai. They were to become partners and both knew it was important to build a rapport and be able to rely on each other. Fortunately Nikolai was an outgoing individual, quite the opposite to Alan, and that helped. Nikolai was a soldier and they had common ground in their approach to many things. This proved useful in the months ahead while they were undergoing their training.

During the daytime, at least at the beginning,

they spent a lot of time at the Moscow Institute of Energetics and Moscow University on courses as mature students. They got some odd looks to start with, joining in the middle of a term, but soon came to be ignored by the majority of students as objects of only passing interest.

The lecturers, who were research scientists in their own right, Alan was sure, knew why they were there. It was never discussed, but by the attention they received and the way certain aspects were highlighted it was obvious. They had been told to give them a good education in the basics of the technology the pair were to use to convince the Iraqis that they were buying the genuine article.

There were two main lecturers, Yusuf Mitikin from Moscow University and Vasily Radishchev from St. Petersburg. Vasily was a great brute of a man, not an academic in appearance.

As part of the history of the subject they visited Dubna and saw the cyclotron in which Red Mercury was first produced.

The most difficult aspect of the assignment was to insinuate themselves with the Iraqis without arousing suspicion. They attended many embassy trade functions and military demonstrations as members of the Russian political machine.

They had decided that some show of honesty was required and Nikolai let it be known that Alan was a British subject who was not exactly welcome in the UK and that he had some sort of grudge against his country. If he had tried to pass as a Russian and got caught out then they would have lost all credibility and the assignment would have to be aborted with the Iraqis on their guard.

He must have played the dissident fairly well because it was in fact Alan the Iraqis approached first.... He'd never forget the man, Aziz Ruboek, he was a highly placed military adviser to Saddam himself.

Alan had told Anna of his shock at seeing again the man whom he had last seen being driven in a jeep around the square in Ur. However his shock had turned to delight, here was a focus for his revenge. If he had any doubts on what he was doing for MI6 from that moment they became fully justified.

Alan said Aziz never smiled, at least not in his presence, and had an expression similar to a beast of prey considering its next meal. He was also extremely direct in his conversation, unlike many of his countrymen who seem able to approach their real interests only from an oblique angle.

He asked Alan whether there was any truth in the rumour that the Russians had sufficiently developed the military potential of Red Mercury. He was extremely well informed and knowledgeable on the subject and for the first time Alan appreciated the grounding he had received from Yuri and Vasily.

Alan's role dictated that he become reserved and secretive, pretending that he was unaware of what Aziz was referring to.

"There is no need to be shy with me" Aziz had said "after all we are friends of the Russians aren't we? And they want to unload all their unused weaponry on the Middle East, much of which is bought through the black market at highly inflated prices." Alan had not reacted. "Not that we don't find it very useful" Aziz added.

"We were standing in the middle of a large salon in the Iraqi Embassy so I contrived to look furtive and told him that even if I could help him this was certainly not the time and place to discuss it." Alan told Anna.

"OK," he'd said "when and where?"

"I will get my Russian colleague Nikolai to set up a meeting" I replied and excused myself from him. I then discreetly approached Nikolai who had been talking to a Georgian politician and at an opportune moment drew him to one side and told him I'd had a direct approach from Aziz Ruboek. Of course I let the Iraqi see me talking to Nikolai and hammed up the situation a bit." Alan had smiled as he told this part of the story. Anna was beginning to get writer's cramp and suggested they break for coffee.

She got up while Alan made only modest protestations.

As she made it she noticed the bad weather had seemed settled in for the day. She reappeared with two steaming mugs of coffee and placed Alan's on the window sill in front of him then pulled up another chair and joined him while they took a break.

"Is this working better?" he had asked.

"Yes, I think so although I expect when I transcribe it and add some filling of my own you

In Pursuit of the Red Kite

won't recognise it." She realised that she seemed to be taking over what was his report and said. "However if it's not the way you want to see it we can use my copy as a draft for you to correct."

"I appreciate what you're doing to help me and I'm already not sure how to repay you," he'd replied.

"I'm sure I'll think of something" she'd said before she realised how her comment might be taken, this in turn had caused her to blush. She had stood up all business-like and said, "enough of this sitting around, back to work."

"OK, where did we get to?"

Anna read him in from her notes and he resumed the narrative with his next meeting with Nikolai and Aziz in the restaurant of the Intourist Hotel where Nikolai had chosen a quiet table apart from other diners.

Alan said he had felt tense now that they were beginning the task for which they had been prepared. Nikolai on the other hand seemed totally relaxed and portrayed his normal outgoing and gregarious nature. Looking back now he reflected on how he had enjoyed the Russians company and would miss him. This despite Nikolai's attempt on his life.

Aziz had watched them both throughout with his hawk-like and unsmiling eyes.

There was a little verbal sparring during the early part of the meal but Nikolai seemed to know when to stop and begin the serious matter of discussing Red Mercury armaments.

"Alan here has told me of your discussion the other evening at the embassy and I would like to know what makes you think that such weapons exist and if they did that they would be available."

The Iraqi had replied, "I have first class intelligence. Obviously I cannot and will not go into that issue. Suffice it to say that we are convinced such weapons exist within the armoury of the Russian military forces. Perhaps I should say Saddam Hussein is convinced and I am to establish the necessary facts for him."

"I see" said Nikolai deliberating over what he had heard. He turned to look at Alan who shrugged which he took as agreement. "Let me ask you and I will be as direct as you appear to be, what is in it for us?"

"What do you want other than money, of course?" said Aziz.

"Total secrecy in anything that should develop from this meeting or any future meetings and that nothing can be traced back to us. There is to be a proper means of covert communications set up and that there are cut outs to prevent any link between ourselves and Iraqi military intelligence being discovered."

"So you are telling me that these weapons do exist?" The Iraqi asked.

"I'm telling you nothing until there is a guarantee that should we be able to assist you, nothing rebounds on us to damage our political careers or endanger our lives........and yes, you are right, we do want money, a large amount each and deposited in numbered Swiss bank accounts of our choosing." He stared at Aziz who returned his gaze without expression. "We also want two-thirds of that money deposited before the material is shipped out and the remainder on delivery."

"What do you call a large amount of money?" said Aziz.

"Two million US dollars each."

"You don't come cheap do you?" Aziz replied, to which neither Nikolai nor Alan had responded. He continued,

"But let us suppose that we can agree to your terms, we are going to need to be convinced that the weapons have been made and tested and could be used immediately if we wanted."

Nikolai had continued with his own agenda and ignored Aziz. "You realise of course that anything we should provide is at tremendous risk to ourselves. If it were discovered that we were letting this technology out of Russia we would never reappear from the Gulag alive. You see, Russia believes she leads the field in this technology and despite detente shares little of the development knowledge with the USA, Britain or South Africa who are the other major powers interested in the potential of these weapons. At this moment in time the balance of external opinion is that we have not achieved success and that all that exists is a scientific probability."

"That is what we had heard" said the Iraqi,

"but knowing you Russians as we believe we do we think you have made the breakthrough. What leads us to this view is the recent testing of small atomic devices in Novya Zembla. Which is not, of course, making you too popular with your partners in the West, especially with the non-proliferation treaties still in force.

As with the West, we have heard your public denials and that you are only testing high- powered conventional explosive, but like the West, quite frankly we don't believe you."

"I couldn't help thinking that the Iraqis had convinced themselves already in this matter," said Alan to Anna, "and that our reluctance to confirm either way was only fuelling that belief. To a con artist it was a classic situation, the sucker was selling it to himself."

Nikolai had taken up the running. "If you are already convinced we have the technology why do you need more proof from us and what do you mean by proof anyway?"

"We want to check the scientific proof."

"Ah," Nikolai had said "that is not possible. That is not for sale. We would not want anyone else to be in a position to manufacture the weapons."

"We don't want to manufacture them. We could not afford the plant and we don't have sufficient skilled labour for the task, although I know skill can always be purchased at the right price" added Aziz.

"We will need to think about what you have said before we commit to you," Nikolai said to Aziz.

"I think you need to convince us that adequate personal safeguards can be guaranteed and that the money is readily available." He stood up to leave and I followed. There was no question as to who would be paying for the meal.

"How do I contact you?" asked Aziz.

"You don't," said Nikolai, "we contact you," and with that he turned and left the restaurant with me on his heels," concluded Alan.

Alan made little further reference in the report on the detail of the negotiations that took place between primarily Nikolai and Aziz and the formulation of a strategy to suit both parties and their respective masters.

Aziz did not probe too deeply as to how Nikolai came about his information nor Nikolai on how Aziz was able to arrange for the necessary transfer of cash into his and Alan's selected accounts.

What took a long and frustrating time for both Nikolai and Alan was in the way every piece of information they provided Aziz with was taken away and over varying periods of time seemingly authenticated through some other source.

They knew they were being tested but were unsure as to how, for there was no other power sufficiently advanced in the development of Red Mercury fusion weapons as the Russians.

Alan, as he told Anna, even then began to suspect the South Africans. His theory was that one of the large chemical manufacturing companies was paying Iraq something towards the cost of the information that they were getting out of Russia and then validating its credibility. Neither he nor Nikolai was too concerned, they were getting regular payments into their accounts. It had been later agreed they would receive a third of the cash for information, a further third when they could actually demonstrate the effectiveness of the weapons and the final third on delivery of the first consignment of arms. It was the second part of the plan that was the most difficult to stage manage. The Russians had told Britain that whether or not the weapons existed there was no way any outside observer would be permitted to witness their testing. So it had been agreed that some elaborate device would be developed to simulate what the Iraqis expected to see.

To further complicate matters, as each of the powers were maintaining the stance of having no knowledge of the hoax that was being perpetrated, a conventional witnessing of a test was out of the question.

It was the natural characteristics of the two nations that solved the problem, deviousness and secrecy.

The Iraqi intelligence network in Russia had hooks into the military and political apparatus and had found the weaker links in many departments where certain persons' proclivities had been discovered, exploited and then used as subtle levers to obtain a regular supply of information. These friends of Saddam would witness and report back their findings to Iraqi intelligence independently of any information provided by Alan or Nikolai.

In Pursuit of the Red Kite

It was agreed that Alan and Nikolai should find out when there was to be a test series and the Iraqis would persuade one of their observers to be at these tests and report back their findings.

The tests would be carried out on the military range at Novya Zembla. The fusion bombs would be fired from hand-held launchers. As the effective area of blast was some 600 metres from the centre, the observers would be in bunkers at about one kilometre and would watch the tests on TV monitors. The soldiers firing the weapons would be approximately one kilometre from the epicentre of the blast and would be provided with blast resistant suits fully protected from radiation. It was nevertheless a very dangerous role these men would perform.

The mini nuclear explosion that the selected witnesses would see would be the result of conventional explosives and sophisticated special effects.

"It was some three months from the first time I met Aziz" Alan continued "till the actual testing was carried out." He smiled at Anna. "How the special effects were stage managed I will never know but the Iraqis were convinced it was a reality and that's all that mattered. We had bets on how long it would be before the Iraqis would be pressing to arrange a sale."

Anna was unable to resist asking Alan what it was that made these mini atomic bombs so attractive.

Alan asked what she meant.

"Well, it's not something that you may feel needs to be said in your report, because you are dealing with the initiated, but to someone like me I don't fully grasp why these mini nuclear explosions are creating so much interest when one big bang would do the whole job."

He had laughed at the way she put it. "What it is," he told her, "is that these nuclear devices are so small that anybody can carry them around in, say, a briefcase which, as a terrorist weapon, has frightening potential."

"Also, a soldier can carry several of them and fire them from a hand-held launcher. This would be lethal to the opposition. In addition, the fall out and contamination would be reduced."

"The device we are talking about is reputedly no larger than a cricket ball including its detonator which can also be set off by a radio signal either by whoever plants it or someone more remote."

"Does it exist then?" queried Anna.

"I am not sure" Alan replied. "I think it may do and if it doesn't I don't think we are far off seeing it become a reality." He looked worried and for the first time Anna shared his concern.

"It was only two days before Aziz made contact with Nikolai and said that the Iraqi military were in the market for the new weapons," Alan had continued. Nikolai told him that it would not be easy and at first the supplies would be limited. A plan now needed to be devised to steal the devices from the Garrison store where they were reputedly held and because they were such a new development each one was coded and accounted for."

"This statement caused Aziz much concern and he became very angry but Nikolai kept his cool" said Alan. "He told Aziz to calm down as there was a plan already in hand. What was happening he explained was that the Russian black market had obtained sufficient information from which to produce dummy casings to simulate the actual devices even to the point of serialising the numbers. These dummies would be substituted for the real thing, he explained. Aziz still looked angry and Nikolai only smiled at him."

"How do I know I will not get the dummies?" he demanded.

Nikolai only shrugged. The question wasn't worth responding to, he implied.

"Because, dear Aziz, I will not provide them or steal them for you. That is something you will arrange yourself."

"Me? How's that?"

"With all your friends in the military I'm sure you could exert sufficient pressure in the right places to substitute the dummies for the real thing. Also you must bear in mind that Russian soldiers are not getting paid at the moment and therefore I'm sure corruption if rife?"

"It would be discovered; you have already told me everyone is accounted for, apart from that it's impossible to get them away without a major problem."

"On the contrary" teased Nikolai as he led Aziz to the destined conclusion. "These devices lend themselves to such an operation by their miniaturisation. Why a man could carry one out in each of his pockets if he's got the balls for it." At this Nikolai had collapsed in mirth at his own humour. If looks could have killed, Aziz would have finished him off there and then.

"Now," Nikolai began, "we come to the final piece of the jigsaw. What we do is sell to you the dummies at the agreed price. You give these to your contacts in the armoury, they switch them over and you walk off with your bomb. Now what could be simpler?"

"The theft could still be discovered if the dummies are ever used by your military" grumbled Aziz.

"So what does that matter to you?" challenged Nikolai.

"We have taken some precautions in that matter also" he told Aziz. "The dummies have the serial numbers of the last bombs produced, so assuming they use them in sequence it will probably be sometime before any dummies are found.

This seemed to satisfy Aziz, Alan had told Anna, because he then went off to discuss it with whoever would sanction the expenditure.

"A week later we had two thirds of our money and gold bullion to cover the cost of twenty bombs had been handed over to our masters or as Aziz believed the Russian Mafia."

"We met him once more before he left for Iraq on the same plane as the bombs. We asked him

In Pursuit of the Red Kite

for the remainder of our money and I'm sure he had intended to renege on the deal. It was when I produced a radio transmitter and told him that should he think of not arranging final payment then he would simply be blown out of the sky. Once payment was in our respective banks, he could take off and we would signal him the frequency at which each of the bombs had been set. If he tried to tamper with the bombs before then that too would have a disastrous effect."

"He hated us you know. He promised if the bombs didn't work he would kill us personally. We told him it was a pleasure to do business with him and that if he needed more devices we would have more dummies made and he could help himself to a few more. I think that and the threat to blow him out of the skies is what convinced him that he could trust us. Anyway we got our money, then did as we were instructed and went to ground for two years. Myself in the Friary in Provence, which you know about from Hans?"

Anna nodded. She had heard part of Alan's story from her father but what bothered her was whether her father had had a role in the hoax and what danger he might be in.

"Where does my father feature in all of this?" she had queried.

"He doesn't. He had nothing to do with it."

"Then how come you knew him and came to seek him out?"

"He was one of those who taught me the basics of Red Mercury. I felt we got on and spent some time between lectures in each other's company. I knew he was a man I could trust and I needed someone to talk to which is why I turned up in Vienna." He smiled at her "And why I am sitting here enjoying the company of his daughter."

She remembered his reply and smiled to herself.

She hit the "save as" button on her PC. She was looking forward to dinner that evening. She instructed her printer to make a copy as she went to take a bath and prepare for the evening before cooking the meal.

In Pursuit of the Red Kite

CHAPTER 23

November 1993

In The SAS unit headquarters in Southern England, Harry was meeting with Commander James Morris. He had come straight to the point. He had told the Commander that Alan was presumed to have killed the Russian agent he had been working with. A body had been discovered in Provence and Alan had gone AWOL. He omitted any detail and the Commander expected none.

"So what is it you want me to do?" he asked Harry.

"Before I go into that" Harry put his head to one side as though trying to recollect something from the past "didn't Alan get himself into trouble with you people?"

The Commander stared at Harry. Why was he asking questions he already knew the answer to? Instead he played along with the security officer's farce.

"Yes."

"Dishonourable discharge?"

"No!" Commander Morris scowled.

"Hmm" said Harry. "What we need Commander is to find him before it gets out of hand." As if to emphasise the point he said, "You know what the Russians are like, they're making a big thing out of it."

In Pursuit of the Red Kite

"So he's been tried and found guilty in absentia, is that it!" demanded the Commander.

Harry shrugged. "Have you anyone here who knew him. Who knew him well enough to try and work out how he might think or act?"

The Commander turned back to fix Harry with a further stare before replying.

"Yes, I have a Sergeant here who may be the man to talk to. He trained Alan as I recollect. He was also the only person who defended Alan when the rest of the unit assumed their own version of the facts when they heard of what happened in Iraq. As it was, I was pretty sure it was the Para's who gave their own somewhat prejudiced view of what happened to them. We were unable to prove anything," he shrugged, "and then it seemed to be yesterday's news and the powers that be suggested I drop the whole matter."

Harry waited for him to go on.

"I guess I could have done more, but by then Alan was away and out of touch....guilt by inaction," he apologised at the memory of an injustice.

Harry looked at him questioningly as he said "Then maybe you can help him now."

The Commander took the point, picked up the 'phone and rang the gate.

"Is Sergeant Joe McMichael on the camp? I see....Tell him my office ASAP."

"I thought you chaps said 'at the double'" said Harry trying to lighten the atmosphere which had been anything but friendly.

The man in question had spent the morning with little to do. In fact since his last tour of duty in Iraq things had been a little quiet for him with the unit. When he was not coaching the new entries to the service he spent much of the time in the canteen where he would chat with various members and catch up the latest news.

He had chosen a table in a corner where he had appeared to be drinking whilst reading a paperback. Any watcher would have noticed that he did not turn the pages. Once again his thoughts were about his future and what he would do when he was no longer fit enough for active service with the SAS.

Many, he knew, had either gone into body-guarding those whose careers led them into the riskier aspects of life or as mercenaries to whichever revolt against a foreign power was popular at the time. The first had little appeal; the second none whatsoever. Joe could see no moral justification for it and it was always possible you could find yourself fighting against someone who had been your friend or colleague in an earlier life.

The problem, he had convinced himself, was that he was no academic. At school he had not achieved very high grades in any of the subjects he had sat for. He had done much better in sports and physical activities. It was this aspect that had led a school advisor to suggest to Joe that he consider a military carcer. It was in following that advice that had led him to his current situation.

He also acknowledged that he liked the outdoor life. One of his favourite pastimes when not on military service was to involve himself in Natural History. He had joined an evening class at the local high school but due to the demands of his military career it had foundered.

It was as he was again considering where he would go from here, unless they offered him a desk job, that a young soldier snapped to attention in front of where he sat and said.

"Begging your pardon sir but would you report to the Commander's Office right away. Sir"

Joe picked up his paperback and made his way to the outer office of the unit's Commanding Officer. As he went he could not help wondering what the summons could be about.

When he entered, the Commander's secretary looked up and on seeing who it was picked up the phone. Joe heard him say "McMichael's here Sir." He Paused "Yes Sir"

He put down the phone, looked up at Joe and told him he could go in. Which Joe duly did.

Inside the office the Commander had got up and gone to the window and stared across the parade ground towards the barracks whilst waiting for Joe to arrive. There was a unit going through its paces and they could hear the muted instructions from the drill sergeant.

"So the Russians are after Marks too" he stated more to himself than Harry.

"We're putting together a joint team" said Harry. "Also we want to get to him before the French

Police find something to go on. "Of course the French don't know of our interest in the matter." he added in explanation.

There was a knock on the door and they both looked round as Sergeant Joe McMichael entered on the command, saw Harry, saluted his Commander then came to attention in front of his desk.

"Relax Joe" said the Commander "we want you to help us out with a little problem."

Harry was introduced and he outlined what he wanted of the Sergeant who, despite his commanding officers instruction to relax, appeared fairly tense to Harry.

Harry had his doubts as to how much help the man would be.

When he had finished outlining the task he asked Joe if he had any questions.

Joe took his time in responding until Harry began to wonder whether he should break the ensuing silence and repeat the question.

"OK" began Joe. "A Russian agent is found dead in France but so far the French police have found nothing to link his death to Alan. We don't even know whether they were together, do we?"

Harry admitted they didn't know. It was the only reasonable assumption they had been able to come up with so far. If Joe was right, a possibility they had already considered, then they had to rely on Alan turning up at his Swiss bank. Although as the trail was already more than a month old it was likely this would only reveal that Alan was already on the move.

Harry had phoned the Swiss bank and was due to fly out the following day himself.

"No, we don't know for sure" he replied. "And that's partly the reason I am here. I am trying to find out the most likely set of circumstances. I appreciate at the moment I'm grasping at straws but someone who knew the man might just give us a pointer as to how he might think." He paused, but Joe was not going to add anything so he went on. "Commander Morris here" Harry turned to the Commander who was also prepared to listen but not join in "tells me you were of the opinion Alan had a rough deal and as you and he got on well during his time with the squadron I thought you may be the man to help us find him?"

Joe was fighting an inner battle, would he be aiding his friend or would he be simply helping to throw him to the wolves.

He decided to play for time before committing himself.

"So have you any suggestions? I mean it's unlike you Secret Service people" he raised his eyes seeking confirmation of his guess at Harry's status. Harry smiled but said nothing, which seemed to satisfy Joe who continued "not to have some ideas of your own?"

"Of course... you're right Sergeant, I do have a theory." He paused as though marshalling his thoughts. "I have been studying the local ordnance survey maps of the area and have made certain assumptions as to the sort of distances they might have covered, assuming that Alan and the Russian were coming out of cover at the time and place the accident took place." Harry avoided the word murder for two reasons. Firstly it would seem that he may have prejudged the situation and secondly he did not wish to get on the wrong side of the Sergeant assuming that he may have been a friend of Alan's.

"There was one possibility that I considered to be worth a look at. I'm assuming that the French haven't already covered it as they have been requested to keep the Russians fully informed as to their enquiries."

"You think they will?" asked Joe.

"Well, the Russians said that they'd not flood the area with agents if they were kept in the picture and so yes, I think they will."

From Joe's expression Harry could tell he didn't share that opinion.

"So, what's that possibility?"

"Well, I found a Friary marked on the map. It is within a day's hike of the area where the body was found."

"So you think they stayed in a Friary for a couple of years?"

"I said it's a possibility, in addition" Harry added "they found a pair of rope sandals among the articles in the Russian's rucksack which could have come from somewhere like that."

"Is that all?"

"No, they also found the remains of some home-made bread and when they carried out the autopsy, found similar remains in the stomach."

"But isn't that all a bit tenuous?" asked Joe. "There are too many assumptions for my liking. Why do you think they were together? What makes you believe they or the Russian went to ground in that area? What leads to the assumption the body was within a day's march of where the Russian may have hid?"

Harry shrugged. He realised he'd been doing that a lot since he'd arrived at the camp. "We don't know the answer to any of your questions Joe. We have to start somewhere and, yes, we could be way off the mark."

Joe fully appreciated the futility of the situation but had come to realise his old friend was desperately short of allies right now and it seemed Alan had made some high powered enemies.

"OK. So how do I get there?" he asked Harry.

"I suggest you go as a hiker on a walking holiday in Provence and you call at the Friary to see if they'll put you up for the night. Then, carry out some discreet enquiries to establish that is where in fact Alan stayed."

"Who will be my Russian counterpart?" Joe asked.

"This first investigation you do on your own.

In Pursuit of the Red Kite

A quick in and out. Then depending on the result you may have to team up. You report directly to me on anything you might discover and I decide what we tell the Russians. If that's a dead end then we are not sure where to begin searching," said Harry almost to himself, "even if he was there I'm not sure where that gets us now. He could be anywhere in the world."

"Wasn't he supposed to report in or something?" asked Joe.

Harry sighed. "Yes he was, which is why we are fairly convinced they met up. Otherwise he wouldn't have failed to contact us. My guess is the Russian must have spooked him and now he believes there is a plot to get rid of him."

"And is he right?"

Harry adopted an indignant expression "No, of course not, there is no hidden agenda by H.M.G., we can only assume that the Russians were not playing the game, which is why we have to find him first, or at least have somebody alongside their man while we try to locate him."

Joe seemed unaffected by Harry's little outburst, he gave the impression of a man who had heard it all before.

"When do I leave?"

"Tomorrow morning."

"How?"

"By plane to Marseilles and then by train up to Aix and from there you work out your own route in."

In Pursuit of the Red Kite

He looked at his commanding officer and then back to Harry "Do I get any cover?"

"You go in on your own passport as a physical training teacher from a school, who is on a hiking holiday in the area. You know enough to be able to describe what that entails if questioned."

"What if they check?"

"It's extremely unlikely that they will check every holiday maker in the area for alibis. We'll chance it."

Harry told Joe that they would provide him with some basic civilian clothes, well worn camping equipment and adequate reserves of French Francs.

The Commander who had said nothing throughout the exchange now asked "Anything else Joe?"

"Not at present Sir except what will be said to the squadron about my sudden departure?" said Joe who knew he was now being dismissed.

"We'll say that you had some personal matters that required your absence for a few days. There will be a car ready to take you to Heathrow in the morning and all the kit will be in the boot," said Harry as Joe turned to leave.

Neither man made any move to shake hands, it did not somehow seem appropriate.

"Thank you Commander for your help" said Harry after Joe had departed. He stood up "I'll get out of your way and thanks again for your assistance."

The Commander grunted as he watched Harry get up to leave. He went over to his desk, opened a drawer and took out an A4 folder which he offered to Harry.

"I think you might want this."

The Commander had, since his call from Harry, assumed detailed information on his two men was what the services were after and had looked through their records.

"Copies of our records and profiles on Alan Marks and Joe McMichaels. They may be of some use."

Harry took them from the Commander's outstretched hand.

"Thanks," he smiled. It was the first indication that the SAS genuinely wanted to help.

Seated in the back of the car on his return drive to London, Harry read the file. It added little to what he knew already about Alan. Joe was an efficient soldier but would he be a good tracker, Harry wondered as he put the closed file on the seat beside him.

CHAPTER 24

November 1993

Just as the man from MI6 had predicted, Joe had no problem in getting into France the following day. The car arrived as arranged, a black Ford Sierra pool car with a plainclothes driver, a garrulous individual, who kept Joe awake all the way to Heathrow.

He flew to Paris and then on Air France down to Marseilles. He took the train to Aix and then a local bus to Forcalquier. From there he would follow a somewhat circuitous route to the Saumane area. He would stay well clear of the area in which Nikolai's body had been discovered.

Once in Saumane he set off towards the Friary. He would be sleeping rough. That night he spent camped against a rock outcrop out of the wind and partly screened by a few stunted trees. He did not cook as he did not want to draw any attention to himself.

He broke camp at around six the following morning and began his trek to the Friary at a steady pace. If the terrain was not too difficult he had estimated he would reach it before midday.

From a cold bright start the day warmed up at around ten and Joe stopped for a break and to remove a layer of clothing which he tucked under the straps of his rucksack. He sat on a rock and surveyed the scenery as he drank from one of his bottles of

"Badoise". He called in at a farm around mid-morning where he was able to buy cheese and bread. He spent a little time with the farmer before continuing on his journey. The old man who came to the door tried to engage him in conversation but soon gave up at Joe's excruciating French. Despite this he indicated they would share a glass of wine together.

They ate at an old timber table that had been put outside the farm many years earlier and nodded and smiled at each other as Joe rested up. The sun was warm and the atmosphere pleasant. Apart from the occasional phrase in French from the old man, the only other sounds were of birds and the farmyard chickens.

Joe almost wished he was on vacation and not assignment. He could quite happily have spent a few days in the area.

He left the farm and continued his journey towards the Friary. The terrain became harder but to Joe this presented no problem and he was in sight of his destination just after midday as planned.

The Friary was a large grey crumbling edifice that from a distance didn't look inhabited but as he got nearer he could see some of the windows were not shuttered. He waited until evening before making his approach and seeking a bed for the night

The large entrance doors with a small inset postern gate were shut when he made his approach that evening. Joe pulled at an old brass ring and heard a faint sound somewhere inside. It was a minute or two before he heard the slap of sandaled feet approaching the door and with a rattle of bolts the postern gate was opened inwards. Joe noticed it was on a safety chain as he saw a tonsured head appear in the gap between door and frame. The Friar was wearing a brown habit buttoned down the front. He asked Joe what it was he wanted. At least Joe assumed that's what he'd said.

"Do you speak English?" Joe asked.

"Just a little" the Friar replied in what Joe felt to be a very passable attempt at his own native tongue.

"Good. My French is almost non-existent" Joe replied. "I was hoping to find shelter for the night, that is, if it's possible?"

The Friar seemed to relax and he smiled in welcome.

"Yes, you may stay here if you wish, though I would tell you the accommodation is fairly basic."

"I'd be most obliged" said Joe as the Friar eased off the safety chain and stood back to allow Joe into the dimly lit hall.

Joe followed the man through the plain corridors whose only decoration consisted of pictures of Christ and the Holy Virgin. They passed several robust timber doors, all closed with no note or number to give any clue as to what lay beyond.

At a turn in the corridor they stopped and

entered a room which was small and plain. It had a single timber framed bed, a small table with a wash bowl on top and a chair. The window was shuttered, the friar crossed the room opened the shutters and Joe could see the clear night sky beyond.

"This is it" said the friar who had introduced himself to Joe as Brother Marcus.

"This will be fine" Joe looked around "Where can I get some water for the washing bowl?"

"Don't worry, I'll bring some for you and I may be able to get you something to eat" he added.

"That would be great....I was told I would be well looked after here."

"Oh...You know someone who has been here before?"

Brother Marcus' curiosity was aroused. It was very infrequent that they had guests at the Friary and he wondered who had mentioned its existence to their latest visitor.

"Yes."

"May I ask who that was?"

Joe reached inside his jacket for a photograph of Alan. He had avoided using a name as there was no way of knowing what name Alan had used if in fact he had stayed here. He handed over the black and white picture, which had been provided by Harry from MI6, to the Friar.

Brother Marcus took the photo and held it close to the light.

"Oh yes, Brother Alan. He stayed for two years and left here only a month or so ago." He suddenly became a little suspicious of the coincidence. "Is he well?"

"Oh yes, he's fine." lied Joe. "We met up when he got back to England. I often take hiking holidays in Provence and it came up that he had stayed here. I included your Friary on my route as he'd told me what an attractive area this was."

This seemed to satisfy Brother Marcus who excused himself to fetch the water and some food for Joe.

Joe looked around the cell and thought to himself that he would most definitely not want to take Holy Orders. He didn't mind a Spartan existence but to spend one's life cooped up in such a small space in a plain unattractive building would not be the life for him.

He put his rucksack on the chair and sat on the bed.

Within ten minutes Brother Marcus returned with a pitcher of water and some bread and cheese.

As he went to leave he said with a sparkle in his eye, "we begin our offices at five thirty in the morning should you wish to join us or if you prefer you may have breakfast in the dining room at seven o'clock."

Joe declined the offer of early prayers with a smile but said he would be pleased to join them for breakfast. Brother Marcus told him where to find the dining room.

Left on his own Joe lay back on the bed and

wondered just how he might use the confirmation of Alan's presence in the Friary to help track him down. His own opinion was that it would be of no use at all. If he had been in Alan's position he wouldn't leave any clues to his future whereabouts with anyone.

This opinion was borne out the following morning at breakfast when he tried to get some indication from the Friars. Having already stated that he had met Alan in England recently, which was why he had come to seek shelter at the Friary, he couldn't now ask where Alan had headed for.

It was an innocent remark by one of the other brothers that confirmed the fact for him. The Friar commented that he was pleased to hear Alan was well and back in England as they had no idea of where he had been headed on leaving the Friary.

Joe returned to England where he was to report to Harry at MI6 having first telephoned from France with the confirmation of Alan's presence in the area.

When Joe got back to England he went straight to Harry's office. Harry asked Joe if he had any thoughts on what he would do if he'd found himself in Alan's position.

"Well, I've been thinking about that quite a lot over the last few days" replied Joe. "Obviously I would change my name and appearance and stay away from anyone who might recognise me. To do that of course would require forged sets of identity documents to allow me to travel wherever I needed. I would also need an untraceable access to money." He paused. "If I could arrange all that, then I think I would try and create some life insurance for myself to get the hounds called off."

"What do you mean?" Harry asked him.

"Well I have assumed that what he knows could be extremely embarrassing to someone therefore I would put together some irrefutable proof of what I had been engaged in."

"Why?"

"Well, again assuming I'm right and that's why you and the Russians are so keen to get hold of him, then I would threaten to publish it if anything were to happen to me. That way I may not have to spend the rest of my life looking over my shoulder and being unable to mix with family and friends."

Joe had more or less confirmed what Harry had expected him to say.

"How would you go about producing such a document?" he pursued Joe's philosophy.

"I haven't really thought about it at all.....as it's not me that has the problem." replied Joe.

Harry decided to change tack. "You know you'll be working with the Russians, don't you?"

"Yes."

"We're not sure why Nikolai was killed and whether Alan was in fact responsible. But if we assume the Russians were trying to kill him and that he was acting in self-defence, it is important that we are there when he is traced. We don't want a summary execution by the Russians, we want him back and to find out what really occurred."

Joe said nothing but he had his own view of the situation. Whatever the greater picture, Joe had no intention of letting Alan be sacrificed as some pawn in a political game. He felt he was one of the few people who had liked Alan and had not been influenced by the issues surrounding his departure from the SAS.

Harry got up from his desk and wandered around the office. It was important to get Joe on board as part of the team and he didn't feel that they had achieved this so far. For sure Joe did not trust the service.

"Where would you go from here Joe?"

"Your guess is as good as mine....He really could be anywhere, does he have any aliases he could use that you know of?"

"We had provided him with three sets of identities when he began the assignment. We're keeping a lookout, but I'd be very surprised if he used any of them" replied Harry. There followed a silence as Harry seemed to be considering the imponderables of the case. It was broken by Joe for whom the silence had become uncomfortable.

"What do you want me to do now?" He asked.

"I think I'll have to put you on standby Joe. I'll talk to the Russians and as soon as there are any leads we'll bring you back into the hunt."

After Joe had left Harry went back over

everything they now had by way of leads. The Russians had been in touch with the French Surete but they had found nothing so far. It seemed the police were chasing a cold trail and it was unlikely they would be of much more use. Still, he thought, I've got to try everything. What Harry had not told Joe was what he had discovered from his trip to Switzerland.

His plane had landed at Geneva International Airport and he had taken a cab directly to the bank.

He was taken through security to a small office where M'sieu Dubois was already standing to welcome him.

He came round the desk with hand outstretched "Welcome to Geneva Mr. McReady" the manager said "may I introduce you to Catharine De Farge."

Harry turned towards the woman sitting in the chair alongside the manager's. She returned his smile as M'sieu Dubois invited him to take a seat in the one remaining chair in front of his desk.

The office was plainly furnished and devoid of any personal decoration.

"How can we help you?" the manager asked before adding, "Oh, the reason I have asked Catharine to join us is because she attended to Mr Marks when he visited us here."

Harry noticed Catharine blush at the manager's explanation, an expression that was missed by M'sieu Dubois from where he was sitting.

He bent and picked up his briefcase, opened it and took out some papers which he placed in front of the manager.

"The one on top is a copy of our deposit to Alan's account, the second confirmation from your bank that the transfer was complete. The next is a photo taken of Alan just after he began working with us."

He looked at them both "Could you confirm that this is the man we both know?"

The manager looked at Catharine before saying that it was their client. Catharine added a weak yes and Harry noticed she no longer looked so relaxed.

Harry continued "I am well aware that you may not be able to answer all my questions simply due to client confidentiality but it is also important to my government that we locate Mr Marks as soon as possible. I am not at liberty to give you more detail than that regretfully," he added with a raise of his shoulders and a rueful smile implying that if it were possible he would take the manager into his full confidence.

"I understand completely," said M'sieu Dubois, "please let me try."

"As you know Mr Marks has a considerable amount of money in his account with you. We know this because some two years ago we paid a fairly large sum into it at his request."

The manager nodded.

"What we need to know is whether he has been to the bank recently, if he has made any withdrawals, redirected his account and if to your knowledge he has taken up temporary residence in Switzerland?"

By way of an answer the manager said "The reason I have asked Madam De Farge to join us as I said previously, is because she attended to Mr Marks when he came here which deals with your first question. The second and third come under client confidence and I cannot comment on those. The last is one I have no knowledge of. But for your information we have never had a contact address for our client."

"Isn't that unusual?" Harry asked.

"Maybe, yes," M'sieu Dubois replied" but not something we would refuse a customer's business over"

"Does he have a strongbox?"

"Sorry again I cannot comment."

Things had not gone any differently from his expectations. He reached out and gathered up his papers.

"Thank you both for your time" he said and got up to leave.

Both Catharine and the manager got up. "Would you see our guest out?" M'sieu Dubois instructed Catharine

"Yes sir. Please follow me." she said to Harry.

At the main entrance doors she went to press the release button but Harry stopped her. "Madam De Farge, I believe you can give me a little help here"

"I don't think so"

"Then let me explain a little more. Mr Marks is being investigated by the French police for a murder. Anybody who has been in contact with Mr Marks is likely to be fully investigated together with their families." He stopped and watched the effect his words had on Catharine.

She had paled and her eyes were darting from side to side looking anywhere but at Harry.

"When do you take lunch?" he asked.

Catharine looked at Harry like an animal caught in the headlights. "In about an hour." she replied.

"Well I suggest we meet at the coffee shop just a few doors along from here and continue this conversation in a more private place. Maybe, just maybe, I can keep you out of any further investigation."

"OK I will be there."

"Good I will see you then." Harry leaned across her and pushed the release button and let himself out of the bank. Catharine watched his departure, her mind working overtime. Jean, her husband was not the forgiving type. What had she got herself into?

Harry did not like this part of his role, he was not a natural bully but sometimes life did not always turn out the way one would have liked. He sensed that Catharine might have a possible lead to Alan's whereabouts and that was what he had come to Geneva to find out.

The hour till her lunch break dragged by. Catharine could not concentrate and found she could not wait for the appointed time to arrive. And was it a twist of fate that had decreed that Harry had chosen the same café where she had first had coffee with Alan?

Harry was already at the café when she got there. He had secured a two-seat table away from the entrance. He stood as she entered but did not attempt to shake hands. Before he sat he beckoned the waiter over who took their order. Neither ordered food.

Catharine waited for him to speak. She was not going to make any confessions on a subject that Harry may not be interested in. As it turned out there wasn't much left after he had finished questioning her.

"Madam De Farge I believe you know a little more about Alan than perhaps you are willing to admit."

"What makes you think that?"

"Your reaction and body language during and after the meeting"

"Oh," Catharine looked down.

"So are you going to tell me what you know?

Or do I inform the French you may be able to help them with their enquiries."

Catharine sighed "Well I did meet up with him outside work. We had coffee, here in fact, and we went out for dinner a couple of times."

"Where was he staying in Geneva?" Harry waited as Catharine deliberated on her reply.

"He was staying in a small hotel not too far from here. He may still be there for all I know" Catharine replied.

"Has your husband met him."

Before she realised the trap, Catharine said "No"

"Why don't we drink up our coffee and you can take me there." Harry beckoned the waiter to emphasise his suggestion.

They left the café and as Catharine had said the walk to the hotel took only a few minutes.

The woman sitting at the reception desk looked up as they entered. She noticed the age difference and concluded the worst. "Can I help you" she asked.

Harry produced the photograph of Alan and laid it on the counter in front of her.

"Do you recognise this man."

She studied it for a moment and then looked at Catharine for a moment before replying. She remembered the German, Paul Gerhardt, and this woman leaving the hotel together one morning about a month ago.

"Yes I do" she pulled a register from a shelf below the counter." That's Herr Paul Gerhardt."

Harry was watching Catharine's expression and from the look of surprise he deduced that the she did not know anything about Alan's alias.

"Did he produce a passport?"

"Oh yes, we do not accept anyone who cannot meet the legal requirements."

Harry did not believe what she had said but went on "Is he still here?"

"No he left after four days" she replied checking the hotel register.

"Thank you Madam"

He turned and with Catharine following left the hotel. Outside he stopped and faced Catharine.

"Thank you Madam De Farge. That's all for now."

With that he walked away leaving a very worried woman behind.

Later he informed a distracted D.G. of his progress.

What Harry did not learn was that after he had hung up Sir Ian picked up the 'phone and asked to be put through to the KGB Headquarters in Moscow. In the spirit of cooperation he would tell the Russian that Alan had been to his bank but the trail from there seems to have gone cold. He would not mention the name Alan was now using.

CHAPTER 25

November 1993

When the plane from Moscow landed Hans planned to take a taxi to his apartment. He passed through the green channel without challenge and made his way to the landside exit.

"Dad!"

He looked up and saw both Anna and Alan and his heart sank. He instinctively knew that they had become closer in his absence. Under normal circumstances he would have been pleased for Anna who had taken some time to get over her previous marriage. He liked Alan and wouldn't have objected to him joining the family under more normal circumstances. Now he was concerned that his daughter's association with Alan could lead to further unhappiness and possible danger.

With an effort he pulled his face into a smile of pleasure at seeing them. Anna hugged him, which pleased him. Hugs had been few and far between recently.

As they walked to Anna's car the conversation was light. They asked him how he had enjoyed the seminar and he gave them a brief run through of the subject matter. He told them of the endless dinners and speeches that had followed until they felt quite sorry for him.

Their light mood was infectious and Hans

found he was able to put aside his earlier concerns for a while.

Anna was more animated in her conversation and told her father of the progress they had made on the report and how pleased Alan was with the result. Hans looked at Alan for confirmation. He caught Alan off guard and saw the expression on his face. Alan said "yes" in response to Anna, but Hans could tell he too was worried about where the situation could be headed.

When they arrived at the apartment he invited them in but they declined and suggested that if he was not too tired they would dine together that evening. It was agreed he would ring Anna later to confirm.

Meanwhile in Moscow Andrei was not having a good day. It had begun with having to say goodbye to his lover at three am that morning. He was going back to Jordan for a two week holiday which meant that Andrei would be sleeping alone for a while.

When he got to his office he slumped behind his desk and looked at the pile of paperwork which had begun to increase over the last week. He was determined that today nothing would prevent him clearing his desk. He had been the butt of Yuri's bad humour ever since they had learned of Nikolai's death

in France. As each day had passed the situation

became worse. Yuri had found him extra tasks and leads to follow. Andrei considered himself an organised and methodical man and his routine had been thrown into disarray by the boss. He sighed and reached out for the pile. He would sort it into groups.

He found several telephone messages which demanded his attention. Suddenly he went cold, there had been four calls from a Professor Vasily going back over the last few days. The last one, dated two days ago stated that the Professor would be leaving the Intourist Hotel in three days' time and had some information the Colonel might find interesting. Andrei checked Yuri's diary. He would be out most of the morning.

Andrei reached for the phone and asked to be connected to Professor Vasily. A few anxious minutes later he was told that the Professor was out but that a message had been left. Andrei told his secretary that when the Professor rang back she must put him through even if it meant interrupting him. There were to be no more bits of paper, it was imperative that he speak with the Professor.

It was nearly twelve thirty before the Professor returned his call. Their conversation was short and to the point. Vasily would be at the office for a three o'clock appointment with Yuri. Andrei shuddered, the man did not sound at all pleased.

When Vasily arrived he was shown into Andrei's office where he took a seat facing Andrei who had done his best to appear both helpful and efficient when they had spoken earlier.

Andrei picked up the phone and dialled

In Pursuit of the Red Kite

through to Yuri, who was back at his desk, it was engaged. He apologised to the Professor and assured him the Colonel would not keep him long. He then attempted to deal with his dwindling in-tray but was aware of Vasily watching him and couldn't concentrate. Any attempt at conversation had met with a terse response.

Vasily sensed Andrei's discomfort and smiled at him.

Far from being reassuring it reminded Andrei of a killer shark about to pounce.

He tried the phone again and was relieved to find it disengaged. He was asked to bring the visitor in. He led the Professor to Yuri's office and stood aside to let him enter. As he passed, Vasily brushed against the aide and smiled directly into his eyes, a look that did not go unnoticed by Yuri. He knew the Professor was bisexual and Andrei's obvious disquiet amused him.

Yuri, who knew the Professor well, invited him to sit down and after the usual pleasantries asked the purpose of his visit.

The Professor leaned back in his chair and steepled his fingers before beginning to relate the reason for his visit to Moscow and how an Austrian Professor, Hans Frieberg, was taking an interest in "Red Mercury" with a view to writing a paper on the subject.

"As I recall you had an interest in the subject yourself a couple of years ago and I wondered if there was any link?" Vasily looked questioningly at Yuri.

In Pursuit of the Red Kite

Yuri did not show any reaction to Vasily's comment. Inwardly he found this news at getting what might be a lead on his investigation into Nikolai's death most welcome. Could it be the beginning of a trail to discover the Englishman's whereabouts?

Since he'd heard from Sir Ian that there was no trail in France he had begun to believe nothing would turn up. But now maybe there was a straw to grasp on to.

Vasily explained with more than a little dramatization, how he had been approached by Hans and at their dinner later how the conversation had led up to his involvement in the Red Mercury hoax.

At the conclusion Yuri thanked Vasily and said he would make a record of their conversation and maybe follow it up a little further to see if any other persons involved in the original plot had been approached.

The Colonel knew that Vasily would be unaware of Nikolai's death and he was not about to enlighten him. Vasily was useful, but if allowed to believe he was important, the man would become even more unbearable, Yuri had learned this from past experience.

Andrei was summoned to show the Professor out and once again Yuri was amused at the body language of the two men. Andrei's expressed almost naked fear.

In parting Vasily remembered to tell Yuri that two other delegates had spoken with the Austrian

In Pursuit of the Red Kite

Doktor in the bar after dinner at the University. He was unable to confirm whether there had been any further discussions between the parties. Yuri noted the names and again thanked Vasily for his information, knowing that the parting comment had been staged and not previously forgotten.

Back in Andrei's office the Professor perched himself on the edge of his desk.

"Why did it take so long for me to see the Colonel?"

Andrei winced but said nothing.

"You thought I was not important, was that it?" demanded Vasily.

Andrei mumbled something about that certainly not being the case.

"I did not mention how you kept me waiting."

Andrei looked up and his expression of relief was exactly what the Professor had expected.

"I would not wish to get you in any trouble young man. I am staying a further day in Moscow, as you know, why don't we have dinner together tonight?"

Fear grabbed at Andrei who could find no excuse at that moment.

"I will telephone you later and let you know where I have booked a table," Vasily said standing up to go.

Once the Professor had left Andrei sank into his chair. He knew exactly where the Professor's

In Pursuit of the Red Kite

invitation was leading and he could not bear the thought of such a brute touching him.

Half an hour later Yuri received a call from Andrei on the intercom.

"Can I have a word with you Colonel?"

"Of course, come in now" said Yuri.

Andrei entered and stood in front of his desk, he was not invited to sit.

"Yes, what is it?"

"Colonel, I have to apologise, there were earlier messages from the Professor which had got to the bottom of my in-tray. I hope it wasn't important, but as soon as I found them and saw that it was one of the people you wanted to speak to concerning Red Mercury and Nikolai's death, I got him in right away!"

"How long ago was the first message?" asked the Colonel in a dangerously quiet voice.

"Three days."

"I see, so the professor was kept waiting three days" roared Yuri.

Andrei cowered back at the verbal assault.

"I suppose it's only the fact that you'd rather have me on your back than him on yours that you're confessing now, right?" continued the Colonel.

Andrei looked down at his feet but said nothing.

"Get out" Yuri waved towards the door and Andrei beat a hasty exit.

In Pursuit of the Red Kite

Once Andrei was out of earshot, Yuri laughed at his own witticism and his aide's obvious discomfort. "The horns of a dilemma" the Colonel said out loud, again breaking into laughter at the double entendre.

The expected call from the Professor came an hour or so later but Andrei was able to refuse the invitation despite the threat of exposure of his earlier incompetence. As he hung up he let out a long breath, a narrow escape.

It may have been his new found humour or maybe the old ways were fading. Whichever way, Yuri decided to telephone Sir Ian and tell him about a possible new lead to Alan's whereabouts.

He was undeterred in his resolve to impart some possible news when Harry came on the line to report that Sir Ian was in a cabinet meeting and could he help.

Yuri explained about the conference in Moscow University and Vasily's suspicions of the Austrian Professor.

Harry asked Yuri whether the Professor had also spoken to any other delegates on the subject. After a pause Yuri stated that he didn't know.

"It might therefore be a genuine research project and not related to our investigation," he said to the Russian.

"Maybe. In fact quite possibly you are right, but do you have any better ideas at the moment?"

Harry not wishing to upset Yuri agreed that it

was certainly worth investigation and said that he would arrange for Joe to meet with Dimitri Vorschek. They would set up surveillance on the Professor's movements and see where that led them. He told Yuri of Joe's visit to France and confirmation as to where Alan had stayed for the past two years. From the way it was passed over by the Russian, Harry realised he had already known.

They concluded the call by making the necessary arrangements for their agents to meet in Vienna the day after tomorrow.

Joe would meet Dimitri at the hotel Inter-Continental on Johannegasse in the Karlsplatz district, not too far from the Technical University where Hans Frieberg lectured. Yuri had done his homework. They would meet up as business acquaintances. It was agreed neither MI6 or the KGB would inform or involve the Austrian Embassy or Security Services. This was to be a strictly covert operation.

CHAPTER 26

November 1993

On the evening of the same day that Harry and Yuri had made their plans, Hans, Alan and Anna were having dinner at their favourite restaurant in Vienna, the Drei Husaren on Weihburggasse.

The food here, according to Hans was reputedly excellent, as was the atmosphere and if they were lucky they would have a good pianist to accompany the meal.

During the course of the meal he told them of his discussions with some of the professors that Alan had identified as being involved in the Iraqi hoax plot. He went on to say that he had managed to get hold of some fairly useful confirmation of the conspiracy on tape. A tape which was now locked in the University safe he assured them.

At the end of his narrative both Alan and Anna sensed that Hans still had something on his mind which he was having difficulty with.

"Hans, what's up?" Alan asked. "You look as though something is troubling you and I've felt it ever since we met you off the plane?"

Hans shrugged. "I guess I'm not cut out to be a secret agent, I think I may have aroused suspicions in Moscow." He replied.

"What makes you think that?" Anna asked her

father.

Hans told them of how he had caught Piet, the South African and Vasily deep in conversation and how he had felt they were discussing him.

Alan, who knew how easy it was for the imagination to over react when involved in covert work tried to reassure Hans that he was probably imagining it. In truth he felt the Professor was more than likely correct in his suspicions.

The mood around the table became quiet and introspective. It was finally broken by Alan.

"Were you able to get any positive material or support for our report?" Alan asked Hans.

"Oh yes," he paused "I let it be known that I was writing a paper on the subject of Red Mercury and the mystery and stories that seem to surround it. The best support I have is on the tape. Come over in the morning and you can hear it for yourself."

"Good" said Alan. "As we told you earlier a large part of the document is completed and Anna has made back-up discs of what has been written to date. We can add the contents of the tape onto the CD"

"Not wishing to be an alarmist, don't you think that we ought to put some of the material we have in a safe place?" asked Anna, "along with the tape recordings. We can always rewrite the text but I suspect that if Dad's right and somebody has become suspicious then we'll not get another chance to talk to anybody else who was involved in the deception.

They'll be warned off."

"You're right. I think I should make a trip" announced Alan. "I will go to Switzerland via Paris and put everything in as safe a place as I can. In Paris I know someone who can provide me with a false set of documents and a new identity." He did not mention to the pair of them that he already had a new identity which he would resume on leaving Vienna.

Having agreed a plan of action Hans said he was tired and wanted an early night.

He offered his daughter a ride home. Alan left with them and went back to his own apartment. As he lay thinking over what Hans had reported he found his attention kept turning to thoughts of Anna and he wished she were with him.

The following morning at around ten they all met up in the Doktor's office. He had taken his tape recorder into the office and it was set on his desk. Anna sat in a chair facing him as Alan perched on the edge of the desk. They listened to each of the recordings of Hans' conversations with Vasily and Piet.

When the last recording had finished Hans looked quizzically at Alan.

"What do you think? Is it good enough?"

"I think it will do." He didn't sound convinced.

"But they are just voices on a tape" said Anna.

"OK, I know names were mentioned but mostly Christian names" she added.

"That's not a problem" said Alan. "Voice recognition prints can soon prove the authenticity of the speaker. It's the content that counts. It's a bit tenuous," he went on, "a clever lawyer could take some of it out of context and weave a completely different interpretation of events around the basis of some of the recordings." Seeing her look of consternation, he added "But not all of it. Yes, I think we have enough," he concluded with more conviction than he felt.

"Where do we go from here?" asked Hans.

Alan got up from the edge of the desk and began to walk around the Doktor's office.

They watched him and waited for his answer.

"I think what I need to do is to get the tapes copied and the originals put in a safe place along with copies of the DFX files you have produced on your P.C." He said to Anna.

"They're incomplete. I will finish them today" Said Anna

"I know, but I think it would be prudent. Especially as Hans feels that the Russians may be becoming suspicious."

"I'm not sure they are" Hans interrupted "maybe I was just a little over-cautious in my comments last night."

"It's not worth taking the risk" said Alan "I think the sooner I start getting the material we have in a safe place, the more secure my position will become."

"Agreed" said Anna. "What will you do?"

"Well" he began and turned to look at both of them. "This is not easy for me to say especially bearing in mind how much you have both done, but I think the less you know at present, the better."

From their expressions he knew they were not happy with his reply, but neither said a word, as they realised he was probably right.

"Also, I have had a rethink, as to how to protect you both from any possible repercussions and at the same time let MI6 and the Russians know of my threat to expose them in the event that anything happens to me."

"How will you achieve that?" asked Hans.

"Assuming the worst case, which is for them to have discovered Nikolai's body and know that I am on the run, they are aware that at some time I will go to my bank in Switzerland for money. By now they will have enquired as to whether I have been there or not.

If Hans is correct and the Russians are suspicious of him then you will be paid a visit and subjected to close scrutiny which may not be pleasant."

From the worried looks on their faces he knew his arguments had hit home. "So what I propose is this. That if or when they question you, you tell exactly what it is you have done. Even give them a copy of my report for them to read. That will overcome how I deliver the threat without disclosing where I am."

Hans was the first to comment "Without sounding like I am simply protecting my own skin I think it's a good plan and I can see the sense behind it."

He looked at Anna who added a reluctant agreement.

"I will also now need to leave as soon as Anna has completed the report, put it onto a CD and make several copies one of which I will let my solicitor have. Unless forced I would rather you didn't mention that or the fact that you have made any tape recordings while you were at the seminar."

"I understand." confirmed Hans.

"One last favour, if I may."

"What's that?" asked Anna

"I was up early this morning and took a trip to the airport to book a flight to Paris. I also took my luggage with me and booked that in too. Would it be possible for one of you to bring the documents to me?"

Anna looked at Hans and said she would do it. That would then not affect any lectures or classes he was giving that day.

That afternoon Anna met up with Alan at Vienna International Airport and handed him a small parcel which he quickly packed into his hand luggage.

Having completed the task he smiled and thanked Anna for all her and her father's help and added somewhat lamely that he sincerely hoped that he had not put them to too much trouble.

Anna said it was OK although not too convincingly but went on to ask how he was going to let anyone know if he was still alive.

Alan told her that somebody would be receiving weekly emails from a laptop he had purchased earlier from one of the airport shops. If those emails stopped and the receiver had not met up with him then it was to be assumed he was dead and the recipient was to release his report to the UK, French and German gutter press.

"May I ask who this someone is? Could it be me?"

"I think I have put you in enough danger as it is don't you?"

To his surprise she reached out and grasped his hand. "I would like to do it."

Alan felt awkward and at the same time wondered what might have transpired if they had met under different circumstances.

"Can you let me think on that?"

Anna opened her handbag, took out pen and paper and wrote down her email address and gave it to him.

Alan took it and put it in his pocket.

"What time's your flight?"

"I have an open ticket as I was unsure as to when you would arrive so I will now book a seat on the next available flight." he replied.

"Well I suppose it's goodbye? You will need to get on your way."

"Yes," and thank you once again.

Anna leant forward and gave him a quick kiss on the cheek before turning and walking quickly away. She did not look back and once again Alan wondered about what might have been.

Enough of that he told himself as he went to left luggage and withdrew his case before leaving the airport. Outside he took a cab to Vienna where he was to take a train to Berlin. In Berlin he would get in touch with his former contact for a further identity and this time he would get himself a gun.

An hour later Joe's flight landed and as he passed through customs he was unaware as to how close he had been to his quarry.

CHAPTER 27

November 1993

Aboard the Austrian Airlines flight Joe had managed to get himself a window seat. They had left the little cloud over the mainland far behind and they headed towards the coast of France into a clear blue sky.

Joe was not looking forward to his assignment. He doubted the motives of the Security Services and he did not want to be party to the death of an old friend on his conscience. He would have to get to Alan before the Russian in order to keep him alive until he got him back into the U.K. There it would be more difficult for him to meet with a "tragic accident". Joe was convinced he was the only one who had Alan's best interests at heart and that a possible jail sentence was preferable to an untimely end.

He was disturbed from his musings by the air hostess asking him to put his tray down to receive the packaged breakfast she was holding at arms length towards him. He smiled apologetically and complied.

Having eaten he tried to settle with a paperback, but his mind was too active and so he closed his eyes and lay back in his seat. Fortunately his neighbour was no more interested in striking up a conversation than he was.

The plane began its slow decent into Flughafen Wien Schwechat. It was five minutes ahead of schedule, not that that mattered to Joe, he was not being met. He would hire a car at the airport and drive into Vienna and straight to the Inter-Continental hotel.

The Russian would not be arriving until later that afternoon and so it had been agreed that they would meet up in the lounge bar at around seven and have dinner at the hotel that same evening. This would give Joe the afternoon to locate the University and trace the Austrian Doktor's whereabouts.

As the operation was strictly covert there had been little information available to Joe. In an overt operation, MI6 would have spoken with the Embassy and names, addresses, photographs and any public record information on the Professor would have been handed to him before he'd left England.

He did know the Doktor's name, qualifications and the University from which he tutored. This had been provided by the Russians from bookings for the seminar.

He tried the simple way first and picked up the local directory. If the Doktor lived in Vienna and did not have an unlisted number then he would find an address, this meant he would not have to surreptitiously approach the University for information and possibly forewarn the Doktor of his interest.

Subject to whatever the Russian might have in mind Joe had decided to stake out the Doktor as a direct approach would only forewarn his quarry that he had been located. This assumed of course that the two Services were correct in their interpretation of the Doktor's motives in the interest he seemed to have taken in certain individuals at the seminar.

Joe had bought a street map of Vienna at the airport and after a quick lunch at the hotel he took his car and drove first to the University and then to the Doktor's apartment in Fleischmarkt in order to familiarise himself with the area he would be operating in over the next few days.

He drove past the Doktor's block and parked the car in Rotgasse. He knew he could park for an hour or so before having to move. He locked it and then walked back to locate the apartment. He noted the ways in and out of the block both on foot and by car.

He would also need to be sure he could observe without being seen himself. This was the most difficult part of any surveillance work and sometimes virtually impossible to achieve. In a tight community any person or car seen hanging around for any length of time would be noted and the watcher would find himself to be the subject of local surveillance.

Here again Joe had been lucky as the apartment was above shops in a busy tourist area where there were cafes and restaurants conveniently located for watching the entrance to the apartment without raising too much suspicion. The rear exit was much more difficult to observe. However as it seemed there was no car park serving the building Joe hoped the Doktor would use the front entrance.

Having located his quarry's apartment Joe decided to spend some time as a tourist before meeting up with the Russian, Dimitri Vorschek, later that evening.

Joe went down to the bar early. He wanted to watch for the Russian and observe the man before officially meeting him. He was to be disappointed. The Russian had arrived first, no doubt to observe Joe.

He was sitting at a table away from the bar. Joe went over and stood at the table. Neither man offered his hand.

"Would you like another drink?" asked Joe looking down at the Russian's glass.

"Yes, thank you." said Dimitri in good English.

Joe took in the lean features and cold eyes of the Russian agent and knew he was looking at a killer. The Russians did not want Alan alive; they wanted him dead like Nikolai. Alan was an embarrassment. Joe wondered, as he had so often over the past couple of weeks, what it was exactly that Alan had done or whether he was just a loose end that needed to be removed.

He walked over to the bar to get himself and the Russian a cold lager. He could feel the Russian studying him. He was simply there to identify the prey.

Joe sat opposite Dimitri and neither man seemed to want to be the first to begin a conversation. It was clear from the outset that there would be no trust between the parties. They would carry out their jobs in a professional manner but that's all there would be to this, hopefully short term relationship thought Joe.

The Russian sipped his lager.

"What information do we have on the Doktor?" he asked.

"Little more than you know already" replied Joe. "I have had a look at the location of his apartment. It will be fairly easy to keep an eye on." he added.

"What about the University?"

"That will not be so easy. I think anyone just hanging around there will soon be spotted."

"But maybe that's not such a bad idea. Make him panic and who knows he may lead us to your man."

"More likely to send Alan away for good, that's supposing of course that he's anywhere around here."

"It's the only lead we have, however unlikely," Dimitri reminded him.

Over dinner they worked out a schedule between them as to who would cover the professor's moves at various times throughout the next day. They both agreed that either the Doktor had met up with Alan or his interest in Red Mercury at the Moscow seminar was purely a coincidence. Neither believed the latter.

It was also agreed that only Joe would approach the Doktor directly; Dimitri would become involved it Joe felt it necessary to add more pressure.

There had been no time limit set for this operation, although both agreed that if there was any connection between Alan and the Doktor it was more likely that their quarry had either flown or had never been in Vienna in the first place.

The Russian had hired a motorbike as his means of transport which Joe realised gave him more flexibility than a car. Both would keep in contact on mobile phones.

It was agreed that the following morning's surveillance would begin with Joe picking up the Doktor as he left his apartment and tailing him to the University where he would point him out to Dimitri.

Joe would then carry out an inspection of the security, if any, surrounding the Doktor's home with a view to breaking in and making a search. Having got in they would then place bugs. These sophisticated devices were voice activated which meant that the listener could set up a recording station which did not need to be manned. Every so often the tape would be checked and replaced by the operator and played back at a separate location.

The problem with this was that they might not receive important information until it may be too late to take advantage of. Ideally they needed more manpower and equipment, but Harry had told Joe before he left England this was not an option.

Joe's plan was to park a car within range of

the apartment and then return to it from time to time to move its location and avoid parking tickets.

CHAPTER 28

November 1993

Next morning, just before lunch, Alan arrived in Berlin following a journey that turned out to be uneventful despite Alan's growing paranoia that he might already be being followed. It was now November, he reminded himself. Throughout he found himself studying, surreptitiously, everybody that came and went on the train. He took a cab to Ku'Damm and walked from there into the side streets looking for one of the budget hotels he remembered from his previous stays

His favourite had been the Hotel Charlottenburg Hof on Stuttgarter Platz and he was pleased to find that they had vacancies. The hotel had barely changed since his last visit some three years earlier. He booked in. His room on the second floor was large and airy and overlooked Stuttgarter Platz.

He unpacked his case and holdall and placed his laptop on the table in front of the window. He looked around for a power point and internet connection although he did not really expect the Charlottenburg to have become that sophisticated. No connection found, he rang down to the desk who confirmed that they had not installed internet in each room but proudly announced that they had a room set aside on the first floor for their business clients.

Having booked in as Paul Gerhardt, he decided he would carry each set of identification documents with him at all times although he hoped to be in a position to dispose of 'Paul Gerhardt' in the very near future.

Having established his base for the next few days, he left the hotel for the Cafe Voltaire where he ordered coffee and to study the street map of Berlin he had purchased at the station.

He had been in two minds as to whether to buy the map. He had been to Berlin several times before and he had a good memory and sense of direction, but caution won.

After a brief lunch he decided to spend a little time getting to know his way around Berlin using the U-Bahn and S-Bahn.

Alan wondered what he would do if he were unable to contact Johan Zeigler, the forger he had met while working with the Russians. Too late now, he thought. If Zeigler had moved or, worse still, had died then he was not sure how to proceed. It might mean trying to locate the embassy envoy who had helped him before. This he did not want to do.

There had been no way he could have checked this out in Vienna. He'd had to make what might turn out to be an abortive trip, but it was the only option he felt he had. He knew that in meeting Zeigler he was putting himself at some risk. But he had balanced this in his mind against the risk of doing nothing and he had decided to trust the forger, after all the man's livelihood was based on a criminal code. His main worry was that if the Russians were seriously after him they would put the word around the underworld in most of the major cities, especially those where crime traded successfully.

After dark he would head south across the city to Schoneberg to the Winterfeldplatz which was Berlin's largest weekly market area and where the Cafe Sidney was located. He hoped to find his man there.

During the day it was a popular coffee stop for Berliners, visiting the market. In the evening, the area took on a different character and became a trade centre for the more nefarious activities of Berlin's Underworld.

It was sometime around eight that Alan found himself seated at a corner table in Café Sydney so that he could see all the comings and goings of the patrons. His reason for coming to the Cafe was that it had been a regular haunt for Johan Zeigler and for Alan it was the only point where he might be able to establish contact with Zeigler, whose address he'd never known. He'd checked the telephone directory but as expected there was nothing listed.

Cafe Sidney had hosted many like Alan and the waiters were well versed in discretion. Apart from replenishing his coffee and cognac they left Alan to his own company.

He'd brought a paperback with him as he expected it could be a long wait and he was unsure as to how many nights he may have to sit there.

Alan had recognised the owner of the cafe from his previous visits and a couple of waiters looked vaguely familiar. He got the feeling the owner recognised him too.

By ten o'clock he was getting bored and

In Pursuit of the Red Kite

couldn't take any more coffee. He decided that as Zeigler had not yet appeared and it was unlikely he would that evening and that maybe he was wasting his time. One more Cognac and he would head back to the hotel.

When next a waiter appeared to take his empty cup and ask if there was anything else he would like, Alan decided to ask about Zeigler.

The waiter looked impassive as Alan described the little bald headed forger and from his lack of response Alan was unable to tell whether or not he recognised the description and simply said that he was not familiar with the gentleman Sir was describing.

Alan did notice however that the waiter proceeded to take some time in conversation with the owner before bringing him his next drink which was placed before him without comment or eye contact. His sixth sense told him that Zeigler did still frequent the cafe but when and how often was the unknown. He fumed to himself in frustration, but he had decided after all, to give it a little longer.

It must have been half an hour later that he was interrupted from his book by a woman who stopped at his table and asked if she could join him. She was in her late twenties and not unattractive, Alan thought, as he waited for more information.

There must have been something in Alan's look that made her realise that some sort of explanation was necessary before he replied.

His silence disturbed her and she looked away

towards the door. Alan followed her gaze and saw a large man leaning against the frame and another smaller man blocking the way to the toilets. There must have been another way out the back he realised.

As she turned back he said "Can I help you?"

"I think it is you who needs help" she replied looking frustrated at having lost her poise.

"You'll just have to be a bit more explicit. I've no idea who you are or why you're here." Alan replied.

"You were asking after Herr Zeigler?"

"I asked the waiter if Johan still came here and was there any chance of seeing him. That's all."

"Why?"

"Isn't that between me and Johan?"

"Not if you want to meet him. Herr Ziegler is very particular about who he meets."

Alan smiled. "He must have gone up market since I last saw him then."

As the blonde was about to reply, an angry light in her eyes, Alan held up his hands in mock surrender as he continued "Tell him Alan Marks would like to do some business with him. That is if he is still following the profession I best knew him for a few years ago when I was working with The Russians."

"Wait here" ordered the blonde who turned and walked out of the cafe. The two men left their posts, one opening the cafe door as she passed without

In Pursuit of the Red Kite

any acknowledgement.

Alan looked up to catch the owner's eye. He swiftly looked away and busied himself at the bar.

It was a further twenty minutes later when the blonde returned with Johan who was dressed much more smartly than when Alan had last seen him. Obviously forgery is still a very lucrative business Alan thought to himself as Johan came over and sat down opposite him without invitation. This time it was the blonde who waited at the cafe entrance.

Alan said nothing as he was scrutinised by Zeigler's dark intense eyes. Seeming satisfied Zeigler signalled to the bar owner who was well versed in one of his more illustrious patron's requirements.

"Well......" said Zeigler "what brings you to Berlin this time?" He kept his voice low and it was unlikely to be overheard by the nearest customers some two tables away.

Alan observed the same procedure with his reply.

"I need you to get me a new identity."

"Where for?"

"Does it matter?"

"No just curious. In what name and do you have photographs?"

"Marc Swartz, and yes I do," said Alan reaching inside his jacket for the small envelope containing the three identical images of himself taken earlier that day while at the station.

In Pursuit of the Red Kite

Zeigler took them out of the envelope and studied them.

"Will you keep this hair colour?" He looked up and caught Alan's gaze. "Not that it matters," he added without waiting for the reply.

"How much?" Alan asked.

Zeigler gave a smirk as he said "For an old friend I will charge him only market rate." He paused. "Let's see, in American dollars I will do it for you for only $1000, how's that?"

Alan replied that he was glad he was glad he was an old friend of Johans' otherwise he dreaded to think what it might have cost. The sarcasm was not lost on Zeigler who simply shrugged a take it or leave it. It did not matter to him.

Alan knew he had no choice but to pay the German.

"How soon can it be ready?"

"Be here the same time tomorrow night and I want payment in fifty dollar bills" Zeigler said as he stood to leave. "Please sit down. There is something else you may be able to help me with." said Alan.

Zeigler sat and waited for Alan to go on.

"I need a hand gun." he stated.

"Why do you think I can help?" Ziegler replied

"Oh I'm sure you can or you will know someone else who can for the right price."

Zeigler paused for thought. When he spoke again it was to say that he would make some enquiries and get back to Alan when he picked up his new identity documents. He got up to leave for the second time.

"Do not follow me, it would not be healthy."

"I have no interest in following you or seeing where you live, I simply want what I'm paying for."

Zeigler smiled as he turned to go, but Alan stopped him "By the way Johan if any of your friends try to follow me you will next see them in hospital. Do I make myself clear?"

"How unnecessary of you my friend" sneered Zeigler as he left.

In Berlin Alan had returned to Cafe Sidney at the appointed hour, the money in an envelope in his inside pocket.

He pushed open the glass door and as he entered he saw the blonde sitting at the table he had occupied the previous night. She was alone and looking bored. He walked over and pulled out a chair. She said nothing, simply observed his movements in a dispassionate way.

Alan caught the owner's eye and asked for a black coffee.

After it had arrived the woman spoke.

"You are to wait here. Herr Zeigler will be coming when I tell him you have arrived. Do you have the money?"

"Yes."

"Let me take it to him."

"No. I'll only give it to Zeigler when I have seen he has what I want."

"You don't trust us" she sneered.

"Don't be stupid. This is business."

She got up and left. Alan changed seats so that he could observe the entrance.

He had spent a day killing time in Berlin. To his best knowledge he had not been followed, however the danger would begin if Zeigler asked around. Alan thought it was unlikely that Zeigler would run checks on all his customers. If he did and it got out he was just as likely to become a target for the forger as well.

However what if Zeigler had been asked to watch out for him by the various undercover agencies that knew of his services to the underworld? He mentally shrugged to himself, if this was the case once the exchange had been made and he'd got clear of the quarter, then that would be the time he would be most vulnerable.

He began to wonder if he had been too casual. Should he have prepared some elaborate disguise until he was clear of Berlin. What could Zeigler do other than to point him out. Zeigler did not know what name or nationality he had entered Berlin with nor, he

In Pursuit of the Red Kite

assumed, where he was staying.

As these thoughts rotated through Alan's mind the man in question entered the Cafe. He came straight over to Alan's table and sat down. He smiled at Alan and said "Have you enjoyed our beautiful city?"

"I have" said Alan a cautious smile of his own in place.

Zeigler looked up and signalled for drinks. He turned back to Alan and pulled an envelope from his inside pocket and laid it on the table. Nearby customers paid them no notice as Alan reached over. Zeigler stopped him. "The money."

"I want to see what I'm buying."

Zeigler shrugged and took his hand off the envelope.

Alan picked it up and slid out the contents. A slightly battered Austrian passport with three years to the expiry date slipped out. His own face stared back at him. He flicked through the pages and noted various stamps from earlier trips abroad including the United States.

He closed the passport, put it back in the envelope and reached inside his jacket for the money which he handed to Zeigler.

Zeigler inconspicuously counted the notes.

"Only just enough" he said to Alan smiling.

"What about that other issue?" asked Alan.

"Ah yes I may be able to help you there."

Zeigler replied

"When and how much?"

"For you the same price as the documents."

"When?"

"Do you have the money?"

"Of course. I can be back to suit you."

"Then I will meet you back here in an hour." Zeigler replied. With that he got up and left.

Alan still wondered if Zeigler planned to turn him in.

Once outside Alan walked for a few blocks as he checked for a tail. He could discover none, either that or they were extremely good. He slowed his walk. He would find a cruising cab just to be on the safe side. He would return within the hour with the money. Part of the money he had obtained in Switzerland and carried with him at all times

As before they went through the same routine at the Café and on departure Alan found himself the owner of a 'Beretta' from which someone had thoughtfully removed any identification.

"There's a full clip and two spare clips in the bag." Zeigler informed him as he saw Alan's questioning look.

He still did not trust Zeigler. Had he imagined the look that passed between Zeigler and a man sitting alone at the bar? He would keep a watch but was aware that he was not on home territory and he would need to consider how to reduce the odds a little.

In Pursuit of the Red Kite

He had noticed a park not too far away from the café.

The day had been overcast and there was no light from a night sky. From his training in the SAS he would possibly have an advantage over anyone who might be following, as they were more likely to be accustomed to an urban environment.

He did not look back as he walked towards the park. When he got there he was pleased to see that it was un-gated. He walked briskly while looking for a place to conceal himself. Several clumps of trees and bushes were available and he took to a side path that twisted and turned away from him. This gave the added advantage of his disappearing into the trees before any pursuer was aware.

His precautions paid off. As he watched from his place of concealment the man from the café came round a corner. Not seeing Alan in front of him he began to hurry on ahead. Later Alan was to ask himself why he did it but instead of making his escape in the opposite direction he decided to follow the man from a distance.

At the far end of the park the man crossed the road and turned down a side street. Alan followed but as he turned down the street his quarry was nowhere to be seen. Suddenly he heard a small noise behind him and instinctively ducked, moved forward and turned to face the man from the bar who stood there smiling and wielding a wicked looking knife.

From his stance Alan could tell the man had not been trained in armed combat although that did not make him any the less dangerous.

"The gun!" demanded the man.

Alan ignored him. The man moved forward raising his knife to horizontal, the other arm forming an arc as if to encircle his victim and underline the threat.

Since arriving in Berlin and knowing the company he would have to be mixing with Alan had carried his own knife strapped to the underside of his left arm with the hilt closest to his hand but out of sight.

His pursuer shrugged as if to say he didn't care if he had to attack or not and stepped closer to Alan. At this Alan whipped out his own knife but instead of retreating his attacker grinned and lunged forward. For Alan it was a simple manoeuvre to avoid the incoming blade while at the same time making a thrust of his own. Whether it was due to the speed of the attack or in an attempt to avoid Alan's counter thrust, the result was that Alan's blade entered his attacker's chest, passed cleanly through his ribs and punctured the heart. He was dead before he hit the ground.

Fortunately for Alan there were no witnesses, mainly due to the lateness of the hour. He knew he could not leave the body on the footpath. He had to buy himself time to get away before it was discovered. If he carried it across to the park he would have to be sure that no late night traffic would catch him in their headlights. It was then he noticed that some of the terraced houses in the street had basements, approached from an external stair. Two doors along from where he stood one of the houses

In Pursuit of the Red Kite

had no lights showing. On closer inspection he saw that the basement window was not only barred but had the blinds drawn. That's where he would place the body. As close to the outer wall to avoid easy discovery from above but in a position that anyone opening the blinds in the morning was in for a nasty shock. At least it would give him a few hours to get away.

Alan now realised how his attacker had got the drop on him. He must have taken one of the stairs down to the basements and waited for Alan to pass. He searched the body in order to remove any ID that might help the police making any early connection between it and Zeigler and therefore start a manhunt that would increase the chances of being captured or eliminated before getting out of Germany.

After concealing the body, he checked his clothing for bloodstains. In the dark it was impossible to tell but whereas it appeared that he had some on his shirt the rest of his clothing seemed to have escaped from any staining.

Back at the hotel Alan spent a restless night thinking about the day's events, the man he had killed and the need to be a lot more careful and use his SAS training to avoid some of the mistakes he had made over the past few weeks in protecting himself since leaving the Friary.

CHAPTER 29

November 1993

Andrei was cheerful. His friend was returning to Moscow sometime today and he would see him at the apartment that night. He pondered on how he would cope if the Jordanian were ever to be posted out of Russia.

When he got home that evening it was to find a note under his door.

He opened it with some excitement only to find the content short and to the point. "I'll see you tonight." He pouted and put the note on the kitchen table as he prepared himself a light meal. He put the T.V. on as background while he worked.

Later as they lay on their backs in the dark Andrei enquired about the Jordanian's leave which he was told had been taken up by a week at some remote village where his family kept a farm. The remainder of the time he seemed to have spent in a succession of government departmental meetings.

Andrei recounted the time he had spent in his friend's absence. He was aware of the Jordanian's interest in the bits of the story he had told over the previous weeks about the dead Russian Nikolai and how they were trying to track the killer.

He felt the Jordanian tense as he mentioned the briefing of the new agent, Dimitri, who was to accompany an English agent in tracing Nikolai's killer. It was when he mentioned the incident with

In Pursuit of the Red Kite

Professor Vasily that the Jordanian sat up and said,

"Was this before or after the briefing?"

"After. Does it matter?"

The Jordanian did not reply.

Andrei was curious at his lover's interest but said nothing.

"What happened then?"

"Well, they rushed off to Vienna to try and pick up a lead from the Austrian Professor," said Andrei. "Still, in my opinion, I think they're clutching at straws. It's so easy to turn the contents of an ordinary conversation into something dramatic. I mean, what would be unusual about a Professor who goes to a conference at which there are colleagues who have an interest in a similar research project, asking questions about matters which form part of his studies?"

He smiled to himself in the dark as the Jordanian lowered himself onto his back.

"You seem very interested in this case my love?" he pushed.

"I suppose it is a bit more exciting than some of the other stuff you seem to spend much of your time doing at the department" the Jordanian replied and left it there.

The surveillance team had a lucky break. It was lunchtime. The students were leaving the University as Joe spotted the Professor leaving with a pretty young woman who he guessed was the Doktor's daughter.

He got out of the car, locked it and followed them on foot to a local cafe where they were to have lunch. He was fortunate enough to get a table within earshot. Having settled himself he took out his trusty paperback and pretended to read.

Over the forty five minutes spent eavesdropping he was able to learn the daughter's name was Anna and that they were hoping to hear from someone he presumed to be a boyfriend, the name of whom Joe had been unable to overhear.

Joe left the restaurant before the couple and was in his car when they returned from lunch. Both re-entered the building and Joe assumed that Anna also either worked there or was a late student. He called up the Russian on his mobile and it was agreed that they should locate the woman's flat and place listening devices in there also.

As he hung up Joe smiled to himself. They were making slow progress always assuming that this would lead them to their quarry.

Joe and the Russian were in position to pick up the pair as they left the University building. It had been agreed that the Russian would follow the Professor and Joe would follow Anna.

Anna left first and Joe almost missed her. She was with two other women, one her own age and

In Pursuit of the Red Kite

the other middle aged. If they had not been going in different directions and had not spent a moment or two in a parting conversation then Joe would almost certainly have lost her.

She walked and Joe again got out of his car and followed on foot. In a side street some minutes later Anna unlocked her car while Joe found himself in a predicament. "Shit!" he cursed aloud. He was on foot, she would soon be driving off and his car was parked some distance away. Anna's car was facing him therefore she would be headed back to the main street. He turned and ran back. As soon as he was on the main thoroughfare he began looking anxiously for a cab.

His luck held. As he flagged one down Anna's car appeared at the junction and indicated she would be turning ahead of his cab.

"Where to?"

"The white car in front, keep it in sight."

"Are you police?"

Joe ignored the question and concentrated his gaze on the car in front. The journey continued in silence until some ten minutes later Anna pulled up outside her apartment.

"Drive past" ordered Joe as his car slowed. He turned to look through the rear window in time to see Anna locking her car door.

"Pull over round the next corner."

The driver did as instructed.

"How much is that?"

"Zwansig Schilling Danke."

Joe gave him a reasonable sized tip and was aware of the man's curiosity as he got out of the cab and walked towards the corner where he stopped, turned and stared back at the cab which hadn't moved.

As if realising that there was no more to be seen or gained here the driver put his car into gear and pulled away. He reckoned he would be able to give the police a good description of Joe should he read of any funny business being reported.

The light was beginning to fade to dusk as Joe approached Anna's apartment. Another entry-phone system protected the dweller from any visitor. Joe studied the list of occupants. There on the second floor was an A. Frieberg. Joe assumed it was unlikely this was the wrong flat as there were no other residents with the initial 'A'. He presumed the daughter was unmarried.

As he walked away from the apartment he telephoned the Russian who reported that Hans had gone straight home. The Russian agreed to come over and pick him up and take him back to his car. That way Joe could show him where Anna lived.

As it would seem suspicious in a quieter area for two men, one in riding leathers, to study the premises, Joe had said he would be outside the apartment entrance. He would mount the motorcycle and they would leave.

While waiting for his lift Joe circled the apartment block. There was no private parking and a secondary rear exit led to a small courtyard where there were unused drying areas and a much used rubbish container. This courtyard exited into a lane that led back to the street where Joe had paid the cab.

When Joe got back to his own vehicle he noticed the red warning light was showing on the recorder. There was conversation going on within the Doktor's apartment. When the light went out Joe replaced the tape with a spare. He took the recording back to his hotel bedroom.

There he played it but it was only a short message between father and daughter. Hans would be half an hour late picking her up for dinner at around eight o'clock. Good, thought Joe, that will give us the opportunity to bug her apartment before she returns later tonight.

Over an early dinner with the Russian they agreed that rather than risk someone noticing regular appearances by a motorcyclist and hire car at the Doktor's and his daughters apartments they would need to vary their routine.

It was agreed that Joe would break into the apartment and place the bugs.

At eight thirty as he approached the building on foot. He parked his car at the end of the lane leading off the courtyard. He felt confident that Anna was unlikely to keep a dog as he had seen a notice inside the common hall saying pets were forbidden in this development.

Before trying the entry phone entry routine Joe went through the back to the courtyard and tried the rear exit door. Over the years, due to much usage it no longer automatically closed itself and the careless tenant did not always ensure it was properly closed as was the case this evening.

Joe found himself in a short corridor that led to a flight of stairs which connected the main hall and lift lobby at each level.

In time he remembered that on the Continent the second floor was the home equivalent to first floor.

Getting in was no more difficult to Joe than getting into Anna's fathers flat.

He had decided to place three bugs, one in the kitchen, one in the bedroom and one near the phone.

Once inside Joe had opened the curtains in order to obtain as much light as he could to assist him. He did not want to put on the lights and risk someone noticing.

When he had finished he closed the curtains.

It was in the bedroom that he knocked against a small table and he heard something hit the floor. Thankfully whatever it was it didn't sound as if it had broken. It was a photograph of two people. He took it to the window, his curiosity aroused, and was able to see a smiling couple in the Prater Gardens. They were surrounded by the halo of the giant Ferris wheel. The girl was Anna, her male companion, a boyfriend or relative.

Joe sat in his car wondering how to get to Alan before the Russian if they managed to pick up his trail. In fact it was imperative that he did so as having now met Dimitri he was convinced that the Russian's orders were to eliminate his friend. Secondly would he be able to persuade Alan that he should return to the UK and possible safety? If Alan had believed the UK a safe haven then surely he would have gone back there. He looked at his watch, it was approaching ten. He had promised to meet up with the Russian in the bar at ten thirty to discuss the evening's progress. He started up the car and pulled slowly out into the evening traffic which soon built up as he got closer to the hotel. Joe was a worried man, he needed time to think and he didn't have any.

At the hotel the Russian confirmed that the Doktor and his daughter had eaten alone and showed little interest as Joe simply told him that the devices had been installed in Anna's apartment.

Joe would use the time between now and a possible reappearance of Alan to think up a plan of action.

Before they departed for the night they agreed that they would go to the University the following morning and meet with the professor.

The next morning they took a cab to the

University and, having paid off the driver, made their way to the main entrance. Inside there were students and tutors of all ages rushing to and fro. There was a reception where a harassed woman was fending off a group of what Joe presumed were students. Dimitri took his arm and nodded to a signboard that indicated where the various departments were to be found.

Nuclear physics appeared to be the most likely and with an air of familiarity for the University's layout both headed for the lift to the second level. As they came out of the lift a further sign facing them directed them to the right. At the end of the corridor the space opened out to form a reception area.

There were two desks, one with a sign that said reception at which a matronly Frau Hecht was sitting.

She watched the men approach with a look of enquiry on her face. "Gentlemen how may I help you."

"We have come to see Professor Freiberg." said Dimitri.

"Doktor Freiberg." corrected Frau Hecht. "Have you an appointment?" she asked, although she knew full well that there was nothing in Han's diary for that morning and he was in his office catching up on paperwork.

With a note of exasperation in his voice Dimitri said, "No. But I am sure he will see us as we have a matter of importance to discuss with him." His attitude did not win him any favours with Frau Hecht.

"And may I ask what it is about?"

"It is an entirely private matter and is of no concern of yours."

Frau Hecht reddened but decided she would not risk any more questions just in case there was good reason for the visit by the two men. She picked up her phone and rang through to Hans and briefly explained that she had two men wishing to speak with him on an undisclosed matter which they said was important. She made the last statement sound questionable.

When she had hung up she nodded towards the door to Han's office. As the pair made their way towards the office door it opened and Hans stood back for them to enter.

"Gentlemen please take a seat." He indicated the plastic stacking chairs set in front of his desk.

The pair sat as directed.

"Now, how may I help you?" Hans asked with a smile.

This time it was Joe who spoke first not wishing to put the Doktor's back up early in their conversation following the Russians approach with the Doktor's secretary.

"We are trying to locate one of our employees who seems to have gone missing," Joe began, "and we are aware that he may be visiting Vienna."

"And you think I may be able to assist you?" asked Hans. "Before I do, however, I would like to see some identity or authority which gives you the right to seek this information."

Harry had anticipated just such a reaction and had provided Joe with a letter, on government headed paper, which he now produced and handed to the Doktor.

Hans took his time in reading it before giving Dimitri a questioning look.

The Russian did not look pleased and made no attempt to hide it before also producing a similar letter from his government.

Eventually satisfied, Hans handed their letters back.

"How may I help you?" Hans look took in both of them.

"Well we know that he studied here and that you were his tutor."

"When was this?"

"About two years ago."

"I'm sure you realize that I have a lot of new students every year and it is not possible to remember them all. Anyway try me with his name, who knows maybe I will remember him." He realized that this was probably the visit he had hoped would never happen and knew that whatever he said would need to satisfy these two if he were to feel safe for both himself and Anna. He remembered that Alan said it would do no harm if he stuck to the truth and told all he knew. It still felt however that he would be letting Alan down.

"His name is Alan Marks." said Joe.

Hans looked down for a moment before replying. "Yes, I have seen him. But not for a week or so." He hoped this small lie would give Alan a little more time to get clear of Vienna and disappear into France. Anna had told her father that Alan had taken a plane to Paris.

"Did he say why he wanted to meet you?" asked the Russian.

"Yes, two reasons. The first was fairly straightforward, for a reference, and the second was to advise me that he had written a report to you," he looked at Joe, "as his employer, who I understand, required a report of his recent activities. " He looked questioningly at Joe.

"That's correct." Replied Joe who had no idea that a report had been sent to MI6 if indeed that were the case.

Joe hoped his expression did not give him away but this report, if it existed, may provide a useful lead to Alan's whereabouts. He would need to ask Harry when next they spoke.

"Do you have a copy?" asked Dimitri.

"No," replied Hans. "He copied it onto a CD which I assume he kept with him."

"What about the computer file?" asked Joe

"Oh no, he asked my daughter to delete it from her computer as she had kindly typed it out for him. Which, of course, she did. He said he would be posting the CD to his office in London, for their eyes only." the Doktor added, "so I'm afraid I'm unable to help you there." Dimitri looked at Joe. He clearly did not believe Hans inability to produce a copy of the report and was frustrated by the answers he was getting.

"Do you know where he is now?"

"All I know is my daughter saw him off to Paris but he gave us no idea what his future plans were and we made no arrangements to see him again."

Dimitri stood up "Thank you Doktor."

Joe got up looking somewhat surprised at Dimitri's action. Obviously he felt there was nothing more to gain from Hans. He shook the Doktor's hand and said that they may be back if they thought there could be something else that Hans could help them with.

Back in reception they saw that the other desk was occupied by Anna who looked openly suspicious of them. She got up and strode into her father's office closing the door behind her.

Dimitri nudged Joe. "Go to the loo."

Joe asked Frau Hecht where he could find the toilets. She directed down the corridor past the lifts.

In his office Hans mouthed to Anna, "pretend we are having an argument about having told the two agents Alan had flown to Paris."

Outside Dimitri listened intensely as Hans suspected.

In Pursuit of the Red Kite

After the agents had left Anna asked her Dad, "What was that all about?"

"I suspect that Alan relied on us to tell them where he was headed."

"Why?" said Anna although as she asked, realized the purpose behind Alan's actions.

Hans smiled as he saw that Anna had bought into the deception. "I imagine that's the last place he is headed for. Did you see him check in?

"No he said an open ticket and wasn't sure of the next flight out. So I came away," replied Anna.

It was agreed that Joe would try and keep an eye on the Doktor and his daughter's movements while Dimitri would get in touch with his office and get them to check all flights to Paris over the last three weeks. Like Hans he suspected it would turn out to be a dead lead. He was however convinced that the Doktor and his daughter knew more than they were saying. Perhaps a little more pressure needed to be applied. He may need to request another pair of hands as he believed Joe would not go along with him on that approach.

Joe reported into Harry on what he had learned that morning and asked whether a report had turned up. Being told that nothing had arrived he suggested that maybe if Alan had a solicitor then maybe that is where the CD might be headed.

Harry said he would look into it at his end. In the meantime told Joe to try and persuade Anna that if there was an open link between her and Alan then she should warn him of the fact that they wanted to protect him whereas they were fairly sure the Russians wanted him eliminated. Get her to take a note of your mobile even though she will probably say she has no way of contacting Alan.

To do this Joe knew it would have to be away from either her's or her father's apartments as the Russian would know what he was up to once the bugs picked up the conversation.

The Russian agent had decided to follow his own agenda. He knew that he and the Englishman would not work well together. He had no intention of sharing any information should he come across Alan Marks when Joe was not there.

Earlier that morning he and Joe had sat in a small coffee house opposite the entrance to Hans' flat and as the Doktor had exited the apartment block Joe had pointed him out.

The Russian, who was already wearing his biking leathers, picked up his helmet and left the cafe. He had followed the Doktor to the University and seen him enter.

Joe had left the café ten minutes later, located the Doktor's apartment from the lobby and with little difficulty had broken in and installed the listening devices. Now all they could do was wait.

As with all surveillance work there are many hours of sheer tedium and the Russian felt this was to be no exception. As a man of action, he found working outside the old USSR extremely frustrating. He had been told in no uncertain terms that he must cause no political embarrassment and handle the case only as directed.

As he sat astride his motorcycle in a side street adjacent to the University from where he had a good view of the main entrance, he speculated on how he would have handled a similar situation back home. He would have had a team of operatives watching every entrance for a start and if after a couple of days nothing had transpired he would have had the Doktor taken in for a little subtle questioning. After the man had been taken from his flat in the small hours and then left for the day in some basement cell to allow him time to explore his own imagination he would have been only too prepared to talk. He sighed, he could never quite understand how it was that the West continued to maintain a good living while the Russian Empire had crumbled.

CHAPTER 30

November 1993

Before leaving Berlin Alan decided that he would email Anna saying that she could remain in contact if she wished. Then having deliberated long and hard he decided that he would phone her first. He also made some additional copies of the CD and sent one off to his solicitor in Colchester with instructions to place it with his will.

He had signed in at the hotel as Paul Gerhardt but the person leaving was to be known as Marc Schwarz.

It was as Marc that he would take the train to Amsterdam Centraal. His new worry was that he had made an enemy of Zeigler and depending on how he took the loss of a henchman, may have endangered his latest identity. There was nothing he could do about that now.

At Berlin Hauptbanhof he purchased a cheap mobile which he would throw away after speaking to Anna. He hoped that anyone chasing him had not got onto his link with the Freiberg's but he would take as few chances as possible from now on.

At the station he found himself a reasonably quiet location having first bought himself a coffee. He decided to give Anna a call at the University where Frau Hecht put him through. He thought it best not to mention his encounter in Berlin.

In Pursuit of the Red Kite

"I'm glad you rang me here" she said.

"Oh, why?" said Alan slightly puzzled.

"Well, I have not mentioned it to Dad, but I think I have had a visitor in the flat."

"What makes you think that?"

"I don't know exactly. Intuition? Paranoia? I could well be wrong, it's just that some items seem to have been moved. Nothing is missing. But you know how it is when you leave things in certain positions and the next time you see them something doesn't look right. The degree of movement can be quite small but somehow you know it's not where you left it."

"Yes" agreed Alan his mind racing. "Can you give me a for instance?"

"Yes, a photograph of me and my cousin at the Prater?"

"Yes?"

"Yes. Well I had it at the front of my bedside table. Now it's towards the back."

"Anything else?"

"Oh similar minor things in the kitchen and by the telephone I think." She paused. "Look I'm not 100% certain, but last night when I walked into the flat I felt odd. Not in danger exactly but that someone else had been there."

Alan knew only too well that intuition should

not be lightly dismissed but wondered if maybe the stress of the situation was beginning to play tricks on her imagination.

"Has Hans had his flat entered, do you know?"

"He hasn't said but it's usually such a mess he'd only notice if an intruder tidied it up for him," she laughed in an attempt to lighten the situation.

"Hold on let me think about this for a minute."

He sat staring at the phone. Were they all beginning to imagine things, he wondered. Why, if it had been entered, had they chosen her apartment. It could only be because someone's suspicions had been raised in Moscow and the Professor was under surveillance. Of course it made sense if the KGB and MI6 were desperate to follow any possible lead that might trace him.

He thought again of Zeigler but the timing was wrong. It seemed that any intruder must have entered the flat at about the same time as he had met the forger in Berlin, therefore the two couldn't be linked. The most Zeigler had learned was that he needed another identity. The reason why had never been discussed. He mentally crossed out the Berliner and came back to Hans' trip to Moscow as being the only possible connection.

He convinced himself that theft had not been the reason the flat had been entered. He had not said anything to Anna but his real concern had been aroused when she said she had thought the photograph had been moved. Which, in turn, meant that her flat was being watched, and probably bugged.

He put these thoughts to one side as he considered what else he may do if he were the hunter and not the quarry.

Almost certainly they had bugged the phone and installed listening devices to keep any possible contacts under surveillance.

Without the aid of electronic sweeping equipment they would never be sure that all devices could be found. He had to assume Anna's flat was compromised and for that matter Hans' also. Maybe he could use this to his advantage.

"Alan, are you still there?"

"Sorry I was trying to think if we could use this to send them off on a fool's errand." he replied.

It had not gone unnoticed by Anna that Alan had said 'We'

"So what are WE going to do?" she asked.

"I'm going to get us some insurance" he said.

"How?"

"I will email you tomorrow."

They discussed what his future plans might be without any real decisions being made.

"Alan, have you considered going into hiding again?" she asked.

"Yes, but only as a last resort. Having recently got out I have no real desire to become incarcerated again." He tried to sound more positive than he felt. "Look I'm going to hang up now and will contact you tomorrow."

"Yes. Speak to you later." As she cradled the phone she caught Frau Hecht's eye. Nothing was spoken but the look said 'I think you should not get so involved.'

When Anna left work there was a light drizzle of rain in the air and she walked with head bowed to where her car was parked. So she was startled when she heard a voice and looked up to see a man standing alongside the vehicle.

"Miss Freiberg. May I have a word with you?"

She recognised Joe as one of the men who had visited her father.

"What do you want?"

"Did your father tell you the reason for our meeting with him."

"Only that you were trying to trace an ex-pupil of his." she replied cautiously.

"Well I'm not sure how to convince you of

what I have to say and I don't wish to alarm you either but if you can help me it will also help Alan."

"How's that?

Joe noticed that she did not ask who Alan was.

"My employers, who are also Alan's, need to get in touch with him urgently."

"Why?"

"I'm afraid I am unable to go into the detail but I can tell you it is on behalf of the UK government." Joe replied.

Anna was unsure as to whether or not she was hearing the truth from this man.

Joe sensed her indecision and pressed on. "It could be a matter of life or death." he added.

To Anna this did not come as a great surprise, but for it to be said out loud increased the worry that had been building up inside her since Alan had departed.

"OK, suppose I believe what you say. How do I know that I can trust you and that I am not increasing any danger that Alan may already be in?"

"The reason I am talking to you here without my colleague is that he works for another power who also have an intcrest in contacting Alan. I am not so sure that their interests coincide with mine, which is to ensure that Alan is safe."

Anna decided that she would go along with

Joe's wish as she could see that whatever followed could not increase the danger to Alan and it might only improve his chances of survival. "Just suppose that Alan should contact me what do I tell him?"

"Tell him what I have just told you and that my name is Joe, his former sergeant

in the SAS. Here, give him my phone number." Joe passes Anna a slip of paper on which he has written his number. "And ask him to contact me."

Anna said nothing. So Joe added "I can do no more than ask for your help. Should you be able to pass my message on it is then up to Alan as to what he decides. But do warn him of other interests in his welfare."

"OK," said Anna. "And I take it we did not have this conversation and your colleague is not to know."

Joe smiled his thanks and turned and walked off into the rain which had become heavier as they had talked.

Anna got into her car but did not start it up immediately. She wanted to sit and consider what she had just heard and what effect it may have on both her and her father because like it or not they seem to have been drawn into Alan's future survival.

As he travelled towards Holland Alan had time to consider what his followers knew of his whereabouts. How large a surveillance team was there? Alan was fairly convinced it would be a small unit, two to three men only. He conjectured that maybe they had had Anna's apartment under surveillance but because it had coincided with his trip to Berlin they knew that he was not staying there. Either they had been misdirected to Paris or they were relying on the listening devices to divulge his latest whereabouts.

He had the Beretta wrapped in a watertight wrap in his holdall and he had to get the gun across the border into Holland. He was aware that there were likely border checks and this proved to be the case. Fortunately he had anticipated the problem and purchased a roll of tape before boarding the train. He chose a seat alongside the aisle in an almost empty compartment so he was able to take out the wrap unnoticed. As the train approached the border into Holland he took the package into the toilet at the end of the carriage. He closed the door and took out the roll of tape and taped the package behind the toilet, at floor level. He stepped back. It was not visible and would only be discovered if someone were deliberately looking for something.

It was the best he could do. If discovered at least it would not be connected to him.

Luck was with him, Customs Officers got on at the border and went through his compartment and checked all passengers papers and opened some luggage including Alan's holdall.

As soon as they had left and the train continued on its way, Alan quickly retrieved the package and put it back in the holdall. There were no further interruptions to his journey.

Alan's email to Anna had been short. He had told her that he was on the move again and had told her that he had told the hotel he had left that morning that he was going on a walking holiday in the Austrian Tirol and that he had left no forwarding address. He did not tell her that he had been staying in Berlin although he had convinced himself that his visit would be traced.

Dimitri was frustrated and had little to report to Moscow and had nothing further to add that might verify whether they were targeting the right individuals or following a dead end. He had been told to give it another week and continue to check with HQ every other day unless something specific turned up.

His luck was to change however. In Berlin Zeigler's man's body had been discovered and the police were looking for the murderer. His bar had been visited and he had been questioned. He told the police that the victim was a frequent visitor to the bar but that he did not know where the man had lived or what he did. The police did not believe that was all Ziegler knew but were unable to gain any more information from him.

One of Zeigler's underworld contacts called into his bar that same morning and in the course of their conversation mentioned that he had heard that the Russians were looking for a Paul Gerhardt. If he came across him it may be worth something. The man smiled as he said this as it was general knowledge in the underworld that the Russians were extremely poor payers.

Zeigler had smiled but said nothing. After his contact had left Zeigler shut himself in his office to consider what he now knew. He could avenge his man and at the same time strengthen his links with the Russians who still had a strong influence in Berlin in both legal and illegal matters.

This time he would be the helpful citizen. He picked up the phone and rang the Russian Consulate. After being passed through several offices a voice enquired how could they be of help.

Zeigler replied that he understood that he had heard that they were interested in finding a Paul Gerhardt and that he may be able to help.

"Excuse me a moment" the aide said and put Zeigler on hold.

When he came back it was to ask where a contact from his office could visit Zeigler who gave him the address of the bar. He was told that someone would call round and see him later that morning.

At just before midday two men in long overcoats arrived at the Bar and asked for Zeigler who had watched them enter. He got up introduced himself and led them into his office. Once inside they removed their outer coats to reveal identical dark grey suits, white shirts and nondescript ties.

They did not introduce themselves and simply said they were from the Russian Consulate to pursue the call Zeigler had made.

Neither smiled as Zeigler took in their appearances and it was the older man with greying hair at the temples who was to do the talking.

"You know this Paul Gerhardt?" he asked.

"Yes but not well." replied Zeigler who went on to add "I do not know him well but over the years he has called into this bar when he is in Berlin usually in the name of Alan Marks.

"And that's how you know his name?"

"Yes."

"What else do you know about him?"

"That's it except that I believe I heard him tell my barman that he would be leaving today to take a walking holiday in the Austrian Tirol." replied Zeigler.

"Where exactly."

"I did not hear more."

"Would your barman be of any more help?"

"No, I have already asked him once I knew it may be of interest to you."

Zeigler didn't know why but something about the Russians' presence was making him uncomfortable.

The younger of the two turned and muttered something to his companion which Zeigler could not pick up despite having a reasonable understanding of the language.

The older man grunted by way of reply and turned back to Zeigler.

"Herr Zeigler we are not sure you are telling us everything you know about this man."

Zeigler found himself breaking into a sweat "Well there was something else but it was something my barman thought he saw Paul Gerhardt looking at while he was sitting alone at the Bar."

"And that was?"

"He said it looked like another passport. Austrian he said."

"What else?"

"It was in the name of Marc Schwarz but he was reasonably sure the photo was that of Paul Gerhardt."

"Should we talk to this barman of yours?"

"He will not be back again before the weekend."

"How convenient." said the Russian taking no care to hide his sarcasm. He turned to look at his colleague and nodded. They both rose to leave.

"We may be back to talk to you again Herr Zeigler and next time it would be wise to have your barman available."

"I understand," replied Zeigler who hoped that occasion did not arise and as for seeking a closer connection to the Russians, he now felt that that would be a seriously wrong move.

Joe having retrieved the recordings from Anna's and Han's apartment's, had taken them back to the hotel. Having played them he realised that there was no further information from those sources than they already knew. What was now paramount was to obtain a copy of the report. What had not come to light was the fact that in addition to the CD, Hans still had the recordings of his conversations while at the seminar in Moscow.

Joe was therefore of the opinion that the Freiberg's were of little more use. With that he rang the Russian's room on the Intercom and suggested that he come over and listen to the latest recordings for himself.

The Russian listened in silence and then asked Joe to replay them. By the time the Russian had heard them for the second time he had become angry.

"This is getting us nowhere."

"What do you think we should do?" Joe asked him.

"I must report to Moscow and get their instructions," said the Russian.

"OK, I'll contact my people although I'm fairly sure I know what they'll say" said Joe.

"What's that?"

"That we should get some evidence that a CD exists and continue to follow any leads on Alan's whereabouts."

The Russian had calmed down a little. "I suppose you're right. There's not much else we can do, is there?"

"No," said Joe "as I see it there isn't."

"Right," said the Russian, "let's assume those are our orders, how do we go about it?"

"We still need to find where he went from here. One thing I am certain of it is not Paris."

"Then how about we abduct the girl," said the Russian, "that will ensure the father's attention and if there is any further information they are holding back

that should bring it out."

"Yes," said Joe rather dubiously "you're probably right."

"And I suggest we do it as soon as possible."

"We will need to find somewhere to hold her, somewhere she won't be found too easily," said Joe.

"Then tomorrow I suggest we find a suitable place. They are aware of our interest in them and I suspect they will try to continue with their lives much as normal." suggested Dimitri. "Tomorrow is Friday, they'll be at the University. If we pick her up on the way home we have all weekend for your man Gregori to come up with any evidence as to where to find this Alan Marks."

Dimitri had earlier decided to tell Joe that they had been given another pair of hands to help out. "Where is he?" Joe had asked but Dimitri had said it was better if they were not seen together and would not let Joe have any details. As there was little Joe could do in the circumstances, he had to accept it.

They agreed they would each speak with their respective leaders before abducting Anna but neither saw that there was likely to be any resistance to the suggestion. They would be cautioned not to cause a diplomatic problem, but both knew their leaders would be paying lip service to their masters in the matter.

All that was about to change. Dimitri

received a call from Moscow while in his room prior

to going down to the restaurant for dinner. The call was from Andrei who told of the break- through in Berlin and that the new name to search for was a Marc Schwarz who was on a walking holiday in the Austrian Tirol. Dimitri listened but from past experience believed that would be the last place they would find their quarry. He thanked Andrei but said he wanted the watch kept on all flight listings and at all borders to be maintained and that he be kept up to date.

CHAPTER 31
November 1993

Dimitri, having considered the contents of his conversation, decided not to tell Joe immediately of what he had learned. He decided that he would still go ahead with the abduction but use the additional man on his team to carry out his plan.

Next morning saw the Russians driving through the quieter parts of the city. They were looking for a small warehouse or office that would be closed and was too small to warrant major security installations or surveillance

It was nearly midday before they spotted a likely candidate. It was a small factory with a yard to the side and with offices over the front. There was also a loading dock on the side and adjacent to it was a door which they discovered led to a boiler room.

It would well serve their purpose without the need of entering the main building. Neither of them found any alarms or security systems on the premises.

They parked the car and walked past the building. The street was quiet and there were only a couple of vans and a car parked nearby to indicate that there might be other people around. It had been a milk servicing depot but now seemed unoccupied, even the gate that once closed the yard off from the road was unused. It had been locked back open at sometime in the past before dropping on its hinges and sitting permanently on the ground. Their biggest problem was going to be one of timing. Anna usually left the University at around 4.30 to 5.00pm, which meant they would need to be sure that the intended prison was suitable and be back in time to snatch Anna on her way home.

They could not afford to delay the operation to the following week or risk trying to abduct Anna from her apartment. Therefore they would need a daylight entry to the factory. It was agreed Gregori would wait in the car and that Dimitri would break in to the boiler room. His assistant sat with the car window open listening for any alarm bells. If there were any, he was to drive into the yard, pick up Dimitri and be clear before any police arrived. It was an unnecessary precaution. Within twenty minutes Dimitri had returned and, as they drove away, he told Gregori that the boiler room had not been secured by the previous owner before their departure, probably because it did not lead directly into any other part of the premises. At least it was dry. They would however need to provide some temporary sanitation and at least a chair and bed if they were to hold their hostage for any length of time.

In London at MI6, Harry was called into Sir Ian's office.

"You wanted to see me?"

"Yes sir. I got a call last night from Joe in

Vienna on this "Red Kite" matter. It seems they have not yet made contact with our man."

Sir Ian's mind raced. "Complications?" he asked Harry.

Amanda who had been sitting ready to take dictation had discreetly left the office closing the door behind her.

"Yes. It seems that Alan has produced a CD on which it tells the whole story of what happened in Iraq. It has been prepared for publication in the event of anything unnatural happening to him."

"Do we have any proof?"

"Not yet. Our man asked for instructions and I suggested he obtain a copy if possible."

"When will we get it?"

"Therein lies the problem, I don't know for sure. It may be necessary for a little more pressure to be applied on the Doktor to extract more information. Also we need to know what exactly it is Alan wants."

Sir Ian stared distractedly at some distant point. "His skin," was all he said.

Harry sat waiting. He knew the signs and procedure. Sir Ian would be considering the political implications of the matter and would be seeking to ensure that his political masters be involved in any decision making. This problem was best shared.

Sir Ian reached for the phone and asked Amanda to connect him to Moscow. As he waited for the call to come through he decided to dismiss Harry.

Just in case there was any future "misunderstanding" of the conversation.

"Yuri?"

"Yes Sir Ian. So you have heard about the damned SAS man?"

"I have. What is the view at your end?"

"I am seeing the deputy president later this morning. What is the British view?"

"Like you we will be discussing it. But I suspect it will be a case of let us wait and see what the demands are."

Sir Ian did not need this, he thought to himself. "How did they discover the documents existed," he asked simply.

"Not only did they interview the couple but they placed listening devices in the Professor's and the girl's apartments" said the Russian, somewhat puzzled by the question. "Why?"

"Well," said Sir Ian, "remember that our quarry is also a trained professional. What if he discovered the devices and has told you a story to play for time to get away."

The Russian was no longer amused. "Maybe, Sir Ian. Time will tell." He cursed the English Knight as he hung up the telephone and roared for Andrei. He would vent his anger on someone.

Sir Ian felt it was a hollow victory. At the end of the day it made no difference. They would have to follow it up and hope that Alan had not already departed leaving his friends to face the music.

He called Amanda on the Intercom. "I need a few minutes with the P.M's secretary," he said. "Tell him it's urgent."

Sir Ian was expected. The door to number 10 opened as he got out of his car and crossed the pavement. He was greeted by the policeman on duty with a small salute which he ignored.

"Come in Sir Ian." The PM's secretary had a questioning smile of welcome as Sir Ian rose from his seat in reception to enter his office. Once inside and seated he reminded himself that it was an urgent matter.

Sir Ian had the grace to look slightly uncomfortable as he gave a brief resume on the current situation regarding "Red Kite". Throughout the P.P.S. said nothing but looked increasingly concerned at what he was hearing.

When Sir Ian had finished he said, "Thank you Sir Ian. I will need to acquaint the Prime Minister of the situation. Please keep me closely informed."

As Sir Ian got up to leave the P.P.S. added "Oh by the way, I think we should try and ensure nothing happens to "Red Kite" don't you?"

"Most certainly." agreed Sir Ian taking his

leave.

As the door closed the P.P.S. allowed himself a rare show of frustration. "Damned Politicians. Now Alan had to kept alive!"

CHAPTER 32
November 1993

Anna looked into her father's office before she left the University, it was ten to five and the Professor would be there for at least another hour, he told her, before he left for the weekend.

They would not see each other until Sunday lunch time when they would be driving out of the capital to a village inn for some food and relaxation.

Anna had bought food at lunchtime for an evening meal at home. She was in a good mood as she left the University and made her way to the side street in which she had parked her car. It was only as she turned into the street that she was aware of footsteps behind her and as she turned a man came alongside and said "Anna Freiberg?"

She stopped. "Yes what do you want?"

"There is a matter I need to discuss with you." As he saw recognition dawn upon her he also saw her expression change from one of enquiry to one of fear as he added, "It concerns our mutual friend, Alan Marks."

Anna did not know whether to bluff out the situation by pretending she did not know what he was talking about, but felt that her reactions had already told the lie to that. Not only that but she knew she had been seen by this man at the university when he had met her father.

"What is it you want to discuss?"

In Pursuit of the Red Kite

"Not here. I have a car parked in front of yours."

"Oh Hell," thought Anna, "if he knows my car, what doesn't he know?" She was now genuinely frightened.

She walked with Dimitri to his car and it was only as he opened the front passenger door to let her in that she saw a shape sit up in the back seat as a second man appeared.

As she turned to make a run, more on impulse than for any other reason, she felt a hard object pressed into her side.

"Don't even think about it," Dimitri warned her. "Get in."

She did as she was told as the man behind her spoke for the first time. "I have a gun trained on the centre of your spine and I don't want to be forced to use it should you try anything stupid."

Despite her fear Anna knew these were the men out to trap or kill Alan. What could she do? At the moment, nothing. She sat and cursed herself at how easily and without any fuss she had been picked off the street.

They made no attempt to blindfold her or tie her up for which Anna was grateful. The journey, which lasted about ten minutes, was completed in silence and Anna knew roughly where she was in relation to the City. As they turned off the main thoroughfare though and entered the back streets she soon lost her sense of direction.

At the depot they drove the car straight in and pulled up at the boiler room door. Anna was told to get out and was taken into the boiler room where she was told to sit on an old wooden chair. The rest of the space contained a cheap put-you-up bed covered with a coarse blanket, a bucket which was empty and a large carafe of water. On a small table was a plastic mug. They warned her that if she called for help it was unlikely that any one would hear. If she was heard and managed to escape and contact the police, then it would be the worse for her father. Anna believed them.

The two men stood back.

"I'm not going to insult your intelligence by telling you won't be hurt provided you do as you're told. It goes without saying." Dimitri paused. "I will tell you what you have to do if you want to see your father again."

Anna's gaze flickered between the two men. The other, whose name she was not going to hear, said nothing. She was more frightened of him than Dimitri whose eyes did not have the same dispassionate coldness as his colleagues.

"The man, your friend Alan Marks," he continued," has, I believe, produced a report on a certain incident in which he was involved some years ago and which my Government is anxious to read." He waited for corroboration on what he had learned from Anna's father earlier but Anna said nothing "OK," he continued, "you, or your father, need to persuade him that your safety depends on my getting a copy of that report and that he remains contactable until he receives further instructions."

Anna found her voice. "How do you propose I do that?"

Dimitri pulled out a mobile phone. "Give me the number" he demanded.

Anna told them that when Alan had left it was without giving her a means of contact. She said she had asked for one but Alan had told her that it was for her own safety that there be no future contact.

The two men said no more but exchanged unbelieving looks. They took Anna's handbag and emptied it to see whether or not she had a mobile phone or some written record of events that might assist them. There was nothing to find. They left the boiler room without saying another word switching the light off as they went. They would let her worry as to what might happen next.

The Russians got into the car and drove it out of the depot to park up several streets away. They did not want to risk anyone investigating its presence in the yard.

As they sat in the car the Dimitri's assistant Gregori asked him "What's so important about this report, surely anything can be denied or suppressed?"

"I guess until they know what it says and how it's authenticated they will take no chances. Alan is only one man. He may have involved others who are looking to make money out of it also. Until we know what it's about, our governments cannot consider an effective damage limitation plan." Dimitri hit the steering wheel in frustration. "However ridiculous it might seem, at the moment we all have to play along. Alan is trying to save his own skin and so far it has worked. I have also been told to keep him alive at least for now."

His colleague shrugged as if to say he was used to his instructions being changed at short notice. "What's new," it implied.

At the same time and in London Harry initiated an independent course of action to that apparently being followed by Joe and Dimitri. He had put himself in Alan's position. What would he do to ensure that his name would be cleared if he were captured or, worse still, eliminated? What else would he do as well as changing his identity? He could go to ground and hole up until, at some future date, he would re-emerge when he believed any hunt had been called off. From there he could tell all and with the story exposed to the world his welfare would no longer be of any importance to anyone. Whether it was believed or not almost did not matter. Those who wished to damage the government would use it as a whip to beat the establishment.

"I have to believe that at the moment that is not the route he is going down," Harry told himself. "Where would I secure the evidence I am using as a bargaining factor?"

He remembered that they had the address of Alan's solicitor somewhere on file. It was with that thought that he had set into motion the next step. He would have the offices searched. This could not be done officially. It would have to be a burglary and, if discovered, it was extremely unlikely it would be traced back to the department. With that decided Harry felt better. Some action was better than doing nothing.

The following night Tony Treadwell's offices in Colchester were entered, the simple security system bypassed and his clients files inspected after the padlock on the security bar was picked and put to one side. The intruder found nothing of interest in Alan Marks' very thin file; but nor did he find a will which he considered odd. Surely there should be one somewhere. In the partner's office he found a small fireproof safe which was not so easy to access. He was however rewarded as among the wills it contained he found Alan's.

Tucked inside he found an untitled CD. He took it out and decided to risk booting up a PC to read its contents. Again he was in luck. He had found what he was looking for.

He shut down the computer, put Alan's will back with the others and relocked the fireproof safe. He carefully looked around to ensure that there was no evidence of entry. Lastly he replaced the locking bar on the general filing cabinet. He left the premises from the back, having first reactivated the alarm system. Unless someone specifically wanted to get Alan's CD out in the near future, it would not be missed.

While travelling to Amsterdam and on passing through open countryside Alan had gone to the toilet and thrown his mobile phone from the train. He would get another in Amsterdam on his arrival.

When he arrived at Amsterdam Centraal Alan decide that he could not stay at a hotel as throughout Europe it was necessary to be registered in and the passport retained. This made him more traceable and, on reflection, he wished he had been more careful in the recent past.

Outside the station he got into a cab and asked the driver if he could recommend a good B&B in the outskirts of the city. The driver was only too willing to oblige as, not only would he get a fare, but a commission from the owner of the B&B as well.

As in all major cities traffic was slow and it was some twenty minutes later before they pulled up outside a three story terraced house in the Plantage district of Amsterdam. The driver escorted him to the door rang the bell and when an elderly woman opened it he told her that if she had a room he had a client for her.

Alan did not interfere in their business transaction and when the driver turned smiling to face him Alan paid him the fare plus a generous tip.

Once inside Alan introduced himself as Marc Schwarz and they agreed they would converse in English as Alan's knowledge of Dutch was virtually non-existent.

Before showing him his room on the second level, his hostess led him down the hall towards the back of the house and showed him where he would take his breakfast. Between the Hours of 7.00 and 9.00 am, she informed him. She also asked him how long he might require the room. Alan was unsure himself but agreed to pay a week in advance and take it from there.

His room, in keeping with the rest of the house, was well maintained and apart from a wide single bed had a comfortable chair, a small table, some built in wardrobes and a small TV hung on the wall opposite the end of the bed. He would share a bathroom at the end of the landing with two other rooms on that floor.

The view from the window, to his pleasant surprise was across a canal towards the Hortus Botanicus gardens. This was a better view than he had had from any of the recent hotels he had stayed in since leaving the Friary.

When he'd unpacked and made himself comfortable and before leaving to go back into the city centre he taped his Beretta to the underside of the bed. He kept his knife strapped to his arm.

Walking along The Dam he found himself a shop selling cheap mobile phones and then found himself a quiet table in one of the older pubs on the street.

In response to his call all he got was the answer phone message on Anna's phone. He hung up and decided to give it half an hour and would try again. In the meantime he would sip his beer and watch the world go by.

An hour later there was again no response from his call to Anna. As he had no plans for the evening he decided to find somewhere to eat. He found a Thai restaurant on a barge on one of the many canals that surround the centre of Amsterdam and had a very enjoyable meal after which he tried Anna for the third time. Still no luck. He began to worry although he had no good reason to. She had her own life to lead and it was unlikely he would ever see her again.

Still he felt uneasy and decided that he ought to try and check and maybe make an unnecessary nuisance of himself. He rang Han's mobile.

It was picked up almost immediately

"Hello, Anna?"

"Hans, its Alan Marks here."

"Oh, I was hoping it was Anna. I've not heard from her which is most unlike her."

"I spoke to her yesterday evening and told her I would be phoning her today," Alan said, "but all I get is her answer phone." he said. "I know I should not expect her to stay in just because I was going to make contact. She's probably out with friends," he added.

Before they could take their conversation any further Hans said, "I have to go Alan there's a call on the land line," and he hung up.

Alan tried Anna one more time without luck and decided to return to his lodgings.

He would try again in the morning.

In England Harry received a call at home. He went into his study to take it. It was the agent who had broken into Alan's solicitor's office.

"Hello. McReady here."

"I believe my trip to Colchester was successful," his agent told him." I found a CD containing the report I think you are after."

"Can you get it to me ASAP?" Harry asked.

"Do you want me to put it in a cab?"

"No. Can you deliver it yourself?"

"Yes, Sir." the agent cursed to himself. Having been up all night he had hoped to get some sleep. He would now have to put that off for at least another couple of hours.

When he arrived Harry offered him coffee which he turned down with thanks. Both were relieved at the refusal. Harry so that he could read the report and the agent so that he could get home to his bed.

In his study Harry read through Alan's report before making a copy and calling for his driver. The copy was to be given to Sir Ian Rush.

After speaking to Alan Hans received a further call that night. The call he had taken was from an unknown source simply telling him that his daughter was being held captive and unless he told the caller the whereabouts of Alan Marks then he would not see her again. He was told that they would call back the following day and before he could ask any questions the caller hung up.

Hans had no way of contacting Alan and sharing the problem with him. Not that

Alan could necessarily help him.

Hans suspected that Anna's captors were the two men who had come to his office and he remembered that they had both left him contact numbers. He would phone each of them and threaten to go to the police tell them of the threat and give the police their numbers.

It was a hollow threat and, on reflection, it would almost certainly increase the danger to Anna. He had to do something. He would phone the one called Joe as he said he was a friend of Alan's, which may or may not be true. His instinct told him that the

Russian was not to be trusted in any way.

After spending most of the night worrying he rang Joe.

Having listened to the Doktor, Joe told him that he knew nothing about the abduction. He would see what he could find out and ring Hans back if he had any news. In the meantime he recommended that Hans told them everything he knew and could only hope it was sufficient to secure his daughters release.

After taking the call from Hans Joe immediately rung Dimitri .

"What the fuck are you up to," he demanded.

At the other end of the line he heard Dimitri laugh. "I think we need to put some pressure on them. I'm sure they know more than they are telling."

"And if they don't?"

"Then we release her of course," replied Dimitri.

"And why wasn't I told? This is supposed to be a joint operation."

"This way we are doing the good guy, bad guy routine and they might tell you more than me."

"What's the next move?" Joe demanded.

"We let the Doktor stew until the morning then we interrogate him at his home."   "I will be there," said Joe. He did not envy Anna's night in captivity.

"I don't think that would be a good idea," said

Dimitri you should remain the good guy."

Reluctantly Joe could see the sense of what was being said and agreed that he would stay away from the meeting with the Doktor on the understanding that Dimitri shared anything he learned and that Anna was not to be harmed.

Dimitri agreed he would. Joe no longer trusted Dimitri but at least knew that whatever was discussed would be picked up on the bugs he had placed in Hans flat.

When Alan phoned Hans the next morning, he had decided on a course of action to divert the attention of his pursuers from the Doktor and his daughter. But before Alan could begin, a frantic Hans informed him that he had received a call saying that Anna was being held and unless he was to disclose Alan's whereabouts then he would not see his daughter again. Alan immediately told Hans to give over the tape recordings he had made of the conversations in Moscow after making a second copy. As for the report there was no way Hans could provide a copy as Alan had taken all copies with him. Hans would just have to hope the abductors believed him as the men were unlikely to believe that copies of the report had not been made but at least they would know what additional information was available should Alan feel the need to make good his threat against The Establishment to ensure his own safety.

In Pursuit of the Red Kite

    Sir Ian had read Alan's report which Harry had handed to him as soon as he entered the office. On reading it Sir Ian came to the view that in the current political climate, if published, it would not harm the image of the UK or the Establishment and in fact there would be those who would applaud the feat. He decided that in view of his last conversation with the Prime Minister's Secretary he would speak to Yuri in Moscow and suggest that any activity against Alan Marks should be dropped.

    The Russian was not to be so easily persuaded until he had read the report for himself so Sir Ian agreed to forward him a copy and agreed that they would speak again later that day.

    During their later call it was agreed that should the whole affair become public knowledge it would not harm either country's image and the Russian told Sir Ian that he would be recalling his man. It was not Yuri who spoke to Dimitri but Andrei, to whom he delegated the task.

    It was an extremely frustrated Dimitri who then told Gregori that the whole operation was off and they were to return to Moscow.

    "What about the girl?" Gregori asked him.

    "We are to let her go."

In Pursuit of the Red Kite

"And the Doktor?"

"We do nothing. He will see his daughter soon enough," Dimitri replied with a shrug.

It was a little over half an hour later when they returned to release Anna, who had not enjoyed her time alone in the dark over the last 24 hours. Despite the coarse blankets she had been unable to sleep due the cold damp atmosphere of her prison.

They had agreed that they would not let her go until they were away from the depot.

They said nothing to her as they led her out of the boiler room. Gregori would take her back to the car while Dimitri relocked the premises, having first removed any sign of its occupation.

As Gregori led her by the arm to the car he heard another car approaching and looked up to see it coming towards him slowly on the opposite of the road. He took Anna round to the front passenger door and helped her get in. Looking back towards the depot there was no sign of Dimitri. He had walked round to the driver's door when the approaching car pulled up alongside him and the driver wound down the window.

"Excuse me"

Gregori turned and went over to the car where the driver seemed to be holding a map.

"Can I help?" he leant down to the window. As he did the map was whisked to one side and he found himself looking at a silencer. It was the last thing that registered in Gregori's brain before the

In Pursuit of the Red Kite

bullet tore into his head just above his right eye taking a large part of the rear of his skull with it as it exited.

His body was thrown backwards onto the road. Anna, who witnessed the incident, reacted instinctively in self- preservation, which she could not later explain to herself, opened her door and threw herself onto the pavement.

The killer was not interested in her however. He put his car into gear and drove off just as Dimitri came out from the depot and took in the scene of both Anna and Gregori lying on the ground; one on each side of the car. Only one of the bodies was moving. He rushed to Gregori and seeing there was nothing that could be done for him, went round at Anna who was getting up as he approached. She looked terrified and was shaking violently.

"Get in the car," he ordered, which she did without argument.

Dimitri went back to the body and removed all documents from his pockets together with his wallet he then got back into the car, put it into gear and drove off.

For Anna this was the stuff of fiction not real life.

"But what about your partner?"

"There's nothing we can do for him," Dimitri replied keeping his gaze on the road ahead.

"He can't be left there. Don't you care?"

This time Dimitri turned towards her as he asked, "What would you do in the circumstances. Call the Police?" he sneered, "and what good would that do us. We would be the only suspects. We would be arrested." he concluded.

They drove on in silence eventually broken by Anna.

"Why?"

"I have been wondering that too," replied Dimitri.

"And what do you think it's all about?" Anna said

Dimitri took his time in answering "Well it could be that whoever it was assumed Gregori was Alan because he saw the two of you together. Or if not, and its unlikely to be his own side, then there is a third party out there that has an interest in the demise of Mr Marks and we have lead them to him. Except, in this case, Gregori took the bullet meant for your friend.

The journey to Anna's apartment was completed in silence. On arrival Dimitri signalled for her to get out which she did before he leant across and handed her handbag to her before driving off.

Anna almost ran to her apartment and after fumbling for her keys let herself in. Once inside she locked and bolted herself in and it was then that the shock of the last half hour hit her. She started shaking and despite herself, burst into tears and leaning against the door slid down onto the floor where she stayed.

After a while she started thinking rationally

and realised her father must be beside himself with worry. She got up and went into the living room and picked up the phone. Hans picked up almost immediately.

"Anna is that you, where are you?"

"At home, Dad. They have let me go but I don't know why. What's happened?" she replied.

"Thank God, I have been so worried about you. They threatened me with your safety if I did not give them the whereabouts of Alan. Which, of course, I don't know. I did however get a call from him. He said I should give them the tape recordings I made in Russia and that might satisfy them. I thought your call was from them to say they were coming round here."

Anna told her father what had happened and how one of them had been shot and left on the road.

Hans said he was coming round and she should not to open her door to anyone else.

Dimitri was not looking forward to making the call to Yuri. The situation demanded that he make immediate contact and not leave it till his normal reporting in time.

Back in his room he got through to Andrei who reminded him that Yuri could only be connected if it was an emergency. Why was Dimitri calling he asked.

"It has nothing to do with you," snarled Dimitri "now if he's there put me through. Or I'll have words with you when I return to Moscow.

Andrei believed him. The threat was real. "Hold on I'll put you through."

Dimitri laughed. "Good. Just do it."

Yuri came on the line "Why are you trying to frighten my secretary. Is it important?" He sounded amused.

Dimitri told him what had happened in Vienna and the conclusion that he had come to. There was a another party interested in the death of Alan Marks "What have you done about Gregori?" asked Yuri

"I left him where he fell. I reasoned that way the police would think he was a tourist who had got into the wrong part of town and that it was a robbery that had gone bad," Dimitri replied.

"Well done, you made the right decision." Yuri told him. "Now I think you should get back here as soon as possible. As far as this case is concerned it's over."

Dimitri was not going to argue with his instruction to return to Moscow, however he was very aware that nothing about this operation had left him in a good light and he felt very concerned about his future.

In Pursuit of the Red Kite

When Hans arrived at Anna's apartment they both had hugged each other tightly for some minutes before going into the living room where Hans saw that she had been watching the television and had the news channel on.

Anna turned to her father and told him that the police had found the Russian's body and it was reported that a tourist had been found in a quiet industrial area of Vienna. He had been shot and killed. There was no obvious motive other than robbery as his documents and money had been taken. The body had been found by a dog walker, the report continued and the police were looking for any possible witnesses to come forward.

"What should I do Dad?" Anna asked her father.

"I'm not sure but my gut feeling is to do nothing," he replied. "In fact, after what they have put you through, I have no sympathy for him at all. I think we should stay well out of it. Is there any way you could be involved? Not unless Dimitri goes to the police although I doubt he will. No we do nothing." he concluded.

CHAPTER 33

November 1993

In Moscow Yuri sat pondering the situation in Vienna and at the loss of an agent. In his business it was not an unusual occurrence but could it have been avoided? He asked himself.

It was probably this feeling of self-guilt that made him decide to ring Sir Ian in London and tell MI6 what had happened in Vienna. It was possible that his opposite number already knew. That depended whether or not Dimitri had bothered to tell Sir Ian's man, Joe, of the situation before he left for home. Knowing his man he concluded that this was probably unlikely.

Yuri's reasoning was correct as when Harry, on Sir Ian's behalf, phoned a very frustrated Joe, he learned he had spent most of the day wandering around Vienna having heard nothing from Dimitri. He told Harry he had been unable to take in the beauty of this city as his mind was continuously elsewhere trying to think of ways to get hold of Alan Marks.

"What?" exploded Joe when he learned of the killing of their agent. "Those bloody Russians. Serves them right."

After he had vented his frustration at Harry's expense he said "What happens now, if anything," he added.

Harry told him that the Russians had pulled out of the operation as a shift in the political climate had meant that they no longer felt worried by Alan's threat of their involvement in the Iraq operation.

"However of more concern was why Gregori had been murdered," he told Joe. "The Russian's conclusion was that there was possibly someone else after Alan's life. So you see Joe it's still important that we find him and bring him in."

"Yes I can now see why you have now put me in the picture." The sarcasm wasn't lost on Harry. "Is it OK if I discuss your views with Hans and Anna?"

By way of explanation he told Harry that he felt that Anna was in contact with Alan. "I believe that he phones her although there is no way she can get back to him. In other words we are in the situation where we are awaiting his next call."

In London Harry looked at his watch. He was already late for his next meeting and did not want to prolong the discussion especially as he had no further information to hand. Before Joe could go any further, Harry said, "Yes, you should let the Doktor know what's going on. Look Joe I'm going to have to go now. Keep me abreast of any developments your end at any time and I will get back to you with anything I hear OK?"

"Yes sir," Joe replied as the line was disconnected.

Harry got up and walked over to the window

and once again watched the river traffic as he mulled over in his mind the latest turn of events. Now that the Russians had apparently pulled out of the operation, who could it be that had killed their agent? If it had been a random street robbery that had gone wrong then why had the killer chosen a quiet part of Vienna especially at the weekend when it was extremely unlikely that they would find a victim. No, Harry was convinced that the killer had knowledge of what had been taking place, had followed Dimitri and had assumed that Gregori had been Alan. Who was the third party? They obviously had inside information. Somewhere there was a leak.

The more he thought about it the more he was convinced it had to be at the Russian end as Joe had not been involved in the abduction of Anna.

He turned and went over to the door and opened it to see if Amanda was at her desk.

"Amanda. Is Sir Ian in? I need a word with him if he's free."

Amanda looked up from her computer and smiled. "He's in. I'll check to see if he's available."

Harry returned the smile and leant up against the door post while she phoned through on the intercom. In answer to her request she raised her eyes from her screen and indicated that Harry was free to enter.

"What is it Harry?"

"It's about the Red Kite case sir." Harry

replied. "The more I think about it the more I am convinced there has been a leak of information and that there is someone else out there who wants our man dead."

"And?"

"I also believe it's still to do with this operation but it may have become a personal vendetta."

"I'm not so sure," said Sir Ian. "I agree it does seem a little odd. Obviously the killer doesn't know what his victim looks like. Unless, of course, it was an internal falling out between agents. Unlikely," he added almost to himself. "One thing we now know is that whoever it was will be aware from the TV coverage that he has killed a supposed Russian tourist and not an Englishman. So it's now even more important that we persuade Red Kite to fly home," he smiled at his own play on words. Harry dutifully smiled back at his boss.

"Have we made any progress in making contact?"

"Not exactly," Harry replied.

Sir Ian continued looking at him for explanation.

"It seems we are dependent on him ringing Anna and for her to talk him into making contact with us."

"And she has agreed to help?"

"Yes."

"OK, keep me in the picture. I will ring Yuri in Moscow and let him know our views. Although I suspect he will have lost interest."

Harry returned to his office, on the way making himself coffee. Sitting at his desk and after further deliberation he decided he would attend any meeting with Alan should he decide to trust the department enough and agree to meet up.

Alan's call to Hans came through as he sat with Anna in her apartment later that evening. He had decided to spend the evening with her while they took in the recent events that had disrupted a quiet academic life to one of international intrigue. They had cobbled together a meal of whatever was in Anna's fridge at the time.

"Hans. What news?"

"Anna is safe." Hans replied. "The whole issue appears to have evaporated. I was told by Joe, who rang earlier, that the Russians have pulled out and you are probably not aware that one of their agents was murdered. Right in front of Anna," he added.

"That's great news. Sorry about the agent though. I don't know how to apologise enough for all the trouble and stress I have put you both through."

"It was Anna who has borne the brunt of it," Hans replied.

Alan could tell from the tone of Hans' voice that the apology was not enough. However he would just have to ignore it so he asked if Anna was there and could he speak to her. Hans hand went over the mouthpiece and Alan had to wait while the pair decided whether Anna, who was obviously there, would speak to him.

"Alan we have had Joe on the phone and he is most anxious to talk to you." Anna told him.

"Anna I'm truly sorry for what has happened, as I said to Hans."

"OK that's in the past." Anna replied in a voice that was slightly warmer than her fathers. "Please speak to Joe. He is extremely worried. From what I understand they now feel there is a threat against you from another source and they have no idea where from. Just speak to him and if you still don't trust him then it's between the pair of you and you can continue on the run if that's the life you decide on."

Alan sensed the concern in Anna's voice and decided he would make contact with Joe.

"Have you got a number I can get him on?"

"Yes, wait a moment." she went to find the number of Joe's mobile. "It's 07786-543251," she told him on her return.

"Thanks Anna." Alan would have liked to continue the conversation but could think of nothing to say that might repair the damage between them. "Once again I'm sorry for having involved you both in my problems," he added somewhat lamely.

"That's OK, good luck" She said before hanging up.

Alan stared at his mobile. He had got to like Anna and there had been times when he had fantasized about getting to know her better. But for now he had to know what was going on and what, if any, this new threat was. He decided to phone Joe immediately and find out what he had to say. Was this just a fabricated plot to get his attention and persuade him to 'come in?' Of all people Joe was probably the only person he could trust enough to give him the truth, at least as he himself believed it to be.

Alan had been sitting on his bed as he made the call to Hans. He got up and went over to the window and looked out across at the park as he dialled the number Anna had given him. The number rang for a while and as he was about to hang up he heard Joe's voice.

"Hello?"

"Joe it's Alan Marks."

"At last." Alan could hear the sense of relief in his old sergeant's voice. "Good to hear from you

Alan."

"I hear they want me to come in," Alan said.

"That's right and for what it's worth I believe they intend you no harm and are in fact more concerned about your safety."

"What, after I threatened to expose them?"

"My understanding of the situation is that they feel any exposure would no longer embarrass the establishment."

"Then why was I to be killed by the Russians?"

"I don't know but I believe that having seen your report they felt that it did not pose sufficient a threat and therefore called off the search. Although I have to say that at the beginning if they had got to you I believe you would no longer be with us."

"Are you saying that both MI6 and the Russians have read my report? Where did they get it from?"

"No idea," Joe replied.

"Now that's worrying as the only copy out there is with my solicitor," Alan told him. "That means they must have broken into his office and either copied it or stolen it. I'm not sure whether to be pissed off or pleased that they did as it seems the pressure is now off me."

"Ah, that's where you could be wrong."

"How come?"

Joe told him of the conversation he had had with Harry, how the Russian agent had been killed in Vienna and that the view was that it had been a case of mistaken identity and confirmed that there was still danger to Alan

As his comments sank in Joe found himself waiting for some form of response from Alan. At last Alan came back on line.

"OK I'll come in but I set the time and place and the Russians are to be kept out of it."

"Good. How do we keep in touch," Joe asked him. "Can I phone you?"

"No." Alan told him. "After each call I make I throw away the phone and get a new one. That way I can't be traced. I'll ring you," he added.

"I'll tell London we have made contact and that you are willing to come in."

"OK Joe. But get them to make me up another set of documents in the name of Alan Marks as I got rid of my set some time ago and I don't want to disclose my current identity even to the supposed good guys."

That evening Joe reported to Harry in London that he had spoken with Alan and expressed their concern about his safety and that Alan had agreed to come in at a time and place to suit him.

Harry understood Alan's concern and agreed

to go along with his request. He went onto tell Joe that he would be coming over to oversee the operation bringing all the necessary documents with him.

CHAPTER 34

November 1993

In Vienna Joe decided to phone Hans and bring him up to date. There was no answer so he tried Anna who picked up almost instantly. Joe had reasoned that although it was probably no longer relevant or of interest to the Doktor or his daughter that should Alan remain in touch with them then they should let him know.

To his surprise Anna showed more concern about Alan's welfare than he would have expected. Joe had believed that both Hans and his daughter would prefer to distance themselves from the whole situation. So when it came to the part where he said that there may be someone other than the Russians who wished to eliminate Alan he had noted that there was a real concern in Anna's reaction.

Had there been some sort of relationship developing between the pair of them? If so it was the first time that Joe had appreciated it and would it now complicate matters? The conversation that took place later that evening between Anna and Alan would have provided him with the answer to his question.

It was around 9.30 pm when Alan's call came through to Anna and almost before he began Anna launched into the content of what she had learned from Joe. Despite the trauma of being kidnapped and the problems he had visited upon her and her father it was clear that she had a genuine concern for his survival.

"Alan is it true that you are still in danger?"

"I have no idea," he replied. "I'm not sure I entirely believe the spin they have put on this incident with the Russian agent. It could well have been a random street crime."

"But to shoot someone and just drive off certainly doesn't seem like a robbery gone wrong to me," she replied.

"I don't know. I have to give it more thought. Still it's nice to hear you sounding so concerned," he joked, trying to lighten the atmosphere. From the silence that followed his remark he realised Anna was not taking things so lightly. He hastened on, "I have agreed to return to the UK for a de-brief and it appears my threat no longer has any power over my previous employers. It does seem that I have put both you and Hans through a lot of unnecessary trouble." he added.

"That's true."

"How about I take you both out for dinner."

"When?"

"Well how about when I meet up with Joe? After that I may well have to spend some time back in the UK."

"Sounds OK and I'm sure Dad will go along with that," Anna told him.

"There's a catch though."

"What's that?"

"I'm proposing to meet him in Amsterdam. I'll pay your fares and expenses as I would like to see you again. Oh, and Hans of course," he added. He could hear the smile in her voice as she told him he had a deal. Now all he had to do was let Joe know. He was fairly sure that neither Joe nor his employers would be too pleased at this turn of events. Still he did not really care what they thought.

His last call that night was made from his room. He was correct in thinking the attendance of Hans and his daughter at a sensitive situation would not be well received. It was finally agreed that they would have dinner the night before he returned to England. After giving it consideration, Joe agreed that provided he was also at the dinner there should be little problem with Harry at MI6. That was how it was finally left. Joe insisted that they now proceed as quickly as possible and that he should meet up with Alan within the next two to three days.

Alan, realising the problem he had given Joe, agreed to this arrangement. As it turned out Hans was unable to get the necessary time off from the university at such short notice and Anna would come on her own two days later.

When Joe reported in to Harry he could tell that things were not working out to the department's satisfaction. They liked to conduct operations in accordance with their own planning. At the end of the discussion Harry raised an issue with Joe that he had been told to instigate.

"Joe I believe that in order to keep Alan safe we need a decoy. What do you think?"

The question hung in the air for nearly 30 seconds before Joe finally said OK, he would go along with the plan.

Harry breathed a sigh of relief. "Joe I am not coming over for the dinner but will meet you at the venue the following morning. By the way do we know where that is?"

"Not yet. I have to tell Alan that everything is agreed before he will tell me where we are meeting. By the way do I tell him about there being another 'Alan Marks'?

"No keep that to yourself. Simply tell him that I will have a set of documents in his name as requested. This will mean of course that we have to leave Holland separately as two Alan Marks passing through customs at the same time may prove awkward and we don't want anything going wrong at the last minute. Alan and I will fly out of Schipol and you and the decoy will travel by ferry."

"OK sounds like a plan," Joe replied.

"Thanks Joe, the documents and passports will be waiting for you at the hotel reception."

CHAPTER 35

November 1993

Alan rang Joe the following morning and gave him the name of the hotel where he would meet them. It was the Park Plaza Amsterdam off Dam Square, a four star hotel in the city centre where he had booked a table for 8.00pm the following evening. This would give Joe sufficient time to arrange accommodation for both he and Anna and to settle in.

After he had ended the call Alan found he no longer felt like visiting the numerous galleries and attractions that Amsterdam had to offer. Instead he moved his chair to the widow and whilst watching the activity in the streets below and in the Botanical Gardens, found himself once again thinking about Anna and attempting, unsuccessfully, to get into a paperback.

They had, after a bit of a rocky start, seemed to get on well especially when they had been working on his report. What was it that he found attractive apart from the fact that she was good to look at, had expressive brown eyes and when she smiled her whole face lit up? They were of a similar age, or so he believed, although on reflection he was not sure as to how old she was.

He told himself that so far women had not featured much in his life. Those that had had been a disappointment or, he corrected himself with a smile,

In Pursuit of the Red Kite

too expensive.

Half way through the morning he gave up and took himself back into the city centre where he found a barge on which he could take coffee and be distracted by the teeming life around him.

The next day it had been agreed that Joe and Anna would meet up at the airport at the check-in desk for their flight to Amsterdam.

Anna had risen early to check all her luggage, for the third time, in order to make certain that she had packed those items of clothing that would most flatter her. She acknowledged to herself that she wanted to look her best for Alan.

As she left her apartment she double-locked the front door and pocketed the key. She walked the short distance to where her car was parked and put her case in the boot. Her attention was on the trip ahead and she failed to notice the small Peugeot that had been parked further down the street pull out and follow her from a discreet distance.

At the airport she left her car in the long term car park and made her way to the departure lounge where she met up with Joe. They would take the first flight available to Amsterdam. The ticket queue was short and it appeared the plane would not be full.

Having passed through passport control they bought themselves some magazines, found an empty table, ordered coffee and settled down to wait for their flight to be called.

The flight was uneventful. Anna had a window seat and, as there was little conversation between Joe and herself, she slept most of the way. She woke to find they were circling Schipol. Once through customs they made their way to the bus rank as Joe could see no point in hiring a car for a couple of days in Amsterdam. Several passengers from their flight seemed to have come to the same conclusion and the bus was soon filled.

They got off at Dam Square and walked across to the Park Plaza hotel. At reception Joe asked whether there was a package for him. The receptionist pulled a small bulky envelope from the letter rack and handed it to Joe. As Anna began her registration he excused himself and told her he would see her in the reception seating area. On his return he booked himself in and booked a further room for the decoy who was arriving later that evening, under the name of Alan Marks. Joe was given the room next to Anna on the second floor.

They agreed to meet at 7.30 pm in the bar that evening and both went to their rooms to unpack and settle in.

Alan spent some time in getting himself as smart as possible from his small collection of clothes. While he had been in the centre he had bought himself a new shirt and pair of slacks which after some moments of indecision he put on before attempting to clean the walking boots that had been his constant companions since leaving the Friary.

At last he felt he had done the best to make himself presentable for his meeting with Anna.

He took a cab and was dropped off in Damrak at some distance from the hotel which he approached with caution. He was still unconvinced that his life was under threat but told himself 'you can't be too careful'.

Despite his caution nothing seemed out of place.

He pushed through the entrance doors and walked over to the bar. It was a little early and he was the first to arrive. The next was Joe who at first held back before crossing to the bar counter where Alan had perched himself on a stool from where he was able to take in the whole area and see anyone entering. They both smiled as they shook hands.

"Thanks Joe for getting yourself involved in something that now seems to be of little or no importance."

"That's OK, at least I've got to see you. After you left the service I thought I would probably never see you again, so it's turned out for the best." He paused and looked around to see whether Anna was in sight. "Before Anna arrives let me give you your new documents. You'll be flying out from Schipol with Harry and I will go back by ferry."

"Thanks Joe . Oh, sorry you haven't got a drink yet. What'll you have?"

"Lager would be good."

Alan called the barman over and ordered Joe's drink.

"I've something for you." He reached inside his jacket and drew out an official looking document. "This is my new will. It's a copy but in case anything should happen to me could you see that it gets to my solicitor whose address is on the front."

"No problem," said Joe as he inspected the address. It was something he thought might be safest in the decoy's luggage. He would put it in later.

The barman returned with the lager and at that moment Anna appeared at the entrance to the bar. She had dressed to impress and both men took in the view as she walked over to join them. She said hello to Joe as she gave Alan a radiant smile which made him catch his breath. He had forgotten just how good she looked and how much he had missed her.

The conversation was kept on a light note as they sat and drank until a waiter appeared to say that their table was ready in the adjoining restaurant. A couple of hours later Joe made a diplomatic exit, leaving them alone. Alan however found his old problem recurring in how to entertain a woman he was more than physically attracted to and although the subject had not been raised he still felt guilty about the trouble he had put Hans and his daughter through.

So it was half an hour later that he made an excuse to leave offering first to see Anna to her room. An offer that she turned down with a smile saying that it had been a long day and that she could do with an early night.

Alan walked her to the lift and took her hand as they waited and with a final 'See you in the morning' watched her enter before leaving the hotel. On the way back to his bed-sit he berated himself at his lack of confidence which always seemed to desert him when he was in the presence of a woman he felt could mean a lot to him, given time.

CHAPTER 36

November 1993

Harry had caught an early bird flight to Schipol from where he took a cab to the hotel, arriving just after 8.00. He checked in at reception and asked to be directed to the breakfast room where on entering he saw Joe already sitting at a corner table.

He crossed the room, shook hands and pulled out a chair.

"Morning Joe. I trust you slept well?"

"Yes, not too bad Sir."

"Is Anna up yet?"

"No idea. It was agreed we would meet you and Alan in here any-time after 8.30 so I'm not expecting her before then."

"Good. Did you tell Alan of the arrangements and give him his set of documents?"

"I did."

Harry looked around. "Any chance of a coffee while we wait?"

Joe looked up and caught the eye of a waiter who at that time of the morning was fairly busy.

"Two coffees, please."

The waiter managed a "Yes, sir" while making it appear that he was being unnecessarily bothered with trivia when there were more important

In Pursuit of the Red Kite

issues in his life.

Harry asked "You have not mentioned to Alan that we are putting a decoy in place have you?"

"No"

"Good. He flew in last night and I gather you pre-booked a room for him in the name of Alan Marks. He has been told to keep out of site. Oh, and are you ready to leave as soon as we have had breakfast?"

"I'm packed. All I have to do is pay the bill," replied Joe.

"No I'll settle all the bills for this little escapade," said Harry with what he hoped was a comradely smile.

Earlier at the bed-sit Alan had settled his account, packed his small collection of belongings and caught a cab from the end of the road.

This time he was dropped off outside the hotel.

Having paid the fare he made for the entrance only to be nearly knocked over by a Middle Eastern looking tourist hurrying away from the hotel. A brief apology and the man crossed the pavement and dived into a waiting white cab. As Alan watched the cab drive off he could see the man in the back leaning forward issuing instructions to the driver.

He turned and entered making straight for the

dining room where he saw Harry sitting at the far table.

"Are you the first?"

"No. Joe has had all he wants and has gone up to collect his bags."

"Anna?"

As he mentioned her name there was a tap on his shoulder and he turned to greet a smiling Anna.

"Good morning."

"Morning," Alan replied. "Oh, and this is Harry." He indicated Harry with a movement of his head.

Anna made no attempt to more than nod at Harry who realised that she must, by now be very suspicious of anyone associated with Alan and the recent attempts on his life.

As if by magic a waiter materialised at her side.

"Madam?"

"Just coffee, please."

The water hurried off as Anna asked where Joe was, to be told by Harry that he was collecting his luggage from his room. Having said it he glanced at his watch but said no more.

One cup of coffee and some small talk later Harry got up and said he would go and see what seemed to be holding Joe up. Anna looked questioningly at Alan who simply shrugged by way of response.

Ten minutes later Harry appeared at the entrance to the dining room and called Alan over. He looked an extremely worried man.

He came straight to the point "Alan, I'm afraid Joe's been delayed. He shouldn't be long though"

Alan said nothing and went over to talk to Anna and tell her what Harry had just told him.

On going to see what was holding Joe up Harry had received no response at his room and had gone along the corridor to the next room where he had booked in the decoy. He had knocked on the door.

A worried looking Joe opened the door a fraction and when he saw it was Harry had told him to come in after first checking that there was no-one else in the corridor.

Inside he was greeted by the site of their decoy stretched across the bed with a bullet through his head.

"Also there was a second shot to the chest," Joe pointed out. It was a 'double tap,' a professional execution. Not only that, but all his luggage is missing!" He looked enquiringly at Harry.

"What do we tell Alan and Anna and, more to the point, what do we tell the Police?"

Harry said "I know this sounds callous Joe, but we do nothing. I'll put the 'do not disturb' sign on the door and close it to give us time to think up a plan. Whatever else you, Alan and Anna must get away from here as soon as possible. I will notify my office from here and act as liaison if that's what is seen to be the best course to take." What Harry had hoped to avoid was Alan finding out that they had placed a decoy as a diversion to ensure his safety. Now he would have to be told. The decoy, who had booked in as Alan Marks and bore a close resemblance to him, had paid for it with his life.

Back in the hotel lobby Alan turned to Harry. "What's the problem?"

Harry turned away so that Anna, if she looked towards them, would not learn what he was about to tell Alan.

"There's been a bit of an accident."

"To Joe?"

"No. We put in a decoy and he has been shot."

"What! Was he registered in my name?"

"Yes"

"Then I think it's a case of mistaken identity poor sod." He looked accusingly at Harry. "Why wasn't I told?"

Harry ignored the question "You have a good point and could well be right. Which of course means you could still be at risk. That's for later." He paused before continuing. "Now you should follow my original plan which is to get you back to the UK. I will have you picked up from the airport and taken to a safe house until we know a little more."

He realised Alan was no longer listening to him. "What is it?"

"I bet that guy who nearly knocked me over when I arrived was the killer. He looked Middle Eastern and he was also carrying military luggage which, now I think of it, seemed out of place for him. I saw him get into a cab and he was certainly in a hurry. I wonder if he can be tracked through CCTV."

"Good idea, but unless you noted the cab number I don't think we'll get far."

"I didn't get the number but it was white and there aren't too many of those about I'm fairly sure."

"You boys seem to be having a very serious debate."

Anna had got tired of waiting and had come over to see what was going on. The men looked at each other. Harry said "Sorry Anna but something has come up which I have to attend to urgently and Alan and I have a plane to catch."

"Can I do anything?" she asked.

"No thank you. I'll settle all the bills at this end and I apologise for having to be so rude but if I could ask you to leave as quickly as possible that would be a great help."

Anna looked at Alan for more explanation but he could only shrug. Suddenly Anna got angry "So it's a boy's thing is it. And where's Joe?"

"Still in his room. He is helping me create a diversion until Alan is safely on his way back to England. I will explain things to him but for now Alan is my first priority.

"Of course. I'm sorry I don't mean to add to your problems," she replied. She turned to Alan." It was good to see you again and still in one piece."

"I'm sorry it wasn't for longer." he replied. "But maybe I can come over and see you once this business is put to bed. He looked questioningly at Harry who said, 'yes of course.'

"Don't leave it too long," Anna replied, and with that she turned and left them, heading towards the lift. She did not look back.

Alan turned to Harry "You know I can't help thinking but it seems that whoever was after me has been following Anna which would explain the killing in Vienna and the decoy being shot here. Someone concluded that by association he was me."

"Yes I was thinking along similar lines. It seems the only likely explanation. Now we have two hours before the flight back to London. I suggest we make our way to the airport. You have your luggage with you. I have none. I will need to make some calls but I can do that from the airport," he concluded.

Alan was still dwelling on the possible link between Anna and himself. "What if Anna reads about the killing and comes to the same conclusion as us, she will be devastated?"

"There is nothing we can do about that but it is unlikely that it will be reported in the Austrian press."

"You are probably right." He collected his

luggage from their table and when a worried looking Joe had returned they both headed for the exit and took a cab to Schipol airport. Harry would travel separately.

At the airport they checked in and went through to airside. Alan wandered about and finally bought himself some magazines to read while he waited for his flight to be called.

Harry found him and they sat and had a coffee.

The flight to London was uneventful and as promised there was a car waiting to take Alan off to a safe house. There had been little conversation between the two men during the flight. They were each preoccupied by thoughts of what had transpired earlier that day. Alan got into the car that, as promised, was waiting for him outside the terminal.

On arriving back in London Harry was sent straight through to Sir Ian Rush's office but not before Amanda had signalled to him, by passing her hand across her throat, indicating that trouble was in store. Harry grimaced at her only to be treated to a wide grin as she picked up the phone and announced his arrival.

Harry knocked and was told to enter. Sir Ian was standing with his back to the window and with the light behind him Harry was unable to clearly see any expression on his face.

"Take a seat Harry." This was delivered as an order not a request. Sir Ian remained standing. "And in your own time tell me about this mess in Amsterdam that has got the Dutch so worked up. They linked your decoy's registration details back to the SAS and suspected there might be more to his death than simple robbery so they approached us. I saw no point in denying we knew anything about it. So I mentioned that you had told me of Alan's suspicion of the man that bumped into him at the hotel entrance. They followed this up and traced the white cab and interviewed the driver. Alan's suspect was dropped at the Iraq Embassy. After that they have no further knowledge as to whether he has remained inside or left the country."

"So it was not the Russians after all who were trying to eliminate our man. It feels like a revenge killing to me."

"Speculation, Harry!"

"I'm not so sure Sir. If you look at the whole picture it makes a lot of sense."

"Remember it was Nikolai who first tried to take out our man."
"True. But what if there were two quite separate services trying to make sure that news of the project never got out. Then when the Russians realised it would not cause them political harm they were no longer interested in a cover up."

"Then you come back to someone in Iraq either concerned as to how the report would affect their personal safety or simply wanting revenge for the consequences of the mission on Iraq," concluded

Harry.

"In view of what has just taken place I think Alan Marks should publicly be dead."

"What have you in mind?"

Sir Ian took some time before replying. "We should arrange a mock funeral in his home town and to give it some credibility we should try and persuade Anna and her father to attend. Of course explain to them why we are doing it but without mentioning anything about what happened at the hotel in Amsterdam."

"We will need to come up with a plausible story and one that will fool any assassin into believing he had succeeded.

I'll leave that to you Harry. By the way we should record the funeral. You never know there could be someone out there tasked to make sure Alan's truly dead."

"Of course and we don't know what name Alan uses at this moment in time. We brought him back on papers we prepared. He hasn't told us yet what name or names he has been known by. He probably still doesn't trust us

"Well we can arrange a new identity for him but if he's officially to cease to exist he will need to get any personal finances moved to his new persona or he will have problems in the future especially if he has made a will that disposes of all his assets to a third party. In order for this deception to work the normal course of events must be followed. Does he have any property?"

"No we provided him with accommodation once he began working for us and until he began the Iraq operation." said Harry.

"OK. Well I'm sure that this matter has given you a lot of extra work Harry. Best you get to it. Oh, and you will need to arrange something with Joe."

"Yes Sir." There must have been a note of sarcasm in his voice as Sir Ian gave him a quizzical look before returning to his desk and sitting down. Harry was dismissed.

As he passed through the outer office Amanda looked up.

"We're going to be a little busy. Any calls?" he asked.

"Yes Holland's been on twice.

Harry sighed "You had better get them on the line."

"Who do you want first? Your friend at the Ministry, or the police?"

"Ministry, to see what the official line is going to be."

As he sat down at his desk Harry knew he had some fences to rebuild with the Dutch authorities. Sir Ian, in his opinion had not handled his conversation with them as well as he could have.

His phone rang and the caller who identified himself as Jan Homma appeared only to be interested in what Harry would do about collection of the body once the Police investigation was completed. Harry told Jan that his department would take care of all arrangements from the UK. This seemed to satisfy the Dutchman who then hung up.

His next call was to the police. He got up and went to the door and called across to Amanda to get them on the line.

Five minutes later he was connected to an Inspector Pieter Mann who despite the problem Harry had left behind for them seemed more friendly than his previous caller.

"How can I help?" Harry began.

"Why did you not report this when you were in Amsterdam?"

Harry assumed that Sir Ian must have mentioned something for them to know he had been there although a thorough check of airline movements may have brought him to their attention. Of course; he had signed for all accounts at the hotel reception thereby proving his presence. Maybe the Inspector was just fishing to see what response he would get.

"Because I was unaware of anything untoward happening after we all dispersed after breakfast. I had a plane to catch and my colleague was staying on in Amsterdam a little longer."

"H'm," was the only comment from the Inspector. Harry decided to see if he could learn anything else about the identity of the man in the white cab.

"I understand you traced a possible suspect to the Iraqi Embassy. I don't suppose you have an image of what he looks like?"

"As it happens we do. I suppose you want a copy?"

"Well you never know, he maybe someone we have in our databases over here."

"If you have, you will of course let us know."

"Certainly," Harry promised the Inspector before bringing their conversation to an end.

CHAPTER 37

November 1993

Deep in the heart of the Iraqi National Intelligence Service, a messenger knocked on the door to the section leader's office.

"Yes? Come in"

The messenger entered, came to attention, saluted and then crossed to the desk, carrying with him a large khaki holdall.

"This has just been delivered for your attention Sir. It came in the diplomatic bag from our Dutch embassy."

"Put it on the desk."

The messenger did as instructed. Stepped back and saluted before leaving the room.

Aziz Ruboek spent a minute or two before attempting to open the bag. There was no lock on the zip which he pulled back to reveal dirty washing on top of a passport and a sealed envelope addressed to a solicitors office in a town called Colchester in England. He opened the passport which was in the name of Alan Marks and turned to the back to see the face of one of the men who had nearly cost him his life at the hands of Saddam Hussein.

As it was it had cost him his career and, if it had not been for some quick thinking, thereby turning a defeat into successful counter strategy, he would by now have been a dead man.

When it had been discovered that the Russians and British had successfully duped Saddam, on his advisors' recommendation, to buy those supposed miniature nuclear devices, all hell broke loose and some heads did roll quite literally. Aziz was able to pass a certain amount of the blame on to the scientists who had assured him that the devices were genuine. Thinking on his feet he had come up with the suggestion that Saddam should adopt a similar strategy against the West.

"And what would that be?" an angry Saddam had asked.

Aziz had put forward the concept that it should be rumoured that Iraq had developed a nuclear device of its own. Once the West picked up on what appeared to be leaked information at the highest level of Iraqi intelligence the West would believe that the Iraqis had developed 'weapons of mass destruction.' This would cause great concern among the Western Allies at a time when terrorism was on the rise.

That simple turn around began the rise of fear of what Iraq might do to the West until finally, after attempting to discover whether or not it was true, it led the West into a war that was to cost them dearly.

Having been removed from Saddam's group of advisors, Aziz had been allowed to resurface in the current Military establishment, albeit at a much lower rank. This was a situation which continued to give him reason to seek revenge on those who had nearly cost him his life and the fall from favour.

He had made a promise to himself that the perpetrators of his fate would pay with their lives.

Over the past three years he had been able to infiltrate the KGB but not MI6 and it was through that agent he had learned of the identities of his two targets, although not their locations.

Only a few weeks ago he had heard that the Russian appeared to have been killed by the Englishman which to some degree had spoiled the anticipation of his own plan. However it had put him onto the trail of Alan Marks.

Now he had before him proof of the demise of the remaining target of his revenge.

He opened the envelope and read the contents of Alan's will. Whereas the envelope had been addressed to a solicitor in England it had been prepared in Amsterdam with instructions that it be referred to the English solicitors of which the Principle was acting executor. This seemed to be confirmation that the hunt was over.

However, Aziz was not a man easily convinced so when Andrei's partner, Hussein, rang him from Moscow, he instructed him to remain there until further notice. He detected from the response that his agent had hoped to be relieved from this assignment. Aziz told Hussein to find out what the reaction in England was to the death of their agent. If there was to be funeral, as would be normal, then Hussein should go to see for himself where and when it took place and report back. He gave Hussein the details of where to find Alan's solicitor. He also warned Hussein that he must take special care not to be seen, although how the man would achieve this he was uncertain. There was little more he could do but

Aziz felt he had covered all the angles short of killing the man himself.

Hussein, aware of the danger he was likely to be in if he was to appear uninvited to the funeral, would approach the task he had been set some other way.

CHAPTER 38

November 1993

At the Safe House deep in the Cotswolds Alan was being looked after by a retired couple in a small Lodge House attached to a country estate. The three bedroom, two-storey building had been converted from its original use to make a comfortable residence some ten years earlier. A gravelled drive led up to the main house.

Alan, who had been there only two days, was already feeling trapped and although his hosts, an elderly couple, did their best to entertain him, the generation gap between them did not provide enough common ground in which to create a comfortable relationship.

He was allowed to go outside the Lodge but could only stay within the grounds of the estate which consisted of about three acres of gardens surrounded by agricultural farmland.

His room was a small double in which there was a single bed, a comfortable chair, a desk on which there was a TV and a laptop computer. Below the desk was some shelving containing a collection of fiction and factual books, mostly in paperbacks and from their condition he guessed he was not the first person to have taken refuge here.

There was a telephone in the hall on the ground floor to which he was given limited access. All outgoing calls would be monitored by MI6 and if they felt that the person Alan was trying to contact presented a security risk then the connection would not be made. Added to which, they had taken his mobile from him. This only added to his increasing frustration. While he was there he had time to think over the events of the past few weeks and the thought that kept coming back to him was how he had felt so little concern for the two men who had died. He had not killed Nikolai but had felt no compunction at disposing of the body. In Berlin he had told himself that the death of his attacker was a case of self-defence and he had barely given it a thought until now. As part of his training with the SAS he had learnt to kill efficiently. The real question was whether he wanted to get involved in tracking down the decoy's killer and meting out some form revenge. His concern was what effect, if any, he might feel in killing in cold blood.

It was an issue he debated with himself much of the time. He finally concluded that he owed it to the individual who had sacrificed himself unknowingly in order that he, Alan, might live. Decision taken, it was then a question of how he would carry it out.

After having been in the Lodge for a week he received a call from Harry to enquire how he was and update him on what was happening.

Harry told him that the body had been released and returned to the UK and that arrangements had been made for the funeral. It was then that he told Alan of the deception that was planned in order that the world believed that Alan Marks was dead.

Alan still felt angry that someone else had been sacrificed to ensure his safety. He was told that, like himself, the man had had no other relatives. Like Alan, the Army had been his family.

Harry went on to tell Alan that the Dutch police had forwarded onto him an image of the man he had bumped into at the entrance of the hotel. The man, who was suspected of being an Iraqi, was assumed to be the killer.

What he did not mention was that Sir Ian had sent a copy on to the Russian head of the KGB, Yuri, in Moscow though he did not expect to learn anything more as the Russian had shown little interest since his agent had been killed.

Yuri had asked Sir Ian to forward the photo directly to himself and not through the office as he had become increasingly convinced that any leaks of information to the killer had been from Moscow.

He opened up his emails and the attachment sent from MI6. A grim smile appeared on his face as he recognised the photo of the man in front of him. It was his secretary's lover. Everything now fell into place and his suspicions were fully confirmed.

He printed off the image which he laid on his desk, sat back and reviewed the situation. He could probably salvage the predicament he was in. Namely, a leaky office, via his secretary, and the loss of

Nikolai and Gregori to Alan Marks and the Iraqis. He felt on reflection that the investigations into people employed by the KGB should be constantly reviewed, long after they appeared to be committed to the department.

Having heard that MI6 had also lost a man to the Iraqi he guessed that they may be considering some reparation and if he could feed into that then both his problems would be solved for him without being personally involved.

That evening after the office staff had departed he made a call to Sir Ian who he guessed would be available despite any time difference.

"Sir Ian"

"What's the purpose of such a late call?"

In Moscow Yuri smiled to himself. "I may have some information for you on that photo' of your suspect."

"You have? Well that sounds promising."

Any revelation from the Russian was still hard for Yuri to admit to but on balance, if it would help him clean out his own stable, then it would be worth it.

"The man in the photo is the lover of my secretary."

"I see." He waited for the Russian to continue.

"He is here on a Jordanian passport. But as they must be false papers he is either a mercenary employed by the Iraqis or he is an Iraqi agent."

Straight to the point, Sir Ian asked Yuri what he was going to do about it.

"Well, I seem to have two choices. One, I arrest the pair of them, or two, I use them to feed the Iraqis with selected information. I will have to think carefully about which course of action I take." He paused, "the only thing that might happen is if the Iraqi is recalled we will possibly have lost a conduit into the Iraqi secret service. I'm still considering what I do."

"Well, let me know what you finally decide. Oh, and by the way, we are arranging a funeral for our dead agent, Alan Marks, I will let you know when; should you feel you would like to attend," Sir Ian told the Russian.

"Of course," promised Yuri before ending the call.

He put his phone down and wondered how events would turn out. He would do nothing for now but keep a close eye on MI6, not that that had proved very successful in the past. He would let Andrei become aware that Alan Marks had been killed and that a funeral was being planned. That would put the Iraqi off his guard and maybe, just maybe, should MI6 decide to take any further action it could only be to his advantage.

Sir Ian went over their conversation in his mind. It was likely that the assassin would not return to Moscow if the Iraqi secret service was now convinced that their mission was complete. On the other hand they may still feel there was much to be gained by keeping their agent in place especially if they assumed that the British and Russian secret services shared little information. It might be just possible that a trap could be set should the Iraqis attend Alan's funeral themselves.

Sir Ian thought that on balance, if it were him he would pull his agent out. He picked up his phone and dialled Harry's number.

"How are the funeral arrangements going for Alan Marks?"

"I have spoken to Doctor Freiburg in Vienna, who has, in turn, spoken to his daughter and they have agreed to be present at the funeral which is now scheduled for this coming Friday. Rightly or wrongly, I told them that Alan was still alive but that they would be helping to maintain that situation by attending." Harry replied. "They were of course somewhat alarmed to learn of the events in Amsterdam. The SAS will also attend," he added.

"Good. Make sure there is coverage of the event just in case the Iraqis should put in an appearance," he reminded Harry.

"Yes Sir." said Harry with a hardly discernible amount of sarcasm in his voice, while the expression about 'grandmothers sucking eggs' passed through his mind.

"Oh, and Harry see what you can find out about Yuri's secretary and his partner. The Russian has told me that he is fairly convinced that the image I sent him is the same man who is in Russia on a Jordanian passport. He gave me no more than that but an address would be useful. By the way I don't think we need to alert him as to our interest."

"With your agreement I think I will approach that can of worms by using the Dutch police who are investigating the murder in Amsterdam."

"Good idea Harry." Sir Ian replied with just the right amount of patronisation in his voice. "By the way does Alan Marks appreciate that if he is officially dead then his current Will comes into effect and any assets he may have will go to all and sundry."

"I will speak to him on that issue and help him arrange the necessary transfers before it is too late. Thank you for bringing it to my attention."

"Bugger, I should have remembered that myself." Harry said to himself. He hated it when he forgot something important, especially if it was the boss who reminded him. He got up and went over to his door and asked Amanda to get hold of Alan's solicitor, Tony Treadwell, in Colchester and the Registrar for Births and Deaths.

The first call was to the solicitor who was surprised to learn that his client had apparently "died" and that a funeral had been arranged for the coming Friday. Harry gave out only sufficient information to ensure that the solicitor was to do nothing until officially notified and to ignore Alan's current Will as a new one was being prepared. Tony understood that his friend had only officially died.

Harry's timing had been fortunate as the solicitor received a call the following morning, from a foreign sounding man who said he was a friend of Alan Marks from the SAS and he had heard his friend had died and was being buried locally. Was it true and where would the funeral take place?

The solicitor, having been notified of the event, confirmed to the caller, who had not given a name, that sadly what he had heard was true and gave him the time and place of the funeral. As the solicitor was about to ask the caller his name the man thanked him and hung up.

Because of the earlier conversation with Harry, Tony Treadwell decided that he perhaps should let him know of the call he had received. He dialled the number and reached Amanda who after listening to Tony put him through to Harry.

"I don't know if it is of any interest but I had a call from a man saying he was a friend of Alan's from the SAS who had heard of his death and wanted to know when and where the funeral was to be held. I told him but before I could find out his name he hung up on me. I hope I did nothing wrong?"

"No that's OK, but if he, or anybody else for that matter, should ask about Alan do your best to get a little more information about them. Perhaps, before you answer their questions."

"Yes of course." replied the solicitor before asking "Would it be alright if I attended the funeral to increase the credibility of your plot."

"That's perfectly OK." Harry told him before, after a few pleasantries, ending the call.

Harry sat back in his chair and put his hands behind his head as he considered this new turn of events. The Iraqi would have found Alan's solicitor from the copy of his Will in the holdall he had taken. So it appeared either he or someone above him was simply being thorough. Therefore it was unlikely that they would now find the assassin attending Alan's funeral. The bigger question was whether the Iraqi would remain in Moscow or return to Iraq.

Earlier he had been in contact with the Amsterdam police and decided it would do no harm in making a further call to see what, if any, progress had been made as to where the assassin resided. He would also need to find out if Yuri's secretary still had a lover or whether he had been withdrawn once the Iraqis felt their mission had been completed. He would have to get Sir Ian to follow that line for him as he doubted the Russian would be forthcoming with himself.

CHAPTER 39

December 1993

Harry's call to the Dutch police had proved fruitful. He now had an address in Moscow for Yuri's secretary. He did not enquire as to how they had traced the address as it was unlikely that they would be prepared to identify their sources to a foreign security service.

On Friday of that week Harry attended the funeral on behalf of MI6. It was a wet day. The grey skies looking set for the rest of the day as a light drizzle filled the air. No more mourners were present than expected either at the church or at the graveside. The service was short with the vicar reading from a short report on Alan's time in the SAS. No mention that he had died in the employ of MI6. Harry had taken the precaution of having several agents on watch to see who approached the funeral despite the fact that he believed that any foreign agent with any sense would stay away. As the coffin was lowered into the ground he noticed that Anna had tears in her eyes and that her father had his arm around her shoulders.

Harry, accepting that it was a very cynical thought, felt it increased the credibility of what they were staging to convince any onlooker that the funeral was genuine.

He was not to know that throughout the journey to England Anna had been thinking about Alan and come to realize that however attached to

Alan she became she would always be concerned that one day she could be attending a real funeral, bearing in mind the apparent nature of his work. She also knew that much of the time he would be away from any domestic arrangements that they might be put in place. She persuaded herself that they had no future together.

Harry thanked the Doktor and his daughter for their help. He would phone Alan later and bring him up to date with events. Tomorrow he would go to the safe house and release him from its security.

On arrival Harry was offered tea, which he accepted, before settling into the lounge with Alan whilst the old couple left on a trip to the nearest town to get some shopping. Alan assumed this a regular pattern of behaviour at such times.

"I have managed to get your affairs in order, not without some difficulty with your Swiss bank," Harry began. "I have given them your new identity details but you will have to go there to provide signatures for the new set of accounts and to transfer any money to a new account with another bank."

Alan nodded, "OK"

Harry opened his case. "These are your new driving licence, passport, national insurance number and bank account details." He handed the bunch of documents over to Alan who went through them one by one before looking up and thanking him.

"I suggest you no longer use your old solicitor or any other body you may have used in the past."

"Makes sense."

Harry was not fooled into thinking that Alan had no plans for his future but nevertheless told him that he could if he wished remain in the employ of MI6 who, Harry stated would continue to pay him a salary for the next six months under his new identity. If Alan had not committed to MI6 by then the salary would cease and he would no longer be in their employ.

"Thanks for the offer but at the moment I am not sure what I will do in the future. Let me think on it and I will get back to you." Alan then changed the subject.

"Have you learned any more about the killer?"

Harry had expected this question to arise at some point and had discussed his response with Sir Ian before leaving London. He had half expected Sir Ian to say it was not a good idea, on the basis that if Alan were to go after the assassin it could result in some international embarrassment. However that was not the case. Sir Ian's reply had been "I don't see a problem with that."

Again he reached into his case and pulled out a small folder which he handed over.

"What you have there is an image taken from CCTV which the Russians have confirmed that the man is in fact known to them and a watch will be kept on his movements within Russia. If his mission is

In Pursuit of the Red Kite

now over he may well leave. Probably back to Iraq. Incidentally it appears he is the lover of Yuri's secretary. The second image is Yuri's secretary Andrei."

"I see," said Alan, more or less to himself, as he studied the photos, before closing the folder.

"What will you do when you leave here?" asked Harry.

"Again I'm not sure. I will probably rent somewhere close to London where there is easy access into town. That of course is once I have been over to Switzerland to see my bank manager," he paused "In the meantime I will put up in a B&B or a cheap hotel for a few days."

"Will you let us know what you decide as soon as possible?"

"Sure."

Their discussion over both men stood and shook hands. Harry picked up his case and made for the door. "Thank the old couple for me please."

"I will." Alan watched Harry get into his car and drive off before closing the door and going to his room to finish his packing. He felt that the sooner he got away from the Lodge the better, in order to get back to some form of reality.

On their return Alan told the old couple that he was leaving and could they get him a cab to take him to the nearest station.

"No need for that I will take you there myself," offered the old man.

"That's most kind," said Alan. "I will get my bags."

While at the safe house Alan had made some minor changes to his appearance in line with the new passport documents that Harry would be giving him. He had shaved his hair and would add padding to his cheeks before any document checks at airports etc.

At the station his host did not get out of the car. As he entered, Alan turned to wave goodbye but the car was already driving out of the car park.

It was still early afternoon when Alan arrived in London. On the train he had decided to go directly to Heathrow and try and get on a flight to Geneva where he would put up in a small hotel for a few days.

Having connected with the Piccadilly Line he was at the airport in half an hour. He had no trouble getting a flight to Geneva. His flight would be leaving just after 6.00pm so he spent the time finding some reading material and getting a meal.

From the airport in Geneva he took a cab into the centre of the city. He paid off the cab in order to take stock of the vicinity before walking the short distance to the apartment.

Before leaving London he had found an Internet Café and booked himself into an apartment on Rue Verdaine in the old town of Geneva. He had taken the apartment for three nights although he doubted he would need them. The room was well equipped and apart from going out to eat he would stay in and watch television that night.

In Pursuit of the Red Kite

Midway through the following morning he visited his bank to set up a meeting with M'sieu Dubois to transfer his funds to a new bank before he became officially deceased. He spotted Catharine de Farge at a desk behind the row of tellers. She was keeping her head down. Either she had seen him enter or was genuinely busy.

He asked the pleasant middle aged woman who was at the counter for a meeting to be arranged between himself and M'sieu Dubois. She picked up the phone and spoke to the Manager's secretary and a meeting was set for three thirty that afternoon. Alan thanked her and again on his way out looked over towards Catharine who still had her eyes glued to her computer screen.

Alan returned to the bank at the appointed time and was shown into the manager's office. This time there was no sign of Catharine.

The greeting was fairly formal but it was obvious that M'sicu Dubois remembered him.

Having produced the necessary confirmatory letter from MI6 the formalities were soon accomplished and Alan now found that the man with the name of Marc Schwarz was more legitimate than he had been some two weeks earlier.

His next destination was a travel agency. He had decided to enter Russia as a tourist. He found one in Ruc Vignier not far from his apartment, where he was able to book on a ten day tour that was centred on

Moscow. As luck would have it the tour began the following day which would mean he would only need the apartment for one more night. He would pick up the tour at Geneva International Airport for a direct flight to the Russian capital.

However, he had other plans for the evening in front of him. He would have an early dinner and then go for a drink in the bar where he hoped to find Nicole before she met up with someone else. He had convinced himself that although he was attracted to Anna, there was no likelihood of any future between them, this being partly due to the stress and danger he had put her and her father through over the past few weeks.

He found himself in the hotel bar at around nine o'clock, a little early perhaps.

There were few customers at the tables and nobody sitting at the bar. More importantly there were no girls around either. Suddenly, he thought, what if Nicole was having a night off or worse, no longer worked there?

He ordered himself a long drink. He had no intention of drinking too much.

It was about half an hour later that unescorted women began to arrive, singly or in pairs. Ten minutes later Nicole entered the bar with a female companion.

They were talking and at first she did not spot Alan, which gave him the opportunity to compare his memory with the woman he now saw in front of him. At the moment he decided that he was not

In Pursuit of the Red Kite

disappointed, she turned and looked towards the bar.

On seeing him she stopped and smiled. She excused herself from her companion and came over. Alan got down from his stool, not quite knowing how to greet her. Nicole took the initiative and took both his hands in hers and reached to kiss him.

"Well I never thought I would see you here again." were her opening words.

At an attempt at gallantry Alan replied, "how could I possibly stay away?"

Nicole climbed onto the stool next to him as he asked her what she would like to drink. "Well, as it's you, I will have a gin and tonic please."

Alan suddenly felt as anxious as a schoolboy on his first date and asked, "are you available this evening Nicole?" and in attempt to regain his poise added, "or do I have to fight off any German bankers?"

Nicole made him wait as she pretended to be considering alternatives. "No, I think I can fit you in," she said at last. "No pun intended."

They spent some time at the bar making small talk until by unspoken agreement Alan settled his bar tab and they got off their stools and headed for the lift.

If possible that night turned out to be better than Alan's memory of their first time. As before their lovemaking was both gentle and passionate and once again Alan was amazed at the number of positions in which two bodies could be both aroused and satisfied. By the morning, after very little sleep, Alan realised he felt very comfortable with Nicole and began to have thoughts of suggesting some form of regular arrangement.

As if reading his mind Nicole said "It would become very expensive my love. I am a working girl whose career is very short and therefore I have to make a lot of money in a short time." Seeing the look on Alan's face she relented and added, "unless of course I find myself a multi-millionaire who could persuade me to take early retirement."

"I do understand," he said "so how about once more before breakfast?"

Breakfast was delivered while Nicole took her shower.

After breakfast Alan made his departure. At the door he turned and as he was about to make some comment Nicole put her finger on his lips, "Maybe." she said before pushing him out of the room.

"Sure." was all he found himself replying. Neither really expected to see the other again.

CHAPTER 40

December 1993

Back at the apartment Alan tidied up his few belongings, pulled back the bed covers on a bed in which he only slept in for one out of the three nights he had booked, before locking the door and leaving. As arranged he left the keys as instructed and went outside to find a taxi to take him to the airport.

He located the tour operator and group he would be sharing the next 10 days with at the check-in for the Moscow flight. The flight to the Russian capital was uneventful. At Sheremetevo International Airport the group had no problems getting through customs. Their guide led them to a waiting tour bus that took them directly to their destination, the Moscow Intourist Hotel. The hotel, located on Lenina Prospekt overlooked Red Square, opposite the Golden Onion Domes of the Kremlin.

Alan had stayed there in the past. He had paid a single room supplement and was directed to a room on the second floor. Not the best he had ever stayed in but adequate for his needs. As the tours organised by the tour company were optional, and could be decided once they were in Moscow, this gave Alan the ability to do more or less as he pleased without seeming out of place with the tour group.

He had a loose plan of action. If all went well he intended to complete his assignment just before leaving to return to Geneva.

That evening he joined the welcome dinner in the hotels main restaurant. It would be a kindness to say the food was only bland.

The following morning he had booked on the tour that took in the city and central areas of Moscow in order to re-familiarise himself with its layout.

The district where Yuri's secretary lived was the Prospekt Mira area. Off the Garden Ring the area links into Yaroslavskoye Highway and the northern suburbs of Moscow. His apartment was on the fourth floor conversion of one of the massive six-storey Stalin era buildings. Each floor had six apartments off a central core.

The tour Alan took that morning would take him along the highway bounding the district in which Andrei lived with Hussein and he could get some idea of the distance from the hotel.

On the way back to his room before lunch Alan took the time to obtain a detailed street map of the area. He also had purchased a travel guide of Moscow in English which gave a better idea of the facilities available in the area. He was looking for locations where he might spend some time observing his prey without looking suspicious and later be identified by the locals.

Moscow was in the grip of winter and Alan

decided to add to his limited wardrobe an overcoat and a typical hat with ear flaps which many of the Muskovite males seem to prefer. It would help him blend in.

His major task was to obtain a gun although this depended very much on his contacts of some two years ago still being in business. If they were, he was most likely to find them in one of the small bars in the Arbat where he would go for his evening meal.

As luck would have it he found one of his previous contacts in the second bar he came to. The man, who he had only known as Oleg, was sitting at the bar facing its entrance and Alan could tell from Oleg's expression that he had been recognised.

Oleg got off his stool and held out his hand. Alan went over and shook it.

"Well. It has been a long time has it not?" he smiled as he held onto Alan's hand. "Is it business or pleasure. No, I think it is business. Am I right?

Alan returned the smile and retrieved his hand. "As usual you are right. But I think there is time for a little pleasure also. What can I get you to drink?"

"You are the visitor. I will buy the first drink." Oleg turned and beckoned to the barman who had been waiting in readiness to take their order. He turned back to Alan.

"Shall we get a table and you can tell me what you have been up to and what it is you want."

As it was still fairly early in the evening there was no problem in finding an isolated table. Having got themselves comfortable and after what Alan considered a reasonable amount of polite small talk he came to the point.

"I need a pistol and silencer." He looked questioningly at Oleg.

"That will not be too difficult here in Moscow," his host replied. "When?"

"As soon as possible. I am here as a tourist for a few days and then I have to leave."

"OK. I will have something for you. Probably not tomorrow but the day after if that fits your plan."

"That's great," Alan told him. "Business over, let us have a serious drink." He raised his empty glass as he said it. The rest of the evening was given over to pleasure. The following morning was not so pleasurable. Fortunately he had booked on a tour that was taking the group beyond the capital to visit "gardens of interest."

He got a seat to himself where he was able to close his eyes and drift off.

Alan had an early dinner that evening in the hotel restaurant. He took a small table to himself before looking round. There were few diners, it would fill up later. A couple of tables away he noticed one of his group. A woman he assumed to be in her thirties. They had not spoken together on the tour so far. She saw him looking and smiled. He returned the smile and nodded. She went back to eating as Alan's starter arrived.

As he ate he sneaked a few looks her way and saw that she appeared to be engrossed in a paperback which she held in her left hand, which partly obscured her face, and used her fork in the right to eat her meal. All he could see was that she was wearing a high collared blue blouse, modest silver earrings and a silver bracelet. She had dark brunette hair which came down below her shoulders. He wondered how tall she might be. 'That's enough,' he told himself. He was in Moscow with a job to do and he could do without any further distractions. 'That is of course if she might be attracted to me anyway', he said to himself.

Finishing his meal and agreeing for the cost to be charged to his room he collected his outdoor clothing. He walked to the nearest Metro, Ohotny Ryad on the Sokolnicheskaya line, change at Chistyie Prudy onto the Kaluzhsko-Rizhskaya line to Prospekt Mira. He would walk from there.

It was only a short distance to the apartment block where Andrei and Hussein lived. It was a dark night. Low cloud had prevented any light from the skies. The street lighting was poor. Nevertheless he turned his coat collar up and the earflaps down before crossing the road to the entrance of the block. Entry was by an entry phone system alongside a list of occupants.

He did not hang about despite the fact that there were few people on the streets but what he had noted was that there were agents' boards indicating apartments for sale.

He made a note of one of them and the contact phone number. He would arrange a viewing on the pretext that he was looking for a place to buy. That would give him an idea of a typical layout of an apartment and of the common parts of the building.

Alan increased his area of inspection of the surroundings before taking the Metro back to his hotel.

In the morning he would contact the agent and arrange a viewing.

The next day he went down for breakfast and as he entered the restaurant he saw the woman from the night before who again looked up and smiled. Alan felt he should do the right thing and go over and introduce himself and at least say 'good morning'.

"Guten Morgan frauline," he began, "Marc Schwarz."

She held out her hand, "Sophia Schmidt."

As Alan took it she said, "will you be dining alone?"

"Well, yes." he replied.

"Would you like to join me?"

Alan who would have preferred to be on his own first thing in the morning did not feel he could refuse. "Yes, I would be pleased to." He pulled out the chair opposite as a waiter appeared to assist and ask him what he would like to drink.

Throughout the meal each maintained a steady stream of small talk mainly from Sophia whose main interest seemed to be whether or not he was married or in a steady relationship.

At some stage the thought came to Alan that if he were to turn up to view an apartment with a woman that would increase his chances of appearing to be a serious buyer. He wondered how he could he engineer the situation. His opportunity came when asked why he had decided to visit Moscow.

"Well I am considering buying an apartment here," he replied.

"That's interesting. Have you seen any that you like?"

"Not yet but I saw one advertised in the Prospekt Mira district that could suit me. In fact that reminds me I must make an appointment to view."

He watched as Sophia took in what he had said.

"I know this will seem really forward of me as I don't know you, but would you mind if I came along too?" she paused, "I would dearly like to see what a Moscow apartment looks like."

Alan pretended to give the question some thought before saying that he could see no problem with her request. He would go and get the agent's number and make an arrangement that fitted in with both their itineraries.

When he returned he phoned the agent and from the way the agent was keen to be available, Alan guessed that there was not a lot of interest in the property.

As Sophia seemed to have nothing planned for the afternoon that day it was agreed that they would meet up with agent at 14.30pm. at the entrance to the block. Alan then excused himself, having agreed to meet Sophia in the hotel foyer at 13.30pm.

Alan had nothing planned for the morning and as there were no tours arranged for that day ("day at rest" according to the tour itinerary) he decided to visit the Kremlin and learn a little more about Russian history.

When he had got up that morning, the day had not decided what to provide. As he stepped outside the Intourist lobby the decision seemed to have been taken. A blustery wind accompanied by a fairly constant drizzle greeted him. He was not to be put off. He turned up the collar of his coat. Fastened his ear protectors and strode across Red Square towards the Golden Onion Domes.

After a morning of culture Alan found himself a small café where he had a light lunch before meeting up with Sophia in the lobby of the hotel. She was sitting reading a German newspaper which she folded and placed on the low table alongside her seat.

She got up and they left the hotel outside where if anything the wind had got stronger. She pulled out a plastic rain hat and having arranged it to her satisfaction, took his arm as they headed for the Metro.

At the apartment block the agent was already

waiting for them and introduced himself as Alexi Tourinof. He had a pass key which opened the main door. He stood back and indicated that they follow him inside before closing the door and shutting out the weather.

"The apartment I will show you today is on the fourth floor. There is a lift and stair that links all the apartments to this lobby. There is also an escape stair which leads out of the back of the block where the car parking is located. Each apartment has one space and there are some places for visitors. I will show you after you have viewed the apartment." He paused to ensure that they had taken in what he had told them. "Now we take the lift to the fourth floor." He crossed the lobby and pressed the lift call button. Movement was heard higher up the shaft and some seconds later the lift appeared behind the lattice grill surrounding the shaft. The car itself was enclosed in a similar lattice design.

The apartment they were shown looked out onto the car park and the backs of adjacent similar buildings to the one they were in. Alan could understand why perhaps the agent had been keen to show them around.

It consisted of a combined kitchen / living area, a double bedroom, a reasonable sized bathroom and off the entrance hall were several storage cupboards, one housing the central heating boiler. Water he was told was supplied from a large tank at roof level and each apartment paid a fixed rate within the service charge.

Alan had seen that each landing level looked

to have the same layout. There were six apartments to each floor. Each apartment had the number and nameplate of the tenant on the door below which was a security eyepiece that allowed the occupier to check on who was outside before opening the door.

The apartment itself was uninspiring and if he had been a serious buyer would not have bought this one.

"I will leave you to have a look around on your own and will be downstairs in the lobby when you are finished and to answer any questions you may have," the agent told them.

Sophia asked Alan what he thought with a smile on her lips having guessed from his expression that he was not exactly impressed.

"It's not for me," he told her.

"I'm not surprised." she said.

They took the lift to the ground, thanked the agent and told him that they had no more questions and would get in touch once they had viewed others in the area before making any decision.

He looked disappointed but not surprised at their comments.

On the way back to the hotel Sophia asked Alan if he would be dining later. Alan felt a little embarrassed in saying that he had agreed to meet with an old friend that evening.

Seeing her suddenly appear rejected he relented and said, "but how about tomorrow evening. We could go and find something with a bit more atmosphere."

"Yes that would be a nice thing to do," she replied.

They parted at the hotel reception. Alan hoped that Sophia would not become too attached over the next few days. He did not want the complication of another woman in his life, especially now. If things went wrong with his plans, apart from anything else, he did not want her to be the subject of a Russian police investigation.

CHAPTER 41

December 1993

Alan went to meet Oleg at around 19.30pm that evening. As he entered the bar he saw that Oleg was deep in what looked like a negotiation with another man. Oleg, who was facing the door, saw Alan enter and, as his colleague turned to take a drink, signalled with his eyes that Alan should take a seat away from the bar.

Alan did as directed after buying his first drink of the evening. He promised himself that he would not stay and repeat the previous session with Oleg. He would leave as soon as their business was completed on the pretext that he was meeting another fellow tourist for a meal at the Prague Restaurant at around 21.00pm. It was his intention to check it out as Hans had recommended it after he had returned to Vienna. He would take Sophia there the following evening, if it looked OK.

It was nearly a quarter of an hour before Oleg concluded his conversation with the man at the bar. At times it had appeared to get a little heated but as the man left he was smiling to himself.

Oleg picked up a GUM carrier bag and his drink and came over to Alan's table.

"Well, he looked pleased with himself." Alan smiled at Oleg as he said it.

"These Georgians are easily pleased," Oleg replied also smiling.

Alan eyed the carrier bag. "I see you have been shopping."

"For you my friend," and he opened the bag for Alan to see two cellophane wrapped shirts. He looked questioningly at Oleg.

"Well I noticed how poor your taste was in shirts and I thought I would try and improve your wardrobe." Before Alan could respond Oleg said, "what you also need is underneath the shirts."

"Do I get to see the merchandise?"

"Take the bag to the bathroom and have a look inside then let me know if that is what you want and if there is anything else. Oh, and by the way there is no rear exit." He laughed as he made the last remark.

"You realise I am deeply offended that you should think that of me," Alan responded with a smile.

He took the bag to the bathroom as suggested which he was pleased to see was unoccupied and selected a cubicle at the far end. He bolted the door, lowered the seat, sat down and opened the bag. He removed the shirts and found two packages wrapped in cloth. The first contained a Walther, the second a silencer which he screwed into the barrel before testing the weight. There was a full chamber, which he hoped would be adequate. Returning to the bar he sat down.

"OK?" asked Oleg.

"The weapon is fine but a bit light on

ammunition."

"You may find your coat a little heavy," said Oleg.

Alan had left his outdoor coat draped over the back of his chair.

"You think of everything."

"Of course."

"What do I owe you?"

"Let's start with a large Vodka and then we will negotiate."

"Oh dear," said Alan, putting on a glum face.

Oleg laughed as Alan looked at his watch.

"There is a problem my friend?"

"Only that I am meeting somebody at 21.00pm for dinner," Alan told him.

"Is she very attractive?"

"Not too bad."

"And is she Russian?"

"No, she is Swiss."

Oleg gave a dismissive shrug. "Swiss women are cold," he advised Alan. "Still good luck, I'm sure you won't need it." He looked at his own watch. "We still have nearly an hour. Do you have far to go?"

"I don't think so. It is the Prague Restaurant which has been recommended to me by a friend. Is it far from here?"

"No. Less than five minutes walk from here. I will give you directions as you leave."

Alan was back in the hotel by 21.30 after first checking out the Prague Restaurant and went straight to his room for an early night.

The next few days he played the tourist. But in the evenings he would excuse himself from the group and go to Prospekt Mira to check out his target. Each time he went he was pleased to note that both Hussein and Andrei's lights were on in their respective apartments.

As he walked past the apartment block he realised it was no guarantee that each would be there when he wanted but it the best he could do without raising suspicion.

He was also having a bit of a problem keeping Sophia at arm's length without making her think she was unattractive. The truth was, he admitted to himself, under any other circumstances he would enjoy the possibility of a more intimate relationship.

Their evening at the Prague went off very well and they had returned to the hotel a little inebriated. By some unwritten etiquette of seduction each had thanked the other for an enjoyable evening before making an unsteady way to their respective rooms.

Alan had planned his strike on the apartment

for the penultimate evening of his stay in Moscow. After due consideration, he had decided that he would attempt to gain access to the block as a delivery man with a parcel for Hussein. In order to not raise the man's suspicion he would ring another bell and say that he was delivering a parcel but that the address was partially illegible. He would ask if he had got the right number. Hopefully whoever answered would let him in after telling him that the number he wanted was on the fourth floor. On the night, and as he approached the apartment block, he decided that the number he would ring to gain access would be that of Andrei.

The other option open to him was to use the escape stair from the car park. When he had been shown around by the agent he had seen no evidence of any security alarms on the door. Probably this was due to the fact that most of the residents would use this route to take shopping from their cars into the lobby area before taking the lift. However he would not take this option unless Andrei refused to open the main entrance door.

On approaching the block he was relieved to see lights on in both apartments. Hussein was where Alan wanted him. There was, however, still one worry in Alan's mind. What if the man who opened the door was not the man he had bumped into in Amsterdam? At the very least it would be embarrassing. No doubt he would think of some story based on poor information from his company having sent him to the wrong address for a man with a similar name.

At the entrance to the block he looked at the name plates and saw that there were two apartments at

Andrei's floor where the occupiers name had an 'A' as the first initial and he did not know Andrei's surname. He did however know the number. For a second or two he debated with himself as to whether to call on a number other than Andrei's. He went for Andrei's.

After about twenty seconds there was a voice on the answer-phone.

"Yes?"

"I have a parcel for a Mr. H. Jaffari?"

"You have the wrong apartment and the wrong floor."

"Then I am sorry for troubling you it's just that the delivery address is handwritten and not very clear." Alan replied.

"You need the fifth floor. Apartment 11, I will let you in." Andrei told him.

"That is most kind."

The buzzer sounded and Alan pushed the door open. The lift was parked at the ground floor. Alan crossed over the lobby, opened the gate and, on entering, pressed the button for the fifth floor.

As the lift slowly ascended Alan failed to notice that at the fourth floor Andrei's door was slightly open. Andrei was a jealous and therefore suspicious lover. He saw a man carrying a parcel and assumed it was a genuine delivery and not simply a male caller who was visiting Hussein. He was unsure of his partner's fidelity which was a constant cause of worry to him and had, in the past, often been the cause of arguments between them. Satisfied, he closed his door and went back to preparing his evening meal.

At the fifth floor the lift finally came to a halt and Alan got out. The light on the landing was minimal, which was to his good. The parcel he was carrying contained the Walther fitted with its silencer. He held the parcel horizontally in front of him and through an opening in the rear he was able to put his hand inside and grip the gun. He checked that the safety was off before ringing Hussein's bell and taking a step back.

He heard a door open inside and footsteps approach the door where there was a pause as Hussein used the spy hole to check out his visitor.

Alan had lowered his head so that his face was not fully visible from within.

The door opened as Alan raised his head to see that his suspicions had been right. Here was the man who had bumped into him in Amsterdam and matched the image from the Dutch CCTV camera, the man he was convinced had killed the decoy. However there must have been something of Alan's appearance that rang a bell in Hussein's mind as he seemed to suddenly look wary and began to step back inside his apartment.

Alan knew he may never get this opportunity again and pulled the trigger. The bullet hit Hussein in the upper torso and he fell back, dead before he hit the floor. Alan took no chances and now having more time to place his second shot fired it into the head.

Hussein had fallen partially blocking the

doorway. Alan stepped over him taking as much care as possible to not step in the blood. Before moving the body Alan removed his outer coat. He knew that despite taking precautions there was a strong likelihood that he would get some blood on his clothing which he could not remove until he was back in his hotel room where he had already taken the precaution of purchasing a new set of clothes. He got hold of one of Hussein's arms and dragged him into the apartment having first discarded the parcel and placed the pistol on a hall table.

On the floor below Andrei's suspicious mind had made him reopen his door to listen to how his partner would greet the delivery man.

He had heard the bell ring and the door open but was surprised that he had not heard anyone speak. Then he heard a heavy thud followed by the sound of scuffing as if something heavy was being dragged across the floor.

He crept up the stairs in time to see a pair of feet disappearing into Hussein's apartment and the door being pushed to. He crossed the landing and pushed open the door.

Alan was taken completely by surprise as the door which he had partially closed reopened to reveal a short squat man in shirt and jeans on the threshold. Both stared at each other for a split second before either reacted. It was Andrei first, who seeing his dead lover laid out on the floor, threw himself at Alan. Alan dropped Hussein's arm and stepped back but not in time to avoid Andrei's rush. He tried to maintain his footing but slipped in a pool of blood and both crashed to the floor, Andrei on top of Hussein's body.

Andrei managed to get his hands around Alan's throat. Alan was surprised at the strength of the grip and remembered that it was likely that Andrei had had military training before taking up a secretarial position with the KGB. He managed to get both his arms between Andrei's and forced the grip to be broken. At the same time he looked to see how far away he was from the Walther. Andrei saw his glance and also turned and immediately tried to get up and reach for the weapon. Alan grabbed hold of him and they struggled each to get on top of the other and gain an advantage in reaching the weapon first. Alan won but only in as far as getting hold of the butt before Andrei grabbed the barrel. They fell back on top of Hussein before rolling off onto the wooden tiled floor of the hall.

Alan was the stronger and fitter of the two and gradually managed to manoeuvre the gun into a position beneath Andrei's throat. He saw the fear in the man's eye's as he realized what was going to happen and renewed his efforts to move the gun away. He was too late. Alan pulled the trigger and ducked to avoid the spatter of blood, bone and brains that erupted through Andrei's skull. He was only partially successful. As gravity caused the matter to fall back he could not avoid getting some on his face, hair and shirt.

Alan extricated himself, stood up and surveyed the scene. He was still holding the Walther. He decided he would make it appear that Andrei had committed suicide after killing his lover. He wiped the gun to remove his prints then placed it in Andrei's hand with the finger around the trigger. It was the best he could think of. He questioned whether or not the position was credible assuming the man had been standing when he pulled the trigger. However, the variations on position and the after-effects of a struggle were too numerous to consider. He left the scene as it was.

He then went into the bathroom to check his appearance before putting his overcoat back on and leaving the apartment. Before he left he went down to Andrei's apartment to ensure that there was no evidence of there being anything untoward. He was glad he did because Andrei's door was slightly ajar and if had been left like that an alarm might have been raised that something was amiss which would have caused a police investigation to be carried out, possibly before he had left Moscow. Not that he expected anything to be linked back to him. Still there had been that viewing of an apartment earlier in the week which may be considered suspicious. He would take no avoidable risks. Outside the apartment he searched for a cab and fortunately found one without too much difficulty. The less he was seen in public the better chance he had of returning to his room and cleaning himself up properly. The winter attire, he felt, was adequate in hiding his stained garments.

Back at the hotel he quickly crossed reception and took the lift to the floor where his room was situated. Once inside he removed all his clothes, putting those which had picked up any blood, into a plastic bag which he in turn placed in his old hold all, before taking a bath.

It was still only 9.30 when he finished and he

was still too awake to settle.

He decided to go down to the hotel bar and have a drink.

Some of his group were already there including Sophia. She was talking to a pair of more elderly women who had travelled together. Alan got himself a drink and nodded to a couple of men standing at the bar. Both smiled and welcomed him to join them. He couldn't help thinking that each had used up all their common ground and were pleased to find someone else to talk with.

Sophia had had her back to him when he entered the bar and it was only sometime later as she turned to look around the room that she spotted him. She raised her glass and smiled as she excused herself from her companions. Alan assumed he should do the same before joining her.

"Well I didn't expect to see you here tonight," were her opening words.

"Nor did I," admitted Alan.

"Shall we sit?"

"Why not?" He looked round for a table. There was a corner table with divan seats which he indicated with his glass while looking questioningly at Sophia. She nodded her approval and they went over and made themselves comfortable.

They spent the next couple of hours discussing the tour and the places they had visited. It must have been around half eleven when Sophia said that she was ready to call it a day.

"You may walk me to my room," she told Alan who remembering the last time he had done so they had both been the worse for wear. They had not drunk so much this evening and were both relatively sober as they left the bar.

They had said nothing to each other as they made their way to Sophia's room. At the door she turned to Alan.

"Coffee?" was all she said.

"Sounds good," He replied.

"Come on then." She turned and opened her purse, took out the key and led him into her room.

It was extremely tidy. The maids had been in to turn back the sheets otherwise apart from a suitcase on its rack he would have believed that it was unoccupied. He closed the door behind him.

What he did not expect was Sophia's reaction. She turned to face him, put her arms around his neck and pressed her body into his and gave him a questioning smile.

"What about the coffee?" he asked.

"Later."

That simple reply was enough to fully arouse him as they began to remove each other's clothing. Sophia stood back from him so that he could see the beauty of her figure. He reached out for her but she stepped back opened up the bed and laid herself back on it with her hands behind her head and her far leg bent across the other. The first coupling was frantic and Alan wondered whether or not he had been too forceful? Had he been driven by the events of the earlier evening? Sophia had said nothing after they parted and lay on their backs each with their own private thoughts.

After a while she turned on her side and appeared to go to sleep.

Alan found himself wide awake and the thought kept entering his mind that he had experienced the same basic action as a primitive conqueror who having plundered a village would kill the men and celebrate by raping the women. Finally he drifted off to sleep. Only to be woken by feeling a hand stroking him. His body was aroused before he fully woke to see a serious looking Sophia staring into his eyes.

She pushed back the bedclothes before straddling him. As she did so she took him and directed him into her body. Alan was able to faintly see her by the dim light that entered the room from the half drawn curtains to the window. She leant back as she slowly rotated her hips. He reached up and cupped her small breasts, the nipples firm beneath his hands. Her eyes were closed and a determined look was on her face which set into a more angry expression as she procceded to increase her body's motion.

Alan realized that she was not with him. She was exorcising her own demons.

Was it revenge against an unfaithful husband, was it a lack of confidence or was it about someone she wanted but who had not been responsive. He would never know but it made him feel better about his own earlier selfish satisfaction.

At around 5.00am he was again woken to find Sophia sitting up alongside him.

"I think it would be a good idea if you were to return to your own room," she said. He was being dismissed.

"Of course," he replied. He gave her a quick kiss before getting up and putting his clothes on. As he made his way to the door he turned to see Sophia watching him. Her face was expressionless.

He did not see her at all the following day either at mealtimes or on the final day's tours. Much of the day he kept wondering why he felt no remorse at having killed two men the previous evening. Was he impervious to any concerns about taking another human's life? Until now he had always felt that killing was acceptable only if you are being threatened or if you are at war but not simply in cold blood. Had he the right to act as some avenging angel. He had to admit that killing Hussein made him feel a lot better and that Andrei was unavoidable collateral damage.

At some time during the day he would have to dispose of the bloodstained clothing which was now in his hold all. He decided his best course of action was to weigh down the holdall and drop it into a river, one of the nearest rivers being the Moskva, a few blocks away from the Kremlin.

It was dark early in Moscow and at around 8.00pm that he found himself on the bridge that led to the Cathedral of Christ the Redeemer waiting for a fall in pedestrian traffic and little on the river beneath. He leant on the parapet with his hands holding the hold all over the water. Earlier that day he had gone to a supermarket and purchased some tins of beans, these, he had used as weights for the hold all.

It was probably about fifteen minutes or so before he felt the conditions to be safe enough to let go. The bridge was quiet and there was only distant traffic on his side of the river headed towards him. He smiled to himself at the thought of letting go on the wrong side and dropping his package onto a passing boat.

He turned back the way he had come. He had decided to return to the Arbat district and see if Oleg was at his usual bar. It was his last night in Moscow and he felt he would like some company other than his tour companions. If he was honest with himself he was just a little worried about bumping into Sophia as he assumed from her silence that the previous night would be a cause of embarrassment.

Oleg was where Alan expected him to be and the smile of welcome appeared genuine. They settled into a gentle drinking routine. There was no macho bout between them as that which had taken place at the start of Alan's holiday.

Also the bar served some snacks which saved Alan finding somewhere to eat with only himself for company.

On his return to the hotel he packed his few belongings into his new hold-all as there was a fairly early departure for the airport in the morning. Having completed the task he looked at his watch. It was coming up for 11.00pm, he might as well turn in.

He was awakened from his sleep by the phone ringing. He looked at his watch. It was just after 1.00am. He picked up the receiver.

"Hello?"

"It is Sophia and I am feeling lonely."

"Can I help?"

"Will you come here or shall I come to you?" she asked.

"I will come to you in about five minutes," he replied as he eased himself into a sitting position. He hung up and dressed himself before picking up the room key which he used to quietly close the door behind him.

At Sophia's room the door was ajar and he let himself in. By the poor light he was able to see the bed and a covered figure in it.

Before he began to undress she said, "I hope you don't mind me calling on you for company?"

"Not a bit. To tell the truth I thought you were avoiding me."

"No. As it was the last day I decided to spend it shopping and I have to admit I didn't get up too early. A bit of a disturbed night," she chuckled as she said it.

Alan quickly undressed and got in beside her as she held the covers back for him.

This time their lovemaking was more gentle and to please each other rather than to satisfy some personal inner need.

It was during the small hours that Alan awoke. Sophia was on her side with her back to him. He gently lifted the covers so as not to wake her.

As with the night before it was indicated that he depart in the early hours but not before agreeing to meet for breakfast.

They sat together on the bus to the airport and on the plane to Geneva but there was little conversation between them, each deep into their own thoughts.

Having been cleared at passport control they collected their luggage, cleared customs and headed towards the exit. As they arrived at the airport lounge Alan stopped and Sophia turned to see why.

"I---" but before he could continue Sophia raised her hand and put a finger on his lips.

"No Marc. Thank you for making my holiday memorable but I believe it ends here."

All he could think of by way of a reply was to

say was, "if that's what you want then I can only thank you also for making my holiday very enjoyable too."

Sophia gave him a warm smile and squeezed his hand before turning and heading for the exit. She did not look back and the last he saw of her was as the automatic doors closed behind her.

He decided to get himself a coffee before taking a taxi into the centre of Geneva where he would find himself a hotel and decide what he was going to do next.

CHAPTER 42

December 1993

Alan sat in his hotel room looking across the street at a modern office block. His mind was not on the view from the window. He again found himself in a position of not knowing how the rest of his life was to be constructed. He had the offer of employment with MI6 and that was all.

Where should he live and should he buy himself somewhere or rent a property? The latter was the safest option, at least until he knew what he would be working as. And there was the next decision he had to make. What marketable skills did he have to sell to the business world?

No answers came immediately to mind. He still kept thinking of Anna in Vienna and despite his earlier decision in Geneva wondered whether he should try making contact with her. Apart from Marie in London there had been no other woman in his recent life with who he had had any form of a relationship that had been anything other than short term and physical.

He told himself that after a bit of a rocky start they seemed to have become reasonably friendly. Could that be developed into something more meaningful and did he want it to? Would recent events that had affected both her and her father be an obstruction?

However that would be something he would think about later. Later that morning he booked himself on a flight to Vienna.

It was a week later when the management company for the Moscow apartment block received several calls complaining about the smell seeming to be originating from the fifth floor. The manager tried to make contact with each of the tenants on that floor and by the end of the day had made contact with all except Hussein. At that point they decided to call in the police.

They came well prepared for a forced entry. The manager met them and they tried several times to get a response from ringing the bell and banging on the door. The smell on the landing was far from pleasant and the police seemed to be aware without actually telling the manager what was causing it.

It was agreed that a forced entry should be made and the police broke in. As the door flew back the smell became overpowering, the manager gagged and turned away while the police held their noses and their breath. The two bodies were very visible from the lobby. The man in charge held his arm up to prevent anyone going in and to preserve the scene of the crime.

One of the other apartment doors opened and as the tenant came out and saw the gathered crowd. He stepped back in as a policeman called and told him to wait as he went over to begin questioning him. The leader got on the phone and called forensics and for a

SOCO to be appointed.

On hearing what had happened to Andrei and Hussein, Yuri immediately instructed that all airports be checked as to who had departed from Moscow to learn from the passenger manifests that a certain Marc Schwarz had left a week earlier, bound for Geneva. It was a name that he recognized from a report he had received from the embassy in Berlin. He smiled to himself. The Brits had cleaned out his stable for him and maybe, just maybe he could use the information in the future. For now he would do nothing.

Harry was working his way through a large pile of correspondence that seemed to have found its way into his in-tray when Sir Ian Rush knocked on the door jamb to his office. Harry looked up.

"Sir?"

"A moment of your time Harry?" Sir Ian said before turning and heading back towards his own room.

Harry sighed, that's all he wanted, more work. He picked up a note pad and pen.

As he crossed reception Amanda looked. He gave her a questioning look. She beckoned him over.

"What did he say?" she mouthed.

"A moment of your time." he mouthed back

In Pursuit of the Red Kite

"That's probably OK. I don't believe you're going to get the cane." she replied in similar fashion but with a smile.

"In your own time, Harry!"

He turned to see Sir Ian standing in his doorway.

"Coming."

He looked back at Amanda. "But I could be wrong," she mouthed.

"Close the door and take a seat," said Sir Ian.

Harry did as instructed but taking his time about to show that he was no mere lackey. An action that Sir Ian failed to notice, as he himself remained standing, hands behind his back, and facing away from the window at Harry.

"I have just had a call from our colleagues in Moscow," he began

"The KGB?"

"Yes. Yuri has been on and it would seem that he's had a bit of a tragedy over there."

"Oh. What's happened?"

"From what he was saying it appears that his secretary has committed suicide after having first killed his lover. The man who we believe killed our decoy," he added just in case Harry had forgotten.

Harry smiled. "I do feel so sorry for him. Perhaps when you next speak to him you will pass on my condolences."

"Now that's enough Harry," Sir Ian admonished but with a similar smile on his face. He was silent for a moment.

"Yuri tells me he has leaked the matter to the Iraqis," he informed Harry, before changing the subject. "Do we know what is happening with Alan, or Marc Schwarz as he is currently known?"

"There's been nothing as yet. In fact we have no idea where he is. I assume he went to Geneva to sort out his future finances but I don't know for sure," Harry replied.

Sir Ian returned to his desk and sat down. As he did so he said, "he'll be back."

"What makes you so sure?" Harry argued the point having got comfortable in his seat.

It wouldn't hurt the boss to have his time disrupted he thought although acknowledging that perhaps he was being a little petty.

"Think about it Harry. What marketable skills has he got, eh?"

Harry thought for moment. "He could be a mercenary or an interpreter."

"I am aware that his training makes him ideal material as a mercenary but I think our man has somewhat higher moral standards." Sir Ian countered. "Yes, he may become an interpreter if he can find such a position. Not easy in business nor in the diplomatic services and I don't somehow see him as a holiday rep."

"How about as a trainer, in the SAS?

"With his official record I don't see the SAS taking him back either as a soldier or a trainer, do you?"

Harry suddenly recalled how Alan had been recruited and made to look as though he had received a dishonourable discharge from the service in order to improve his credibility with the Iraqis.

Sir Ian studied Harry's face "No he'll be back you'll see. In fact I'll put a fiver on it!"

Harry looked suspiciously at his boss for a moment then smiled and said, "Done."

He stood and they shook hands.

"Now Harry if you'll excuse me I must get on."

"Of course." Still smiling Harry turned and left the room.

As he crossed reception Amanda beckoned him over and held up a note.

"Two calls," she informed him.

"Who from," he asked without looking at the note.

"One from the Dutch police. The other from Alan Marks or Marc Schwarz as I believe he is now known."

"Bugger!"

"I beg your pardon."

"Has he had a call from Mark Schwarz?" Harry nodded towards Sir Ian's office.

"Not that I'm aware off. Why?"

"If I'm right the old bugger has just shafted me for a fiver."

Later that day Harry was again called into Sir Ian's office.

"Harry I believe you owe me?"

Harry had been prepared for this and handed the money over.

"Thank you." Sir Ian smiled broadly as he took his winnings. "I have been thinking how we might use Marks when he returns. I have had '5' on the phone to me. It seems they lost an agent who had been infiltrated into a plot on the opening of the channel tunnel and asked if we had any spare hands especially as it had been discovered the French were also involved, which sort of made it an International problem rather than just a Home one. I said I'd see what I could do and get back to them"

"And?" Harry felt obliged to ask.

"Well, unless you have any better suggestions, I think he fits the bill." replied Sir Ian with that smug smile Harry really hated.

Printed in Great Britain
by Amazon.co.uk, Ltd.,
Marston Gate.